Praise for
the novels of the Nine

Gift of Magic

"The exciting story line is fast-paced from the onset . . . Lynn Kurland spins another fabulous fantasy."　　　　*—Genre Go Round Reviews*

"With her storytelling gifts, Kurland weaves a magical combination of action, fantasy, and character exploration that is truly wonderful! A journey well worth taking!"　　　　*—Romantic Times*

Spellweaver

"One of the strongest fantasy novels welcoming in the new year."　　　　*—Fresh Fiction*

"Kurland weaves together intricate layers of plot threads, giving this novel a rich and lyrical style. Not only does mystery and danger abound, but also the burgeoning of a love and trust that is wonderful to behold. Kurland is an elegant spinner of tales!"　　　　*—Romantic Times*

"A magical world with a Celtic setting, *Spellweaver* is a romantic adventure with surprises and danger around every corner. Beautifully written, this tale is filled with mages, witches, spells, and shapeshifting, but also with plenty of intricate details of the incredible world around them."　　　　*—Romance Reviews Today*

A Tapestry of Spells

"Kurland deftly mixes innocent romance with adventure in a tale that will leave readers eager for the next installment."　　　　*—Publishers Weekly*

"Captured my interest from the very first page . . . Lynn Kurland's time travel series might occupy a favored place on my shelves, but I think she truly shines in the Nine Kingdoms books."　　　　*—Night Owl Romance*

"Once again [Kurland] uses her gift for place and character to weave an adventurous tale that will have readers breathlessly awaiting the next chapter. Good stuff indeed!"　　　　*—Romantic Times*

continued . . .

Princess of the Sword

"Beautifully written, with an intricately detailed society born of Ms. Kurland's remarkable imagination." —*Romance Reviews Today*

"An excellent finish to a great romantic quest fantasy . . . Readers will relish Ms. Kurland's superb trilogy." —*Genre Go Round Reviews*

"An intelligent, involving tale full of love and adventure." —*All About Romance*

The Mage's Daughter

"[A] perfect ten." —*Romance Reviews Today*

"Lynn Kurland has become one of my favorite fantasy authors; I can hardly wait to see what happens next." —*Huntress Reviews*

"*The Mage's Daughter*, like its predecessor, *Star of the Morning*, is the best work Lynn Kurland has ever done. I can't recommend this book highly enough." —*Fresh Fiction*

"I couldn't put the book down . . . The fantasy world, drawn so beautifully, is too wonderful to miss any of it . . . Brilliant!" —*ParaNormal Romance Reviews*

"This is a terrific romantic fantasy. Lynn Kurland provides a fabulous . . . tale that sets the stage for an incredible finish." —*Midwest Book Review*

Star of the Morning

"Kurland launches a stunning, rich, and poetic new trilogy. The quest is on!" —*Romantic Times*

"Terrific . . . Lynn Kurland provides fantasy readers with a delightful quest tale starring likable heroes." —*Midwest Book Review*

"Entertaining fantasy." —*Romance Reviews Today*

"An enchanting writer." —*The Eternal Night*

"A superbly crafted, sweetly romantic tale of adventure and magic." —*Booklist*

More praise for the novels of Lynn Kurland

Till There Was You

"Spellbinding and lovely, this is one story readers won't want to miss."
— *Romance Reader at Heart*

With Every Breath

"Kurland is a skilled enchantress . . . *With Every Breath* is breathtaking in its magnificent scope, a true invitation to the delights of romance."
— *Night Owl Romance*

When I Fall in Love

"Kurland infuses her polished writing with a deliciously dry wit, and her latest time-travel love story is sweetly romantic and thoroughly satisfying."
— *Booklist*

Much Ado in the Moonlight

"A consummate storyteller . . . Will keep the reader on the edge of their seat, unable to put the book down until the very last word."
— *ParaNormal Romance Reviews*

Dreams of Stardust

"Kurland weaves another fabulous read with just the right amounts of laughter, romance, and fantasy."
— *Affaire de Coeur*

A Garden in the Rain

"Kurland . . . consistently delivers the kind of stories readers dream about. Don't miss this one."
— *The Oakland (MI) Press*

From This Moment On

"A disarming blend of romance, suspense, and heartwarming humor, this book is romantic comedy at its best."
— *Publishers Weekly*

Titles by Lynn Kurland

STARDUST OF YESTERDAY
A DANCE THROUGH TIME
THIS IS ALL I ASK
THE VERY THOUGHT OF YOU
ANOTHER CHANCE TO DREAM
THE MORE I SEE YOU
IF I HAD YOU
MY HEART STOOD STILL
FROM THIS MOMENT ON

A GARDEN IN THE RAIN
DREAMS OF STARDUST
MUCH ADO IN THE MOONLIGHT
WHEN I FALL IN LOVE
WITH EVERY BREATH
TILL THERE WAS YOU
ONE ENCHANTED EVENING
ONE MAGIC MOMENT
ALL FOR YOU

The Novels of the Nine Kingdoms

STAR OF THE MORNING
THE MAGE'S DAUGHTER
PRINCESS OF THE SWORD
A TAPESTRY OF SPELLS

SPELLWEAVER
GIFT OF MAGIC
DREAMSPINNER

Anthologies

THE CHRISTMAS CAT
(with Julie Beard, Barbara Bretton, and Jo Beverley)

CHRISTMAS SPIRITS
(with Casey Claybourne, Elizabeth Bevarly, and Jenny Lykins)

VEILS OF TIME
(with Maggie Shayne, Angie Ray, and Ingrid Weaver)

OPPOSITES ATTRACT
(with Elizabeth Bevarly, Emily Carmichael, and Elda Minger)

LOVE CAME JUST IN TIME

A KNIGHT'S VOW
(with Patricia Potter, Deborah Simmons, and Glynnis Campbell)

TAPESTRY
(with Madeline Hunter, Sherrilyn Kenyon, and Karen Marie Moning)

TO WEAVE A WEB OF MAGIC
(with Patricia A. McKillip, Sharon Shinn, and Claire Delacroix)

THE QUEEN IN WINTER
(with Sharon Shinn, Claire Delacroix, and Sarah Monette)

A TIME FOR LOVE

Specials

"To Kiss in the Shadows" from TAPESTRY

Lynn Kurland

DREAMSPINNER

BERKLEY SENSATION, NEW YORK

THE BERKLEY PUBLISHING GROUP
Published by the Penguin Group
Penguin Group (USA) Inc.
375 Hudson Street, New York, New York 10014, USA

Penguin Group (Canada), 90 Eglinton Avenue East, Suite 700, Toronto, Ontario M4P 2Y3, Canada
(a division of Pearson Penguin Canada Inc.) • Penguin Books Ltd., 80 Strand, London WC2R 0RL,
England • Penguin Ireland, 25 St. Stephen's Green, Dublin 2, Ireland (a division of Penguin
Books Ltd.) • Penguin Group (Australia), 707 Collins Street, Melbourne, Victoria 3008, Australia
(a division of Pearson Australia Group Pty. Ltd.) • Penguin Books India Pvt. Ltd., 11 Community
Centre, Panchsheel Park, New Delhi—110 017, India • Penguin Group (NZ), 67 Apollo Drive,
Rosedale, Auckland 0632, New Zealand (a division of Pearson New Zealand Ltd.) • Penguin Books
Rosebank Office Park, 181 Jan Smuts Avenue, Parktown North 2193, South Africa • Penguin China,
B7 Jaiming Center, 27 East Third Ring Road North, Chaoyang District, Beijing 100020, China

Penguin Books Ltd., Registered Offices: 80 Strand, London WC2R 0RL, England

This book is an original publication of The Berkley Publishing Group.

This is a work of fiction. Names, characters, places, and incidents either are the product of the author's
imagination or are used fictitiously, and any resemblance to actual persons, living or dead, business
establishments, events, or locales is entirely coincidental. The publisher does not have any control over
and does not assume any responsibility for author or third-party websites or their content.

DREAMSPINNER

PUBLISHING HISTORY
Berkley Sensation trade paperback edition / January 2013

Berkley Sensation trade paperback edition ISBN: 978-0-425-26219-1

An application to register this book for cataloging has been submitted to the Library of Congress.

PRINTED IN THE UNITED STATES OF AMERICA

10 9 8 7 6 5 4 3 2 1

DREAMSPINNER

Prologue

❦

A gentle breeze whispered over the waters of Lake Cladach, carrying with it a goodly amount of the last of winter's chill. The waves rolled up endlessly onto a fine sandy beach on one side of the pier and up against a haphazard collection of smaller rocks that turned into boulders as they retreated from the shore on the other. Those boulders were just the right size for a lad to sit on and try his luck at catching something for supper.

Rùnach of Ceangail walked down a long, weathered dock and stopped at its end. He looked out over the lake as it sparkled with the dying rays of an early spring sunset. He could bring to mind innumerable occasions when he had either sat on one of those rocks by the shore or made himself at home exactly where he was currently standing, with rod and tackle, and pitted his skill against the inhabitants of his grandfather's lake. He had, as a matter of honor, never used magic to lure the fishes his way, nor cast a spell to make them visible, nor otherwise done anything to give himself an unfair advantage.

He knew from experience that there was more to the lake and its environs than met the eye. The waves laughed as they lapped against the rocks, the birds sang, the trees reached back into their timeless memories and told tales that were strange and unchanging, the flowers chattered, and over it all the wind murmured endlessly of the things it had heard. Only now it was just wind, just water, just trees with their branches moving gently. He heard no song, listened to no tales, could not tell where the fish were biting.

It was odd how one's self-imposed prohibitions as a youth could become one's life-imposed limitations as a man.

He would have given quite a bit to have escaped those constraints, but sometimes escape wasn't possible. Escape was especially difficult when what a man wanted to do was flee his beloved, well-meaning, but somewhat stifling family.

That was something, that thought, given how long he had been without family. And now to want to leave them behind . . . he shook his head. It said more about him, surely, than it did them. Then again, he had been to two weddings in the previous fortnight. Perhaps he could be forgiven for wanting to run.

He looked out over what was, he was quite convinced, the most beautiful lake in the Nine Kingdoms. He would have given much to have simply turned himself into something with wings and hurtled out across that deep blue water that was rather less still than usual, but he was who he was so he simply let the thought slip past him without holding on to it. He put his hands on a bit of railing that overlooked a rocky patch of beach and settled for clutching wood.

He looked down at his hands dispassionately, rather thankful for the shadows that showed less of what they were than did the harsh light of midday. They were useful hands, which was an improvement, but they were not the hands of a mage. They weren't the hands of a swordsman either, though they bore a web of scars that perhaps a swordsman would have been proud of. Only he hadn't won his scars in any battle with swords. He didn't particularly care to think about the details of how he had earned them, truth be told.

He looked back over the lake and suspected it might be time to be on his way. He had already said his farewells to his sister Mhorghain and her husband Miach, and his brother Ruithneadh and his wife Sarah earlier. He'd taken tea with his grandmothers and argued loudly and at great length with his grandfather Sìle before, during, and after luncheon. That only left his grandfather Sgath to exchange opinions with about his plans.

A discreet cough sounded from behind him.

Rùnach turned and saw Sgath of Ainneamh, lately of Lake Cladach, standing at the end of the dock, looking as if he was considering whether or not he dared approach. Rùnach smiled wryly and waved his grandfather on.

Sgath, who it had to be said looked not much older than Rùnach himself, walked over the well-tended wood and joined Rùnach at the end of the dock. Rùnach studied his grandfather thoughtfully. He wondered, at times, whom he resembled more, Sgath or his mother's brother Laìdir, but the truth was he couldn't have said. He hadn't looked in a polished glass in a score of years, and before then he'd limited his admiring of his visage to what he could see of it in a well-polished sword—

"Off on an adventure, are you?"

Rùnach looked at Sgath warily. "I was considering it."

"Leaving me to face Sìle's grumbles for who knows how long," Sgath said. "That seems rather unkind."

Rùnach sighed deeply and turned back to look out over the lake. His mother's father Sìle had done slightly more than grumble at him that day.

What in the bloody hell are you thinking? his grandfather had bellowed directly into his ear directly after breakfast. Sìle had shouted quite a few more things at him, but he didn't have the energy to bring the particulars to mind at present. They mostly had to do with Sìle's inability to understand how Rùnach could possibly prefer life out in the wilds of the Nine Kingdoms to a comfortable, elegant existence in Seanagarra, arguably the most beautiful place on earth.

Rùnach hadn't been able to answer. He'd simply soothed his grandfather with compliments, been charming during the day, and slipped out when his grandfather had been distracted by the menu for supper.

He released the railing. He rubbed his hands together—gingerly, for they still pained him—then turned and looked full at his father's father. "If it eases you any, I imagine he'll go back to Seanagarra to grumble where he can put his feet up on his own stool and make a proper job of it."

"One could hope." Sgath paused, then looked at Rùnach. "You know I don't like to agree with Sìle if I can help it, but out in the middle of nowhere, son? Surely there is somewhere comfortable you could choose to land instead."

"Where would you suggest I go?" Rùnach asked.

"Back to Buidseachd?"

Rùnach pursed his lips before he could stop himself. He had spent half his life there, haunting the library at the schools of wizardry, pretending to be the servant of the most powerful master there whilst in reality being kept safe by that same master. He took a deep breath, then shook his head. "Soilléir has been enormously kind to feed and house me there for all these years, but I can't impose on his hospitality any longer. And, because you won't ask, I'll answer and tell you that he did offer."

Sgath sighed. "You need to make your way in the world, I suppose."

Rùnach looked at him seriously. "And what else am I to do, Grandfather? Remain here at your home for the rest of my exceptionally long life, eating at your table, loitering in your salon, drinking your very fine wine?"

"I can think of less tolerable guests."

Rùnach couldn't bring himself to smile. "My other choice is to give in and return to Seanagarra with Sìle, to take up the life of a pampered elven prince."

"Oh, I imagine Sìle would find something useful for you to do," Sgath said.

"What?" Rùnach asked, more sharply than he'd intended. He dragged his hand through his hair, then looked at his grandfather wearily. "Let me attempt that again, more politely this time. With what task, Grandfather, would he saddle me? I have no magic, no sight, nothing but the hard, grim realities of a mortal life coupled with elven years. I could walk through the halls of Seanagarra, but I would see nothing of Sìle's glamour, hear nothing whispering in the wind, feel nothing coursing through my veins besides my dull, unmagical blood."

"And that, my lad," Sgath agreed quietly, "would be terrible." He paused, then rubbed his chin absently. "And staying here would be intolerable as well?"

Rùnach sighed, because he had seriously thought about asking if Sgath might need an extra stable hand. He had considered that request for the space of approximately five heartbeats before he had put it aside with other things he couldn't bring himself to consider. He shook his head. "It wouldn't, and perhaps I will return one day and beg a patch of dirt from you. But until then, I need to go and do something I can do."

"And what can you do, Rùnach?"

Rùnach would have taken offense at that question from his mother's sire, but not from Sgath. Then again, Sgath generally went about his life in a most unmagical fashion, wearing any one of a rather large collection of crumpled felt hats sporting fishing lures whilst waxing rhapsodic about the current batch of wine he had pressed himself and left curing in a special root cellar he'd built for just that purpose. If anyone would understand what Rùnach wanted, it would be Sgath of Ainneamh, elven prince and husband to the granddaughter of the wizardess Nimheil. Most people mistook him for a rather rumpled farm holder.

"I thought," Rùnach said carefully, because in all the time he'd been contemplating it, he had never dared voice his thought, "that I might take up the sword." He paused. "In spite of my hands."

"Well, your hands are healed well enough, aren't they?"

Rùnach found he could do no more than nod.

"A logical choice, then, given your skill with a blade in your youth," Sgath said, not sounding in the least bit horrified. "Where will you do this taking up?"

"Perhaps with some lord who needs another lad in his garrison,"

Rùnach said slowly, "though I suppose I would do well to engage in a bit of training first."

Sgath only looked at him steadily.

"Perhaps somewhere where I can regain some of my very disused skills," Rùnach added.

"South?"

Rùnach nodded.

"An interesting direction," Sgath conceded. "Many things to the south."

"So there are."

"How far south are you considering?"

"South and a bit west. Until there is no more of either."

Sgath laughed a little. "Not many places that fit that description, are there? And nay, you've no need to elaborate. I know what you're considering without your needing to say anything. I will tell you I think Gobhann is a mad choice, but one I can't say I wouldn't make myself were I in your boots. You do realize it's a magic sink, don't you?"

"Miach said as much, yes," Rùnach agreed. "I doubt I'll notice."

Sgath only sighed. "Very well, when do you want to go?"

"Now."

Sgath slid him a look. "And how is it I already knew that?"

"Because I've been a terrible guest," Rùnach said with a sigh. "Prickly, unpleasant—"

"Snarling, moody, sour," Sgath finished for him. "Not at all like the very charming, elegant young man who used to be first in the lists in the morning when Sìle would notice and last to come in, again, when Sìle would notice."

It had been so long since he'd been anything akin to that, Rùnach felt a little like his grandfather was talking about someone else. He couldn't say he had ever been charming or elegant, but he had been passing fond of a decently fashioned blade.

"Eulasaid has prepared a thing or two for your pack," Sgath continued. "Clothing, delicate edibles, that sort of thing. Sìle made his own contributions, which aren't, as you might fear, poisonous serpents or rocks."

Rùnach managed a faint smile. "Did he?"

"He did."

"Good of him."

"He's been pacing in the great hall, accompanied by a formidable glower."

"Has he?"

"I don't think you'll have words, but you never know. It is Sìle, after all." Sgath put his hand out and reached for something on his far side. He turned and handed it to Rùnach.

It was a sword.

"Just steel," Sgath said with a shrug.

Rùnach drew the sword halfway from the sheath. He had to stop, because just holding the hilt long enough to do that had left his hand cramped beyond reason. The steel glinted dully in the faint twilight of evening. The hilt glinted a bit more intensely, which led Rùnach to believe there were things there he would have to examine later. He resheathed the sword and looked at his grandfather. "Thank you."

"You're welcome." Sgath smiled. "Sìle provided you with a knife—here it is—though I'm not sure what it's fashioned from."

Rùnach wasn't going to speculate. He took the slim, sheathed dagger and slid it down the side of his boot.

Sgath tilted his head back toward the house. "One more thing, if you're interested. Just the right thing for a hasty exit, if that's what you're about."

Rùnach looked, because it would have been impolite to have refused yet another gift he was uncomfortable accepting. Then he felt his mouth fall open before he could stop it.

A horse stood there. Well, perhaps *stood* wasn't the right word. A horse occupied space on the greensward in a way that gave the impression that it was on the verge of sprouting wings and flinging itself up into the air.

It was a chestnut lad with a white blaze beginning in the center of his forelock and sweeping majestically down to his nose. His profile, something he turned his head to show Rùnach, was unmistakable. Rùnach looked at his grandfather and knew he must have greatly resembled a boy of ten-and-two looking at his first properly folded sword.

"An Angesand steed," he managed.

Sgath only lifted an eyebrow briefly. "His sire was Geasan, his dam Maiseach, who you might recall is descended from Màthair of Camanaë."

"I thought only Lord Hearn was so interested in bloodlines. When did you start memorizing names of steeds?"

"Ah, Rùnach, lad, what else have I to do but argue with Hearn's get about breeding lines and pick flowers for your grandmother's table?" Sgath asked with a smile. "Tùr of Angesand is, as you may or may not know, the youngest of Hearn's five sons and the most opinionated of the lot. He was discussing bloodlines with me when he was eight." Sgath shook his head slowly. "That lad has a feel for it that not even any of his very illustrious line of progenitors can match. And aye, since you're obviously asking, Tùr has come to oversee the breeding of my sweet Maiseach, several times as it happens. But that one there . . . well, Iteach is a horse without peer." He shot Rùnach a look. "I daresay he would even eat hay out of a simple, unmagical stable if you asked him to."

"Has he offered?"

"He has, actually. He had a look at you before Ruith's wedding and decided he might like to come along on your adventures."

"I won't be having any adventures."

"Iteach feels differently."

Rùnach laughed, because he could do nothing else. "Grandfather, we are standing here talking about a horse having opinions as naturally as if we were discussing what you'd found in your lake before dawn."

"Four very fat, very feisty lake trout, and aye, we are. But what can you expect from a steed that majestic?"

Rùnach considered. "Does he shapechange?"

"Go ask him. Your cloak's over the saddle, if you're interested."

Rùnach thought he just might be.

"And best of luck with your quest."

"Quest?" Rùnach echoed in disbelief. "Oh, nay, don't wish that on me. My only quest is to find myself a position in the garrison of some obscure lord, earn enough to put a roof over my head and food in my belly, and live out my life in obscurity."

Sgath put his hand on Rùnach's shoulder. "Simplicity has always been my desire, as well. But the achieving of it is more difficult." He paused and looked at Rùnach solemnly. "Isn't it?"

Rùnach supposed simplicity and obscurity weren't exactly the same thing, but there was no sense in trying to argue the point.

Sgath released him and smiled. "Somehow, son, I don't imagine obscurity is your destiny."

"It has served you well enough."

Sgath only lifted an eyebrow briefly. "How conveniently you overlook my brushes with something other than obscurity, but we'll leave that for later. Go meet your pony who has chosen you for your obvious appreciative eye. We'll be waiting back at the house. And if you decide to just trot on off, I'll make your excuses for you."

Rùnach took a deep breath. "I've already said my good-byes."

"Then what are you waiting for?"

"I thought I would walk to Melksham."

"A fortnight on foot?" Sgath asked mildly, one eyebrow raised. "As you will. You could leave in the daylight, you know, and make it easier on yourself."

Rùnach shook his head. "I see perfectly well in the dark. 'Tis the only gift left me."

"I think you underestimate yourself, Rùnach, but perhaps we can discuss that later, after you've had enough of adventuring and need a quiet place to land for a bit. We'll be here."

He imagined they would. He embraced his grandfather briefly, then watched him turn and walk back up toward the house, whistling something that sounded familiar. Rùnach listened for a moment or two, then shook his head. Too much trouble to try to place it. He leaned back against the railing of the dock until there was nothing left there but him, the breeze, and a horse worth a king's ransom. He took a deep breath, then walked up the path to meet that stallion who was destined for nothing more interesting than an unimportant stable courtesy of an unimportant lord who would need a marginally skilled guardsman who would live out his very long life in obscurity.

Because regardless of what either of his grandsires thought, he was no longer an elven price except by birth. He was also no longer a lad of ten-and-nine, but a man with a rather full tally of years to his credit. He wanted to say that a score of years haunting a musty library at the schools of wizardry hadn't ruined him for polite society, but he feared it had. The only thing he was likely good for was the crusty society of mannerless garrison knights— and he wasn't sure he was even fit for that.

But he couldn't simply loll about and do nothing with his life. He refused to live any longer off the charity of others, though at least at Buidseachd, he'd had his skill for finding hidden spells to trade for his keep.

That was before, when his hands had scarce been equal to the task of even turning pages. Now, he could at least hold a book. A sword was more difficult, but manageable as well.

Which would all lead, he could only hope, to a simple life as a marginally skilled, unremarkable swordsman.

It seemed like the safest thing to do.

One

The pub was as unremarkable as any pub would be on the last day of the week, lit with just the right amount of candlelight reflecting off the dark wood of the floors, tables, and beams in the ceiling. If things were a little more worn than was polite, the wooden paneling sporting more evidence of knives having resided in their soothing embrace than was comforting, and the barmaids more steely-eyed than in other places, who could complain? When a pub owner found himself in the seediest district of Beul, seediest of all cities in Bruadair, he was simply happy to sell his wares in peace.

Aisling slipped inside the door and flattened herself against the wall in as much shadow as she could find and forced herself not to gasp for breath. She wasn't sure she had ever run as she had just run, as if her life had depended on it, and she sincerely hoped she would never need run that way again. She clutched the wood behind her and told herself that there was indeed still an hour before dark, ample time to decide what she was going to do. No one would be looking for her.

Not yet.

She searched through the crowd to see who might be lurking there. It wouldn't have surprised her to find the keeping room full of armed guards looking for her. Fortunately, it was simply full of the usual suspects—working-class lads and lassies who had gathered to eat and drink the cheapest fare the kitchen had to offer. It was Beul, after all, and even a full six days of labor didn't provide much in the way of funds to splash out on fancy foodstuffs.

She looked across the large gathering room to the table where her usual companions were wont to hold forth. To her very great relief, she saw just her usual mates there. Or rather, two of them. A thrill of fear went through her at the thought that any of the other four might have been detained in order to tell those who might want to find her where she might be found—

She pushed aside the thought as a perfectly ridiculous one. She was one of hundreds of weavers who made up the Guild, and she was the least of those who sat before their rickety looms, turning out ream after ream of dull, grey cloth. No one would come looking for her, at least not until her precious few hours of weekly liberty were over and she wasn't to be found where she was supposed to be.

No one, perhaps, save someone who might have a vested financial interest in her presenting herself at her loom at dawn on the first day of the following week. Or perhaps two someones—

She realized she was wheezing, but she blamed that on the smoke in the air. It had nothing to do with having seen not a quarter hour ago a very well-dressed man and woman exiting an extremely expensive restaurant, then pausing to allow themselves to be admired before continuing on toward their carriage. She had gaped at them, convinced she was imagining things, only to hear them instruct the driver of that fine carriage to take them immediately to the weaver's guild. The woman had paused before she'd entered the conveyance and turned to look over her shoulder, as if she felt something untoward looking at her.

Aisling supposed that untoward thing would have been she herself, the woman's daughter.

Her first instinct had been to step forward, but she'd found her way suddenly blocked by a tall, well-dressed gentleman who had paused to ask her directions. If he had thereafter arrived safely at his destination, she would have been surprised. She wasn't sure she'd said anything that made any sense at all, but who could blame her for her alarm? She had just seen her parents, parents she had been separated from at the tender age of eight and not seen but thrice since—

The door next to her opened, startling her so badly she jumped. She put her hand over her heart, nodded to the entering patron, then pushed away from the wall. She still had time to decide what to do, though the sands were falling rapidly through the hourglass. If she returned to the Guild, she would surely find that her parents had come not to rescue her from her last possible months of indenture, but to secure another seven years of her labor for which they would take a hefty advance.

But if she didn't return to the Guild, it would mean consequences so dire she couldn't think on them without horror.

She walked unsteadily across the common room, then collapsed onto the bench set against the wall, thankful it was in the darkest corner of the pub. Perhaps if she could simply sit and think, a solution would come to her.

She looked at the man across the table from her who was cradling his empty mug between his hands and speaking in a low, angry voice. Quinn was the leader of their little band, primarily because he was the loudest. He was not now a handsome man, nor had he been, she suspected, before he'd spent years brawling over his very loud opinions. He looked at present as if he were fully prepared to brawl a bit more with the other member of their group present, a tall, thin man named Euan.

"You're a fool," Quinn snapped. "How many ways must I say this before you understand what must be done?"

"We've been over this dozens of times, and you're still daft," Euan said calmly. "This is Bruadair, remember? No one gets in or out."

Aisling knew that very well. In fact, not only did no one leave Bruadair, no one left the Guild. She had recently been granted the privilege of an afternoon a week to leave the grounds, but that was only because she had proven herself to be so relentlessly trustworthy.

Until an hour ago, of course, when she'd seen her doom standing there, dressed in clothing so fine she could safely say the fabric had not been woven on any loom she had ever touched.

She saw a cup of ale suddenly on the table in front of her. She looked at Euan quickly, had a wink as her reward, then wondered how she might manage to imbibe any of that unexpected gift with any success. She reached for it, but her hands were simply not equal to the task of holding it.

"Aisling, what ails you?" Euan asked, rescuing her cup before she dropped it in her lap.

"Who gives a damn what ails her," Quinn growled. "Aren't you *listening* to me? We have to do this thing *now*, before 'tis too late."

Aisling couldn't have agreed more. She tucked her hands under her arms to hide their trembling, then shook her head at Euan's questioning look. What was there to say? *I am considering running away from the Guild, the penalty for which is death.* That was the fate of weavers who fled, when they were found. It was also the fate of those who dared cross Bruadair's borders, though it was rumored there was no finding necessary there. Death followed them as if it were one of Murcach of Dalbyford's finest hounds, relentless and without mercy. If she didn't return to the Guild or, worse still, tried to escape Bruadair altogether, then she would—

She pushed aside that thought and wished she had a warmer cloak. Not even the fire could mitigate the chill that ran through her, though she supposed that was perhaps more from the cold hand of terror gripping the back of her neck than it was the draftiness of the pub.

The hard truth was, she had to make a choice between two things that were equally terrible. She could return to the Guild and submit to her parents' borrowing against another seven years of her labor mere months before she would come of age and could no longer be forced into submission. They had done it twice before, so it wasn't unthinkable. Or she could flee and most likely find

herself submitting to death from any number of other more unpleasant means.

She put her hand over her eyes and forced herself to breathe
normally. She couldn't sit at that bloody loom for another minute,
much less another seven years. But the consequences of running
away were so terribly dire.

And not just for her.

The Guildmistress had told her very plainly, on that first day
when she'd been granted a bit of freedom, that if she didn't return,
not only would they hunt her down and force her to pay the ultimate price, they would slay the Mistress of Weaving as well.
Muinear, the woman who had taken her on that first horrible, endless day, fed her, soothed her, then put her to bed and told her a
heroic tale of daring battles and romance. The old woman who
had, in all the years since, taken an especial interest in her, loaning
her an endless number of books, telling her an endless number of
obscure tales from less obscure kingdoms, finding an ironclad
excuse for an extra hour or two each fortnight for Aisling to come
and read to her once her eyes had begun to fail her. It was not
exaggerating to say that the weaving mistress had saved her life.

And to repay her with harm . . .

Aisling leaned back against the wall and closed her eyes. What
she wouldn't have given for a timely rescue. Unfortunately, there
was no handsome lad waiting to carry her off to his impossibly
lovely castle and there keep her safe, no fierce swordsman to stand
between her and those who would harm her, no prince wearing a
circlet of silver on his head and carrying untold power in his hands
to wield his sword and drive away those who wanted her for nothing more than her ability to endure countless hours of backbreak-
ing labor.

Nay, it was just her, sitting in a darkened pub, wearing worn
slippers and a threadbare cloak, hoping beyond hope that she
would see a doorway open up before her where there had been no
doorway before.

"You have no concept of what's at stake here, or the things I'm
willing to do to assure success."

Aisling opened her eyes and looked at Quinn giving Euan an icy stare.

"And just so you know," Quinn continued, "a body might get across the border if they knew how to flee."

"Flee?" Euan repeated with a snort. "How?"

"Traders cross the border all the time," Quinn said.

"Traders who are not of Bruadair," Euan clarified, "else they would be dead within the hour. *And*," he added, cutting Quinn off in mid-protest, "even if we could find a man fool enough to test the veracity of that, you haven't solved the very real problem of attempting to cross the border without a specific scrap of paper."

Quinn pulled something from under his cloak and laid it on the table.

It was a trader's license.

Euan's mouth fell open. "Where did you get that?"

"It doesn't matter," Quinn said. "My solution is to walk across the border in plain sight, then trot off to find aid."

"Against Sglaimir's army?" Euan said, rolling his eyes. "Impossible."

Impossible was better used to describe her situation. Aisling wondered if the two sitting at the table might have an opinion on what she should do. She cleared her throat.

"I need help—" she began.

"Oh, be quiet," Quinn said, obviously annoyed. "We've no time for your womanly cares."

Aisling was tempted to tell him her cares were slightly more serious than what hat to wear with which pair of shoes, but she supposed if they were talking about the fate of the realm, they wouldn't care—

Guards burst in the front door. Before she could do so much as decide how best to hide under the table, Euan had snatched up the trader's license, taken her by the hand, and was dragging her out the back of the public room. She couldn't believe those guards had come for her, but she wasn't about to take the chance of being wrong.

"Come *on*," Euan whispered fiercely. "*Hurry.*"

She didn't need to be told that twice. She ran with Euan

through the kitchens and out the back door. She continued to run down the street with him, because it seemed like the most sensible thing to do.

Until she realized Euan had run them into an entire clutch of city guards.

Euan shoved something into her hands. She looked down at it and realized, to her surprise, that it was the trader's license. She looked up and watched as Euan was swallowed up in the crowd of black-garbed men brandishing swords. Before she could say anything at all, she had been taken by the arm and pulled away.

By a Guild guard.

"Nay," she gasped, trying to jerk her arm away from him, "I've done nothing!"

He drew a knife. "If you want me to use this, keep struggling."

She stopped only because it occurred to her suddenly that she might stand a better chance of getting away from him if she feigned acquiescence. After all, that was what she did best.

The guard looked over his shoulder, cursed succinctly, then resheathed his knife in his belt and dragged her off the main street down a side street she'd never seen before. Then again, the pub wasn't in the nicest part of town, so there were several streets she hadn't dared explore.

She ran with him, because she supposed that she might manage to dart away from him if she were moving instead of digging in her heels. That might have been a more appealing proposition if she'd been able to recognize her surroundings, but she couldn't. Perhaps the man knew something she didn't about trouble in places she hadn't considered.

Or perhaps he was merely hurrying to meet someone else who might want to hurry her back to the Guild.

She considered her escape until she found herself suddenly handed off to none other than the finely dressed gentleman who had blocked her view of her parents. The guard melted into what she realized with alarm had become deep shadows. Her hour had come and gone—and she was so far out of any part of town she recognized, it would likely take her hours to find her way back to the Guild.

"Come along now, lass," the man said pleasantly. "No making a fuss. Wouldn't want to draw any attention to ourselves, now, would we?"

Aisling felt as if she were dreaming. She would have pinched herself, but her arm was already throbbing from where the guard had been holding on to her. She trotted along with the fop, because whilst he was speaking kindly, he was as insistent in his own way as both Euan and the guardsman had been in theirs.

She hurried with him along streets, past pubs and music halls, until she realized that her escort had come to a gentle but inexorable halt.

And she was looking at none other than the weaving mistress herself.

Aisling blinked. "Mistress Muinear, what are you—"

The old woman looked behind Aisling's shoulder, then swore. "She's cannier than I gave her credit for being, damn her." She looked at Aisling. "You'll have to run."

Aisling looked over her shoulder as well to see what she would have to be running from. To her horror—as if things weren't bad enough as they were—there strode the Guildmistress herself, bearing down on her, her expression hard and her stride full of fury.

Aisling almost went down to her knees then because she knew she was doomed. Another seven years of her life spent in a grey, soulless, freezing hall listening to the endless clack of looms—

"I'll see to them," the weaving mistress said. She shoved something into Aisling's hand. "You go through the border."

Aisling looked at her and blinked. "What?"

Mistress Muinear took her by the arms with surprising strength and shook her. "I do not matter," she said, her normally watery blue eyes bright and fierce. "Get yourself across the border, gel, then go do what must be done."

"But—"

The old woman embraced her briefly, then turned her around and pushed her. "Go, whilst there is still time."

Aisling stumbled forward, then found herself swept up in a

press of men who seemed to be in a great deal of haste. She looked over her shoulder and could see through the crowd that Guild guards had surrounded the weaving mistress—

"You're Quinn?" asked a voice in front of her flatly.

Aisling looked at the border guard who had taken her license. His expression of absolute boredom was visible thanks to the excessive and unpleasant amount of torchlight. She supposed that light allowed the guards to identify miscreants more easily, but to her it seemed garish and harsh.

"Quinn's wife," Aisling lied, her mouth very dry. "On his business."

"Do you have anything to prove that?" He shoved the license back at her and waited.

Aisling looked down at her hands and realized that what she was clutching in one of them were coins Mistress Muinear had given her. She slipped a pair of gold sovereigns into the crease of the trader's license, and handed it back to the guard. Her hands were trembling so badly he had to snatch it before she dropped it. He slid the gold—she could see it glinting warmly in the torchlight—into his sleeve, then back down into his glove with the practiced ease of a man who had done the like a time or two before. He handed her the license.

"Go on."

She went, because the men crowding in behind her didn't give her any choice. It was only as she stepped across the border and looked back to see a very thin, red line behind her heels, that she realized just what she'd done.

She had just sentenced herself to death—and not just from the Guild's bright swords.

It was, as Quinn had said, common knowledge that to cross the border without leave meant death by any one of several means, ranging from a long, slow, lingering illness to a sudden collapse. It was also said that those of noble enough blood could come and go as they pleased, but she had never met anyone noble to ask them. And given that she was nothing more than a common young woman of a score-and-seven, her blood would not save her.

"Well, get on with ye, girl," said a rough voice from behind her. "Or at least get out of the way!"

She found herself pushed aside by a burly trader who apparently was in a hurry to be about his business. She looked to her left. A wagon was receiving its passengers, having already been loaded with whatever cargo it was carrying.

"Where is that wagon going?" she managed, looking at another man who was moving past her.

"Gairn."

Aisling heard shouts behind her, shouts that made her blood run cold because she recognized the Guildmistress's voice. She turned, because it was what she was accustomed to doing, though she could hardly bring herself to look and see what the woman would do.

The Guildmistress was holding aloft a sword, stained with blood. She looked at Aisling, her gaze making the distance between them seem much less than perhaps it was. It was a look that left Aisling feeling as if she had lost control of her form. She took a step toward the border, but before her foot touched the ground, she found herself jerked backward.

"Oh, nay, you're not going there," a voice said firmly.

Before she could do so much as squeak, she was pulled out of the torchlight, away from that thin bloodred line that meant the difference between life and death.

The thought was halfway across her mind that Euan had caught her and was helping her to safety when she looked up at the man who was pulling her quickly into the shadows. To her surprise, she found it was the peddler she occasionally borrowed books from. Actually, she had once purchased a book from him, a book she had residing in a pocket she had made in her skirts, a book she had paid dearly for and never allowed to leave her person. But why he should find himself where he was at the current moment was one of the more baffling things in an evening that had been full of things she hadn't expected.

"But the weaving mistress—" she protested.

"Dead, most likely," he said briskly. "Count yourself lucky you aren't as well."

He shoved a bundle into her arms, then took hold of her long braid. She started to ask him what he was doing when she saw a knife flash in the darkness and felt a tug on her skull.

She gaped at him. "You cut off my hair!"

"And if they catch you, they'll cut your throat," he said harshly. "Those are lad's clothes. Go put them on."

They were out of the light but still within earshot of a great deal of shouting. Aisling wished she had even some idea what the peddler's name was, because she would have used it repeatedly whilst cursing him, but unfortunately all she could do was splutter at his nameless self. She flinched at the increase in the shrieking coming from the border, then decided that whatever else she chose to do, doing that thing as a lad would be much safer than as a woman. She ran behind an enormous boulder, then threw on the clothes the peddler had given her. She didn't care about their condition.

She retrieved her precious book from her pocket, then shoved it into the waistband of her trousers. She pulled her tunic down, then drew a cloak around her shoulders. She came out from behind the boulder on legs that were so unsteady beneath her, she felt as if she were floating. She stopped and looked at the peddler, who was watching the border closely. He turned his head to look at her, then reached down and picked up a pack. He took her clothes from her, then pushed the pack into her arms. It was so heavy, she almost dropped it.

"What's this?" she managed.

"Your new life," he said, taking her by the arm and pulling her along with him. "There's a carriage half a mile down the road, waiting."

She looked at him in surprise. "Why?"

"Because I paid them to," he said impatiently.

"A carriage—"

"Get in it and don't get out until it stops."

She blinked. "But—"

"There's gold in that pack. Find an assassin. Save Bruadair."

She shook her head, but that didn't clear away the persistent sensation she had of having wandered into a terrible dream. Less than an hour ago—perhaps it was longer, she honestly couldn't tell—she had been looking in the window of a shop and admiring a cloak that whilst grey had at least been cut handsomely. Now she stood outside the border of her country, dressed as a lad, knowing that her flight had meant death for the one person in the world she cared about— and knowing that continuing her flight would spell her own end.

"Save Bruadair?" she repeated, finding herself completely unable to understand how she was to go from merely wanting to save herself to needing to save her country.

He swore at her. "You're dead right now, don't you know? You crossed the border."

She knew it, of course, but she hadn't wanted to face it. "I didn't have any choice—"

"Of course you did," he said briskly. "You could have chosen to crawl back to that miserable guild and spend the rest of your days trapped in a life of endless drudgery. But you chose freedom."

She looked at the ground, because it was safer that way. "What does that matter if I've sentenced myself to death?"

He put his hand under her chin, lifted her face up, and looked at her with absolutely no expression on his face. "You haven't. There is a way to save yourself."

She pulled away from his hand, sure she'd heard him awrong. "How?"

"It won't be easy, or pleasant," he warned. "The usurper who currently sits the throne must be overthrown before he destroys every last bit of—well, his plans aren't important. What *is* important is that the rightful king takes his place. This is not a task for an army, for Sglaimir will see them and slay them before they can touch him. A mage will not manage it either, for his magic will be sensed before he reaches the palace walls—"

"Mages?" she interrupted, trying to laugh. She thought it had sounded more like a gasp of terror than anything else, but she wasn't perhaps the best one to judge. "I don't believe in mages."

He blew out his breath in frustration. "Seek out an assassin, then, one who will dethrone the king for the glory of it—or as much gold as we've been able to muster." He looked at her seriously.

"You have three se'nnights. The bargain must be struck before midnight of the last day or your life will be the forfeit."

She couldn't keep from blinking. "How do you know—"

"Because I know," he said curtly. "Bloody hell, wench, have you no idea—nay, of course you don't." He shook his head sharply. "The details aren't important. You have been granted the gift of a fortnight and a half. Complete your quest and your life will then be yours."

"But quests should be left to Heroes." She might have been a common weaver, but she was very well read in subjects ranging from the movements of stars to the movements of men. It took a certain set of skills to embark on any sort of serious heroic business.

"You were all that was available at the time. And you know where to go."

She felt her mouth go dry. "Do I?"

"Did I sell you that book for naught?"

"Which book?"

"The only book you own!" He glared at her. "*The Strictures of Scrymgeour Weger*, written by Ochadius of Riamh, and gathered, from what I've heard, only at incredible peril to the man. *That* book."

She put her hand over her belly before she thought better of it. There, residing under the waistband of her trousers, was a book for which she had given half of all the meager coins she'd managed to accumulate over the years doing odd things about the Guild. *The Strictures of Scrymgeour Weger* was indeed the title. Just looking at the cover had fair burned her eyes. She couldn't quite bring herself to think about the things she had read inside.

The peddler put his hand suddenly on her shoulder and turned her away from the border. "Run. The carriage is waiting, but it won't wait forever. Find a solution to what you've left behind here while you're still alive."

Her mouth was very dry. "But I know nothing about wars or rulers or—"

"Then every book you ever were given by the mistress of the loom during all the years she had you at her elbow was completely wasted."

"But I am nobody," she protested. "I am no one of consequence, without friend or family or any gifts—"

"Then no one will miss you when you're gone," he said shortly. He put a heavy hand on her shoulder. "There is no one else, Aisling, no one but you. I suggest you go south."

South.

The word echoed in her head like a great bell that had been rung just once in an immense canyon. South. There were many things in the south, many places to lose herself. Scrymgeour Weger lived in the south, on an island, or so it was rumored. She didn't suppose he would have an army at his disposal.

But he might be able to tell her where to find someone who could do what needed to be done.

"Tell no one of your errand or of your homeland."

She looked at the peddler. "Not even the mercenary?"

He shook his head. "Have him meet me at Taigh Hall three months from today."

"And you think he will come?" she managed.

"He will, if he wants the rest of his money." He gestured to the pack. "The first half of his incentive is in there. He can name his price for the rest when the deed is done. Now, go. The sands have already begun to fall. Three se'nnights, Aisling, and no longer."

She turned and peered into the darkness, looking for a different means of escape. Unfortunately, it seemed her only escape lay along a path that was intertwined with the fate of her homeland, a land that had hosted her birth and now would be the reason for her death.

She turned back to the peddler, but he was gone.

Guards shouted in the distance. Aisling felt torn for a moment or two between two terrible alternatives. Then she took a deep breath, turned, and stumbled into the darkness.

South.

A blond man stood in the shadows that were unrelieved by even the faintest hint of moonlight and watched the carriage roll away. He turned his head and looked at the peddler who had appeared next to him.

"So, it is done," he said slowly.

"Finally," the peddler said with a gusty sigh.

The first man frowned thoughtfully. "It goes against my upbringing—"

"Damn your upbringing and all your bloody ideals," the peddler snapped. "I arranged this end of it. If you tell me all this work has been for naught, I will kill you."

The blond man stared off into the darkness, seeing things the peddler couldn't. "Nay," he said slowly, "the pieces are in place."

"I still say a firm hand in the backs of the players wouldn't go amiss."

The other shook his head. "I have prepared my side as I could, as have you. There is nothing else to do but wait."

"I hate waiting."

"Which, if memory serves, landed you in a spot of trouble quite a few years ago with a particular member of your father's family."

The peddler cursed him, then turned and stalked off. The blond man, ageless, having watched countless souls take their turns on the world's stage, looked off into the distance. He forced himself to simply observe. Wringing his hands wasn't in his nature.

Then again, neither was interfering. The world was full of good and evil and both were necessary. After all, if there were no evil, what would there be for good men to fight?

He had already interfered more than he could bear to, even if his only contribution to the upcoming events had been a casual remark about the desirability of sword skill, made to a man who certainly would have agreed. But it had been more interference than he was comfortable with, which meant that he would be stringently limiting himself to nothing more than observation in the future, no matter what hung in the balance.

It was up to others now to see to the measure.

Two

The carriage lurched to a stop, but given that it had lurched almost continually since Aisling had climbed inside it, breathless and convinced she wouldn't live to see the end of the night much less the end of the journey, another bit of jostling wasn't terribly surprising.

The door was wrenched open.

"Last stop," a deep voice said shortly. "Everyone out so as I can be cleaning the seats ye've no doubt befouled."

Aisling found herself taken by the arm, pulled from the carriage, and sent on her way. *Sent* was perhaps too polite a term for it. She was hurled away from the door. She caught herself before she went sprawling, then turned around, intending to protest her treatment, only to find her arms full of her pack that had been sent her way from its recent position on top of the carriage.

Perhaps *sent* was still the wrong word to be using. It had been flung at her so forcefully that she had caught it out of instinct, then found herself knocked off her feet by the weight of it. Perhaps that wouldn't have been so bad in and of itself save for the fact that she had been knocked not only upon her backside but upon her backside in a puddle of—

She looked down, then decided perhaps it was best not to examine too closely what she was sitting in. It wasn't as if she hadn't seen muck and horse leavings in the street before. Somehow, though, sitting in it and wiping it from her eyes whilst trying to recover from a journey that had seemed to go on forever left her wondering why it was she had been so desperate to leave the Guild.

After all, she had been weaving for so long that it took no thought. She could have been sitting comfortably—well, uncomfortably, actually—on a hard wooden bench, creating rough cloth for equally oppressed seamstresses who would in turn fashion it into equally ugly clothes to be worn by those who couldn't afford better. At least she would have been warm—mostly—and dry—definitely—and not hungry. Well, not too hungry. It was true that after years and years of nothing but gruel and the occasional bowl of rather nasty vegetables to stave off scurvy that she had begun to crave even the cheapest of pub fare. It was astonishing, actually, that somehow that seemed preferable to sitting in the middle of a muddy street that was sporting smells she couldn't—and didn't want to—identify.

Not to mention the fact that the weaving mistress would have still been alive . . .

Aisling heaved her pack aside and crawled to her feet. She was in Istaur and there was no turning back. All she could do was press on, see to her quest, then take the rest of her life and do something with it worth the sacrifice that had been made on her behalf.

And when she was capable of thinking on it, she would wonder why the weaving mistress had been near the border at just the moment when she had been most needed.

She thought without fondness about the events that had followed that bit of unexpected aid. Just getting herself and her heavy pack to the carriage had been almost impossible. She'd run along a deeply rutted road in utter darkness, cutting her hands and knees when she'd fallen, wrenching her back when she'd dragged herself upright. The carriage had indeed been waiting, along with an angry, impatient driver who had jerked open the door, pushed her up the step, and shoved her inside.

She'd never been inside a covered carriage before and hadn't known what to expect. She'd fallen into the only open spot, a wholly inadequate space between a very large, fragrant man suffering from gout and a woman who whispered about spies and coughed incessantly, necessitating the windows being up and the blinds being drawn the entire way lest the dust enter and make things worse for her. Aisling thought there might have been a trio of silent men with business of their own facing her, but she couldn't have said because, again, the blinds had been drawn.

Perhaps that had been just as well. She could honestly say she had never wept in the whole of her life, not even during the only other ride she'd ever taken, a journey in a rickety wagon that had left her hanging her head over the side and heaving continually until she'd been put into the care of the Guildmistress. She hadn't wept as she'd realized that her parents hadn't put her there on trial, they had left her there for good. She hadn't wept a fortnight ago either as she'd stumbled in the dark to the carriage waiting for her, even though the vision of the Guildmistress holding triumphantly aloft a sword stained with blood had certainly been fresh in her mind.

Instead, she had simply counted the days and greeted the approach of each new dawn with increasing dread.

She hadn't dared sleep at first, on the off chance that someone from Bruadair—no doubt an assassin trained in the art of following his countrymen to slay them outside the border—had followed her. After that, she had scarce managed to stay awake. Thankfully the gouty gentleman from Gairn, who was traveling to take the waters in Meith, had happily provided her with what his swollen foot told him was an accurate count of the days.

By her count—and this she could hardly believe—by nightfall, she would have been journeying a full fortnight plus a bit. That left her almost another se'nnight to get from Istaur to Gobhann. The peddler's bag of gold was heavy enough that she supposed she might even manage to hire a carriage of some sort to take her from the port of Sgioba to Weger's gates. Though she was well read thanks to Mistress Muinear's insistence, details about Melksham Island had always been rather sketchy, so she could only hope to find what she needed.

Sgioba was the farthest point on the north side of the island where she could make port. If she could find a fast ship, she could make the journey in three days, leaving her ample time to reach Weger's gates, get herself inside, then negotiate with him for the sort of lad she would need.

She pushed herself back to her feet and spared a thought for what sort of decent bread might be purchased at dawn in a port town. Perhaps the leftovers from the day before. They couldn't be any worse than what she'd had at the Guild.

She brushed her filthy hands on her leggings and was grateful that at least the front of her was fairly clean. She reached down for her pack—

And found herself suddenly sprawled face down in the muck.

It took a moment or two to get far enough past the shock of that assault to catch her breath—and that she had to do carefully. She lifted her face out of the mud and tried to blink away the layer of slime that was now covering not only her back but her front. She wiped her eyes on her sleeve, but that did nothing but smear more unidentifiable substances all over her face.

She blinked enough to see a circle of lads surrounding her, pointing and laughing at her. She could hardly blame them, though she didn't care to endure any more of their sport than necessary. She pushed herself to her knees and looked around her quickly for her pack. No sense in losing that to the giggling fools continuing to mock her.

She blinked, but her surroundings were the same: smelly and empty of her pack.

She scrambled to her feet and spun around, looking for the rucksack that contained everything she owned save her book, which she had kept tucked into the waistband of her trousers. She could scarce believe her eyes. All her food, her spare clothes, her gold, everything gifted her by the peddler was gone.

One of the lads gestured back over his shoulder. "He went that way with your gear," he said helpfully. "Don't think you'll catch him, but you might try."

Or words to that effect. Aisling realized that her life—however long that life might be—was going to be made substantially more difficult by the fact that it was a struggle to make out what was being said. Perhaps Bruadair was less provincial than she'd imagined, for the speech there was rather more refined than what she was hearing at present. The accented common tongue she was listening to currently sounded as if the speakers were attempting it with pebbles in their mouths. Then again, they were a rough-looking lot, so perhaps they simply didn't know any better.

She pushed through the small crowd gathered there, then realized immediately there was no point in attempting to run after what was rightly hers. The press of humanity, some of whom smelled even worse than she did, was too thick. She pulled her cloak more closely around her and looked at one of the least grinning of the lads standing there.

"Docks?" she asked.

He waved expansively. "You're there, my lad. You might be overdressed, though. Perhaps we can relieve you of your very fine cloak—"

"Oy, there'll be none of that," said a loud voice from behind her.

Aisling found herself taken by the scruff of her neck. She didn't have time to protest that before the possessor of that gruff voice had dealt out several hearty shoves and a cuff or two. Lads dispersed without hesitation. She opened her mouth to offer thanks, then got a good look at the man who had rescued her. Her jaw continued on its way to her chest.

She had never seen anyone that large before in the entirety of her life. Perhaps her life that consisted of the society of women at the Guild and the odd lad down at the pub had ill prepared her for anything else. The Guildmistress might have been almost as tall as the man before her, but she was half his weight. Aisling was profoundly grateful he seemed to be friendly.

"Where're you off to, la—" He paused, then frowned. "I mean, er . . . lad?"

Aisling shut her mouth before untoward substances found their way inside. "Sgioba," she mumbled.

Then she froze. Aye, she had business in Sgioba that consisted of getting off her ship and beginning a frantic run to Gobhann, but given that all her funds had just been stolen from her along with every other item of value she possessed save the book of Scrymgeour Weger's strictures hiding in her trousers, she wasn't going to be indulging in that journey as quickly as she would have liked. She didn't even have anything to sell. She couldn't imagine anyone would even care about her book.

She was beginning to wonder, not for the first time, if she'd made a terrible mistake leaving her homeland.

She was currently friendless, fund-less, and covered in the muck of scores of horses and heaven only knew what else. Even if she could find work she was capable of doing—which would consist of weaving cloth and sewing the most rudimentary of straight seams—it would likely take her several fortnights to earn enough for her passage. She didn't have that much time. In fact, she had less than a se'nnight before she was dead.

And at the moment, she realized she wasn't feeling very well, so perhaps the peddler had overestimated the time left her.

"Sgioba, eh?" her rescuer said, looking at her with a thoughtful frown. "Nothing sails there but cargo ships and ruffians."

Aisling wasn't a very good weaver, all her years at it aside, but she was rather skilled with a map. At least she was in theory, and theory told her that even if she managed to sneak aboard a ship that would take her in a direct line across the strait to Bere, it was still a se'nnight's journey on foot to Gobhann. That was time she didn't have. Sgioba was where she would have to go.

She looked at the man. "I have no choice."

He considered. "You've no gear, I see," he noted. "Nothing to be done about that, I suppose. Perhaps you would welcome a wee wash, though. Then we'll see what a bit of pretty speech does for your passage."

Aisling could hardly believe she'd found a friendly face in a sea of faces that didn't look particularly friendly. She took a deep breath, then coughed out what she'd ingested. "Thank you," she wheezed.

The man winked at her. "My good deed for the day. What's your name?"

"Aisling."

"Interesting name," he said. "Where're you from?"

The peddler's warnings were uppermost in her mind at present, which left her even more unwilling than she usually was to divulge details. "Too obscure to mention," she said, gesturing vaguely behind her. "My village is, I mean."

"Many are, my lad," the man said with a smile. "Let's be off, shall we?"

Aisling nodded and followed him, trying to ignore her smell and pay attention instead to her surroundings. A sentence of death hung over her, true, but still she couldn't help but marvel that she was walking down a street half a world away from where she'd recently been, as freely as if she were simply out for an afternoon stroll. She was aware of the undesirables her companion pushed out of their way as they walked down a long, worn dock, but for the most part she simply walked and breathed air that was full of things she'd never smelled before.

"In a bit of a hurry, are you?" the man asked, taking a rather persistent lad and tossing him into the water without apology.

"Aye," she said, hearing the words come out of her mouth with less haste than desperation.

"Then you will certainly need a very fast ship."

"Is there such a thing?" she managed.

He glanced at her. "If you don't mind a bit of something added to the sails, as it were, aye, there is a particular ship fast enough to see you where you are going."

She had no idea what that extra bit of something might be, but as long as it didn't consist of her flapping her arms, she was all for it. "I don't mind, sir."

"Then we'll see what we can find. Clean up a bit here, lad, and we'll carry on."

Aisling paused in front of a wooden barrel and didn't dare ask where the water had come from. It was cold and mostly clean, something for which she was very grateful. She was happy to use it to wash the grime from her skin, but not her clothing. It was cold, so she thought it best to smell rather than freeze to death. She dried her face on the inside of her cloak, then looked up at her rescuer.

"Thank you."

"No need to, little one." He pointed toward the end of the dock. "Keep going until you can't go any farther. Ask for Captain Burke. Tell him Paien of Allerdale sent you. I've a bit of business back in town—buying pretties for my lady wife, you see—else I would come with you. Tell him I'm sorry to forgo the pleasures of his ship, but I've sent you instead." He laughed a little. "I'm sure he'll thank me."

Aisling had no idea why he found the thought so amusing, but she wasn't going to ask. That might have been because there was a sudden and quite annoying lump in her throat at the sight of the gold coin Master Paien was holding out toward her. She met his eyes quickly.

"I couldn't—"

"Of course you can." He smiled, a warm smile that left her unaccountably comforted. "Do a good turn for someone else when you're able. I've had more than my share done to me of late. And some passing fine victuals at places I thought only existed in—" He paused, then laughed a little. "Never mind my ramblings. Be off with ye, little one, and catch yer ship."

"Thank you, good sir."

He patted her shoulder again with one of his great paws, then walked off, whistling a cheery tune and shoving a few more lads out of his way. Aisling would have watched him go, but she decided immediately that the best thing she could do was hurry to the end of the dock. Whilst Paien of Allerdale might have been of a friendly mien, the rest of the men on the dock were not. If she gained the ship without losing her coin, it would be a miracle.

Unfortunately miracles were apparently not hers to claim that day. By the time she had reached the ship Master Paien had indicated, all the while trying to avoid seedy-looking men and even a pair of women dressed in red silks who looked as dangerous as the men, she was missing not only her coin but her cloak and her boots. She wasn't entirely sure her eye wouldn't swell shut soon, and she was fairly convinced her lip was bleeding. Whatever else might be said about her, one could certainly say that brawling was not an occupation she should be considering anytime soon.

Things were just not going her way. She shouldn't have been surprised, she knew. The journey there had been terrible: uncomfortable, unpleasant, and with absolutely no privacy in the coach. That, added to her constant fear every time they paused that she had been followed and caught, had made for a horrendous journey indeed. She hadn't spent very much time doing anything but hiding behind the hood of the peddler's cloak and wishing she could ignore the sensation of the carriage standing still and the world spinning endlessly beneath her . . .

She stumbled to an ungainly halt behind a stocky man who directed other less burly lads to carry things to a ship bobbing not-so-gently against the wood of the dock.

"Excuse me, sir," she began.

He elbowed her aside. "No time, lad."

"Are you Captain Burke?"

"If you have to ask, lad, you should be back at home, hiding behind your mama's skirts, now *move*."

"Paien of Allerdale sent me," she blurted out.

Captain Burke swung around, almost taking her head off with his arm. He frowned. "Did he, now?"

"He gave me a coin as well," Aisling said, wrapping her arms around herself.

"Where is it?"

There was the rub, truly. She took a deep breath and looked up at him with as much courage as possible. "I lost it."

"Had it stolen from you, no doubt," Captain Burke said with a grunt. "And no wonder, what with you being such a wisp of a thing. What are you thinking to be out in the world?"

"I have no choice," she said, trying not to sound as desperate as she was. "I must reach Sgioba as quickly as possible." She took a deep breath. "I could work on your ship."

"Doing what?" he asked with a snort. "Looking for your beard? Lad, you're about to find yourself in the bay if you don't leave me be."

"I can sew your—" She gestured at the canvas bits hanging from the crossbars of the mast of his ship. "Well, whatever those things are."

"Sails," the captain said, blowing out his breath. "You useless landlubber, begone!"

Aisling caught him by the sleeve. "Please," she said quickly. "*Please*. I need to get to Sgioba."

He raised his hand. She realized he intended to strike her only because another hand caught his wrist and stopped it from coming any farther toward her. The captain started to swear, then shut his mouth abruptly around his words. He shook off the restraining hand, then schooled his features.

"Just a lesson in manners," he said gruffly.

A male voice spoke from behind her, the words pronounced in an elegant way she could understand perfectly. "Not taught by you, I don't think."

"Of course, my lord."

Aisling looked over her shoulder. A man stood there, cloaked and hooded. He was quite a bit taller than she was, though she didn't consider herself particularly diminutive. Hadn't the Guildmistress complained endlessly about the space her legs took up in order for her to weave in the workroom?

The man reached out and handed the captain two gold sovereigns.

"That should suffice for his passage and mine," he said, his voice sounding as hoarse as if he'd been shouting for weeks on end. "And I am no lord."

"Of course, my l—" The captain bit his tongue around what he obviously intended to say. He shot Aisling a look. "Best polish his boots for him, boy, lest he humors me by allowing me to pitch you over the side."

Aisling managed to nod, only half heeding what he had said. She was too busy looking at the man's hand. It was horribly scarred, as if it had been . . . well, she supposed she couldn't say in truth what the scars were from. If the scars troubled him, he didn't show it. He simply tucked his hand back in his sleeve and stood there, silent and unmoving. Aisling looked up at his face but could see nothing of his features save a rather handsomely fashioned nose that protruded slightly from his hood.

"Thank you," she said, feeling that was somehow woefully inadequate. "I will of course repay you—"

"No need."

"If he says no need, take him at his word and get your arse on board, lad," the captain snapped, "before I forget your passage has been paid."

Aisling didn't doubt he would if it suited him. She ran up the ramp spanning the distance between the dock and the ship, because she was accustomed to doing what she was told. And because she wasn't, in truth, free as yet. Until she reached Gobhann and bargained with Scrymgeour Weger for one of his mercenaries to aid her, she was still captive. She knew this because she had earlier found a note tied around a packet of dried fruit. She had subsequently tucked that note very carefully inside the cover of Weger's book where it would remain hidden. She supposed she could have just as easily thrown it away given that its contents had been indelibly burned onto her mind.

Go to Gobhann, talk to Weger, find a lad capable of doing what needs to be done with absolute secrecy and silence. Say nothing of your errand or your life will be the forfeit, no matter how many fortnights have passed.

All of which she fully intended to do. She would walk up to Weger's gates, knock, ask to speak to the lord of the keep, then present her problem to him along with a bag of gold—

Which she didn't have any longer. She shivered as she stood in the midst of the commotion of a ship getting ready to launch. She felt horribly exposed, mostly because she had not a bloody thing to her name save that book of Weger's strictures she had tucked into the waistband of her trousers for safekeeping. No pack with supplies, no gold, no cloak with more coins sewn into the hem. She didn't even have her hair to sell any longer. She wondered if it might be easier to simply go and heave herself overboard—

And then she saw past all the ropes and barrels and gear that littered the deck, past the other ships that crowded the one she stood on, past the buildings that had blocked her view of something she had never seen before.

The sea.

She realized her mouth was hanging open only because her mouth had become rather dry after a few minutes standing in the same place, unmoving, practically not breathing.

It was . . . glorious.

She walked over to the railing, because she couldn't not go have a closer look. She clutched the wood and looked out into the bay, seeing what she had never before imagined. It moved ceaselessly, that sea, sparkling in the sunlight, continually slipping past the ships bobbing against the docks.

"Shut your mouth," the captain snapped suddenly, "and try not to look as if you've never been away from home before."

She hadn't realized he was standing next to her. She looked up at him, mute. He started to say something else, then sighed.

"Never seen it, have you?"

She shook her head slowly.

"You'll never be free of it now, lad, not with that look on your face."

"Won't I?" she managed.

"Nay," he said in a tone that was suddenly almost kind. "Best find yourself something to do either on a ship or near the shore. You'll wither, else." He put his hand on her shoulder briefly. "We men of the sea require a certain amount of salt air every day or we just waste away." He nodded wisely. "Keep that in mind—nay, damn it, put those kegs on the *port* side, ye bloody fools!"

Aisling watched him stride away, continuing to instruct his men politely about their duties. She thought about what he'd said, then looked back out over the sea. She suspected he might be right. She listened to the men and lads shouting as they did whatever it was they did to get the ship underway, heard the gulls crying above her, smelled air that swept through her and healed something inside her she hadn't realized was a wound.

And then she remembered whom she had to thank for it all.

That man was standing a few paces away from her, his hands—both scarred, she could now see—gripping the railing. The wind caught his hood suddenly and tore it away from his face.

Aisling wasn't impressionable. In fact, she had almost prided herself on her steely pragmatism and her ability to remain unaffected by most everything. Jewels and silks on display during those rare moments when she had seen fine ladies wearing them during the daylight on their way to some fancy occasion or other had left her unimpressed. Fine carriages, well-bred horses, men dressed and powdered and perfumed had hardly merited a yawn. She might have lifted an eyebrow now and again over something she'd read in a book, but she couldn't say that counted for anything much.

But that man standing there . . .

She was, she reminded herself, not a giddy maid. She was a woman of a reasonable number of years, too old to be swayed by a pretty face.

But she wasn't swayed; she was stunned. She had never in her life seen a man so handsome. She hardly knew where to begin describing him. His hair was dark, his profile noble, his features refined and flawless. The captain had been an absolute fool to call him a lord. Surely only a prince could be so beautiful—

And then he turned to face her.

She continued to stare at him without a change in her expression only because she had mastered that art at an early age to save herself the trouble she had watched less discreet gels find themselves unhappily experiencing.

The left side of his face was horribly scarred, as if he had caught his cheek against some unyielding surface that hadn't wanted to release him. It wasn't so much a single scar as it was a web of scars that started at the corner of his mouth, ran up his cheek to the side of his eye, then traveled over to his ear. It looked as if he might have scraped his face against the same bit of rock that had perhaps taken hold of his hands.

She looked into his very green eyes and smiled faintly. "Thank you, good sir, for the passage."

He pulled his hood back over his face, nodded, then moved away.

"Sew a seam, can you?"

Aisling jumped at the sound of the bark next to her ear. She steadied herself and looked at Captain Burke. "I can, actually."

"I have a thing or two needing mending. You'll do it and earn a pair of boots and a cloak if you're quick and careful." He scowled. "Paien of Allerdale will owe me."

Aisling followed the captain, feeling the boat already rocking beneath her feet. It reminded her unhappily of the carriage, only at least here she had air to keep herself from being ill. She didn't dare ask the captain how long the journey would be. As long as she talked to Weger and convinced him to sell her a mercenary—

Which she would have no way of paying for.

"Coming?" the captain demanded.

She nodded, because she had to have something to put on her feet and around her shoulders. She passed the tall, dark-haired man who had paid for her passage, but he didn't look at her, and she didn't attempt further speech with him. One of his hands was resting against the railing, but the other was holding on to the throat of his cloak, as if he didn't want his hood blowing back and revealing more than it had before.

She understood and hoped he would take her thanks as payment for his generosity. She supposed that in time she would find her feet steady beneath her, grow accustomed to the freedom she would soon be enjoying, and then she would repay the kindness of both Paien of Allerdale and the stranger before her.

But first, her own life, which would be much better seen to with a cloak and boots at her disposal. She followed the captain, hoping sincerely that whatever it was he had for her to sew would be something she and her straight seams could manage.

Three

Rùnach stood at the railing as Burke's ship limped into port, three days later than intended. That certainly wasn't the captain's fault; the weather had been absolutely terrible. If he hadn't had such a strong stomach, he might have spent his share of time along with the other passengers, heaving his guts out over the railing. Instead, he had simply found a spot above decks where he was out of the way of most of the weather and passed the time contemplating the irony of sailing not to Bere but to Sgioba as a way to ease his sense of haste. Given how much time the weather had cost them, it would have been quicker to simply sail to Bere, then cross the rest of the island on foot.

He supposed he could have avoided the whole thing by flying from Lake Cladach, but he had purposely avoided that. He had left his grandfather's house on his own two feet, because he had wanted to make a point of leaving behind in a very pedestrian fashion all things magical and beautiful. He had no intention of discontinuing the practice now.

Iteach had walked along behind him obediently for a goodly part of that first night, stood guard over him whilst he slept, then apparently grown bored with it all. Rùnach had lost count of the shapes the beast had taken as he himself had simply continued on his way.

He had paused just outside Istaur and waited until his horse had resumed his own shape and was paying him a decent bit of attention so he could come to some sort of understanding with him. He had made it clear that he would continue on toward Gobhann via ship and his horse would, well, his horse would do as he bloody well pleased, apparently. Iteach had tossed his head at the suggestion that he change himself into something that might fit into a pocket, replaced his equine self with a remarkably fine-looking hummingbird, then flitted off. Rùnach had honestly had no idea whether or not he would ever see him again.

He watched idly as seagulls flapped lazily alongside the ship as it slowed, wondering what it would feel like to fly again. He could remember with perfect clarity the last time he'd flown. It had been with his brother, Gille—a notoriously inventive shapechanger—and their flight against the canopy of heaven had lasted well into the wee hours of the morning. He remembered thinking at the time that that sort of flight might not happen again for a bit. It was a sad testament to his arrogance that it had never occurred to him that that flight might not happen again *ever*.

"Excuse me, sir," a young voice warbled beside him, "but there is a bird sitting on your larboard side."

Rùnach looked to his left and was greeted by the sight of a smirking seagull. He lifted an eyebrow at it and had an ear-piercing call as his reward.

"Lianaich preserve us," the lad breathed.

Rùnach blinked. "Who?"

"Lianaich," the lad said, looking at Rùnach as if he had grave doubts about his intelligence. "Guardian of all honest sailors. She was the daughter of Seòladair, the great sea captain who sailed into the mists of Guasachdach with only three half-mad lads as crew. During her father's greatest voyage around the world, he fell ill, went fully mad before he perished, and it was left to Lianaich

to squelch a mutiny and bring back the treasures due the king of
Meith, else she would be turned into a mast."

Rùnach knew several of the descendants' of that particular
king of Meith, but couldn't bring to mind a one of them who would
have turned a sea captain—or his daughter—into a mast. But perhaps he wasn't as well-read as the average galley lad.

The lad made a shooing motion at the seagull, but it only
squawked at him, which left him backing away, making signs
Rùnach assumed were of ward and other seafaring usefulness.
He would have assured the boy that it was only his horse masquerading as a rather obnoxious bird, but he was interrupted by
the boatswain calling the hands to their stations. The kitchen lad
disappeared belowdecks, leaving Rùnach to his watching.

The port of Sgioba was every bit as squalid as he'd expected it
might be. There was a certain amount of wear one might expect to
see in a port, but this went far beyond simple sea air. He had no
fear for himself, but he certainly wouldn't have brought his sister
to such a place.

Then again, for all he knew Mhorghain had traveled here more
than once when he'd been unaware she was even alive. He found
himself rather more grateful than usual that she had someone
now to look after her, though perhaps she would do just as much
looking after her husband as he would her.

He looked about himself for the tall, painfully thin lad he'd
paid passage for, but didn't see him. Now, that was a lad who would
have been better off to stay at home. Perhaps he'd found sense
and was hiding behind a barrel until he could rush down the
gangplank and hie himself off to whatever relative he was seeking, hopefully without finding himself robbed yet again.

"Do you have dreams, my lord?"

Rùnach almost fell over the railing. He pulled himself back to
himself and found Captain Burke standing next to him, watching
him closely.

"What?" he managed.

The captain leaned against the railing with the ease of one who
had done it innumerable times and knew just how comfortable he

could get before he fell overboard. "I wouldn't say this to just anyone, but I have the feeling you'll understand." He hesitated, then
shook his head. "My dreams are troubled."

Rùnach suppressed the urge to swear. Did he have the sort of
face that led people to divulge details better left undivulged? He
had gone out of his way to keep to himself and keep his face covered, lest he draw unwanted attention. Apparently he hadn't been
diligent enough.

"Sounds terrible," Rùnach said, trying to imbue his tone with
just enough sympathy to allow the captain to feel as if he'd been
heard, but not enough to encourage him. "Bad ale, no doubt."

That the captain didn't respond to that but plunged straight
into a description of his troubling nocturnal visions said something perhaps about the seriousness of them. Rùnach tried to pay
attention, but truly he had no desire to listen to anyone's dreams of
barnacles and leaky hulls and—

Rùnach held up his hand suddenly. "What did you say?"

The captain frowned, as if he were slightly disappointed in
Rùnach's ability to listen. "I said I had dreams of streams running
through my belowdecks."

"I'm no seaman," Rùnach said, "but aren't mice generally the
only thing running belowdecks?"

Captain Burke drew himself up. "Not on my ship. Well," he
amended, "not often. And if it were just mice troubling my dreams,
I wouldn't be so unsettled. Unfortunately, 'tis those streams that
won't leave me be."

It was obvious that the captain wasn't going to let *him* be until
he'd unburdened himself fully, so Rùnach leaned back against the
railing alongside his host and folded his arms over his chest, set-
tling in for what he could tell would be a fairly long conversation.

"Are these ordinary streams, or something different?" he asked
politely.

"Well, that's just the thing," the captain said slowly. He looked
at Rùnach. "Apart from the fact that they're running places they
shouldn't, there's what they seem to be made of that's alarming."

Rùnach felt time slow. He supposed that sensation might have been exacerbated by the slowing of the ship as it rolled into port, but then again, perhaps not. He couldn't say that he had retained many of the gifts he'd taken for granted in his former life, but he'd seemingly been blessed with a pair of them. He could see perfectly well in the dark, something not even his father could manage, and he had a nose for . . . well, it was almost as if he could sense the trails left by magic before that magic had carved its way into whatever surface it would choose.

He managed to suppress the urge to flee simply because there was nowhere to flee to. He gave Captain Burke a look he hoped wasn't too pained. "And what do you think these rivers are made of?"

The good captain looked as uncomfortable as Rùnach felt. He had to take a deep breath, seemingly bolster his courage with a selection of hearty curses, and scowl fiercely at a ship's mate or two before he spat out the word with as much haste as possible.

"Magic."

Of course. Rùnach decided that the most sensible course for him would be to get as far away from his companion and his speculations as quickly as possible. "How interesting," he managed, though he found it anything but.

"Or it might have been dreams." He looked at Rùnach. "Rivers of dreams found within a dream."

Rùnach shivered. He shouldn't have found any of it unsettling. He wasn't troubled by dreams from his past or his future, a fact for which he was enormously grateful at the moment. The truth was, his life was nothing but easy movement from one blissful night's sleep to the next. And soon his days were going to be filled with the hard, honest work of a man doing things in a perfectly normal way, which would lead to more restful nights' sleeps thanks to an abundance of honest toil. Dreams about rivers and magic and rivers of magic—

"They seemed to be pulling at my ship," Captain Burke continued thoughtfully. "Pulling it apart at the seams, if you like, one board at a time—nay, but a splinter at a time, eating away at the foundations of it all." He looked at Rùnach. "A mystery, isn't it?"

Rùnach didn't like the picture that painted for him. He'd had enough experience in a former lifetime with magic lurking beneath foundations of all sorts of things to be happy he would never need encounter it again.

"It is indeed a mystery," he agreed, and it was one he had no interest in investigating further. "I'm sure it will all clear itself up soon enough." He fished about in his pocket and pulled out a gold coin. "Give that to the little lad with no boots, won't you? He'll need gear, I imagine."

The captain looked faintly disappointed—perhaps he had hoped for a solution to his restless nights—but he took the coin just the same. "He's been sewing for what silver pennies I'm willing to give him, but I'll give him this as well. Very generous, my lord."

"I told you," Rùnach said, "I am no lord."

The captain shrugged. "Quality displays itself."

"You might be surprised," Rùnach said under his breath, but he supposed the captain hadn't heard him for his sudden bellowing at one of his men. Rùnach was happy to see him go off to attend to his own affairs and leave tales of his nightly perturbations behind.

Rivers of magic, rivers of dreams. What rot. The sooner he was away from a man who dreamed either, the happier he would be.

The ship docked, and none too soon to Rùnach's mind. He suppressed the urge to look for that scrawny lad and make certain he reached his destination in safety. It was none of his business. He instead walked over to the side of the ship and put himself at the head of the line to disembark, because he had things to be doing and no time to aid foolish boys who should have remained at home. He had the work of a simple soldier before him. No overwhelming quests, no dangerous forays into places better left unexplored, no marching off into the gloom to right wrongs that could be better righted by someone else.

And no rivers of magic and dreams running inside banks no mortal could see.

Nay, he would gain Weger's mark over his brow, see what glory and riches it brought him, then live out his life in relative obscurity in some place where he wouldn't have to think too often about what he had been.

It was much safer that way.

I t was almost dawn—after a night spent walking thanks to that irascible stallion of his who had given him a final view of his tail feathers as he'd flown off to do heaven only knew what—before he realized that he was being followed.

He cursed his stupidity. It wasn't as if he wasn't accustomed to looking over his shoulder to see what lurked in the shadows. When one lived in a university full of mages, one tended to want to know what was loitering out of sight. Why he hadn't been just as aware in a forest of ancient trees, he couldn't have said. Perhaps the lack of sleep on board Burke's ship had been more detrimental to his wits than he'd suspected it would be.

He continued on for a bit until the opportunity to duck into the shadows appeared, then he slipped off the road to his left. He stood behind a sturdy tree and waited for his would-be companion to pass him.

He was somehow not terribly surprised to find it was the lad whose passage he'd paid for. Of course, the youth was again without either cloak or boots. He was limping along at a good pace, though, so perhaps he'd managed breakfast before he'd been robbed again. That haste didn't seem to be keeping him warm, something Rùnach could understand. Even for spring, it was damned cold still.

He opened his mouth to call out, then shut it with a snap. To his surprise, not only had he been followed, but his follower was being followed. Rùnach reached out and yanked the lad directly in front of him off the road and into the shadows, then clamped a hand over his mouth before the boy could so much as squeak. He endured a feeble elbow in his gut, but then even his captive seemed to sense there was something amiss, for he went completely still.

And in that moment, Rùnach realized something very important.

The lad he was holding captive was not a lad.

He saved that as something to think about later and concentrated on the man sauntering down the road toward them. The man had neither sword nor bow, which made Rùnach very uneasy. He would be the first to admit that he was a very poor judge of who had magic and who didn't, but the sight of a man walking through the woods without any sort of protection bespoke either bravado Rùnach wasn't interested in challenging or magic he didn't want to encounter.

He held his breath as the man in the road stopped, tilted his head to one side, and listened for things perhaps only he could hear. He frowned thoughtfully, then walked on.

The lad—or, rather, the lass—Rùnach was holding tried to pull away from him. He tightened his arm around her waist.

"Scream if you like," he breathed, "and alert that man out there to our location. I guarantee he'll have much more in mind than simply joining us for the breaking of our fast."

She went still again. Rùnach stood with her in the dark, grateful for the shadows of the trees, and waited until he could see the man no longer.

He considered the possible identity of that traveler for a moment or two, then shook his head. There were many dark-haired men in the world, many who looked as if they had a hint of elven blood flowing through their veins, perhaps even a few who looked as if they might have sprung out of Ceangail—

Nay, it was impossible. It was still quite dark and whilst his sight in the dark was excellent, he was extremely weary and, he could admit now that he was no longer on board, still a little seasick. He was imagining things. He had not just seen whom he'd thought he'd seen.

He waited a bit longer just to be safe, then removed his hand from his companion's mouth. She jerked away from him and spun around to face him. She was bleeding down the side of her head, which led him to believe she had had a bad night. He started to reach out to touch her head only to have her duck away from his hand.

"And just what was that about?" she demanded in a furious whisper, gesturing down the road.

Rùnach wasn't sure if she was angry with him or terrified by what she'd seen. Given that she'd apparently been robbed thrice in the past se'nnight, perhaps she had more reasons for fury than he wanted to know. Or perhaps she thought she might warm herself with a bit of perfectly reasonable indignation.

"That was about you following me," he returned, quite reasonably he thought, "and someone else following you. I didn't care for the dance, so I decided to make a change to the pattern."

She put her shoulders back. "I wasn't following you. I simply happened to be going in your direction."

Rùnach suppressed the urge to roll his eyes, then undid the catch of his cloak. He reached out and swung it around her shoulders, then started to fasten the clasp for her before it occurred to him that he wouldn't have done the like for any lad he knew. He pulled back quickly, then returned to folding his arms over his chest. It was a handy thing, that, because it kept him from reaching out to finger either her shorn hair or her very pale cheeks.

And then he realized what she'd said.

"My direction," he echoed. "To where?"

"That, good sir, is none of your business," she said, lifting her chin. "And while your generosity does you credit, I cannot accept this—"

"Keep the cloak," he said shortly, "and save me the sight of your shivering self whilst we discuss exactly where you think you're going on this road that only leads to one place."

She stepped backward. "I must be on my way. I fear I cannot repay you for the cloak."

"No need," he said, waving away her words, "but let us discuss this road you're thinking of taking—"

"Again, none of your affair." She nodded firmly, as if she perhaps sought to convince them both of her determination. "I have business."

He watched her turn and walk out onto the road, then considered a bit more. He supposed it was possible that she was fleeing something unsavoury—an unfortunate betrothal, or an iron-handed father, or perhaps even a controlling mother—but that would surely lead her to seek refuge with a grandmother or a great-aunt who would be equal to the task of sheltering her from such annoying relatives. He supposed it was possible that there existed the odd hamlet tucked along the coast, supplier of meat and wool for those who braved Gobhann's unforgiving walls. Perhaps the lass before him was simply on her way to such a place.

He sighed heavily. Obviously he was going to have to take time and see her safely to wherever she was going. He stepped out onto the road and started after his self-appointed charge. It took him no time at all to catch up with her, then he walked beside her, keeping a careful eye on the road ahead. He saw no other traveler, which was only mildly reassuring. The woods were thick, and dawn not yet arrived. He watched her as they walked, wondering what she was about. She was continuing doggedly on her way, ignoring him for the most part save for those wary looks she occasionally favored him with.

"Where are you headed?" he asked finally.

She quickened her pace and said nothing.

"There isn't much to the west," he noted.

She glanced at him briefly. "I appreciate the aid, but I'll be fine on my own from here. Manly business ahead, and all that."

"Manly business?"

"Aye," she said firmly. "Manly business of a sort I must keep to myself."

Well, he couldn't imagine she could have any business save plying a needle on some poor tunic, so he contented himself with the thought that she was no doubt traveling toward some sort of landhold where she would seek refuge from whatever simple, womanly concern had been too much for her. Nothing else made sense.

He shouldered his pack, then almost went sprawling. He caught himself heavily on one leg, then turned, his sword halfway from its sheath before he realized it was simply his damned horse nosing him so enthusiastically.

The subsequent whicker sounded too much like a laugh for Rùnach's taste.

The woman next to him gasped. "Where did that come from? You didn't have him on the ship."

"You would be surprised where a man might acquire a horse," Rùnach said grimly. He took up his journey again, ignoring the way his mount continued to clomp along behind him, and tried to concentrate instead on where he was going.

He resigned himself eventually to the necessity of depositing his companion at her destination, for it didn't look as if she would merely trot off the road toward it on her own. He supposed he would also need to think of her as a him for at least the duration of their acquaintance, which he hoped would be very brief. He had business of his own, the business of getting on with his very ordinary, unremarkable life. He had neither the time nor the heart to look after a lass who should have been safely ensconced in her father's house.

Time wore on, and his patience wore thin. She didn't seem to be preparing to leave the road and pick her way through the woods to her aunt's house, so when the wood had ended, he stopped and looked at her.

"Don't you have family in the area, then?" he asked, feeling rather exasperated.

"Nay," she said, looking at him in confusion. "Why would you think that?"

"Then where are you going?" He gestured impatiently to his left. "There?"

She followed his pointing finger, then her jaw went slack. Rùnach followed her gaze and had to agree. It was one thing to think about Gobhann from the comfort of a decent seat in front of a roaring fire; it was another thing entirely to stand several hundred paces from the place and realize that there was nothing to it save unrelenting grey walls topped by unrelenting grey clouds. Did Weger attract that sort of weather simply by virtue of who he was, or was there a spell set over the place that cast it perpetually into gloom? Rùnach didn't suppose he wanted to know, though he wouldn't have been surprised by either.

Mhorghain had warned him it was a bit sparse, but his sister was obviously a master of understatement. At least at Buidseachd there had been ample heat, an excellent kitchen, and a generously stocked library. He didn't dare hold out any hope for any of the three inside what faced him. The walls were sheer, the front gates forbidding, and the general aspect enough to give one pause.

But if what lay within was the purchase price for the rest of a useful life, he would pay it gladly.

He looked at his companion, who had turned the color of her hair, which he discovered, thanks to a rapidly lightening sky, was so pale a yellow as to be almost white. She was filthy, as if she'd been rolling in the street and failed to find any sort of mirror to use in ridding her face of the smudges on her cheeks and nose. Her hair looked as if it had been much longer at some point and then cut carelessly with a knife. He started to suggest that she perhaps trot back the way she'd come when she turned and looked at him.

And then he, who hadn't dreamed in a score of years, felt himself falling into a dream without any hope of saving himself.

He clutched at Iteach's mane and was actually rather glad for his mount's rather pointed snorting directly into his ear. He shook his head, looked at the beast in annoyance, then found himself helplessly looking into eyes that were neither green, nor blue, nor grey, nor any other color he could name. They were all those things, only possessing a sort of translucence that left him feeling as if he weren't quite firmly settled inside his poor form.

Very well, so he couldn't say she was beautiful, though perhaps that had to do less with the fairness of her face than with the fact that she looked to be under extreme duress. But nay, she wasn't beautiful. Then again, in all his years before he'd gone with his family to the well, he had seen more than his share of absolutely breathtaking women. He supposed in the arrogance of his youth he had been well aware of the fairness of his own visage, the lure of his magic, and the appeal of his parentage. Beautiful women, elvish or not, had put themselves in his way, hoping to catch his eye. He had even considered coming to an understanding with one of them, a princess of Cothromaiche. It was possible that he had enjoyed those attentions perhaps more than he should have.

But at no time had he ever looked at a woman and—

He shook his head sharply. He was weary, that was it. Weary and frustrated and needing to have found a barn and slept the night before instead of having spent it walking. The wench was naught but a silly gel who would have been better served to have found a simple, unremarkable man to wed and settled down to making his suppers and providing him with sons.

"You can't be in earnest," he said with a heavy sigh. "Gobhann?"

"Aye," she said, pulling his cloak more closely around her and lifting her chin. "I have business there that cannot be delayed."

"The only business you should have, my *lad*, is taking up your place again behind your mother's skirts. Now, why don't you let me turn you around and set you on the right path?"

He reached for her, but she backed away.

"I don't need aid."

"I didn't say you needed aid, I said you needed sense," he said, reaching for her arm and taking hold of it. "Let's go—"

"Look out behind you! There in the woods!"

He released her and turned around, drawing his sword as he did so. He braced himself, ready for anything, but fearing he would see there the man he had seen earlier that morning.

But he saw nothing.

His horse chortled, a particularly equine sort of snorting laugh that grated on Rùnach's nerves. He took a deep breath and looked at Iteach.

"Are you trying to help?"

The damned horse only lifted an eyebrow and snorted again. Rùnach rolled his eyes, reached for his temper, and strode off across the muddy spring ground toward a place he was quite sure wouldn't improve matters any. Whatever other failings his erstwhile companion might have had, the inability to sprint was not one of them. Whether she would make it to the gates before he did, however, was yet to be determined.

He dashed after her and contemplated what he'd seen in her face. If he hadn't known better, he might have thought there was desperation in her look. Perhaps that had less to do with determination than it did with a desire to find somewhere warm to sit and have something decent to drink. Obviously the task that lay next in front of him was to tell her that she would find neither inside Weger's formidable gates.

At least his legs worked as they always had, which aided him in getting himself quickly to the gates before his companion. He knocked politely, then put himself in front of her when she tried to elbow her way past him. He shot her a warning look.

"Go home."

"I must speak to Weger," she said firmly.

He couldn't imagine why. Obviously she had absolutely no idea what she was in for. Indeed, he couldn't bring to mind a single reason why a woman would want to go inside those gates and subject herself to what he suspected would be months of absolute hell.

He wished—absently, lest he think about it overmuch and grieve—that his sister Mhorghain hadn't chosen it as her habitation for so long, which led him to feeling that if he could save another wench the horrors of the work inside, he should.

"He wouldn't be interested in anything you had to say," Rùnach said.

She tried to elbow him out of the way. "I am a lad, just as any other. Why would he let you in and not me?"

"I have a sword?"

She opened her mouth, then shut it abruptly. Rùnach left her thinking on that and pushed her aside to put himself between her and the gate. It opened without haste, which he had expected. He steeled himself for the first test, grateful that in that, at least, he had been prepared by his sister and her husband as to what to expect—

Though it would have helped, he supposed, if he'd had a sword to hand.

His sword, as it happened, had been filched from his side with remarkable swiftness. He watched, Iteach's nose on his shoulder, as a woman who had no business even looking at Gobhann faced the gatekeeper and brandished that pilfered sword.

The gatekeeper rested his sword against his shoulder and scratched his cheek absently with his other hand.

"Well," he said, finally.

Rùnach couldn't have agreed more. The lad—er, woman, rather—holding his sword with both hands and struggling to keep it aloft might have done a fair amount of damage with it if she lost control and had it nick some poor fool as it fell toward the ground. But use it for its intended purpose?

Not anytime soon.

"Which way to the lord of Gobhann?" she said, her voice quavering dangerously.

The gatekeeper blinked. "I beg your pardon?"

"I must talk to Scrymgeour Weger *today*."

The gatekeeper, who was reputedly named Odo, looked at her as if he couldn't quite understand what he was hearing. "Today?"

"Before midnight, at least," she said.

Odo frowned. "I think you might be better served if you were to turn around and retreat back out the gate."

She put her shoulders back and fixed a look of determination on her face, a look she turned and favored Rùnach with very briefly. "I *will* go forward. If either of you stands in my way, you'll pay a very steep price."

Rùnach looked at Odo. Odo only shrugged, then gestured toward the stairs. The woman glanced at those stairs—empty ones, thankfully—then looked back at the gatekeeper.

"Thank you. I'll speak highly of your good sense to your master."

"Well, thank you, ah—"

"No need to exchange names," she said. "I just need an hour to speak to your master, then I will be on my way."

Odo frowned but didn't stop her as she walked unsteadily past him. Rùnach watched her reach the stairs, then looked at Odo.

"Master Odo," he said, inclining his head.

Odo lifted his finger and flicked it backward, indicating that Rùnach should remove the hood of his cloak. Rùnach supposed there was no point in delaying the inevitable flinching he would have as his reward. Why Miach of Neroche couldn't have attended to his face while he'd been about that bit of repair work at Seanagarra, Rùnach couldn't have said. Then again Rùnach hadn't asked. He had wanted hands that worked, which he had gotten, for the most part. Anything else had seemed just too frivolous. He suppressed the urge to take a deep breath, then reached up and lifted the hood back off his head.

Odo studied him for a moment or 'two, then leaned over and had a quiet word with one of the pair of lads who waited at his heels. The lad scampered off and up the stairs, bypassing the woman carrying Rùnach's blade. Rùnach watched for a moment, then looked at Odo.

"She's absconded with my sword."

"That one's trouble," Odo agreed, then he blinked. "Did you say—"

"I meant *he* has absconded with my blade," Rùnach said hastily. No sense in subjecting the gel to unnecessary attentions she was obviously trying to avoid.

Odo pursed his lips. "Then 'tis a good thing I've seen that *he* gets upstairs without incident." He considered Rùnach for a moment or two. "You remind me of someone."

"Do I?"

"Your sister, I imagine." Odo drew his sword and handed it to Rùnach. "We'll see if you make as good a showing as she did on her first day. Give that back later, if you're alive to do so."

Rùnach accepted the blade. "Thank you."

"Well," Odo said with a small smile, "you might not say the same a handful of hours from now, but then again, perhaps you might. That's a mighty set of scars you bear."

"They help me remember what not to become."

"I daresay." He looked over Rùnach's shoulder. "I'll see to your mount."

"He would likely appreciate that."

Odo waved him on. Rùnach would have thanked him yet again—he had decent manners, even in trying circumstances—but he suddenly found that whilst his companion had been waved through the gauntlet, he most definitely wasn't going to be enjoying that same concession. The bellow of a war cry approximately two handsbreadths from his ear almost left him leaping out of his skin.

He turned and lifted his sword, hoping his attempt at reaching the uppermost courtyard wouldn't end right there.

Four

Aisling made her way up the stairs, finding it very difficult indeed to keep her filched sword upright. Thank heavens she had no intention of becoming a mercenary. Better that she consider something that didn't require doing anyone in with a blade or being startled by the unexpected. She almost went sprawling thanks to a young lad slipping by her and racing up the stairs. Perhaps he was going to tell Weger he had guests.

She didn't want to think too hard about how that set her heart to racing.

She climbed many long flights of steps, some broken in half by passageways that led to places she didn't want to investigate, some briefly bursting out into courtyards only to wind back into darkened stairwells. She decided then that when she started her own life, she would begin a regimen of healthful trots about whatever village she settled on. She was wheezing already, and she was sure she had only climbed four or five flights of stairs.

But she climbed on because she had only until midnight to do what needed to be done to save not only her country but her own sorry neck. She would have had more leeway, of course, if it hadn't been for the inclement weather that had turned a three-day voyage on that rickety ship into almost six. Admittedly, she could have perhaps calculated amiss—

Nay, that wasn't possible. She had counted the days as if her life had depended on it, which it did. The third se'nnight ended at the stroke of midnight that night. Her task was set out before her and the time appointed mercilessly.

That she had managed to get past the gate was heartening. Perhaps it would be easier than she thought to simply continue on until she could go no further, at which point she could only assume that she would come face-to-face with either Weger himself or one of his aides. She would ask for a private audience, state her business, then be on her way. Perhaps Fate would smile on her and she would find a mercenary desperate enough to travel to Taigh Hall with only the promise of a princely sum as inducement.

She paused at the top of the sixth flight and looked over her shoulder. To her surprise, the man who had so generously paid her passage, then subsequently and rather inadvertently loaned her his sword, was fighting his way up the stairs behind her. Perhaps he had borrowed a blade from someone else. She considered telling him that assaulting Weger's men at every turn wasn't going to win him any affection from the lord of the keep, but perhaps it was better to keep her mouth shut. Obviously he had business in the keep just as she did, so perhaps it was better to carry on and leave him to his own affairs. She raised her eyebrows briefly at the things the man and his sparring partner were snarling at each other, added *learn curses out in general circulation* to her list of things to see to when she was free, then turned back to the stairs in front of her.

It was as she climbed that seventh staircase that things began to occur to her, most likely because she realized that there were men waiting in the shadows, men with drawn swords, men who watched her but did not approach. Perhaps it wasn't so much that the man behind her had been sparring with men she hadn't noticed, but that those men had formed a gauntlet he'd had to fight his way through. If that were the case, why hadn't she been favored with the same?

Perhaps that was yet to come.

She reached the top of the staircase and walked out into a courtyard full of statues, realizing only then that she was chilled to the bone—and very uneasy. She had skill enough for sniffing out the dangers lurking in the hierarchy of a weaving guild, but here she was completely out of her depth. It had occurred to her that she would need to talk quickly to convince Scrymgeour Weger to give her aid, but she hadn't considered that she might be putting her own life at risk as she did so.

She looked around her carefully. The middle of the courtyard itself was empty, surrounded by low, wholly inadequate walls, and full of fog. And then she saw that what she'd thought were statues obscured by the fog were actually more grim-faced men who stepped closer and formed a large circle around her, all watching her with glittering eyes. She hardly had the chance to even attempt to raise her sword before she went sprawling thanks to someone having pushed her from behind. She managed to hold on to her sword, but she supposed that was just dumb luck. She crawled to her feet and realized it had been her morning's companion who had nudged her rather ungently out of his way.

He was also keeping her behind him, putting himself between her and the man who had stepped forward and engaged him. She would have thanked him for that, but she imagined he wouldn't be particularly interested in anything she had to say at present. He was too busy keeping himself alive. He shrugged out of his pack at one point, then flung it away from him before he was decapitated by his foe.

The battle didn't go on for very long before her companion's sword was slapped out of his hand. It went sliding across the wet stone, past her. She followed its journey and saw the toe of a boot pin it against the stone. Aisling looked up the leg, up, and still up a bit more, until she saw a face that sent a cold, heart-stilling terror through her.

Scrymgeour Weger.

It could have been no one else.

"I heard," he drawled, "that a warrior of uncommon ferocity was making his way up my steps, so I came to see who it was. Which one of you two feeble women was mistaken for someone with sword skill?"

Aisling found herself again pulled behind the scarred man, which she didn't object to as it gave her time to decide how best to be about her business.

She looked around herself. She was still surrounded by very fierce-looking men who were watching her as if they could have as easily killed her as looked at her. Worse still was the giant of a man standing there with his arms folded over his chest, who would likely grasp her by the front of her tunic and fling her over his parapet. She could only assume what lay beyond those walls was the sea. She could hear the roar of it—or perhaps that was the wailing of those whom Weger had sentenced to death and were still awaiting it.

It was perhaps foolhardy to think there could be honor in such a place, but all she could do was hope for it. Though it was tempting to simply stand where she was and hide, she knew she had to do what she'd come to do. Her life hung in the balance.

She stepped forward, in front of her companion.

"It was me," she managed. "I am the warrior."

"You?" Weger said with a look that reduced her to the quivering coward she was. "You were the one sending my best men off to lick their wounded pride and not this strapping lad behind you?"

Aisling lifted her chin. She supposed that was less to manufacture a show of courage than it was to keep her teeth from chattering. "He did me a good turn on a ship recently. I had to repay him."

"Not by doing aught with a sword," Weger said with a snort. "I have a better idea. Why don't you take the part best suited for you, which would be to act as his servant for the next fortnight?"

She blinked. "But I wasn't planning on being here a fortnight. I only need to speak to you—"

He waved away her words. "Not now. I'm busy."

"But—"

"I am busy," he said, cutting her off curtly.

Aisling wanted to blurt out that she had until midnight only to talk to him, but he didn't seem amenable to any further conversation.

Weger pointed at her, then used his pointer finger in the most minimal way possible to indicate that she should move.

Aisling hadn't planned on moving, but she moved just the same thanks to the hands that came to rest on her shoulders and set her out of the way. She went, then pulled her cloak closer around her—*his* cloak, rather, the man who was now standing in front of her—and was grateful for someone to hide behind. She leaned slightly to the left so she could see Weger's face, which was as malleable as granite. He simply stared at her companion for several very long minutes in absolute silence. Then he pursed his lips.

"Well."

The man in front of her didn't move. It occurred to her as she stood there that he was the perfect size for her to hide behind. A swordsman, obviously, judging by his muscular build, which was well revealed by the tunic pasted to his shoulders and arms. He was trembling badly, but she couldn't blame him for it. If she'd been fighting her way up those perilous, slippery stairs, she might have been trembling as well.

"Your name?" Weger barked.

"Rùnach," the man said. "My lord."

Weger's expression didn't lighten. "Who's the quivering puss behind you?"

"A lad I encountered on my journeys."

Aisling looked around the man—Rùnach, if that was what he was called—and nodded. "He paid for my passage on the ship after I'd been robbed. Very decent of him."

"Then as *I* said, you'll be very decent and be his squire whilst you're both here, given that you have absolutely no skill and he has two hands that don't work."

Aisling felt her mouth fall open. "But—"

"Paul," Weger called, "take these two and show them to the buttery."

A man stepped forward. "But, my lord," he protested, "I have already a lad with no skill under my charge—"

"And now you have another," Weger said, looking at him mildly, "plus his servant. Does this trouble you?"

Paul looked as if he was torn between marching himself over to the parapet and flinging himself off or speaking his mind. Apparently he decided on the latter. He let out a slow breath. "It seems to me, Master Weger, that my skill might be, ah, better used—"

"How I say it should be used," Weger interrupted. "And I say your mighty skill, my good Paul, should be used to see this man and his servant fed. I'll send instructions later on where they are to be housed. Find the lad water as well to wash the blood off his face."

Paul opened his mouth, considered, then shut it. Aisling understood completely. She'd seen the look Weger had sent him and found herself rather relieved that her interaction with both the keep and the keep's lord would be limited to sneaking in a simple question before midnight.

Paul scowled at her, then looked at the man who had named himself Rùnach.

"Come, then. And bring that thing there along with you."

Aisling didn't argue. It was early still. Perhaps she would slip off after sunset, after Weger's work was done and he'd had a decent supper, and corner him. He might be more amenable then to listening to her request.

She walked behind Rùnach as he crossed the courtyard to collect his pack, then forced herself not to wince as she followed after him as he followed Paul. Her feet were very sore, though she supposed they would thaw out eventually. It was safe to say that she had spent the whole of her life that she could remember being cold and wishing that her feet were warm. The first thing she was going to do when she had a bit of money was buy herself a decent pair of shoes.

She descended steps behind Rùnach and Paul, hardly able to believe where she was. At least the inside of Gobhann was less intimidating than the outside. Her first sight of the keep that morning had almost stopped her heart.

Details had been, she had to admit, very sketchy about Scrymgeour Weger's lair. She'd known where it was, mostly, thanks to Ochadius's book. She'd scoured the weaving mistress's library for further details about both those who had escaped its sturdy gates and those who chose to stay inside the same, just to satisfy her curiosity. She had assumed it would be a rather small place, tidy, sparse, with perhaps large lists, stables for horses, and a rather rudimentary garrison hall.

She hadn't expected a fortress that looked as if it had simply erupted from sheer, unforgiving rock. The walls had risen easily a hundred feet up in front of her, terraced back against the mountainside, which had seemed to be, again, solid rock.

The inside of the keep was no less intimidating. More stone as far as the eye could see, with the whole place seeming sparse and uncomfortable. It was obviously a locale meant for the very utilitarian business of learning the art of war.

She followed Rùnach and Paul down three flights of stairs, then along a passageway that filled increasingly with a smell so vile she had to put her hand over her mouth.

"In here," Paul said in a tone that was just south of a snarl. "And be quick. When the food's gone, it's gone."

She couldn't imagine that could be anything but a good thing, but what did she know of men and their stomachs? She caught the rag Paul threw at her, presumably to clean her face with, then walked into a long, cave-like room full of tables flanked by rough-hewn benches. Those benches were currently being occupied by the most terrifying-looking group of men she had ever clapped eyes on.

She felt horribly conspicuous in her bare feet and borrowed cloak, but she seemed to garner little notice. That might have been because Rùnach seemed to be attracting the full attention of the bulk of the men there—and the attention wasn't of the pleasant sort.

She followed him to where things—she supposed they might have been termed *food*—were being slapped on trays and handed over for consumption. She looked down at her quivering, grey bit of gruel accompanied by a slab of dry, grey bread, and was almost felled by the smell of it. She accepted a cup of something she hoped was drinkable, then followed Rùnach over to a table.

He sat, nodded for her to sit between him and the wall, then set to his meal with the single-mindedness of someone who hadn't eaten much for breakfast. She hadn't eaten either save for what the captain had given her on board his ship. She had intended to take the coins she had earned sewing the things he'd trusted her with and buy yet more things that couldn't be as awful as the food in the Guild, but events had interrupted her—events consisting of disembarking, then finding herself promptly robbed. Again. She was beginning to think that asking someone for a few ideas on how to keep herself safe might be wise.

Her supper was every bit as disgusting as it looked. She ate it all only because she was very hungry. She poured some of her ale onto the cloth and wiped the blood from the side of her face. She sincerely hoped that would be the last time she ran afoul of ruffians. Highly unpleasant as a group, truly.

Once she was finished with that, she had nothing to do but look about herself and wonder what she'd been thinking. She should have asked Weger to come outside the gate and talk to her there. She was accustomed to the society of women. That wasn't to say that they couldn't be vicious or dangerous or uncouth, but at least after a certain point there had been no tittering over bodily emissions or fights erupting over bread that was just this side of brickish hardness.

At least she had a buffer between herself and the rabble. Of course when someone's stew went flying and the bulk of it landed against the wall above her head, she found she was wearing it just the same. The only thing that saved her from a broken nose was Rùnach's hand reaching out just in time to catch the bowl before it landed on her face. He set it down, then continued on with his meal.

She sipped her drink—she didn't think she dared call it ale, but she couldn't think of anything else it could be—in a futile effort to calm her nerves. She was extremely grateful when Rùnach asked her if she had finished, then indicated he'd had enough himself. She followed him from the dining hall, wincing at the things that hit her in the back but unwilling to draw any attention to the abuse.

Paul led them back up a flight of stairs and down a passageway to a door. He pushed it open, then indicated with a sweeping gesture that they should enter.

"Only the finest," he said grandly.

Aisling realized she wasn't moving only because her feet had become rooted to the spot. "We're together?"

"Of course," Paul said sharply. "Why would you expect anything else?"

"Well—"

"The lad is out of his head with weariness," Rùnach interrupted. "Many thanks to my lord Weger for his consideration."

Aisling peered into the miniscule chamber she had been given—to share with a complete stranger, no less—and wondered if it could possibly have been worse. There was a bed of sorts, a table sturdy enough to sport water for washing, and a tallow candle that was spluttering as it burned. She supposed it was an improvement over the long rows of cots in an enormous room that was stifling in the summer and freezing in the winter that she'd been accustomed to at the Guild, but she wasn't quite sure how.

"Wouldn't leave anything here you want to keep," Paul said from the doorway.

"Then thievery is overlooked?" Rùnach asked mildly.

"Everything's overlooked," Paul snapped, "or did you think this would be a luxurious holiday?"

"Nay," Rùnach said, "I hadn't expected that."

Paul, whoever he was and whatever his expectations were for his time in Gobhann, was obviously not happy about being any sort of host. Aisling realized she was in his way only because he elbowed her so hard as he strode off that she gasped. She also burped, a rather indiscreet thing that would have earned her not only a look from whatever overseer would have been in the weaving room but likely an extra hour or two after her shift doing some menial labor. She clapped her hand over her mouth, then realized that burps weren't the only things clamoring for escape.

Rùnach wasn't facing her, which she thought might be fortunate, all things considered. The half of his face that was scarred was too difficult to look at, and the half of his face that wasn't was also too difficult to look at. At the moment, he simply gave the overall impression of a man too large for the confined space they'd been given to share, though he went inside readily enough and dropped his pack on the floor.

Aisling hovered at the doorway, profoundly uncomfortable. She kept her hand over her mouth because doing so muffled the sounds that threatened to come out. Unfortunately that did nothing to mask the horrendous churning noises her stomach was making. It wasn't inconceivable that what she had eaten at dinner had been slightly more full of life than she'd feared, which led her to thinking that she might want to sit down sooner rather than later. The bed was the closest thing to her, so she perched on its edge and watched Rùnach stand in the midst of the chamber and turn himself around.

How she was going to live in this proximity with the man and not have him learn what she was—

Nay, there was no fear of that. She had her business to see to with Weger that night, then she would leave and that would be the end of it. Given the condition of her form, she suspected that she should be about that business sooner rather than later.

Rùnach fetched a pair of boots that had been sitting by the door and put them down next to her. "Those look like they might fit." He lifted his eyebrows briefly. "Generosity from an unexpected direction, I daresay."

"It makes up for supper."

He looked at her in surprise, then smiled.

She closed her eyes. It was fortunate that she wasn't going to be anywhere around the man. She had no interest in finding a man, actually, and she most definitely wouldn't have wanted the one in front of her if she'd been looking. He was . . . well, he looked a bit like what she'd always thought Heroes of old might look like: noble; grave; impossibly handsome, scars and all. If she ever wed, she wanted a simple, homely farmer who would think she was pretty. He would obviously have to be almost blind for that to happen, but perhaps that was something to think on later. All she knew was that the man in front of her was far too luxurious for her admittedly very pedestrian self.

"I believe we're missing a sword."

Aisling frowned, then nodded slowly. Rùnach had taken his sword from her as they'd left the courtyard, but the one he'd lost that had wound up under Weger's boot was definitely not in her care.

"I left it in the courtyard," she said. "I'll go—"

"Nay," he said easily, "I'll go. You should stay where you are."

She thought she should as well, but unfortunately she had things to see to that didn't include lingering on any horizontal surfaces. She shook her head. "I must come with you—"

"Nay, you mustn't," he said firmly. He shot her a look. "You look as if you're fair to sicking up your supper."

"But I need to speak with Weger."

"Do you?" he asked, looking at her with more curiosity than she was comfortable with. "Why?"

She hadn't realized just how small a chamber it was, nor how large Rùnach was. He had seemed so much more manageable outside the gates. She drew her hand over her eyes. "Because I must."

"I wouldn't badger him today, were I you."

She didn't have a choice, but she wasn't going to say as much. She also wasn't going to argue with a man who seemed twice her size. She would wait until he had left—as he was doing then—then determine how she was going to get back to her feet and out the door so she might be about her own business.

Her stomach still churned violently, which left her thinking that perhaps a small rest wasn't an untoward idea. She leaned over carefully until she was lying on the bed—if bed it could be called. It felt more like wooden slats with a blanket draped over them, but since that's what she was accustomed to, she wasn't going to complain. Her head was swimming, the chamber was swirling around her, and she thought she might be ill very soon.

Perhaps just a little rest before she gathered herself together, put on her gifted boots, and worked her way to wherever Weger kept himself in the evenings. She had to speak to him that night.

Her life depended on it.

Five

❧

Rùnach walked through the passageway that seemed to have a chill wind blowing through it just for his pleasure, then forced himself to climb the stairs with a spring in his step instead of dragging his sorry self up them. It occurred to him to wonder if he might not have been better off to have flown to Gobhann and saved himself the weariness of travel, but he let that thought continue on to the place where all regrets were wont to gather. There was nothing he could do about it now, and he'd had good intentions initially. Hopefully he could retrieve Odo's sword, then manage to get to sleep early.

Though he wasn't quite sure where he was going to sleep.

He considered the young woman he'd left behind in what apparently passed for a chamber here. Poor foolish, desperate lass. What had possessed her to come inside Gobhann's unforgiving walls? She had seemed determined to speak to Weger, though he couldn't imagine about what. She obviously had no sword skill, no

pack full of gold, and no sense of her peril. It must have been
something truly dreadful to have driven her from her home.

He wasn't quite sure what he was going to do with her at present. It hadn't taken him long to decide that the dining hall wasn't
a place to linger after the meal was over. He had given his companion no choice but to come with him—not that she seemed
inclined to argue about leaving—though he wasn't sure the chamber was much of an improvement. There had been an alcove opposite the bed with blankets tossed in it. He supposed it would have
to do for her. He would have given her the bed, but he was substantially taller than she was and it was the only place he would fit.
He would apologize for the lack of chivalry later, after he'd dis-
cussed with her exactly what she was and what the hell she'd been
thinking to come inside such a dreadful place.

He'd left her plotting, he was certain of that. If she hadn't
looked so green, he might have worried that she truly would run
afoul of trouble. He supposed she would be fortunate indeed to
simply run afoul of a garderobe before she started heaving.

He took a deep breath, realizing that he was more worked up
than he should have been over business that wasn't his. He had his
own task to accomplish, then his life to be about. He had spent far
too long locked behind Buidseachd's forbidding walls. That he
had traded one set of walls for another was something he supposed he shouldn't dwell on overmuch.

He came out into the uppermost courtyard he had visited before.
There was no moon, not that that would have mattered much
given the mist that had already draped itself over Gobhann like a
shroud. The chill made his hands ache, which made him more
angry than it should have. He saw Master Odo's sword lying in the
midst of the courtyard, walked over, then leaned over to pick it up.

A foot came out of nowhere to rest on the blade, denying him
his desire.

He straightened and found himself facing Gobhann's lord. He
couldn't say he was terribly surprised to see the man there. He
would no doubt have the odd question or two regarding Rùnach's
intentions. That was understandable. Whether or not those answers

would be sufficient to keep Weger from throwing him off the walls onto the rocks that were reputedly on the shore below was another thing entirely.

Weger flipped the sword up with his foot, caught it, then looked at the blade thanks to the dim light of torches that fought to illuminate anything in the fog.

"Nice blade."

"It belongs to your gatekeeper."

"Thought I recognized it." He shot Rùnach a look. "Think you'll ever be able to use anything like it?"

Rùnach looked at him evenly, refusing to be baited. "That's why I'm here."

"I usually require that my aspirants be at least capable of *holding* their weapons," Weger drawled. "I'm not sure you can even manage that."

"Then throw me over the parapet and have done."

"And have your grandpappy sweep inside my gates and cut out my entrails?" Weger shuddered delicately. "I think not."

"Surely you aren't afraid of him."

Weger shot him a look. "Nay, but I'm terrified of your mother and she is—sorry, was—his daughter. He may have learned something from her whilst I wasn't watching."

"I don't believe you were—or are, rather—terrified of either of them," Rùnach said wryly, "but I also think you would rather let me live than do me in. It would be a shame to miss the chance to satisfy your curiosity and grind me under your heel at the same time."

"There is that," Weger agreed. "And I suppose apart from your hands you're useful enough."

"Thank you."

Weger glanced about himself casually, then looked back at Rùnach. "And I might have the odd question for you, when the company in the evenings grows tedious and I'm looking for something to amuse me."

"I imagine you might."

Weger studied him silently for a moment or two. "Rumor has it you died at the well."

"It was a very near thing," Rùnach conceded, "but nay, I did not."

"Where have you been keeping yourself for the past score of years? Hiding in Sìle's pantry, eating through his larder, or in his library, memorizing spells you shouldn't know?"

"Neither," Rùnach said, refusing to spare any regret for not having chosen either of those very appealing alternatives. "I've been at Buidseachd."

"Ah," Weger said, nodding slowly, "somehow quite unsurprising. Were you brushing up on your considerable skills there, or something else?"

Rùnach supposed it was none of Weger's damned business what he'd been doing, though the truth of it probably wasn't believable. He'd been hiding, true, but he'd also been looking for the sources of his father's spells. Trying to explain why was, well, difficult. He'd had his reasons, but those reasons were too complicated for a conversation out in the open when he wasn't at his best. He looked at Weger evenly.

"I was hunting."

"I don't think I'll ask what," Weger said. He shot Rùnach a look. "I understand your sire also wasn't quite as dead as everyone thought."

"Do you?"

Weger shrugged. "I hear many things, though I imagine you do as well. Perhaps you've heard a few tidings of a recent nature that might delight and amuse your future swordmaster."

Rùnach tried not to smile. He'd heard Weger had a ready ear for gossip, but he hadn't truly believed it until that moment. As for the rest, he supposed those were details he could give easily enough.

"My brother Ruithneadh and his newly made wife Sarah had a little chat with my sire at his home in Dòire, of all places. They decided that for his own health and well-being it might be best he keep to his house and garden."

"Generous of them."

"Ruith thought so."

"And how did Gair react to such kindness?"

Rùnach shrugged. "I wasn't there to hear his dulcet tones or pleasant words, though I understand there was ample of both. I believe Ruith and Sarah were rather relieved to be out of earshot."

Weger grunted. "I have to wonder if he might like a house-guest."

"Have you one you'd like to rid yourself of, my lord?"

"Aye, 'twas a gift," Weger said sourly, "from a certain lad who earned my mark rather recently. I'm not sure who I want to kill first, the gift or the giver. And the latter was the newly made king of Neroche, if you're curious."

"What was his gift, then?"

"If he didn't tell you, I expect I won't. And unfortunately 'tis nothing more than I likely deserve, perhaps, for allowing Miach out my front gates without having had my price out of him before-hand." He frowned at Rùnach. "I hesitate to ask what you'll offer me."

Rùnach untied a purse from his belt and handed it over with-out ceremony. "Gold, gems, and other items from an unmagical treasury containing a part of my inheritance."

Weger hefted the bag expertly, chortled, then tucked it into a pocket on the inside of a very serviceable cloak. "I imagine I will count that with glee. Who's the gel?"

"What gel?"

Weger rolled his eyes. "You might call me many things, lad, but a fool is not one of them. She's not particularly lovely, but she's surely too pretty to be a lad."

"Which is why you put her in with me."

"Of course," Weger said without hesitation. "I can hardly vouch for the honor of the rabble that comes through my gates. The worst of the worst, some of them, though I will admit your sister lent an air of distinction to the place. I don't know what that slip of a thing is to you, but you'd best keep her close."

"I don't know her," Rùnach said frankly. "I paid her passage from Istaur because I saw she'd been robbed, then found her fol-lowing me this morning from Sgioba. I then simply stood back and watched as she paved my way to your luxurious porch here."

Weger huffed out something that might have been akin to a laugh. "Aye, she certainly did. I wonder what she thinks she'll have now she's inside my gates?"

"I have no idea," Rùnach said, "though she seems powerfully interested in talking to you."

"I shudder to think why. Perhaps you would do me the very great favor of finding out sooner rather than later so I can send her quickly on her way. There is something about her eyes that bothers me." He started to speak, then shook his head. "She sees too much. That spells trouble, to my mind."

Rùnach had to agree. "I'll do what I can, but I daresay she's too innocent to be trouble. She almost fainted when she saw Gobhann for the first time."

Weger smiled a self-satisfied smile. "*Everyone* almost faints when they see Gobhann for the first time."

"I didn't."

"Aye, well," Weger said, frowning suddenly, "you're obviously the exception. Sturdy stock in your lineage and all that. I'm sure you'll be wishing you had fainted at some point, but I'll leave that as a pleasure to be savoured later. Now, before I release you to your very luxurious accommodations, answer me this: what are you here for?"

"Sword skill."

"So is everyone else. What are *you* here for?"

"Strength," Rùnach said, suppressing viciously the urge to shift.

"Along with a dozen other weak-kneed men. Come, Rùnach, you can do better than that. What has driven you from wherever you've been keeping yourself for the past score of years—ah, I remember, it was Buidseachd." He looked at Rùnach piercingly. "Why are you here?"

Rùnach decided there was no reason to not be honest. "I couldn't hide anymore," he admitted. "And I don't want a place on the world's stage, not any longer. A simple soldier's life is what I aspire to."

"We don't create simple soldiers here," Weger said mildly, "though what you do with your training after you leave is your business." He held Master Odo's sword out to Rùnach, hilt first. "You can trot down the stairs and give that back to Odo before you retire." He started to walk away, then turned back. "Just so you know, there's a cell beneath your palatial chamber that houses the gift I was sent. A guest, you might term him."

Rùnach lifted an eyebrow. "I wasn't aware you kept guests."

"We keep all kinds of rabble here," Weger said, nodding significantly. "He torments his jailors by singing Nerochian pub ditties whilst having absolutely no sense of pitch or timing." He smirked. "Thought you with your fine tastes might enjoy that."

"How kind of you."

He slid Rùnach a look. "Didn't think I'd make your time here pleasant, did you?"

"I thought it would merely be the swordplay to test me."

Weger rubbed his hands together enthusiastically. "Nay, lad, we're here to mold the entire man. Just consider it my contribution to the betterment of the world." He looked at Rùnach, chuckled in a way that wasn't at all pleasant, then walked off. "Best go see to that sword, then your valet."

Rùnach suspected that might be wise.

By the time he'd delivered Odo's sword to him and run back up the steps, he was wishing desperately for nothing more than peace, quiet, and any flat surface upon which to collapse. He paused outside the door to his chamber and listened to things that echoed in the passageway. First was indeed some off-key warbling sung with great enthusiasm. Rùnach wished that the hoarseness indicated the winding down of the evening's entertainment, though he didn't dare hope for it overmuch.

The other sound was something that, had he been in a different locale, he would have thought might indicate weeping.

He pushed open the door—cursing Weger for not having taken the trouble to install a lock—and found his chamber companion doubled up on the floor. She wasn't weeping, she was gasping in what looked to be absolute agony. He shut the door behind him and wished for the ability to make werelight. All he could do was peer at her by the light of a vile tallow candle.

"What is it?"

She remained doubled over on the floor, but managed to look up at him. "I must speak to Weger," she gasped. "Quickly."

"I think what you must be doing quickly is holding your head over a bucket," he said. "What befell you?"

She pushed herself into a sitting position. She was absolutely grey in the face, which startled him all the more. "Nothing," she said hoarsely. "Help me up."

He reached down and took her hand to pull her to her feet but only succeeded in pulling her over. He squatted down in front of her. "I don't think you're going anywhere, er, what is your name?"

"Aisling," she managed.

Well, that was definitely not a lad's name, but he wasn't going to tell her that as he imagined she wasn't going to be interested in his opinion. Judging by the rapidity with which she clapped her hand over her mouth, he suspected she wasn't going to be interested in much at all for the next little bit.

He managed to find a bucket and get it close enough to her to be of use before she started heaving. It was violent enough that he put his hand over his own belly protectively. Supper had been disgusting, but not vomit-inducing. He knelt on the floor next to her and patted her back sympathetically, though that didn't seem to help her much. He realized almost immediately that a single bucket was simply not going to be enough.

"I'll return," he said, jumping to his feet.

She put her hands over her face and groaned. Answer enough, he supposed.

By the time he'd hied himself off to the kitchens and run back up to his chamber, Aisling was sprawled on the stone, trying to claw her way toward the door. Rùnach set the buckets down and helped her back to her knees only to find she was, as he had thought, not at all finished with her business.

She dragged her sleeve across her mouth at one point, though that did nothing for the tears streaming down her face. He had no doubt those weren't tears from weeping, but from puking. He couldn't blame her, actually. Just listening to her was about to make him ill.

"I must go," she gasped. "I must speak—"

He shoved the bucket near her.

Time passed with miserable slowness.

By the time she was finished, so was he. He leaned back against the wall as she lay on the floor with her cheek against the stone.

"I need to . . . ask . . ."

He reached out and put his hand on her back. She was still breathing, which he supposed was all she could ask for at the moment. Rùnach waited, but she seemed to have forgotten she'd been speaking.

"Ask who what?" he said, finally.

She didn't reply. The only sounds in the chamber were the faint echo of a very raunchy song that Rùnach remembered from an unauthorized visit to a seedy pub in Slighe he had made with his elder brother Keir on the occasion of his eighteenth birthday, and Aisling's labored breathing.

She rose suddenly to her hands and knees and looked at him. He almost fell over in surprise. There was something about her eyes that was altogether unsettling. Otherworldly, to be more accurate. Otherworldly and unsettling—

"What . . . time?" she gasped.

"Almost midnight, I should think—wait, where do you think you're possibly going like this?" he said incredulously.

"Weger."

Rùnach would have pointed out that Weger had already likely gone to bed and wouldn't be amenable to a visit, but he didn't have time before she started to fall. He missed catching her just as he missed catching everything, in spite of all the work Miach and Ruith had done on his hands. He managed to get his hand between her face and the stone floor, but he wasn't sure it had served her any. The pain of it almost sent him tumbling into the faint that the sight of Gobhann hadn't quite managed.

He considered, then with more effort than he had to spare, managed to get Aisling up and in bed. He emptied the buckets down the garderobe, walked back down the passageway, then stacked them outside the doorway. He hoped for her sake that she was finished with whatever was vexing her, but for all he knew, he would be nursemaiding her the whole of the night.

He entered the chamber to find her sprawled on the floor, still trying to get to the door. He squatted down to look at her.

"Aisling, this is madness. You must rest."

She looked up at him, her pale eyes full of things he could not name. "Death."

"What?" he said in surprise. "Whose?"

She reached up and clutched the front of his tunic. "Mine."

He put his hand on her head and smoothed her hair away from her face before he thought better of it. "Why would your life be forfeit for anything, Aisling?"

"Before . . . midnight . . ."

Her fingers loosened and she slid back to the floor, though he managed to soften the ground beneath her face. It hurt just as much as it had the first time, but he ignored the pain. He shook his head, because what she was saying made absolutely no sense to him. She had admittedly been rather anxious to speak to Weger, but what did it matter if it were that day or the next?

He felt her forehead and found that she wasn't warm. Well, there was only one thing to do and that was get her to bed and make certain she remained there. He managed it with an effort, then put both the cloak he'd given her earlier and a blanket over her.

He started to allow himself the luxury of wondering about her, then abruptly put a halt to it. He wanted to stay alive and well long enough to wrestle Weger's mark from him now that he'd given him the bulk of his gold. Aisling had her own troubles, perhaps things that only she could see with those pale, clear eyes of hers.

He had the feeling he might regret finding out what those things were.

"A little house."

He looked at her in surprise and realized she wasn't awake,

though she was definitely murmuring something. Perhaps she was dreaming.

"No . . . doors," she breathed.

"A house with no doors?" he said before he thought better of it. "And what good is that?"

She opened her eyes suddenly and looked at him. He jumped a little in surprise, but before he could wring any more details out of her, her eyelids closed and she slipped into senselessness.

He propped his sword up against the door so its clattering to the ground would waken him, then considered where he might most successfully pass the night. Not in front of her, for reasons that seemed obvious to him. The chamber was small enough that his options were very limited, but he chose to lie down with his head toward the door. Assuming no one plunged him into insensibility by shoving the door open, and Aisling managed to keep herself in bed, he might actually sleep peacefully for the rest of the night, what was left of it.

A house with no doors? It was a ridiculous thought, though he supposed he would have to admit that there were several places in Seanagarra where Sìle had neither locks nor doors. Then again, there were chambers there that were locked as if the innards would tempt the most skillful of lock pickers.

He yawned, then leaned up and blew out the candle before he stretched back out on the floor. If the poor gel was so anxious to see Weger, he would help her in the morning, the first chance he had.

And once she'd had her parley, he would help Weger see her out the front gates and concentrate on his own life.

Six

❧

Aisling woke.

Or at least she thought she woke. She opened her eyes, but the darkness was complete. She lay there, still, and gingerly felt the surface she was lying on. It wasn't soft earth, nor was it rock, though it certainly felt as hard as the latter. She wondered if perhaps they had put her into some sort of chamber where they put all those who were dead until they could arrange something more suitable.

The thing that struck her as odd, however, was how much pain she felt. It was true she hadn't considered death overmuch; she had been too determined to outlast the Guildmistress, win her freedom, and make a life for herself where she would never, ever need sit in front of a loom again. But she hadn't imagined that abandoning her mortal frame would still leave her with such terrible aching in every joint.

She shifted and her body protested so violently, she couldn't even manage to gasp. She felt as if she'd been sitting for days in front of a loom, endlessly weaving until every muscle and sinew had been tormented past what any human could bear. She lay very still, hoping to calm her poor form, and allowed herself to consider something she could scarce credit as possibly being true.

Was she alive?

She rolled over—rather, she took several very long minutes to ease herself onto her side. The chamber was very dark, which was slightly unnerving, but she couldn't hear any movement, which eased her just the slightest bit. Unless death was nothing but dark, cold, agony of body and mind . . .

But nay, that was breath that she was dragging into her lungs. Unless things in the afterlife were far different from what she'd suspected, she was, to her very great surprise, alive. She thought back to the night before, on the off chance she had missed something important.

She was quite certain she had never been so ill in her life. Supper had been disgusting, true, but she'd been astonished at the determination with which it had forced her to relinquish her hold upon it. She had been convinced it had been the first appearance of the curse that would take her life if she failed to do what was necessary before the stroke of midnight.

She fingered the surface beneath her cheek and decided that it was the same bed she'd sat on the night before. She could hardly believe it, but it was impossible to believe anything else.

Perhaps she had miscounted the days—nay, perhaps her companion on the carriage ride had miscounted the days they had traveled. After all, what could a gouty toe possibly know about that sort of thing? For all she knew, the man had been numb from that terrible ride and slept through hours he later failed to bring again to mind. The rest of the journey had been easier to keep track of, but that endless ride in the dark? It was possible, she supposed, that it had taken thirteen days and not a fortnight.

Giving her one more day to speak to Weger and save herself.

That was almost enough to leave her leaping from the bed in joy. Or it would have been, if she'd been able to lift her head with any success at all. She had to admit she felt much better than she had the night before, which gave her the faintest bit of hope that she might manage to do what needed to be done and save herself. Perhaps her endless heaving the night before had simply been fear coupled with bad stew.

She pushed herself up until she was sitting, mostly, and fought the feeling of the chamber spinning around her. It took several more minutes before she managed to get her feet on the floor. She wasn't wearing her boots, but she could feel them there on the floor next to her. Nay, not *her* boots, but rather boots she had been gifted by someone in Gobhann. Perhaps Weger wanted his aspirants properly clothed before he did whatever it was he did with men daring enough to come inside his gates. Ochadius had been very stingy with details of his life inside Weger's gates—leaving most of the details out, actually, no doubt as a kindness to anyone foolish enough to read his book yet brave Weger's gates just the same—but he had been very clear about what happened to those who didn't quite measure up. Over the walls they went, without any concern for where they landed.

She put her boots on, pulled her cloak around her—Rùnach's cloak, rather—then forced herself to her feet. She swayed and felt frantically for something to hold herself upright. Finding nothing, she fell to her hands and knees on the hard stone floor. The door opened immediately and torchlight seared her eyes. She put her hand up against the light.

"Take that away," she gasped.

The torch disappeared behind the wall, but left enough light that she could see that the door had remained open. A thin figure appeared back in the doorway, then came into the chamber and stopped in front of her. Aisling accepted the proffered hand, then managed to get to her feet with a goodly bit of aid. She swayed, but surprisingly strong hands on her arms kept her upright. She realized her rescuer—if that's what he was—wasn't Rùnach, but rather a young lad. He was tall, but extremely thin, as if he hadn't eaten very well for quite some time. If he had been eating in the buttery below, she could understand.

"Who are you?" she croaked.

"Losh," he said. "Who're you?"

She hesitated, then supposed it didn't matter whom she told her name to in this terrible place. She wasn't planning on being there very long anyway.

One way or another.

"Aisling," she said. She stepped back and put her hand on the wall to steady herself. She frowned when she realized he wasn't moving. "What do you want?"

"I've been sent to watch you."

She felt a thrill of fear go through her. Or perhaps it was the last vestiges of whatever she'd had the night before.

"Have you?" she said uneasily.

"Aye," he said, sounding slightly awed. "Weger commanded it."

"Did he say why?"

"Of course not," he said promptly, "and I weren't fool enough to ask him. He told me to watch you, feed you, then bring you to the upper hall when the work was done for the day—if you wasn't still puking."

"The upper hall?" she asked, her ears perking up. That boded well. "Where's that?"

He swallowed, though it looked as though it were rather painfully done. "Never been there meself, but I can find it." He nodded toward the door. "Perhaps a bit of fresh air'd do you good. It's a bit close in here, aye?"

She agreed that it was indeed rather close in the chamber, settled her cloak around her shoulders, and did her best not to stagger as she followed after him. She would have locked the door behind her, but there was no lock, so she counted herself fortunate that the only thing of value she possessed was still tucked under her tunic. She hoped Rùnach had been as thorough with his own gear.

They went all the way to the upper courtyard, which took her longer than she thought it might, but there was nothing to be done about that. Losh didn't seem to require any responses from her, so she let him continue on with his endless stream of babble and concentrated on making sure she stayed on her feet. When they reached the top of the steps, she was more than happy to simply lean against the wall. She was cold in spite of her cloak and far weaker than she cared to be.

Perhaps the night before was simply the curse announcing its presence. For all she knew, she would spend the day growing weaker and weaker until that night brought certain death. All the more reason to find Weger as quickly as possible and have her errand accomplished.

She realized after a few minutes that Losh had stopped speaking and was looking at her closely. She was too weary to try to hide her face, so she simply returned his look.

"What?" she asked.

"Just wondering about you."

"Best not to," she advised. "Let's talk about you instead. How long have you been here?"

"Three fortnights," he said. "On trial."

She looked at him in surprise. "On trial?"

Losh shifted uncomfortably. "Well, you see, my uncle shoved me inside the gates and pulled them shut behind me, and I've yet to have the chance to prove my skill." He looked at her and seemed to shrink into himself. "In truth, 'tis only because my uncle is who he is that they haven't tossed me over the walls."

"But surely he gives everyone who enters a sporting chance."

"Well," Losh said slowly, "I don't know as that's the case. He was full prepared to give me a heave right away, but someone told him my uncle was Harding." He swallowed again, looking as if he were in great need of something strong to drink. "I think it bought me time. Until, you see, I acquire the necessary sword skill."

"Harding?" she asked. "Who is that?"

Losh looked at her as if he couldn't quite believe she could be so uninformed. "He is a very important man hereabouts. Perhaps Lord Weger trades with him, or thinks I'll one day gain my mark, then go vex him." He nodded, as if he were trying to convince himself as well as her. "I've considered that, once I've done what's necessary. That will be soon, I'm sure of it. So until that time I'm anxious to do as Lord Weger says. When he told me to watch you,

I said aye immediately and with great vigor." He looked at her closely. "Are you hungry, or are you going to puke again?"

Just the thought of trying to ingest anything was enough to leave her feeling ill, but she was trembling with weakness. "I'm not sure."

"I says you'd best eat," he offered. "I always find that helpful."

"Perhaps in a minute or two," she said. "I think I would rather just stand here for a bit, if you don't mind. The breeze is bracing."

"It is that," he said, though he looked as if he might have preferred a spot a bit less bracing. "I don't suppose I can argue. Lord Weger told me to watch you, not order you about."

That was something, she supposed. And if Weger had told Losh to watch her, she wasn't going to gainsay him. She was happy to simply stand on even the side of the upper courtyard and shiver. The wind was bitter and ferocious, but it did a fine job of making her feel as if it were blowing not only her soul but her illness straight from her poor form.

She leaned back against the wall, using Losh as a windbreak, and watched the men fighting in front of her.

"Best of 'em," Losh said reverently. "Aye?"

She couldn't help but agree. They weren't pretty men, but they were extremely fierce. There were perhaps a dozen of them there, fighting in pairs, parrying with a ruthlessness that was truly a sight to behold. She supposed any of them would have done for her errand, but what did she know of them, in truth? Obviously, Weger would need to help her choose the appropriate man for her quest—

She almost went sprawling suddenly thanks to a jostle she hadn't seen coming. A hand, scarred and briefly clutching something that dropped at her feet, grasped her forearm and steadied her. She looked up and realized Rùnach was there, breathing raggedly.

"Sorry," he said, then leaned over with his fists on his thighs. "Didn't see you."

Aisling would have said something to him, but she lost her ability to speak abruptly at the sight of Weger suddenly standing in front of them both. He picked up a black ball, apparently what had fallen out of Rùnach's hand, and tossed it at her.

"Hold that," he said to her. "Do the stairs again," he said to Rùnach. And then he walked away.

"Och, and how many times is that, my lord?" Losh breathed.

Rùnach straightened with a groan. "Don't ask, and I am no lord."

Aisling had to admit he certainly carried himself like one, though she perhaps wasn't the best one to judge. She watched as he nodded to her, then turned and trotted back down the steps she had come up earlier.

And that wasn't the only thing that was threatening to come up. She put her hand over her belly.

"I don't feel well," she said, then clapped her hand over her mouth.

"Wine," Losh said quickly, taking her by the arm. "Och, but you've an arm like a girl."

She supposed she would argue with him later. At the moment, she thought perhaps a bit of wine might help settle her stomach. Memories of her last evening's activities were very fresh in her mind, and she didn't think she would particularly want to be washing it off the stone of the passageway.

By the time evening shadows had fallen, she had ventured a bit of soup in the buttery and was happily, if not carefully, following Losh to the upper hall. She was very dizzy, but she hadn't been about to argue with him as to their destination. She had to speak to Weger and she had to do it soon.

She wished she could say she'd spent the afternoon counting and recounting the past three se'nnights of her life like precious pearls in the hands of a rich man on the verge of certain death, but the truth was she'd spent the afternoon asleep. It seemed a poor way to enjoy what could quite possibly be the last day of her life, but she had simply sat down on the bed in her chamber, then woken unable to feel her hand that she had apparently chosen to use as a pillow. She'd had no memory of any of it.

She now followed behind Losh, not bothering to spare the effort to nod at him every five paces as he looked over his shoulder to make certain she was still behind him. She didn't have the strength. It was all she could do to put one foot in front of the other and continue on.

Losh paused in front of a sturdy door, then knocked. The door was opened, Losh tiptoed in, and she followed him. She ignored the jeers and slurs that greeted their entrance. Perhaps it was fortunate most of it sounded unintelligible. She spared a brief thought for Rùnach's perfect elocution—the man who claimed he was not a lord but spoke like a lord's son—then hazarded a look at her surroundings.

The garrison hall was surprisingly large. There were windows all along the far side save where they were broken up by more books than she had ever seen in the entirety of her life. She didn't suppose she would manage to familiarize herself with them, which saddened her, but business was business. She followed Losh across the floor, ignoring the groups of men she passed who were talking of bloodshed and sieges, then sat with her guide on a long bench pushed up against a rather rustic bookcase. It was conveniently close to the hearth at the far end of the hall, though, which put her within leaping distance of Weger himself.

He was sitting in front of the fire, looking like nothing more than a man who had spent a hard day in the fields and was now enjoying a very welcome cup of ale. She was slightly surprised to find Rùnach there, sitting across from him, but perhaps Weger too enjoyed Rùnach's crisp consonants and posh vowels.

"I think he's an elf."

She looked at Losh in surprise. "What?"

Losh nodded toward Rùnach. "Him. He's an elf."

"Don't be daft," she said without hesitation. "Of course he's not. A lord, perhaps, but not an elf."

"Why not?"

She would have snorted derisively if she'd had the energy, but she didn't, so she merely shot Losh a look. "He doesn't have pointed ears, of course."

Losh rolled his eyes. "Have your lived all your life in a barn? There's a difference between them all."

"The only difference is the tales they find themselves in," she said dismissively, "which is the only place they exist." She paused, then looked at him seriously. "I'm sorry to disillusion you, Losh, but that's the truth of it."

And it was. She was very well-read, having devoured all Mistress Muinear's well-loved books over the course of her incarceration at the Guild, everything from science to philosophy. The only reason she'd ever heard of elves had been that Mistress Muinear had occasionally unbent far enough to loan her a glorious, tatty tome full of myths and legends of the Nine Kingdoms. She'd gotten to the point where she'd been too old to enjoy it, but it had provided her with a goodly amount of entertainment in her youth.

Losh was looking at her as if she'd lost her wits. "You ain't serious."

"The Heroes of legend are real, of course," she conceded, "but those other mythical creatures?" She shook her head. "Fanciful imaginings."

"'Tis the fever, isn't it?"

"I don't have a fever."

"Then someone has led you astray," he said seriously. He paused, looked around him as if he stood to impart very secret and important knowledge and wanted no one else to overhear him, then leaned closer to her. "There are elves, and then there are elves. Most mere mortals don't get close enough to tell the difference."

"Then how would mere mortals possibly know what they look like?"

"Because there *have* been those who've gotten close and they've done the rest of us a goodly service by reporting what they've seen."

"How convenient."

He pursed his lips, then continued on. "*Most* elves have pointy ears. Well, the elves of Ainneamh have pointy ears. The ones from An Céin don't, neither do the ones from Tòrr Dòrainn." He paused again and frowned. "At least I *think* the ones from Ainneamh do. I wouldn't know, never having seen one myself, but I've heard they look like something that has stepped out of a dream, all glittering and terrifying." He looked at her seriously. "They look right through you as if you wasn't there. That's odd, isn't it?"

"Weger does that," Aisling said, "and I'm fairly sure he's not an elf."

"I wouldn't be so sure." He looked at Weger, then shook his head. "Since I came here, I'm not sure about anything. Not even elves."

She could safely say she wasn't sure about anything either. She had been convinced she was going to die the night before, yet she'd woken that morning, still breathing. Though perhaps that wasn't going to last as long as she had hoped. Her stomach made a terrible noise that had not only Losh but half a dozen others looking her way. She put her hand over her mouth, but that didn't stop the feeling of her supper beginning to crawl up the back of her throat.

Only this time the feeling was more violent than it had been the night before. Perhaps she'd been granted one more day, as a grace and a warning. She pushed herself to her feet and managed to remain there, however unsteadily.

"Where're you off to?" Losh asked in astonishment.

"Must talk to Weger," she said thickly.

He tried to stop her; she would give him credit for that. She shoved him away from her, a little surprised she was able to manage it, then stumbled across the floor to the hearth. Rùnach looked up as she came, then jumped to his feet. Perhaps she looked determined. Perhaps he feared she would puke down the back of his tunic. She didn't care. She clutched the arm he held out toward her and vowed to weave him something made of any color but grey at her earliest opportunity, then put herself in front of Weger. She cleared her throat.

He ignored her.

She took a deep breath and spewed out words whilst she still could.

"I must speak to you, my lord."

He looked up at her. "Must you, indeed?"

She nodded.

Weger considered her for several heartbeats in silence—though she had no silence inside her head. She could hear her heart beating as if it were a great river rushing in her ears.

He finally looked at the handful of men gathered there and nodded sharply toward the door. "Privacy."

The men grumbled as they rose. Several of them shot Aisling looks that said they were heartily unhappy she had ruined their pleasant evening.

Weger waited until they'd gone, then looked at her. "Talk."

Aisling looked nervously at Rùnach, then back at Weger. "In private, my lord."

"Your master there won't care what your wee concerns are, little lad, so spew them out, but be quick. I have a hot fire and a bit of dessert waiting for me in my chamber. You're standing between me and it, and that place is perilous."

"I need a soldier," she blurted out. She supposed that could have been done better, but perhaps simply stating her needs was the best way to go about it all.

Weger yawned. "For what?"

She glanced at Rùnach, but he was only watching her without expression on his half-ruined face. She took a careful breath, then looked back to Weger.

"For business that I have been foresworn not to reveal."

"Important doings, eh?"

"Very, my lord."

"And just what sort of gold do you have for the hiring of a soldier?"

She felt a little faint. "I had a goodly amount, but it was stolen from me in Istaur. The rest of my goods were taken in Sgioba."

"Not all that handy in protecting yourself, are you?"

"I never had the need," she said. Her voice sounded tinny to her own ears. Not only that, an annoying buzzing had started in her ears. That and the flutterings in her midsection were starting to become quite alarming.

"*Lad*, you had best realize that the need has arisen." He folded his arms over his chest. "What do you have to trade?"

She wished she'd had the peddler's gold. She wished she'd had a bright sword with a gem-encrusted hilt. She wished she had had anything to trade but perhaps something Weger wouldn't even be interested in. But since it was all she had, it would have to do.

She turned her back to Weger and pulled the book from under her tunic. She looked down at it in her hands, though she would be the first to admit she was having a hard time seeing it. There was a very large *O* carved into the cover, and that cover was splattered with a few stains she had always hoped hadn't been blood. It was obviously something Ochadius had treasured, so perhaps Weger would find some value in it as well.

She took a deep breath, turned, and then handed it to him.

He took it with a frown, opened the cover, then froze. The book dropped from his fingers suddenly, but he made no move to retrieve it. It was Rùnach who reached over, picked it up, and handed it back to him.

"Where," Weger asked in a garbled tone, "did you get that?"

"I bought it," she said.

"And what is it you're thinking of doing with it?" he asked, looking at her sharply. "Selling it back to me at a premium?"

"That hadn't occurred to me," Aisling said, wondering why it hadn't. She looked at him hesitantly. "Would you—"

"What, buy back my own damned words stolen from me by some . . . some . . . some—" He spluttered for a moment or two, then slammed the book down on the table by his elbow. He rose and glared at Rùnach. "Get this creature out of my sight before I kill it."

Aisling blinked. "But I need your help—"

He snarled a curse at her, then turned and shoved a chair out of his way before he strode furiously across the hall and slammed out the door.

"And now off we go to bed," Rùnach said, rising and retrieving the book. He tucked it under his arm, then took her by the elbow and pulled her along with him. "I think a sturdy door between you and the lord of Gobhann would be a very sensible thing to have at the moment."

"But I need—"

"You need to be behind a closed door," Rùnach said firmly. "Let's find that, shall we?"

She found that she was perspiring suddenly. "I think I might be ill."

"I imagine Weger feels the same way."

"I'm in earnest." She clapped her hand over her mouth and looked at him in horror.

He cursed, then looked for Losh. "Garderobe," he said crisply.

She arrived at one only because Losh knew where it was and Rùnach managed to carry her there before she lost her supper. And when there was nothing left inside her wanting freedom, all she could do was lie on the stone of the passageway and wonder if each breath might be her last.

Which was becoming slightly tedious, as it happened.

"Hold that book, lad, and follow me. Let's get this one to bed, shall we?"

She didn't protest when Rùnach picked her up and carried her out into the courtyard, down the stairs, and along the passageway to their chamber. She closed her eyes and was extremely grateful for even a hard, uncomfortable wooden bed beneath her back.

She heard Rùnach thank Losh for his aid, then send him off to bed. A stool scraped across the floor. She turned her head to find Rùnach sitting on that stool, lighting a fresh candle. He held her book in his hands and looked at her.

"Best spill your guts, lad."

She couldn't see his ears for his hair, but he didn't look like an elf. He was handsome, true, in a way that was almost difficult to look at, but as for having stepped from a dream . . . well, obviously Losh had listened to too many fireside tales and begun to take them seriously. Elves were creatures of myth, as were dwarves, trolls, ogres, and dragons. Everyone knew that. Even she who had grown to womanhood cloistered in a weaving guild knew that.

"Aisling?"

She looked at him, poor normal-eared man that he was. "I have no tale to tell."

He shot her a look of profound disbelief. "I think you might be the first person in the history of Gobhann to leave the lord of the keep stomping off in a snit. There has to be some tale behind that feat."

"'Twas the book," she said, gesturing weakly to what he was holding.

"May I?"

She would have nodded, but her head was spinning too violently to even attempt it. She simply waved him on, then closed her eyes so she wouldn't have to watch him flip the pages.

"Where did you get this, Aisling?" came his voice from rather far away.

"A peddler."

"Why do you need a soldier?"

She couldn't tell him, partly because she couldn't fight her weariness and partly because if she gave him details, she would die. Though if she didn't find her way back to Weger, she would die just the same.

"I'll tell you about it in a bit," she lied.

"I'm sure you will."

"Wake . . . me," she whispered. "Before midnight."

She felt something be put over her, a blanket perhaps. She opened her eyes a few minutes later and saw Rùnach reading her book. He rubbed his fingers over his mouth, then apparently surrendered to the impulse to smile. She couldn't decide what he found so amusing about that hapless Ochadius of Riamh's troubles, but apparently he found something.

"Midnight," she managed.

He looked at her and smiled faintly. "Of course."

She closed her eyes and surrendered to a weariness that went far beyond anything she'd ever felt before.

She hoped it wouldn't be the last thing she felt.

Seven

❧

Rùnach watched Aisling until she fell asleep, which didn't take all that long. He had no idea what ailed her, not being much of a physick himself. She had no fever, no stuffiness in her head that he could hear, nothing that led him to believe that something had invaded her form. Though given where they were and the appalling conditions to be found there, he supposed she could have been felled by any number of things out of her experience.

He looked at the book in his hands and had to shake his head. Ochadius of Riamh? No wonder Weger had been slightly startled, Ochadius being one of his cousins however many times removed as was polite. Rùnach stared thoughtfully into the darkness. It would take a bit of thinking about that genealogy to place Ochadius, but he had the feeling he was among the younger of Lothar's progeny. That Ochadius had escaped Riamh was unusual. Most who were either guests in the hall or stumbled across the borders didn't find their way out again. That he had gotten himself inside Weger's gates was even more unusual.

That he had stayed long enough to memorize all Weger's strictures was astonishing.

Rùnach would have given much to have had a wee peep at Ochadius's brow to see if he sported any kind of mark there.

He thumbed through the pages carefully, memorizing as he went. Though it was tempting to speculate on how Ochadius had come by Weger's strictures, the more interesting questions were why he'd lost them and how Aisling had come to have them in her possession.

Or if she understood what she had.

A sound at the door startled him. He reached out and caught his sword before the hilt of it slid along the wall and clunked him on the head. He looked up to find Weger standing in the doorway.

"She is well," Rùnach said, "if you were curious."

"I wasn't," Weger growled. "I'm here for a look at that damned book!"

Rùnach waved him in, waited for Weger to perch on the side of Aisling's bed, then handed Gobhann's lord Aisling's treasure.

"I don't think you'll be surprised by its contents. Our good Ochadius was very thorough."

"Damn him to hell," Weger grumbled. "Never should have let him in the front gates. Still, I would prefer to make certain he's written all my strictures down properly." He shot Rùnach a look. "Don't suppose you've had time to memorize what you've read, have you?"

Rùnach smiled. "'Tis a very bad habit, I'm afraid."

"The question is, can you call what you've read to mind?"

Rùnach stretched his legs out, because it gave him something to do besides shift uncomfortably on a stool that was better suited to a serving maid of about seven summers. "I can," he said slowly.

"Everything?" Weger asked pointedly.

"There seems to be an unfortunate gap in my memory where my father's book of spells is concerned," Rùnach conceded.

Weger grunted. "There's a mercy."

"I could rectify that, I suppose, if necessary," Rùnach said, because he thought Weger would be terribly interested in the details. "Keir remembered everything and gave all the spells to Miach before he died. Ruith knows them as well, but as you might imagine, he wasn't particularly keen to spew them out for my benefit. Miach offered, though."

"And what did you say?"

"I thanked him kindly for thinking of me, but demurred." He shrugged. "I don't want them."

"That would have grieved your father sorely, I daresay, did he know. What delicious irony runs through the world's tapestry."

"Poetically put, my lord."

"It was, wasn't it?" Weger said, sounding faintly pleased. "Poetry annoys my guest, so I've become something of a connoisseur of it, especially of the more rustic forms such as the limerick. I prefer those, especially when dwarves and buxom wenches figure as their subjects."

"He does seem to be rather vocal about things," Rùnach agreed.

"Have you heard him?"

"Over the sound of my companion behind you losing all her meals, aye, though the noise was faint. I have the feeling it will grow louder with time." He looked at Weger. "Are you going to tell me whom I have the pleasure of listening to, or must I guess?"

"I assumed you would know."

"Why?"

"Because that damned king of Neroche would have told you, or so I would have guessed. Perhaps he's more closemouthed than I give him credit for being." He slid Rùnach a look. "I don't mind telling you, though. 'Tis the black mage of Wychweald."

Rùnach smiled in spite of himself. "Lothar?"

"The very same," Weger said, "which leaves me feeling a certain obligation to make certain he's well entertained."

"I imagine it does."

Weger shot him a sharp look. "Has the king of Neroche been gossiping about my genealogy?"

Rùnach shook his head. "No need. Sgath knew your father, of course, and grieved for his end, though I will admit our discussing that was a very random and unusual tangent indulged in another obscure conversation between just the two of us after a rather thorough session of tasting what his vineyard had produced the year before." He didn't bother to add that whilst he had never been one for indulging overmuch in after-supper wine, that was the first and last time he had had too much to drink. He was fairly certain his grandfather had been trying to distract him from thoughts of killing his father. "I have never repeated the details to anyone, if you're curious."

"I appreciate that."

"I should point out that Sgath likely thought the possibility of my ending up in Gobhann was so remote that the knowledge would never be of any import." He looked at Weger. "And yet here I am, and there below is your guest."

"And so he is, the miserable wretch. I make certain to favor him with as much culture as possible. Especially the limerick." He smiled unpleasantly. "Call it my little service to the betterment of humanity."

"I'm sure he's enjoying your generosity of spirit."

"Oh, he is," Weger agreed. "I find what he enjoys the most are freeform verses where I simply list mages of note and their opulent residences. I still toss in a few nuggets about buxom wenches and dwarves, just to keep myself from wandering too far afield." He looked at the book in his hands and frowned. "I wonder where your little wench came by this?"

"I have no idea, but she's been keeping it in the waistband of her trousers. I thought I should return it there when I was finished with it."

Weger shot him a look. "I'm surprised at you."

Rùnach held up his hands, which were slightly less twisted than they had been the day before. "I am a gentleman, if that worries you."

"It worried every father of note in the Nine Kingdoms when you were a lad of ten-and-eight, I'll tell you that much," Weger said with a snort, "though I suppose the manners your exquisite mother beat into your thick head likely saved you several skewerings."

Rùnach smiled. "I don't remember being such a rogue."

"I can assure you I never gave it much thought either until you showed up in my courtyard." He started to speak, then shook his head. "As I said before, I had supposed that the lot of you had been slain at that accursed well."

Rùnach blinked. "Did you not know who Mhorghain was whilst she was here?"

"Hadn't a clue," Weger said honestly, "though that makes me a bit of a fool, doesn't it? Then again, it wasn't as if I had been expecting the daughter of Gair and Sarait to stride inside my front gates, then proceed to terrify every man in the place with her superior swordplay." He shook his head slowly. "She's without peer."

Rùnach kept his mouth shut, because he realized in a blinding flash that Weger might have harbored the odd, fond feeling for Mhorghain. That must have put Miach in a difficult position when he'd come inside Gobhann to fetch Mhorghain out. He looked at Weger to see if more details would be forthcoming, but the man had turned his attentions to the book he held. He turned each page methodically, peppering the air first with snorts, then curses that were increasingly vile, and finally resorting to threatening increasingly dire consequences should he ever find Ochadius and his throat within reach.

He finally shut the book with a snap and handed it back to Rùnach. "Well," he said, apparently having run out of other things to say, "he was thorough, I'll give him that." He glanced at Aisling. "I am terribly curious about this one and how she came by it. Ochadius disappeared long ago, though I'm the first to admit I'm not out in the world often enough to frequent the better salons to find out if he's been loitering there by the punch bowl."

"Apparently he's been off somewhere, scribbling."

"I daresay." He shifted so he could look at Aisling, then reached over and with surprising gentleness brushed her hair back from her face and felt her forehead. "No fever, but that doesn't surprise me."

"Doesn't it?"

Weger clucked his tongue. "It shouldn't surprise you, either. You should take better care of your valet, Rùnach my lad, or no one will want the position in the future. Word will get round."

Rùnach imagined it would.

"She's handsome enough, for a simple, unremarkable wench," Weger mused.

Rùnach was beginning to wonder if he had acquired an unfortunate habit of muttering under his breath. "Never said she wasn't."

"Plain, though, isn't she?"

Rùnach considered all the things he shouldn't say—and that list was very long. He couldn't, for instance, say that whilst it had perhaps been wise for her to cut her hair in an effort to pass for a lad, what was left of her hair still looked a great deal like a waterfall of spun gold, sparkling and shining even in the perpetual gloom that was Gobhann. He likely also shouldn't say that not even shorn hair, rough clothing, and ill-fitting boots could help her swagger in any way that didn't mark her immediately as a woman. Or that perhaps despite the clothing and the shorn hair and the dogged efforts to turn herself into a swordsman, she could not hide her face.

Would that she could.

The protestations died on Rùnach's lips only because even though his twenty years in Buidseachd hadn't restored his magic, they had rid him of the unwise habit of saying the first thing that came to mind. He'd indulged in that enough during his youth. He looked at Weger and schooled his features.

"She seems to have an unhealthy fascination with midnights and a question she hasn't had the chance to ask you," he said, finally. "I think she might manage it if she could do something besides puke up what she finds on your delicate platters in the dining hall."

"Do we have platters in the dining hall?" Weger asked, scratching his head. "I thought we just poured it all in a trough and let you have at it with your grubby, blistered hands."

"The luxurious conditions and delicious culinary stylings found at Gobhann are legendary, my lord."

"I'm sure they are, my lad." He looked at Aisling. "She seems restless, doesn't she? I like that. Says she's ready for an adventure."

"It says she's ready for a sewing circle."

Weger shook his head. "That, Rùnach, is exactly what she doesn't need. She would be torn to shreds within minutes."

"Then what is to be done about her?" he asked, not really expecting any answer. She was a mystery, that one. "Something terrible must be driving her."

"I don't want to know what it is," Weger said grimly. "My dreams have been troubled since she came inside my gates."

"For all of the past thirty-six hours?" Rùnach said with as much of a snort as he dared. "I daresay, my lord, that those were nightmares brought on from the slop served in your buttery."

"You don't imagine I eat the same fare, do you?"

"I don't know," Rùnach said. "Do you?"

Weger started to speak, then shook his head. "Better not to think about it, actually." He glanced at Aisling again. "It doesn't seem to be agreeing with her delicate constitution."

"One would swear she was being poisoned."

"One should perhaps learn to sniff one's supper before partaking. We have quite an extensive collection of herbs downstairs. Perhaps some have found their way into her stew." He looked at Rùnach blandly. "Oregano, dill, the odd pinch of lobelia."

Rùnach felt his mouth fall open. "What are you saying?"

"I'm saying lads must find their sport somewhere." He shrugged. "Sometimes a little tampering with the stew is enough amusement for the evening."

Rùnach could hardly believe his ears, but given the fact that Aisling had been puking up everything she'd eaten over the past two days, he supposed it made sense. "But why her and not me?"

"If I were the cook, I wouldn't be worried about that wee thing finding out what I'd done. But you? Even with your feeble hands and all the girlish epitaphs you picked up in Buidseachd, you're enough to give a cook pause. That and you bear a rather strong resemblance to your sister, who, I imagine I don't need to tell you, thrashed Baldric the slop dispenser to within an inch of his life after she stopped puking that first day."

Rùnach pursed his lips to keep from smiling. "She didn't."

"A marvelous wench, that one," Weger said with a sigh. "That whelp from Neroche—well, I was going to say he doesn't deserve her, but I suppose I must concede that he does."

"He does love her very much," Rùnach agreed.

"Please," Weger said, holding up his hand, "spare me the details. Let's speak instead of bloodshed."

Rùnach smiled, mostly to himself. "Or perhaps something even more interesting, such as that poor lass there next to you. Doesn't she deserve to at least have your ear for a bit? You could ease her mind, you know."

"I do not exist to ease anyone's mind."

"Not even a lass who gives you nightmares?"

"Well, there is that, I suppose," Weger said reluctantly. "I'll consider it, perhaps after supper tomorrow that my cook will prepare especially for me."

Rùnach sighed before he could stop himself. "I will think on it with fondness."

"I imagine you will." Weger glanced at Aisling once more. "Don't suppose you'd spare me time and effort and simply exasperate her until she spews out her sorry tale, will you?"

"And how would I do that?" Rùnach asked politely.

"Be supercilious until she cracks." Weger looked at him with one raised eyebrow. "That should come naturally to you, given all the superciliousness you witnessed in your youth from your grandfather."

Rùnach shook his head. "I don't remember my past."

"You know," Weger said slowly, "I once knew a gel who thought much the same thing. And look what happened to her."

"My sister possesses what I do not."

"Aye, a decent amount of wit," Weger said with a snort, "and vast amounts of sword skill. I don't care to discuss what she has running through her veins. I imagine she would prefer it that way."

"If it eases you, you were a powerful influence on her," Rùnach said. "Sìle complains about it endlessly."

"A vile, insufferable man who wouldn't last a quarter hour inside my gates." Weger pushed himself up off the bed with an energy that belied his six centuries of living. "Go run in the morning. I'll decide when you've had enough, then perhaps we'll work in the afternoon. I think if I lash your hand to your sword, you might be able to heft it fairly successfully."

Rùnach refrained from comment. He could scarce hold that damned leather ball of sand Weger had commanded that he squeeze constantly on his runs. Whilst he wasn't a cynic by nature, he had to admit progress was not being made as quickly as he would have liked.

But at least he now knew the source of Aisling's troubles. With any luck, he could see her fed that night and then perhaps they both would have a decent sleep. Though he was happy to see what of the remainder of the night he could use for that purpose. After, of course, he spent half an hour memorizing all Weger's strictures.

Old habits died hard.

He woke to torchlight in his face. He waved it away with a curse, then sat up and rubbed his eyes. Once he could focus again, he saw Losh standing there, looking as if he expected the very stones of the floor to belch up a score of black mages who would then fix their sights on him and subject him to a lifetime of torture.

"'Tis morning, my lord," Losh ventured.

Rùnach frowned at him, then looked at Aisling. She was sitting up, though she didn't look much better than she had the night before. She did, however, look very surprised.

"How do you fare?" he asked with a yawn.

"I'm not dead," she said, patting herself as if she thought she might find the secret of her survival somewhere on her person.

"I imagine things will continue to improve from here," he said, crawling to his feet with all the energy of a centenarian who had spent the night on a stone floor, which was exactly how he felt. "Let's be off for something strengthening."

She didn't move. "You didn't wake me at midnight."

"I tried," he said, though obviously he hadn't. She had looked so wraithlike by the light of that terrible candle that he'd half feared she might just fade to nothing if she didn't sleep enough to at least start to heal. He looked at Losh. "Something to break our fast, eh?"

"If you dare, my lord," Losh said, looking rather green.

"I dare," Rùnach said, "and I am no lord."

"So you say," Losh said, with an added *my lord* muttered under his breath.

Rùnach ignored that, for he was growing increasingly tired of correcting those who seemed determined to accord him what wasn't his—

Well, he supposed he was due that and at least a couple more courtesy titles, but those were things better left in the past.

He started to hold down his hand to help Aisling up, then realized that was perhaps a more gentlemanly action than a man would extend to his companion that he thought was a lad. He instead reached down and took her by the forearms in the most gentle-yet-manly grip he could manage, then helped her to her feet. He held on to her until he was certain she wouldn't pitch forward onto her face, then released her.

"Thank you," she said with a faint frown, as if a puzzle lay before her that she simply couldn't solve.

Rùnach hoped for her sake that it wasn't a contemplation of any upcoming meals, then nodded to Losh, who led them forth out into the passageway.

The buttery could have been reached in the dark by its smell alone. Rùnach had eaten worse on a very long journey he preferred not to think about when he'd had to kill things by stepping on them and tear into them with his teeth—

He pushed aside those memories abruptly and strode into the buttery, prepared to appreciate the best it had to offer. He walked up to the long slab of a table that held all manner of pots and bowls, then folded his arms and eyed the cook as his meal was slapped onto a round wooden trencher.

"Baldric, is it?" he remarked as he accepted the plate.

The cook looked at him uneasily. "Aye, my—"

"I am no lord."

Baldric licked his lips nervously. "As you say."

"I understand my sister came to an understanding with you sometime during her first fortnight here."

Baldric had an attempt at a swallow. "Heard your sister is Morgan."

"So she is."

"A peerless swordsman, that one." He looked at Rùnach with a sick smile. "Don't suppose it runs in the family."

"I imagine that isn't anything anyone would want to test seriously, don't you agree?"

Baldric nodded enthusiastically.

"And this lad here is part of my company," Rùnach said, tilting his head toward Aisling. "Be a shame to find out that he hadn't been fed properly."

"Ah—"

"I couldn't agree more." He handed off his plate to Aisling and stared at Baldric. "And now that we've come to an understanding, I'll have my meal."

Baldric took the other plate he'd been holding, a plate that Rùnach hadn't watched him dish up himself, wobbled a bit, then dropped the plate with a curse.

"Clumsy me," he said, spooning out slop from the same pot he'd unearthed Rùnach's breakfast. He handed it over. "Here you are, m'lord. Hot and tasty."

"I'm sure it will be superb."

Baldric simply nodded several times, as if he strove to convince Rùnach that no beatings needed to be administered. Rùnach could only hope the man would be inspired from then on to leave the lobelia in the infirmary where it belonged.

He sat down at a long table with Losh, Aisling in between them, and set to something that was every bit as disgusting as everything he'd eaten up to that point. If he ever escaped Gobhann, he would make it a point never to visit any other kitchen that could possibly rival Weger's for the vileness of its victuals.

Once the break-of-day misery was over with, he walked back

up to the upper courtyard with Aisling and Losh. Weger was waiting for him, which Rùnach supposed should have made him a little nervous. Weger looked at Losh.

"See if you two feeble lads can get from here to the gate and back again before the sun sets."

"Of course, my lord!"

Weger looked at Aisling. "What, no questions from you, lad? No vexing me, no driving me from my own comfortable seat before the fire with books you shouldn't own?"

Aisling was mute, just as she'd been the entire morning so far, as if she simply couldn't believe she was still breathing. Then again, Rùnach supposed if he'd been puking up his guts for two solid days, he might have looked a bit stunned as well.

Weger shot Rùnach a look of unease, which he returned with a shrug.

"Harding's nephew, see that one there up and down all the stairs, then put him in the sun and leave him to bake until he finds his tongue." He made a shooing motion. "Off with you children and leave me to my sport." He looked at Rùnach. "Come along, old woman, and let's see what can be done about you."

Rùnach glanced at Aisling. First she'd been frantic to speak to Weger, but now she had nothing to say?

He motioned for Losh to take her away. It was her affair, not his, not anything he wanted to get involved in. He had problems enough of his own without taking on the simple, womanly cares of a wench who should have been home learning the gentler arts of stitching and cooking.

Then again, his sister had been thrust out into the world to do things that he never in his life would have wanted for her. For all he knew, Aisling was in like circumstances, without friend or kin . . .

"Are you done with your thinking," Weger asked politely, "or should I watch you dither a bit longer?"

"I have nothing to think about."

"Well, that is likely the first bit of unvarnished truth I've had from you since you arrived," Weger said. "Come along, little lad, and let me see what I can make of you." He tossed Rùnach that accursed black leather ball full of sand. "Give that a few squeezes on your way down to the gates and back. When you look properly wrung out, I'll allow you to stop."

Rùnach nodded, because he'd come inside Weger's gates willingly and with a purpose.

Two hours later, he was wondering if he'd lost his mind. His hands ached so badly he was seriously considering cutting them off, his shins felt as if some terrible feline with double the usual amount of claws had been using him as a sharpening post, and he was almost numb from the chill and lack of sleep. He wondered absently if spring ever came truly to Gobhann or if Weger had struck a bargain with some local wizard to make certain that a bitter wind caressed the western side of the island at all times, just for the pleasure of the inhabitants trapped there.

Gobhann. Had he been mad? Sìle would have only lifted a single white eyebrow and said nothing at all, because words wouldn't have been necessary. The truth was, he had left sanity far behind and strode stupidly full into whatever land lay past absolute madness.

He leaned over and sucked in desperately needed breaths. A hundred times, two hundred, perhaps it had been three hundred times up and down those blasted stairs already that morning. Damn that Miach of Neroche, whose neck he would cheerfully wring the next time he saw him, for remaining mum on the more particular details of life at Gobhann. Mhorghain also could be shouted at for having refrained from giving him tales she'd said would bore him. They had colluded, those two, and he would have words with them next time they met. Assuming Weger's light exercise before the true work began in the afternoon didn't kill him first.

Sadly enough, he suspected Mhorghain had enjoyed it. His associations with his sister as an adult had been woefully few, but he recognized in her the same relentless determination to carry on past where others with sense took a rest that seemed to infect all his siblings. For all he knew, she would have assumed he would have enjoyed the torture.

"Ah, finished so soon?" Weger bellowed from where he was resting his sorry arse on a comfortable-looking bench with his feet stretched out before him. "Another few turns, Rùnach love, then we'll see about starting you on the rudiments of swordplay. I don't imagine you've even *held* a sword before, have you?"

Rùnach was too tired to curse, nor did he have the energy to repay any of the other inmates for their laughter at his expense. He simply nodded at Weger, then turned and trotted back down the stairs. He passed Aisling making her way down them as well, a look of suspicion on her face, her hand resting protectively over her belly.

That one had secrets, he decided, but secrets he didn't want to know, he decided even more quickly.

He had secrets enough of his own.

Eight

Aisling stood at the edge of the upper courtyard and wondered why it was she wasn't dead.

It wasn't a thought she was accustomed to having, but it was, she had to admit, something she had become rather preoccupied with of late. She couldn't believe that she had done such a poor job of counting the days that had passed since leaving Bruadair. It was possible, she supposed, to mistake twelve days trapped in a carriage for a fortnight, but more than that? Impossible. And she herself had been painfully aware of her time on the ship, the passage of the moon overhead as she'd limped away from Sgioba, and the terror of that first day when she'd felt the first pangs of the curse taking root in her.

Only she hadn't died that night. She hadn't died the next night either. It wasn't possible that the peddler had been mistaken in his calculations, but what else could be the truth of it? What if he had meant that she had not three se'nnights, but three fortnights?

She eased along the edge of the courtyard, avoiding the men who

fought like fiends in its midst. The stone of the wall she trailed her
hand along the top of was rough, but worn, as if innumerable hands
had used it to find their way just as she was. She paused at a certain
spot, where the roar of the sea wasn't too loud to hear herself think
and where the sun seemed to have found its way through the gloom.

She peered over the wall, pulling her cloak—which was Rùnach's cloak, actually—more closely around herself. She wasn't sure
how often anyone could see the rocks below given that Weger's
tower seemed to be an unnatural attraction for an endless amount
of gloomy mist. Then again, perhaps that was a boon. Better not to
know what potentially waited below than to have a full sight of it
at all times. She could see them very well at the moment and
wished that weren't the case.

The sea, though, was glorious. She took as deep a breath as she
dared, and felt the air sink into the whole of her. She watched the
water endlessly swirling, spinning, pulling things into itself as it
slipped up to the rocks, then receded. If Gobhann hadn't been so
relentlessly grim, she might have been tempted to see if she could
stay for a bit. Just for the sea.

Though perhaps the lads who were working behind her wouldn't
agree. She didn't need to look at them to know that the ones in the
uppermost courtyard were the most elite of Weger's students. Losh,
who had proved to be a veritable fount of information, had said as
much. In fact, he said much about all sorts of things. She hadn't
been unhappy to have him be sent off on an errand a quarter hour
ago so she could have a bit of peace for thinking.

And the first thought that came to mind was one that left her
wondering if any of Weger's lads would agree to her quest out of
the goodness of their hearts.

"They wouldn't."

She almost fell over the wall. The only thing that stopped her
was a hand catching her by the cloak and pulling her back into the
courtyard. She looked up and realized it had been Weger himself
to save her.

"Excitable, aren't you?" he drawled.

"You startled me."

His smile was particularly self-satisfied. "Then all is as it should be."

Aisling readjusted her cloak, willed her feet and knees to be steady beneath her, and tried to still her pounding heart. She would have made polite conversation with the lord of Gobhann, but she had no idea what the topic should be. Death? Swordplay? Her death by someone's swordplay? She managed to turn herself around and lean carefully against the wall in a way that she wouldn't pitch over backward if he startled her again, which she had no doubt he would try to do if it suited him.

"Well," he said briskly, "you have me here. What do you want?"

She shifted uneasily. "What do you mean?"

"What do you think I mean? You've been angling to talk to me since you trotted inside my gates, so talk."

"Ah—"

"And let it be the truth," he warned, "else I'll toss you over the walls, and sooner rather than later, to save myself any more vexation in the evenings. You said before that you needed a soldier. Why?"

"For business I cannot name."

"Very well," he said, taking her by the arm, "'tis over the wall with you."

"Wait," she blurted out. She supposed that since the moment she'd been waiting for had truly come, she had no reason not to be as honest as she dared be. "I need an assassin."

Weger stopped, released her, then turned to face her. How he managed to lean his hip against that rock wall without taking a tumble himself, she couldn't have said. Years of practice, no doubt.

"An assassin," he repeated slowly. "That's an interesting thing to need."

"It wasn't my choice," she said quickly, "but it is my task."

"And what sort of lad sends a wee lass out to hunt for a hired sword?"

"I—" She shut her mouth because she realized what he'd called her. "I'm not—"

"Of course you are. You can't swagger to save your life, and you couldn't defend yourself against an inebriated granny."

"I am not so helpless," she said, thinking perhaps that a bit of bluster might serve her at the present moment. Never mind that anything she knew about swordplay had come from reading about it in a book. There wasn't much call for stabbing people in the halls of the Guild, though she had to admit that there had been those for whom the thought had definitely crossed her mind.

"I think you're exactly so helpless," he said with a snort. "Tell me what you want this hired killer to do for you."

"Oh, the usual ordinary business," she said carelessly.

He smiled without humor. "The business of killing is generally not ordinary, but we'll leave that for the moment. Does the some-one you want killed have a name?"

She blinked in surprise. "I never said I wanted someone killed—"

"Don't bore me with your hedging," he said sharply. "When you want a lad to do a tidy bit of killing for you, it usually means you already have someone in mind to be on the receiving end of his ministrations. Who is that?"

She looked at him unflinchingly. "I cannot say."

He studied her in silence for a moment. "I could wring the answer from you, you know."

"I know you could, my lord," she said slowly, "but if you knew the price that would be exacted from me for giving voice to that answer, you might have mercy on me."

"What is that price? Death?"

She nodded.

"Well, that makes things a bit more interesting, at least," he conceded. "Let me see if I understand this: If you tell me of your quest, you'll die by some mysterious means, but if you don't tell me of your quest, you'll die by a very pedestrian encounter with the rocks below my keep."

She felt her mouth fall open. "Would you?"

He rolled his eyes. "Odo and I need to come to a better under-standing about who he lets inside the gates." He shot her a dark look. "I won't toss you over the walls because I have apparently lost all good sense, but I would like answers to my questions. Are you sworn to secrecy by someone, or did you decide all this on your own?"

"I cannot say."

"Oh, come now," he said dismissively. "You're not going to die if you tell me at least that."

What she wanted to do was wrap her arms around herself and tremble. What she did was force her arms to remain down by her sides. "There is a curse attached to my errand," she said, because she supposed there was no reason not to be at least that honest. "I was given a certain number of days to find you, convince you to lend me one of your best lads, or my life was to be forfeit."

"A curse."

"Aye."

He laughed, then sobered abruptly when he apparently realized she wasn't laughing with him. He looked at her in surprise. "How old are you?"

"A score-and-seven."

"Then Aisling, my gel, if you're a score-and-seven, unless you were reared in some provincial place—Shettlestoune, perhaps— you should know there is no such thing as a curse. Nasty spells, definitely, but not curses."

"Spells," she echoed with a laugh of her own. "Surely not. Magic and its practitioners don't exist except in books."

He blinked several times, as if he struggled to understand her words. He started to speak a time or two, shut his mouth, and shook his head. "I'm not even sure where to begin with you. Very well, we'll leave magic and curses aside and concentrate on your quest. So, you need a lad."

"A very skilled one, preferably," she said, hardly able to believe she had had so much conversation with Gobhann's lord.

"Just one?"

"I was sent to procure only one." She decided that since she had at least managed to get that far with him, it was perhaps acceptable to give him the barest of hints about what would be required of her mercenary. "There are certain situations that require delicacy, my lord, and this is one of them. Hence the need for a single assassin instead of an entire army."

"Off to overthrow a government, are you?"

Her mouth fell open before she could stop it. "Of course not," she stammered. "I mean, why would I do that?"

"Why else would you want a single man instead of an army?"

"Well, because, ah, in my little village," she said, searching desperately for the right words, "there is a, ah, bad man."

"There usually is," Weger said. "And so you think he's so evil that he needs to die?"

"I don't, but others do."

"And what are his offenses?"

She picked through the worst of Quinn and Euan's grievances, but in truth they hadn't seemed so terrible to her. Since her life had been such a misery all without aid from anything else, she hadn't had much sympathy for lads who complained about their movements being restricted and Sglaimir enjoying luxuries they couldn't. She looked at Weger. "He oppresses our, ah, villagers."

"That hardly seems worthy of death."

"I never said death," Aisling said quickly. "I have simply been sent on an errand to procure a mercenary for others who are more offended by him than I am. What they do with him at that point is none of my affair."

"Meaning, you'll have done your bit and can trot off in another direction and wash your hands of the thing, is that it?"

She hadn't thought of it in those terms, but she had to admit that that was exactly what she intended to do. She took a deep breath and looked Weger full in the face. "That doesn't seem very sporting, does it?"

He shrugged. "I'm not particularly interested in sporting."

She wasn't particularly interested in sporting either, especially since there were truths she could not deny. If she returned to Bruadair, she would die. The Guildmistress would find her, kill her in the most painful way possible, and then Mistress Muinear's aid and the peddler's gold would have been wasted. Well, the peddler's gold was lining someone else's pocket at the moment, but Mistress Muinear . . .

She met Weger's relentless gaze. "I cannot return home," she said honestly. "All I can do is find someone to free my villagers."

Weger considered for a moment or two, then gestured toward his courtyard. "What do you think of these lads here?"

She could hardly believe he was going to help her, but she wasn't going to distract him by saying as much lest he change his mind. She turned uneasily and stood next to him just as uneasily. He was Scrymgeour Weger, after all.

"An unlikely looking warrior is most often the most successful," she said slowly.

Weger turned his head just far enough to look at her. "You seem to know an uncanny number of my strictures, but at least we know where you learned them." He considered, then nodded toward the field. "Choose."

Aisling felt a little faint. "I can choose? In truth?"

"I haven't said I could convince the lad to accept your quest, just that you might select one or two for our consideration." He glanced at her briefly. "I am always curious about a lass who thinks to overthrow a government. I plan to pry all the details out of you whilst you're not paying attention."

"I always pay attention."

His knife was suddenly in front of her face, pointed at her.

"Except now, perhaps," she conceded.

He resheathed his knife with a grunt. "So it would seem. You could stand a few hours of training yourself."

She wasn't sure that would aid her and certainly didn't want to be loitering any longer inside Gobhann than necessary, but she supposed there was no point in saying that. She looked at the men in front of her, wondering who might suit the task at hand. There weren't many, perhaps a dozen, but they were ugly and battered and looking infinitely capable of doing nefarious deeds for any price.

Then she looked across the courtyard and saw Rùnach of a place he hadn't named leaning over, his hands on his thighs, sucking in perhaps a few well-needed breaths, though with much less desperation than the day before. He straightened, then flinched a little as he realized she and Weger were looking at him.

"I think he's too tenderhearted to do anyone in," Weger remarked.

"He's also too pretty," she said. "Assassins should look craggy and unpleasant."

"Rùnach's scars temper his charm."

She didn't think his scars tempered anything, particularly the fairness of his face, but she thought it better to keep silent on that.

"Do you want that one?" he asked, nodding toward Rùnach.

"Can he be bought, do you think?" she asked.

Weger studied Rùnach for a bit. "I think not," he said slowly. "If he agreed to help you, it wouldn't be because you were able to pay for his services. Not that he can wield a sword worth a damn at the moment anyway. In a few months, perhaps, when I've worked the strength back into his hands." He paused. "In his youth, he was a formidable swordsman, but now—" He shot her a look suddenly. "Do not ask me what happened to him."

"I wouldn't dare."

Weger grunted at her. "A show of good sense." He considered her. "Are you in haste for this lad?"

She nodded.

"But you have no gold."

She shook her head.

"Lass, if you can't hold on to your gold long enough to give a decent swordsman something to inspire him," Weger said with a sigh, "you're not going to convince him you'll give him anything at the end of the road, no matter your good intentions. We'll have to think of something. I can't guarantee anyone will agree to such a hopeless bargain, but perhaps I'm more cynical than most. At least you've come to the right place for cynics."

"Your reputation is flung far and wide, my lord," she said seriously, "among those who want aid in escaping prisons made for them by others. Even a simple village woman can understand and appreciate that, no matter how hopeless the situation might seem."

"The hopelessness of it doesn't touch me, so don't look my way for sympathy. You did, however, come inside my gates with nothing but your courage and a bit of bluster. That should count for something." He reached down, then straightened and shoved a leather satchel at her. "Best put your book in there lest it go missing."

"Thank you, my lord," she said, surprised beyond measure.

He considered. "I will teach you at least something before I throw you out my front gates, and I will think on your troubles, womanly though they seem to be. Something will no doubt occur to me, with enough time."

She wanted to tell him she didn't have much time, but she wasn't at all sure of that any longer. She started to put Ochadius's book inside the bag, then paused. "You don't want this?"

"What would I want with that bloody book?" Weger demanded. "*I'm* the one who invented what's in it!"

He had a point there. She secured the book, then pulled the satchel's strap over her head. "There are many useful things in it."

He shot her a look. "What did I say about avoiding mages?"

"'Kill them before they speak,' 'the only good mage is a dead mage,' and several others I didn't take particular care to memorize given that they applied to creatures who don't exist."

He looked at her, laughed suddenly, then pushed away from the wall and walked away.

"Stairs," he threw over his shoulder.

Aisling jumped and hastened around the edge of the courtyard to catch up to Rùnach before he started down the stairs. He was drenched but whether that was from sweat or the mist, she couldn't have said.

"Weger said I should trot down the stairs with you, then back up them," she said.

"Still trotting?" he asked.

"He didn't specify, but I think merely climbing them might be enough."

"Thank heavens," Rùnach said, with feeling. He nodded toward the stairwell. "Let's go then, lad." He shot her a look. "You might manage it today, don't you think?"

She put her hand over her belly before she thought better of it. "I might. Perhaps it was the adjustment of being in such an intimidating place."

"Or the lobelia the cook was putting in your stew," Rùnach said easily. "Let's go."

Aisling felt her mouth fall open, but she had no chance to offer any opinion on his opinions. She simply trotted after him, carefully, and decided that perhaps she would think about mysteries later. For whatever time she had left.

Though she was beginning to suspect that her time breathing might go on a bit longer than she'd dared hope.

The entire situation was perplexing. She couldn't say she knew the peddler *very* well, but she had seen him every Friday at the market. He had never once been, in her presence, anything but painfully exact about the exorbitant prices he exacted from those wanting his wares. Then again, he had been distracted by providing her with new clothing, paying her passage south, and cutting her hair off to help her look like a lad. Perhaps he'd been so eager to see Bruadair freed from Sglaimir's unsavoury self that he'd been confused.

It was possible.

She considered that as she followed Rùnach down to the front gates. The gatekeeper was there, apparently as was his wont, leaning against the wall and watching them. She nodded politely to him, listened to him make a comment to Rùnach in a language she couldn't understand but Rùnach apparently could, then happily stood there while Rùnach caught his breath. It took far less time than she hoped for, so she stopped him before he started to climb again.

"Do you believe in curses?"

He frowned thoughtfully. "What do you mean?"

Her first instinct was to reveal nothing, but if the peddler's threat of her dying wasn't true, perhaps there were other things that weren't true. She had had an extensive education in things that seemed quite logical to her. Those things she had either heard of or read about, those tales of impossible creatures, reports of impossible quests and the Heroes who had been responsible for their successful conclusion, surely those had simply been stories for children. She was as convinced of that as she was that Bruadair did have a curse laid upon it. And whilst it was possible that the peddler had miscalculated the time available to her, she was absolutely convinced that there had been no lie about the punishment for those who spoke of Bruadair outside its borders.

She looked at Rùnach, then shook her head. "Nothing. I was speaking out of turn."

"As you say." He nodded toward the steps. "Shall we?"

"If we must."

"Think on the delights awaiting you in the dining hall."

She looked at him quickly, but he only smiled before he walked away. She supposed as long as he was there to intimidate the cook, she might manage to eat something that didn't leave her retching. It had been the case this morning.

She wished the rest of the mysteries in her life could be solved as easily.

By the time the day had waned and she had eaten another less-disgusting-than-usual meal, she was exhausted and profoundly confused. Rùnach, however, seemed happy to spend a bit of time in Weger's upper gathering hall. She didn't want to argue, on the off chance Weger had decided upon a solution to her mercenary problem.

She soon found herself sitting on a bench near one of the bookcases with Rùnach on one side of her and Losh on the other. She would have been happy to speak further to Weger, but he was engaged in spirited conversation with a very rough-looking man. The truth was, most of the men gathered there were disreputable-looking, so she wasn't sure she could ask Weger to recommend any of them. She considered, then leaned slightly closer to Rùnach.

"Are there any good men here?"

Rùnach leaned back against the books and folded his arms over his chest. "I suppose it all depends on what your definition of *good* is."

"Not what I see there," she said with feeling. "They all look so rough and . . . assassin-like."

He looked at her, amused. "Have you known many assassins, Aisling?"

"I've read about them," she said. She looked at him reluctantly. "I've led a somewhat sheltered life."

"Well, I can't say I've been out in the world of late much either, so perhaps we are not so different."

"What have you been doing?"

He seemed to consider what he should say. "I was a servant of sorts," he said slowly, "to a man who was a very great friend of my mother's. I needed a refuge from events I could not control and he was good enough to provide that for me." He shrugged. "I had the run of a very large library, so in return for that I was quite willing to pour his wine for him."

"A library," she breathed.

He turned slightly to look at her. "Have you never seen one?"

"Only Weger's," she admitted, "though I was made loans of books from a woman who owned perhaps a score of them. I borrowed them one at a time, you know, because they were precious to her."

He studied her. "Why did you come here?"

She took a careful breath, then looked at him. "I have been sent on an errand."

"Have you?"

"Aye." She considered. She started to speak, then realized Weger was standing in front of her. She rose to her feet because Rùnach was on his.

Weger smiled unpleasantly. "I'm still thinking on your problem," he said. "You need someone rough, uncouth, always ready for a nasty adventure." He leaned in closer. "And you'll need someone willing to work for hobnails, eh? That'll be a challenge."

Aisling had to agree about the price, but before she could ask if he'd found such a lad he had sauntered away, whistling.

"We should both be abed," Rùnach was saying. "Work begins at dawn."

Aisling hadn't seen dawn and didn't imagine Gobhann experienced dawn, but she wasn't going to argue.

He smiled briefly. "Things will look better in the morning."

She would have said that wasn't possible, but she had hope for the first time that she might actually go to bed, then wake to see the sunrise.

And if she did, perhaps she would manage to figure out why.

Nine

❖

Two days later, Rùnach stood in Weger's upper courtyard, trying to decide it if was more work to run the stairs endlessly or keep Weger's twelfth most proficient student—something Weger had informed him that morning with a smirk—at bay. He found himself with a bit more time than expected to think about things that puzzled him when his opponent unexpectedly held up his hand for a bit of a rest. He propped his sword up on his shoulder and happily allowed himself the pleasure of just breathing deeply without having to push himself past what he could bear.

Aisling was looking for an assassin?

He had watched her—occasionally, when he had reached the top of the endless stairs and was preparing to descend them again—training with Weger over the past two days. Apparently Gobhann's lord had decided that if the woman couldn't wield a sword, she could at least poke her finger into an assailant's eye and do some damage. Rùnach had serious doubts she would manage even that, but he'd always been too winded to argue.

None of which answered the question of why she had left her home, why she would ever have thought that coming inside Gobhann to look for a mercenary could possibly be a good idea, or why she seemed to greet each day in utter surprise that she was alive to do so.

His training partner made a strangled sound of horror. Rùnach looked at him in surprise, then turned and looked where the man was pointing with his sword.

And then he understood the sound.

He was halfway across the courtyard before he realized that he likely should have covered his face.

Lothar of Wychweald stood five paces away from where Aisling was staring off into the distance, as if she saw things no one else could. Lothar looked rather rumpled, as if he'd recently been in a bit of a tussle, perhaps with his guards. He smoothed his hand down the front of his tunic, then he glanced at Rùnach. He looked away, then swung his gaze back. His mouth fell open.

Rùnach knew he shouldn't have even looked in Aisling's direction, but he was fool enough to rush toward her. He saw the thought that she might mean anything at all to him cross Lothar's face, followed immediately by calculation, then a decision.

Time slowed to a crawl. Lothar pulled the knife from Losh's belt, gave him a hearty shove, then jerked Aisling in front of him. Rùnach leapt forward, but not before he watched Aisling flinch, hard. Lothar smiled, but Rùnach was less concerned with that than he was with the way Aisling was gasping, though that likely had quite a bit to do with the point of the knife that was protruding from her chest. Rùnach flung himself forward and skidded to a halt in front of her in time to catch her as she fell forward.

He turned her sideways so he didn't bump the blade either going into her or coming out of her. He wondered how he might pull the blade free and stab his father's nemesis standing there without wounding Aisling further.

"I am agog," Lothar said with obvious mock surprise. "Fancy meeting someone here who I was just certain was dead."

"You shouldn't believe everything you hear," Rùnach said evenly.

"Oh, I don't know," Lothar said, smiling pleasantly, "I recently had your brother, Acair, as a guest in my hall and heard all kinds of things in return for, well, I think it was for something I neglected to give him." He shrugged. "A bit naughty of me, I suppose, as is what I've done to your little friend here—"

He didn't manage to finish, but that was likely because he'd just enjoyed the feeling of his descendant's fist under his jaw. His head snapped back and he crashed to the ground. Rùnach listened to Weger bark out orders for Lothar to be bound, gagged, and locked in his chamber below. He snarled out a few dire threats for whomever had been fool enough to allow the blackguard out of his prison, which Rùnach heartily seconded.

Weger turned to Rùnach. "I don't think we can take her anywhere with this in her flesh."

Rùnach found that his arms were shaking. "Can she be healed?"

"Aye."

"Then do what you must."

Weger's face was absolutely expressionless. He put his hand on Aisling's back and pulled the knife free without further comment.

Rùnach felt Aisling sag in his arms, which he supposed was a mercy for her. All he could do was hope she wouldn't bleed to death before something could be done.

"Clear the courtyard," Weger bellowed.

Men scattered as if a strong wind had blown them to the four quarters. Weger looked at Rùnach.

"Follow me. Bring her."

Rùnach didn't argue. He picked Aisling up in his arms, again shocked at how little there was to her. She was actually rather tall, but she was so terribly thin, as if she had spent her life not eating very well. Yet another thing to add to the list of mysteries that swirled around her.

He followed Weger across the courtyard and through a gate he hadn't noticed before. It led to another courtyard of sorts, though Rùnach couldn't begin to guess the purpose for that. He continued along behind Weger until he realized that the only thing before him was the sheer face of a mountain. Cut into the side of that mountain was a set of stairs. He looked at them, then at Weger.

"You can't mean me to climb these," he said in disbelief. "Not with this girl in my arms."

"Shall I put her on your back?"

"I think moving her at all is an extraordinarily poor idea—"

"I don't care what you think," Weger said shortly. "Don't fall off. I can't save you."

Rùnach balked. "But—"

"If you want her to die, keep talking," Weger snarled. "If not, follow me."

Rùnach settled Aisling more securely in his arms, made the decision to ignore the wind blowing a gale, and followed Weger. Because for some reason he couldn't divine, he didn't want the girl in his arms to die when he could be a means of saving her.

He decided once he'd reached the top that he would never think about the journey there again. He was no coward, but the route had been heart-stopping. He'd lost count of the times he had slipped and barely caught himself before plunging to his death, taking Aisling with him. He had also been acutely aware that every breath Aisling took became shallower. Perhaps that wasn't her blood dripping down his arm, but then again, perhaps it was.

His need for haste coupled with the terrible wind had left him resorting finally to cursing his father for having taken what might have aided him. He could have carried Aisling out the front gates, healed her right there in the mud, then come back inside within the same quarter hour.

Instead, there he was with a bitter wind lashing him, the woman in his arms dying, and no recourse but to follow a madman who for some unknown reason thought climbing the side of a mountain was going to do something for any of them.

Before he could think too long on that, or find his breath to shout a question about it, they had reached the top of the staircase. Weger fitted a key to a lock, then pushed open a door. Rùnach walked inside, surprised to find the chamber lit by torchlight, but dismissed that in favor of laying Aisling down on a pallet in the middle of the chamber. He stepped over her, then knelt by her side. The sleeve of his tunic was indeed drenched in blood, as was she. She was as still as death, which didn't surprise him. If she survived it would be a miracle. The sooner she was seen to the better.

He looked around himself, then up at Weger. "Where is your surgeon?"

Weger shook his head. "He's useless."

Rùnach didn't consider himself particularly dull, but he had to admit he was baffled. "Then what now?"

"What do you mean, *what now?*" Weger echoed in disbelief. "Do what is necessary! Bloody hell, man, must I instruct you in every bloody step? Take your mighty magic and heal her!"

Rùnach blinked. "What in the world are you talking about?"

Weger threw up his hands in frustration. "Heal her, you fool! Use Fadaire or whatever elvish rot comes first to mind."

"But—"

"Have you lost all sense?" Weger demanded incredulously. "Surely you haven't been so long out of the world that you can't recognize when you have your magic back. It will work here in this chamber, I guarantee it."

Rùnach gaped at his host. "But I have no magic."

"Of course you have magic—" Weger stopped suddenly and his mouth fell open. "You *what?*"

"I have no magic," Rùnach said, through gritted teeth. "My father took it all at the well."

Weger looked quite suddenly as if he would have liked to have sat down. "Bloody hell," he said faintly. He sagged back against the door. "I had no idea."

"You didn't ask."

Weger rubbed his hands over his face and indulged in a selection of very vile curses. "Damn it," he said, finally. He looked at Rùnach. "What are we to do now?"

"Well, if magic will work here," Rùnach said, "why don't you use yours?"

Weger folded his arms over his chest. "I haven't used a word of magic in over three hundred years."

"No time like the present to dust it off then, is there?"

Weger hesitated. Rùnach suspected it was the first time in those same three centuries he'd done so. He considered, then looked at Rùnach.

"I could," he said, sounding as if the words had been dragged from him by a thousand irresistible spells, "but I have no elegant magic."

Rùnach shrugged. "Then use Wexham."

"It will leave a scar."

"I don't think she'll care."

"It will leave a very large, ugly scar," Weger amended.

"Then use Camanaë or Fadaire," Rùnach suggested.

"And have my mouth catch on fire? You ask too much."

Rùnach looked at him seriously. "I honestly don't care what you use as long as you use something that will save her life. Whilst you still can."

Weger looked as if his fondest wish was to turn and flee. But he apparently wasn't the master of Gobhann because he was a coward. He took a deep breath, cursed fluently, then knelt down on Aisling's other side. He took her hand in his, then put his other hand over the still-bleeding spot in the middle of her chest. Rùnach listened to him spit out an eminently useful spell of Croxteth, then follow that bit of healing with a very long string of curses in which Lothar of Wychweald and Rùnach's own father figured prominently.

Aisling took a deep breath. She murmured a handful of things, opened her eyes and looked at Weger, then sighed and fell back into senselessness.

Rùnach smiled in spite of himself. Perhaps the spell had been hastily and roughly spoken, but as with any spell used for healing, there was something left behind, something wholesome and good. If Weger's spell had left a wholesomeness that was better suited to the rough atmosphere of a garrison hall, well, perhaps that was only to be expected. Aisling would live, which was all that mattered.

He smoothed the hair back from her face, then looked at her benefactor. To his surprise, Weger was looking at the woman lying there in front of them as if he'd seen . . . well, his expression was not one of horror or disgust. It was as if he were seeing something he had never expected to see, no matter the location.

"What is it?" Rùnach asked in surprise.

Weger put Aisling's hand he'd been holding in Rùnach's, then lurched to his feet. "I need something very strong to drink," he said thickly.

"What did you see?"

Weger glared at him, spat out another pair of spells that flooded the chamber with werelight and created and filled a hearth behind Aisling's head. "Nothing." He threw a key at Rùnach that he barely managed to catch. "Lock up and make sure I get that back. It's the only one I have."

"And the werelight?"

"Everything inside here will disappear when you lock the door." He took the two steps necessary to get to the door, then paused as he put his hand on the latch. He considered, then turned and looked at Rùnach. "No magic?"

"Not a drop," Rùnach said. Almost without flinching.

Weger pursed his lips. "Magic is a very unmanly way to go about things. Prissy and affected, if you ask me."

"I feel better already."

Weger paused and seemed to be chewing on his words quite thoroughly before he found ones he wanted to spew out. "See her back to your chamber," he said, "then do not leave her."

Rùnach frowned. "What do you mean?"

"What I mean is I want you to keep her next to you at all times." He scowled. "The girl needs a guardian, not only here but when she leaves here. I believe you are that man."

"But I'm not going anywhere with her," Rùnach said in surprise.

Weger was very still. "I would rethink that, were I you."

Rùnach felt his mouth fall open. "Why?"

"Because along with a keeper, she needs a swordsman to win a war for her." Weger lifted an eyebrow. "Are you not a swordsman equal to that?"

"I have no *desire* to be equal to that—" Rùnach heard the words come out of his mouth, then shut his mouth slowly, because it felt as if the entire world had slowed to a smooth, almost imperceptible stop.

Are you not equal to me, son?

I have no desire to be equal to you, Father.

A good thing that is, young one. You with your pitiful scribblings in your book that will never be equal to mine . . .

The conversation in its entirety came back to Rùnach with startling clarity, as if he were standing to the side of the little tête-à-tête, watching his father speaking with his son of ten-and-eight. A son who, as it happened, very much wanted not to be equal to his father, but surpass him in every way.

Only whilst using that power for good, of course.

He had often wondered, in the years that followed when his power was no more and the controversy was confined to mere speculation, if perhaps he would have failed that test if he'd had to face it in truth. Perhaps he would have become just like his father if he'd had the opportunity. He had been, he had to admit, perhaps a bit more proud than he should have been of several things. His skill with the sword. His skill with a spell. The way he could walk into a hall and have all eyes turn his way, the masculine eyes with envy and the feminine ones with admiration that ofttimes had led to swooning.

How many times had Gille complained loudly that Rùnach had taken at birth all the beauty intended for the rest of them before they could claim their share? Rùnach had laughed, for his brothers had not been lacking in handsomeness themselves, but he could admit, now that his face caused flinches of disgust and horror, that there had been a time when he'd been very aware of the elegant figure he'd cut.

Perhaps the well had been a boon.

"Must you think about this all day?" Weger demanded.

Rùnach looked up at him. "What war?"

"How would I know?" Weger snapped. "I just know . . . well, never mind what I know."

"With all due respect, my lord Scrymgeour, what have you seen?"

Weger rubbed his hands over his face suddenly, then blew out his breath. "Nothing I could name," he said, sounding suddenly very weary. He looked at Rùnach. "I'll give you another fortnight, then throw you out. I think I can protect your anonymity that long, though Odo recognized you easily enough as Morgan's brother. I can't imagine others would, but one never knows. Lothar certainly knew who you were—" He started to speak, then shook his head. "A fortnight. No longer."

"But, I don't want to fight her war," Rùnach spluttered.

Weger looked at him in a way that made Rùnach suddenly feel as if he were a lad of ten-and-two who had disappointed someone who had until that point thought highly of him.

"You might, Prince Rùnach, think about someone besides yourself for a change."

And with that, the door banged shut and Weger was gone.

Rùnach shook his head, then he shook his head again. He finally had to get up and walk around the chamber, a dozen times, two score, five score, until he stopped being able to count the turnings.

He realized, at a certain point, that Aisling's eyes were open. For a moment, he feared she was dead in spite of Weger's spell, but she was watching him. He stopped at her feet and looked down at her.

She was, as he had thought at more than one point, not at all plain. She was . . . well, he had no idea what she was. To be honest, she frightened the hell out of him. She should have been at home, sitting by the fire, trying to fatten herself up, not lying in a bitterly cold tower chamber attached to the most austere keep in all the Nine Kingdoms, sporting what he was certain was a very ugly scar on her chest.

He wondered, not for the first time, how she had been chosen to come look for a man to save her village. Had there been no one else? Or had she volunteered?

And why?

"You're making the chamber spin," she said, putting her hand over her eyes.

"I'll stop." He hesitated. "How do you fare?"

"I feel a little . . . breathless."

He imagined she did. He looked at her and shook his head. How she had expected anyone to have believed her a lad, he had no idea. He watched her put her hand over what had recently been a hole in her chest, then flinch. She lifted her head and looked at blood still damp on her tunic and the rather substantial rent, then looked at Rùnach in surprise.

"That man stabbed me."

He nodded.

"Who *was* he?" she asked faintly.

Rùnach had no desire to discuss those details with her, so he wouldn't. He sat down on the floor next to her. "He was no one important," he said easily. "I wouldn't give him another thought."

She rubbed her chest absently. "He seems very dangerous. Why is he here?"

"Perhaps *because* he is dangerous," Rùnach said. "Weger may keep him here because he can do less damage locked in a cell here than he could outside the gates. Why he was free today, I wouldn't attempt to speculate."

She sat up carefully, then looked over her shoulder at the fire in the hearth. The sigh that escaped her was difficult to listen to.

"Let me help you," Rùnach said, holding out his hand.

"I don't need aid," she said, then crawled over to sit against the wall, close to the hearth.

That bothered him slightly, that refusal, though he decided it was perhaps wise not to examine why. He simply turned so he could watch her as she leaned her back against the stone and breathed. It looked painful, truth be told, but perhaps there was no healing that came without some sort of price attached.

"Why am I not dead?" she said finally.

Rùnach realized he should have thought sooner about invent-
ing a decent answer for that. He was absolutely positive Weger
wouldn't want anyone to know what he'd done, not even the
woman who owed him her life.

"Ah," he began, "Lord Weger keeps a, er—" He cast about for a
plausible tale. "He keeps a mage here for emergencies."

She blinked. "A what?"

"A mage."

She laughed a little. "Surely not."

He smiled, because there was something about her laugh that
was like a glimpse of sunshine after endless days of rain. He had the
feeling, daft though it might have been, that she hadn't laughed all
that much in her life. She seemed to savour it just as much as he did.

"What do you mean, 'surely not'?" he asked.

"Because there are no such things as mages," she said, almost
gently, as if she feared to ruin a dearly held belief for him.

Rùnach had to admit there was part of him that wished desperately that he could take Aisling down and have her shout that
over and over again outside Lothar's door until the man went completely mad.

"Ah, well, I suppose the man was a healer," he conceded. "Call
him what you will."

She frowned thoughtfully. "But I am healed completely."

"Potent herbs, I imagine."

She looked at him and frowned again, as if she knew that couldn't
be possible but couldn't possibly admit that anything else might be
responsible. He decided that before she gave herself pains in the head
by any more frowning, he would do well to change the subject. No
sense in not prying a few answers from her whilst she was distracted.

"Where were you raised?" he asked. "I mean, it was obviously
a place without mages."

"Who don't exist," she said absently.

"Of course not."

She seemed to be struggling to find the right words for heaven
only knew what. She crawled to her feet, shunning his help, then
began to pace slowly around the edge of the chamber. She stopped

by the door and put her hand on the wood, much in the same way Weger had not half an hour beforehand. She looked at him bleakly.

"I don't know whom to trust."

"Don't you?" he asked.

She shook her head. "I have spent my life with persons who were . . . untrustworthy."

"Have you?"

"Will you stop that?" she snapped, then she let out her breath slowly. "I'm sorry—"

"Don't be," he said. "I'm not trying to vex you."

She looked at him seriously. "Are you trustworthy?"

He rubbed his chest, wondering how it was that mere words could leave him feeling as if he had been the one with a dagger recently plunged to the hilt in his flesh. It took him a moment or two to catch his breath.

"I can keep a secret," he managed, "if that's what you're getting at."

She considered him for several moments in silence. Rùnach looked at her by the light of a dozen orbs of rather decent-looking werelight and wondered what it was Weger had seen in her that had unsettled the hell out of him.

"Does your mother trust you?"

Had he agreed to go with this wench anywhere? He was quite sure he hadn't, which was a good thing because he wasn't going to spend but another quarter hour in her presence, long enough to get her back to their chamber, then see if he might find a scrap of floor in the kitchens. He took a deep breath then saw, to his shame, that his thoughts were reflected in her face, as if she'd seen them hanging in the air, drawn them to her, and wrapped them around her.

She was opening the door before he realized what she was doing. He shoved himself to his feet, jumped across the chamber, and pushed the door shut before the wind whipped it so forcefully into her that it knocked her over. He took off the cloak he had borrowed from some disgusting pile of unwanted clothes and put it around her shoulders.

"I have three and you none," she managed.

"And we have a fire," he said, taking her by the elbow and tugging. "Come and sit."

She didn't move. She simply looked at him with eyes that somehow saw far more than he was comfortable with. "You didn't answer."

He blew out his breath, then dragged his hands through his hair. He leaned back against the door and looked at her.

"My mother is dead," he said quietly, "but when she was alive, aye, I believe she trusted me." Only he had failed her, just as he'd failed his brothers and sister. If only he hadn't been so concerned about magical fastidiousness, he might have lowered himself to use his father's bloody spells against him—

"I'm sorry."

He blinked, then pulled himself back to himself. He shook his head. "It was a long time ago, so no matter." He nodded toward the fire. "We can at least be warm for a bit, I think. Come, lass, and sit."

"La—" She shut her mouth abruptly. "I am no lass."

He tried not to smile, but it was difficult. "Aisling, my hands may not work very well, but my eyes do."

"Losh thinks I'm a lad," she said, lifting her chin.

"Losh is a boy, which I am not."

She frowned at him, but didn't argue. She put her hand hesitantly over her chest, then looked at him. "I don't think herbs work this quickly. Do they?"

"Generally not," he conceded, "but 'tis possible this chamber has properties neither of us could possibly hope to understand. I wouldn't worry about it."

"What else will there be that is not as I've been told it is?"

There was something in her voice that, well, if he hadn't been such a hard-hearted clod, it might have brought a tear to his eye. He had to fight the impulse to pull her into his arms and hold her until that look of utter betrayal disappeared from her eyes. He reached out and tucked a lock of her shorn hair behind her ear before he thought better of it.

"I'm not sure I would ask," he said quietly. "Come and sit, Aisling, closest to the fire. I don't think Weger would begrudge you that."

She didn't argue as he helped her sit next to the fire, then sat near her in a companionable sort of way. After all, he had no interest in her that extended past a passing curiosity, and he had no intention, no matter what bloody things Weger might say to him, of trotting off to some obscure village in a desolate part of the Nine Kingdoms and mediating what was sure to be a feud between two families fighting over grazing rights. But that didn't mean he couldn't be pleasant whilst they were where they were.

"Weger says you need a mercenary," he asked, because it was the first thing that came out of his mouth. He supposed it was too late to take the words back, so he left them there, hanging in the air in front of them.

She was silent for a moment or two, then she sighed. "My village has been taken over by, ah, someone." She paused. "I was charged with finding someone to aid those who want to see him removed."

"I don't suppose you'll tell me where your village is, will you?"

"I don't suppose I will."

He smiled, in spite of himself. "You are rather cheeky, you know, for a lass who can't wield a blade."

She glanced at him. "I could poke my finger in your eye. Weger taught me how."

"There is that," he agreed.

She shivered. "After today, I think I might need to learn other things."

"I think you might want to," he agreed. "Perhaps tomorrow."

"I don't have much time to learn."

He shifted so he could look at her more fully. "What does that mean?"

She looked calm, but her knuckles where she was clutching her hands together were white. "I am simply in a fair bit of haste."

"Will your village lie in ruins if you don't return to see to it?"

"Nay, but I must find a man to aid them," she said, "and time grows short." She looked at him quickly. "That is all I can say."

He supposed she had said more than she'd cared to, though it was all he could do not to press her for more details. Why the haste? She had been so adamant about talking to Weger before midnight on two consecutive days, but now *midnight* seemed less important than *very soon*. Was destruction imminent or was there more to it than that?

And why was she pretending to be a lad?

He had his own share of secrets, but his weren't nearly so interesting. He also hadn't been stabbed by Lothar of Wychweald, though he imagined that had been nothing but Lothar happily trying to destroy something Rùnach appeared to have interest in.

Weger's reaction to her, however, had been less than random. And there was the language she'd murmured after Weger had healed her. He could say without any pride at all that he had learned the major languages of the Nine Kingdoms well enough to read them and all the languages of magic well enough to be able to cast a spell in any of them. She had spoken nothing he'd recognized.

"Shall we brave supper?" he asked, thinking that perhaps a change would suit them both.

She nodded, though without enthusiasm. He couldn't blame her for that.

He pushed himself to his feet, held down his hand to pull her to hers, then took back his cloak when she handed it to him. He made certain he had Weger's key, then opened the door and promptly lost his breath at the bitter wind that whipped him in the face. He crowded out onto the landing with Aisling, pulled the door to, then locked it and pocketed the key.

"The fire?"

"It will go out on its own," he said loudly. "Not to worry."

She looked at him seriously. "That seems unusual."

"There are many unusual things in the world."

She made no comment, but she did take his hand as he descended the steps in front of her. He was fairly sure he hadn't breathed until his foot touched the courtyard. Aisling's sigh of relief was audible as well.

"You won't say anything."

He looked at her, knowing what she was asking. "Nay."

"Thank you."

He smiled briefly. "No need."

Nay, there was no need to thank him, because he wouldn't tell her secrets to anyone. He wasn't going to be close enough to her for that to be a possibility.

Guard her? Fight in her village squabble? Put aside his own desires to take up the cause of a woman whose eyes laid his soul bare and whose smile left him wishing quite desperately for something sturdy beneath his backside?

He would be damned if he would.

Though he had the uncomfortable feeling he might be damned if he didn't.

Ten

Aisling woke to a blinding pain in her eyes. At first, she thought it was that terrible man again, stabbing her not in the back but in the face, then she realized it was just torchlight. She tried to push it away but someone had hold of her arm and was pulling her up to her feet. She stood in the midst of the chamber, blinking, and tried to make sense of the madness that was swirling around her.

Weger was standing just inside the chamber, handing off the torch to Losh, who was watching the goings-on with enormous eyes. Rùnach rolled up to his feet, rubbing his eyes then shaking his head to apparently clear it. Aisling caught the cloak Weger threw at her. She put it around her shoulders because he barked at her to do so. She had the distinct feeling he was not interested in whether or not she wanted to.

"You must go now."

Rùnach was looking at him as if he'd never heard words before. "What in the hell are you talking about?"

"He's shouting your name to anyone who'll listen," Weger

growled, "which, if you'll pardon my saying so, I find to be a rather dangerous state of affairs."

"Who?" Aisling asked, but they weren't listening to her. She pulled her boots on, yanked the strap of the leather satchel containing Ochadius of Riamh's book over her head, then listened in astonishment to Weger and Rùnach argue in an increasingly acerbic manner. There was talk of a fortnight, a man who knew Rùnach—which seemed to bother Weger very much, though she couldn't account for why—and other things she couldn't quite catch. Then again, she was still having trouble breathing and had been from the moment that man had taken his knife and plunged it into her back . . .

"I don't give a damn what you want," Weger snarled finally.

"And I would have thought you judged a man on his merits, not—"

Weger's drawing of his sword almost left Rùnach without his head. Aisling felt her mouth fall open. They were mad, both of them. She scrambled back over the bed and flattened herself against the wall, trying to stay out of the way. At least Rùnach had managed to get his sword between his face and Weger's blade. The screeching of metal on metal had her clapping her hands over her ears. She would have wondered how it was that Rùnach had his boots on, but perhaps he'd never taken them off the night before.

"Bring his gear," Weger snarled at her. "Follow me to the front gates."

"I'm not going—" Rùnach began, then apparently he lost the thread of his thought in the heat of battle.

Aisling picked up his pack, because Weger had told her to do so, then shouldered it with difficulty. She picked up his cloaks as well because if Weger had his way, she suspected they wouldn't be coming back to their chamber. If she had learned nothing over the past several days, she had learned that Weger never said anything he didn't mean.

The battle that raged was impressive. Weger was forcing Rùnach down the stairs, giving him no choice but to retreat. Aisling followed, slowly, watching them fight in and out of the shadows, spitting curses at each other in languages she couldn't understand, promising all manner of retribution in languages she could. She was surprised to find that even though Rùnach's hair looked as if he'd just rolled from bed and he was obviously furious, he was holding his own.

Perhaps anger was a good thing for swordsmen.

By the time the pair had reached the front gates, Aisling realized that Weger was very serious about throwing them out. The only thing she could say about that was at least they would be much closer to the ground when he did so, as opposed to being two hundred feet up. It would hurt much less.

She stood on the lowest step of that long staircase for a few minutes, then finally set Rùnach's pack down next to her. Several minutes later, she sat down next to the pack. She wondered why anyone would care who Rùnach was. Weger seemed to think having his name noised about was a disaster. Given how many disasters he dealt with over the course of any given day, she was a little surprised that mere babbling would have concerned him any at all.

She found herself joined on her step by Losh, who didn't so much sit as perch next to her. She glanced at him.

"This is perplexing," she said.

He nodded.

"Have any idea what it all means?"

"I wouldn't dare ask," he said faintly. "Don't want to be tossed over the walls—and I daresay Weger would drag me upstairs so's he could."

She had to agree that was quite possibly the case. She was happy to hope that might not be her fate. Then she realized she perhaps shouldn't relax so soon.

Because she hadn't obtained a swordsman.

She supposed, with a sick sort of feeling of fear, that she might manage to trot back up the stairs and look for one while Weger was otherwise occupied. There were men inside Gobhann, steely-eyed, fierce men. Surely one of them would be willing to travel all the way to Bruadair for the glory of it alone.

Though it was not as simple as that, unfortunately. She had been told to send the man to Taigh Hall, but would the peddler truly be waiting for him there? And even if she managed to talk a mercenary into doing what needed to be done, how would the peddler manage to recognize the man she'd sent if she couldn't tell that man what to look for at journey's end?

"It will have to be enough," Weger said loudly. "You have no more time."

Aisling blinked and realized that the men in front of her were no longer fighting. Weger had put away his sword and was simply glaring at Rùnach. Or, actually, Weger's sword was stuck like an arrow in the front wooden gate. Aisling looked quickly to see if Rùnach still retained his sword. She was surprised to find that he did, that Weger's hands were the ones that were empty. She could hardly believe Rùnach could have rid him of his blade, but all signs pointed to it. Weger folded his arms over his chest.

"You learned what you needed to," he stated firmly.

"And what was that?" Rùnach growled, resheathing his sword angrily.

"That perhaps the world doesn't revolve around you?"

"I believe I at least had a vague notion about that before today, my lord."

"Very well," Weger conceded, "there might have been a sliver more altruism in you than I've given you credit for. As for anything else, just what was I to teach you? Considering who your swordmasters were in your youth—"

"That was before."

"And you've forgotten nothing, if that soothes your enormous ego. You must improve the strength in your hands, but perhaps another bit of attention from your brother-in-law would aid you with that, if you could bear the pain of it." Weger shrugged. "Otherwise, it will just take honest sweat and no small number of hours in the lists."

Rùnach looked at him in silence, as if he simply couldn't find anything to say.

Weger walked over to a small brazier burning near the gatekeeper's hut that was in truth nothing more than a wooden roof standing on four wooden pillars and leaning against the rock wall.

Master Odo was reclining on his stool, looking only slightly less bored than usual. Aisling wondered just what that meant, if anything.

She looked at the long, slim rod Weger held in his gloved hand. The end of it was red hot. She fell off the step in surprise, her hands outstretched, when he started toward Rùnach with it.

"Don't!" she exclaimed, wondering how she was going to stop Weger from killing Rùnach.

And wondering, exactly, why she was concerned.

Weger shot her a look that froze her in mid-step, then pressed the rod against the flesh above Rùnach's eyebrow.

Aisling expected him to at least flinch in pain. What she didn't expect was for Weger to peer at Rùnach's forehead, then attempt his singeing again. He looked at Rùnach.

"There's something there."

Rùnach drew his hand over his eyes. "Don't ask me what."

Weger tossed the metal rod back into the brazier. "Well, I can't solve the problem." He nodded to the gatekeeper. "Open the gates, Odo. These two are in a hurry to leave."

Aisling watched Rùnach remain exactly where he was, unmoving apart from his chest heaving. Weger noticed that, finally, then he stepped close to Rùnach and spoke in a low voice. Aisling didn't want to listen, but she was right there and none of it made sense, so she supposed there was no harm in eavesdropping.

"He can't possibly know," Rùnach was saying.

"Of course, he knows," Weger whispered furiously. "He's been shouting at the top of his bloody lungs for hours now, or didn't you hear him?"

"I was busy sleeping."

"I hope you had enough of that," Weger said sharply, "for you'll not have any in the near future. You must go and you must go now."

Rùnach looked at him evenly. "I do not fear death."

"Then perhaps, my dear Rùnach, you might, again, think of others besides yourself. Your sister, for one."

"She wouldn't need my protection even if I were able to offer it."

"Then perhaps you might consider those who cannot protect

themselves, those who might be harmed—or might have been recently harmed—just to see if your glorious chivalry would leap to the fore. Will you put them in harm's way?"

"A coincidence."

"You fool," Weger growled, "you know there are no coincidences where he is concerned!"

"He is restless—"

"He's centuries old, damn you, and not even my gates will hold him forever. If you have even a single useful thought in that pretty head of yours, that thought will tell you to bolt whilst you have the chance and not stop running until you've reached somewhere safe." He folded his arms over his chest. "Besides, didn't you promise to take that gel there to Tor Neroche and find her a mercenary?"

Aisling watched Rùnach look at Weger for several eternal moments, then turn his head and look at her.

She felt her mouth go dry. "I don't need aid," she managed. She attempted to swallow several times, but it didn't go very well for her. "Tor Neroche?"

"Head straight to the palace," Weger advised. "They're less interested in gold than they are immortalizing themselves in legend, unlike this rabble here in my keep. You'll find what you need right off, I imagine."

She hardly dared hope as much. She took a deep breath, then looked at Weger. "Can you guarantee it? My life depends on it."

He reached out and put his hand very briefly on her shoulder. "There is a lad there, Mansourah, who is unimportant in the grander scheme of things, but a right proper swordsman when the inducement is enough. Ask for him, trust him with your details, then watch him hurry off into the sunset to do what you need to have done." He nodded firmly. "I guarantee it."

Aisling calculated furiously. It was perhaps five days to Bere if she ran, a pair of days to Istaur by ship, then . . . well, she supposed if she managed to reach Tor Neroche in less than a month, she would be fortunate indeed.

She looked at Weger. "It would take a miracle to get there in time," she managed.

Weger beamed on her. "And how fortunate you are that a miracle stands here before you. Rùnach, take this child to Tor Neroche. You can find the way, can't you? And introduce her to little Mansourah?"

"But, I have no intention of going to—"

Weger backhanded him.

Aisling was so shocked, she could only stand there and gape. Rùnach faced Weger again, then put the back of his hand to his mouth. It came away bloody. He looked at his hand, then at Weger, then took a deep breath.

But he said nothing. He simply went to fetch his pack, shouldered it, then nodded at Weger. The next thing Aisling knew, he had taken her hand and was pulling her out of the front gates. She went, because he gave her no choice, heard the gates bang shut behind them, then realized they were missing something.

"Your horse."

He shrugged. "He'll find us eventually, I imagine. Or not. He has a mind of his own."

She pulled on his hand until he stopped, then she pulled her hand away. "I don't need aid."

"Don't be—"

"I am not ridiculous," she said shortly. "And I don't need your aid. I don't think I would accept it if you offered it."

He bowed his head and rubbed the back of his neck for a moment or two, then looked at her.

"I apologize," he said quietly. "I did that . . . badly."

"No need," she said promptly. "I appreciate the passage. I'm sorry I cannot repay your kindness for that, nor for the tending when I was ill inside." She held on to the strap of the satchel Weger had given her. "I only have this—"

"Nay," he said quickly, reaching out to stop her from pulling it over her head. "You keep it."

She pulled her forearm away from his hand, then nodded and stepped backward. She pulled her cloak closer around her, because it was cold, then nodded at him. "A good journey to you, then."

He looked at her in surprise. "Where are you going?"

"Tor Neroche."

"But you can't be serious," he protested.

"I have no choice. Now, please get out of my way."

"But—"

She held up her hand, cutting him off. "Aren't there ships that travel from Sgioba to Tor Neroche?"

He looked at her for several minutes by the very faint light of the torchlight atop the walls flanking the front gate, then he sighed.

"Freight ships, I suppose," he conceded slowly, "but the sea is very rough and the hands rougher. Nothing as luxurious as what brought us from Bere."

She suppressed the urge to sigh. "And by land?"

"On foot?" he asked. "You would need at least a month if you ran, longer if you walked. You might manage a fortnight from Istaur with a very fast horse and good weather, but the horse would need wings on his hooves." He looked at her in surprise. "Are you making for Tor Neroche in truth?"

"I have no choice."

"But of course you have a choice. There are soldiers aplenty in the world who could see to your troubles."

"But I must have a particular sort of man," she said, then she found she couldn't say anything else. She had been sent to Gobhann to find a mercenary, yet she had left without one. Weger had sent her off to Tor Neroche, which left her still, for the moment, without a mercenary.

She looked off into the distance and considered curses and quests. The first thing she examined was the condition of her poor form. She wasn't feverish, didn't feel faint, didn't have her heart racing as if it wanted to accomplish a few more beats before it was stilled. In fact, apart from the ache in her chest, she felt fine.

You have three se'nnights. The bargain must be struck before midnight of the last day or your life will be the forfeit.

The peddler's words came back to her as if they'd been the deep, throbbing tolling of the village green bell she could remember from her childhood. He *had* said three se'nnights, not three fortnights. He'd been terribly specific about everything, warning her so direly of the consequences she would face if she didn't fulfill her quest.

He couldn't have been mistaken about the length of time allotted her.

She didn't protest as Rùnach took her by the elbow and tugged her away from the gates. Walking helped. She had walked at the Guild, around and around the buildings, under the watchful eye of the guards, of course, whenever she was allowed to. It cleared her mind, left her feeling grounded.

It served her just as well now. She walked and let the peddler's words resonate in her mind. He had said what he'd said. There was no doubt of that. He was a careful man, of that she was certain. He wouldn't have made a mistake, not when so much depended on his being completely accurate in his instructions.

She continued along with Rùnach for another few minutes until a thought occurred to her that she had never before considered.

What if the peddler had lied?

She stopped so abruptly, Rùnach had to turn around and walk back to her. He looked at her, then apparently saw something in her face that surprised him.

"What is it?" he asked.

She looked up at him searchingly. "Are things different from what they seem, do you think?"

He looked slightly winded. Perhaps he was still unsettled from having been torn from his very comfortable sleep. Perhaps he was still reeling from the ferocious battle he had just fought with the lord of Gobhann. A battle he had won, as it happened, but perhaps he had found it somehow unsatisfying.

"I think," he said slowly, "that sometimes they are. Why?"

She considered just blurting everything out to him right there, but too many years of keeping things to herself prevented that. Well, that and the curse that would fell her on the spot did she dare divulge anything about Bruadair or its inhabitants.

Unless that curse was a lie as well.

She blew her shorn hair out of her eyes. "I'm not sure what to believe. And I have no idea what to do now."

"Walk."

"Do you think so?"

"I'm sure of it," he said confidently. "Weger will begin raining arrows down on us if we don't move soon, so perhaps that is all we need think about at the moment."

"How do you know?"

He reached over and plucked an arrow from a spot of ground near his foot. "The first volley."

She blinked in surprise. "He is a skilled archer."

Rùnach snorted. "'Tis more dumb luck, I imagine, though he'll hit us eventually." He shouldered his pack and handed her the arrow. "Let's trot off into the distance and see if we can't get beyond the reach of his good fortune."

She would have told him she didn't want to go with him, that he was unkind, ill-mannered, ill-tempered, and difficult to look at, but an arrow landed at her feet, almost tearing through her boot. She jumped back, then looked at him.

"Which road to Bere?"

He pointed to the road they'd come from before they'd entered Gobhann.

"Thank you," she said briskly. She nodded to him, then strode away. He would either follow or not. She honestly didn't care.

But she did run.

Three days later, she was bone weary, hungry, and tired of Rùnach following her. She was angry with him but couldn't decide why. He had had his own reasons for entering Gobhann and he'd left it not having accomplished what he'd set out to do. She could understand that. What she couldn't understand was why Weger had been so concerned that someone knew Rùnach. He was handsome, to be sure, and an excellent swordsman, but surely his importance in the world was limited to that.

What she wanted was to sit down somewhere and think until she had sifted through all the thoughts plaguing her. She didn't want to be responsible for Rùnach's having been tossed out of

Weger's gates. She didn't want Rùnach feeling responsible for her. She didn't want to be responsible for the future of Bruadair.

But mostly she wanted to know why she was still alive.

It was a terrible feeling, that of being under a curse she hadn't asked for and didn't want. The sword of that doom hung over her constantly, interfering with every thought, making her jump every time she was startled by a noise or a twinge or a thought. It was made all the worse by knowing that there was no possible way she would reach Tor Neroche in time to stave off the effects of that doom—not even if the peddler had meant three fortnights in spite of what he'd said.

Which left her less than ten days to get to the king of Neroche's palace.

She shivered almost uncontrollably. The very cold spring rain that had begun an hour ago hadn't helped either. In addition to everything else, she was soaked to the skin and feverish. What she wanted to do was find somewhere to get out of the wet, but that didn't look to be a possibility anytime soon—

Or, perhaps it would be. She suddenly smelled smoke in the air. She saw it rising from the chimney of a house well off the road, which she realized only because she had wandered well off the road. It was a pleasant-looking house, cozy, small enough for a man and his wife, or a widow trying to keep herself safe and fed.

She wasn't sure who reached the door first, but she suspected it hadn't been her. She stood looking at Rùnach's back as he knocked softly. It took quite a while for the door to open, but open it did eventually.

"Aye?" came the worn voice, warily.

"Good e'en to you, good woman," Rùnach said politely. "We are two weary travelers seeking refuge from the storm. If there is labor I can offer in return for shelter, you need only name it and 'tis done."

Aisling wondered how it was that that tall, solemn man could say more to a complete stranger in one sitting than he'd said to her in the past three days. Then again, she hadn't been interested in speaking to him, so perhaps she deserved what she got.

His offer won them entrance. Aisling stood just inside the door and was extremely grateful for the chance to at least get out of the rain. Rùnach stepped aside to introduce her—

She gasped.

There, ten paces away from the door, was a hearth. That in itself wasn't noteworthy, she supposed. It was a simple thing fashioned from rock no doubt gathered from a nearby river. A wooden plank had been set into the stone for use as a mantel, perhaps crafted lovingly by a husband at some point in the past. On it were several modest but no doubt cherished items: a pair of candlesticks; a small painting of a man dressed in fine clothes; a simple vase that stood empty at the moment but Aisling imagined would be filled during the late spring and summer when flowers were abundant. On the near side of the fire was a stack of wood, chopped and ready for use. On the far side of the hearth was a woven basket full of snowy white fluff.

And a spinning wheel.

"Aisling?"

She realized her breath was coming in gasps, but she couldn't seem to find enough air in the small house to satisfy her burning lungs. She took a step backward, because she had to.

"Aisling!"

She realized Rùnach was speaking to her. It occurred to her that he sounded rather unsettled, but given that she felt equally as unsettled, she couldn't blame him for it. She felt for his arm until she found it and could clutch it. "That's a spinning wheel."

"Well, yes, I believe it is," he said, his voice sounding very faint thanks to the rushing in her ears.

"I'm not to touch it."

"Why not?"

She dragged her attention away from the wheel and looked up at him. "Because I'll die."

"Of course ye won't, dearie," said the old woman. "There's no magic to it. Just a wheel and some wool I carded myself last year. Very lovely stuff it is."

Aisling looked at their host. She was unremarkable, that old, wrinkled granny dressed in homespun. Aisling supposed that at another time she might have been happy to sit with her in front of her hearth and talk to her about the things she had woven over the course of her life, things Aisling could only hope had been some other color besides dingy grey.

But at the moment, all she could do was look at the woman in horror and wish she'd put her spinning wheel in a different room.

Then again, from the look of things, the house didn't have a different room.

Aisling felt Rùnach put his hand over hers, but it wasn't enough to anchor her in the world. Her hand slipped from underneath his as if it had been water slipping down the face of the slick stone in Weger's upper courtyard. She found herself standing in front of the wheel without knowing quite how she'd gotten there. She stopped because she could go no further.

The wheel was old and weathered and so beautiful she couldn't look away from it. She brushed her hand over the flywheel, not touching it.

It spun just the same.

She heard gasps behind her, but she could do nothing about that. She reached out and touched the wheel as it revolved—

And her world exploded.

She was no longer standing in a humble cottage, touching the worn wooden wheel of a simple village spinner. She was standing on the edge of a cliff, staring out over the ocean. In front of her the sky had exploded into a thousand colors, a thousand scenes of battle, of reunion, of delight and beauty. She stood there struggling to draw in a normal breath, struggling to understand what she was looking at, where she was, how she was going to find her way back into herself—

And then her world went black.

Eleven

❋

Rùnach managed to catch Aisling as she fell only because he'd been halfway to her before she'd started to sway. He lifted her up into his arms. She was utterly senseless, which surprised him. She'd also just been babbling in that tongue he had never heard before, that same tongue she'd been murmuring in Weger's tower chamber. A handful of the words had been the same, which he supposed might be useful at another time in determining just what language it was. He wondered if perhaps she had been calling for help.

She had cause.

"Get out," said a voice from behind him. "And take your witch with you."

He turned around and found himself facing an old woman brandishing a very large boning knife.

"I beg your pardon?" he asked in surprise.

The woman gestured with her knife. "Her, befouling my wheel with her magic. Don't pretend you don't know."

He didn't know, but he wasn't going to argue with that very

well-tended blade. He eased around his erstwhile hostess, exited as expediently as possible, then continued on out into the rain. The door slammed shut behind him and the bolt was thrown home.

Rùnach stood ten paces from the house with Aisling in his arms and wondered several things, beginning and ending with just who the hell she was.

He considered his options and decided that he had only one and that was to find shelter as quickly as possible and see if Aisling was merely senseless or if she was dead. She was absolutely motionless, but the rain so driving and the wind so fierce, he wasn't sure he would be able to hear her breathing if he tried. He started to walk forward, then almost dropped Aisling in his surprise.

His horse stood there in front of him, watching him silently.

Rùnach rolled his eyes. That was all he needed, to have that granny behind him start throwing boiling oil at him for being a sorcerer. Horses appearing from nowhere would do nothing to enhance his already tarnished reputation.

Rùnach pursed his lips. "How did you escape—nay, never mind. I don't want to know. I don't suppose you saw an inn—nay, never mind that, either." He hadn't intended to make any uninvited visits to other locales on Melksham, but then again, he hadn't given much thought to where he would go after he earned Weger's mark—which he hadn't done even though the spot over his brow burned like hellfire. He looked at Iteach. "Well, any ideas, you irascible pony?"

Iteach took a handful of steps backward, tossed his head, then flapped his suddenly sprouted wings. Rùnach spared a brief but very fond thought for his grandfather's foresight, then climbed as gracefully as he could onto Iteach's back. He supposed all those years he'd spent riding served him at the moment, for whilst he had a saddle, his horse had definitely not provided him with any reins. He was fairly sure that hadn't been an oversight.

Screeching ensued from inside the house.

"South, I think," Rùnach said quickly, "and perhaps a bit east—"

Lisssssmòrrrrr . . .

Rùnach blurted out a curse, but only because Iteach had leapt up into the air, not because the bloody horse was inside his head, whispering and rolling his r's in a particularly equine way. He decided abruptly that he would definitely be having words with Sgath. He just wasn't quite sure which ones wouldn't get him boxed ears.

"Well, aye," he gasped. "Lismòr would do quite nicely."

And that was the last thing he said for quite some time. He managed to get Aisling's head on his shoulder and his cloak settled around her, which he hoped would shield her from the worst of the truly terrible weather. He kept his seat only because he'd been riding literally from the moment he could walk. He hadn't done very well on his way to Mhorghain's wedding at Seanagarra, but those were memories perhaps better left behind. It had been so long since he'd been out of Beinn òrain that he'd been a little unnerved by the whole journey, he who had traveled the world before, striding about with all the confidence and arrogance of an elven prince. He had spent the entire trip reduced to a less-than-confident clutcher of reins, wishing he'd asked Soilléir to strap him to the saddle before they'd leapt up into the night sky on the backs of other shapechanging horses. It was little wonder he'd lost what gear he'd brought with him.

He turned his mind away from that. They were useless notes that he'd dropped as they'd flown, notes that wouldn't mean anything to anyone but him. He might have forgotten the contents of his father's book, but a score of years with nothing to do but read and run endlessly up and down stairs in the dead of night to keep his body strong had at least given him the time to retrain his mind to memorize what he saw.

He didn't want to think about the things he couldn't remember.

In time, he saw the faint twinkle of lights at the university. Iteach seemed to be sharing his thoughts of discretion because he landed gently half a league away and his wings vanished. He cantered for most of the rest of the distance, a smooth, elegant gait that left Rùnach feeling as if he were sitting on a comfortable chair in his grandfather's library.

Iteach stopped fifty paces before the walls. Rùnach supposed his steed might have continued on a bit farther in different circumstances, but an arrow sailed through the air with a whistling sound, then went to ground right in front of them. Iteach stopped, snorted, then did a lovely bit of piaffe until Rùnach begged him to stop. Rùnach slid off the saddle, rather more grateful than he could say for a solid horse who didn't seem to mind when he used him to lean on until he'd gotten his feet underneath him.

He carried Aisling across the remaining distance, followed closely by his horse. Perhaps he looked harmless enough, for no other arrows came his way. Or, perhaps they were waiting until they had a sure shot before they wasted any more. He had no idea and decided he wouldn't bother asking.

He stood instead at the gate in the driving rain and kicked at the gate because he had no hands for it. At least, for a change, that wasn't because his hands didn't work. His arms, however, were shaking so badly, he thought he might drop Aisling before he managed to get her to safety.

A small panel slid back and a lamp appeared. That was followed in good time by a long, pointed nose.

"Who are ye?"

"Travelers seeking refuge," Rùnach said, loudly, over the sound of the howling wind.

The gatekeeper seemed to be in no hurry, despite the nastiness of the weather. "We have many travelers here—"

"Oh, bloody hell, just open the door," Rùnach exclaimed. "You know you must offer refuge to all who seek it."

The panel slid shut, the bolt was pulled back, then the gate creaked on its hinges until only the gatekeeper stood in Rùnach's way. He held up the lantern.

"Name, or ye don't pass."

Rùnach opened his mouth, then shut it. He knew that Nicholas had cultivated anonymity at his university, so it was impossible to give the man in front of him the entirety of his name. He wasn't sure if anyone knew who Mhorghain truly was or whom she had wed, but he didn't dare count on that either. He looked at the gatekeeper.

"I am called Rùnach," he said, finally.

The gatekeeper, Master James if Mhorghain were to be believed, pursed his lips, then motioned to a lad who turned and bolted into the darkness.

Master James looked at Aisling. "Ill, is she?"

"Senseless, rather."

"But she's not dead," Master James said, peering into her face. He looked at another of the lads waiting there for something useful to do. "Lead this man to the infirmary," he said briskly. He looked back at Rùnach. "Someone will be waiting for you."

Rùnach could only hope so. He nodded to Master James, then followed the lad along paths that led past gardens and buildings, and finally to a large courtyard surrounded by a beautiful portico. Rùnach would have perhaps admired it another time. At the moment he was simply glad to be out of the rain.

He rubbed his face on his shoulder, trying to get the water out of his eyes. He blinked, then realized that there was someone standing in front of him.

That Nicholas of Lismòr didn't seem to be particularly surprised to see him didn't surprise him at all. His uncle was, after all, the former wizard king of Diarmailt, which wasn't exactly a realm known for its pastoral and unremarkable nature. Strange happenings there, or so the tales went. Rùnach didn't want to know what his uncle was capable of.

Nicholas only nodded gravely at him and sent Rùnach's escort back to the front gates. Rùnach followed the lord of Lismòr around the edge of that large courtyard until they came to a long passageway. Nicholas paused in front of a door, opened it, then stood back for Rùnach to enter.

The chamber was lit by candles driving the darkness back into the corners. A fire burned brightly in the hearth. Nicholas said nothing but Rùnach was suddenly standing there in dry clothes.

Rùnach sighed lightly.

Nicholas undid the clasp of Aisling's cloak, then helped Rùnach get her into bed. Rùnach was willing to pull off her boots, but he could go no further than that. He supposed that didn't matter. Aisling's clothes had obviously been just as enspelled as his.

Nicholas put his hand against her forehead and was very still for several moments. Then he sighed, drew the covers up over her, then went to pull up a chair by her bedside. He looked up at Rùnach.

"Make yourself at home, nephew," he said with a smile.

Rùnach realized he was still standing there with his gear on his back and his cloak almost choking him. He took off his cloak, shrugged out of his pack, and collapsed into the chair opposite his uncle.

"Will Master James see to my horse?"

"What horse?"

Rùnach opened his mouth, then shut it. "Never mind."

Nicholas smiled. "A gift from Sgath?"

"How did you know—nay, don't tell me." Rùnach shivered. "I don't want to know how you know anything."

"I imagine you don't." He reached out and brushed Aisling's hair back from her face. "What befell this lovely gel here?"

"I have no idea," Rùnach said, rubbing his hands together restlessly. "We were seeking shelter at the hearth of an old woman, just off the road to Bere. She saw a spinning wheel." He looked at Nicholas. "She touched it and fainted."

"Is that all?" Nicholas asked politely.

Rùnach blew out his breath. "Of course not. Before she put her hand to the wood, she set it spinning without touching it and after she touched it, she babbled in a tongue I couldn't understand."

"Before she fainted."

"Aye," Rùnach said wearily. "That is the order of events."

"Interesting. Who is she?"

"Her name is Aisling. Past that, I don't know."

Nicholas smiled. "Rùnach, lad, you've lost your touch. I heard tales that you could, in your youth, walk into a ball and leave every lass in the place tripping over anything in her way in order to press her name on you. Fights ensued, or so I was told."

Rùnach pursed his lips. "And who told you that?"

"Desdhemar of Neroche, actually," Nicholas said. "You were kind to her son. I think she appreciated it."

"And I think I might have slipped her a coveted spell or two," Rùnach said dryly, "which I imagine she appreciated more."

"I imagine that's true," Nicholas agreed. He was interrupted by a knock. "Ah, supper. That is most welcome. William, come!"

Rùnach didn't argue as Nicholas drew up a small table between them and his page set down a hearty meal. He attempted a bit of polite conversation, but Nicholas waved him on with a smile.

"Don't stand on ceremony with me, my boy. I've never been inside Gobhann, but I've heard tell of its culinary wonders."

"How did you know I was in—" Rùnach held up his hand. "Again, never mind."

"You give me too much credit," Nicholas said easily. "I overheard you at your sister's wedding saying it was in your plans, and I didn't doubt you would make good on the threat. But I won't force you to delve into the reasons for that choice at present. Eat in peace, my lad. We'll discuss other things tomorrow."

Rùnach was happy to take advantage of the invitation. He tucked in contentedly to food that tasted as if it had actually been made with the intention of humans not only eating but enjoying it, finished with a few sips of an elegant, delicate wine, then sat back with a deep sigh of pleasure.

"Better than Gobhann?" Nicholas asked, his eyes twinkling.

"Please," Rùnach said with feeling, "let's not discuss it."

"Then let us choose a different comparison. Was this superior to Buidseachd?"

"That depends on which table you're talking about," Rùnach said. "The buttery is, as I'm sure you know, vile, but I didn't eat in the buttery."

"Soilléir is a bit more choosey about his fare, is that it?"

"Thankfully," Rùnach said with feeling. "And I was the beneficiary of that for many years."

Nicholas studied him. "And what did you find during those many years you were there? Anything interesting?"

"A few things I gave to Miach at Buidseachd earlier in the year, but nothing else of note."

"And did you find anything interesting in Gobhann?"

Rùnach shot his uncle a sharp look. "Terrible food, endless amounts of work, and Lothar of Wychweald, though I'm guessing you aren't surprised by any of those."

"Encounter him, did you?" Nicholas asked mildly.

"I thought the worst would be having to listen to him sing at all hours, but I fear it was much worse than that." He nodded toward Aisling. "He stabbed her, though I'm not sure why."

"Don't you know?"

Rùnach dragged his hand through his hair. "Have I told you how much I loathe riddles?"

Nicholas only laughed. "Consider it a mystery, then."

"I'm not sure that makes it any more palatable," Rùnach said grimly, "but I'll play, if it pleases you. Nay, I don't know anything about her save she doesn't tolerate lobelia very well. She's obviously too thin, rather delicate, and has absolutely no skill in defending herself despite a pair of days with Weger conducting her lessons. And Lothar I'm sure thought her nothing more than a convenient target."

"In the last, you might be right," Nicholas conceded. He looked at Aisling for a moment or two, then back at Rùnach. "Who healed her?"

"Weger, if you can believe it."

Nicholas laughed softly. "I'm actually surprised he managed an entire spell when what was likely tumbling out of his mouth were curses."

Rùnach nodded, though he found himself suddenly thinking less about Weger's abundant collection of foul epitaphs in several languages than the look Weger had given Aisling after he'd healed her.

As if he'd seen something that . . . awed him.

Rùnach looked at the woman lying in that bed, still as death, and wondered what had felled her and what would remain of her once she woke. *If* she woke.

He looked at Nicholas. "Can you heal her?"

Nicholas smiled. "There was no need for healing, Rùnach. She was overcome by something and had no recourse but to fall senseless."

"What sort of something?"

"Oh, I imagine it isn't really very interesting."

"Isn't it?"

"She'll wake to herself," Nicholas said, as if he hadn't heard Rùnach, or perhaps had heard him but didn't want to discuss the subject further. "I wouldn't have fed you supper if there hadn't been aught to do."

Rùnach could only nod, because he should have realized that.

"Sleep is what you need, my boy. You can have the chamber next door if you like, or William can make you up a pallet here before the fire. Aisling will be safe either way, I promise you."

"I'll stay here, if it's all the same to you."

He listened to the words come out of his mouth and couldn't for the life of him decide where they'd come from. He had the tatters of his former plans to gather up and try to weave back together and Aisling had . . . well, he had no idea what Aisling had.

If I touch it, I'll die.

He frowned thoughtfully. That was an odd thing to say. Had it been her mother to so thoroughly warn her off her own spinning wheel that Aisling had continued to believe it far past the age when she should have relegated the words to a mere childhood warning?

Odder still that she had touched it just the same, as if she simply hadn't been able to stop herself.

Well, that wasn't precisely true either. She had sent the wheel spinning without touching it. An unmagical woman who had walked into Gobhann with no cloak and no boots had smoothed her hand over air and sent a spinning wheel turning. And then when she had reached out and touched the wood, she had gasped, babbled in a tongue he didn't recognize, then fallen as if she were dead.

"Mysterious, wouldn't you agree?"

Rùnach pulled himself back to himself and looked at his uncle. "I'm not sure she's a mystery I want to solve."

Nicholas only smiled pleasantly. "What a terrible liar you've become there in that hovel so loftily termed a school."

Rùnach would have protested further, but he knew there was no point. He could perhaps tell himself all day that he wasn't interested in the things swirling around that very plain, very simple gel from some obscure corner of the Nine Kingdoms, but he would be lying.

The first thing he would start with was that language she had murmured in her unguarded moments.

He looked at his uncle. "How is your library these days?"

"Robustly stocked with all manner of interesting tomes. And when you've exhausted your search there, you might come have a peek at the more dangerous things kept in my solar."

Rùnach found himself unable to keep from smiling. "Then perhaps when our patient awakes, we should make a visit there."

"I do have a lovely hearth."

"I imagine you do, my lord."

Nicholas called William, who helped him clear away the dishes and move the table. "I'll return in a bit," he said, putting his hand on Rùnach's shoulder briefly. "I'll bring you something to read should she sleep longer than you do."

"Thank you, my lord," Rùnach said. "For that and the refuge."

"Always, Rùnach. Always."

Rùnach watched William make up a cot for him in front of the fire. He thanked the lad, then took Nicholas's chair and simply stared at Aisling by the light of the fire and the candles, which had magically dimmed to just the right brightness.

He rubbed his hands over his face and sighed. He hadn't intended to be sitting in comfort at Lismòr, he'd intended to be freezing his arse off in Gobhann. He touched the spot over his brow where Weger had tried to brand him, not once but twice, and wondered how it was possible his face could hurt him so badly yet there be no mark there to show there was a reason he winced every time his hair brushed his brow.

That was a bit of a mystery, as well.

Though he was more interested, he had to admit, in the secrets of the lass lying in the bed in front of him. He leaned forward with his elbows on his knees and stared at her, wondering who she was and where in the Nine Kingdoms she had learned a tongue that he absolutely didn't recognize, a tongue that had left a soldier with almost seven centuries of living to his tally almost speechless with wonder.

"My lord?"

Rùnach jumped in spite of himself. The next words out of his mouth were almost *I'm no lord*, but he supposed there was no point in bothering. He smiled at Nicholas's page.

"Aye, William?"

"My lord Nicholas asked me to bring you these things," he said, handing Rùnach a basket. "Books he thought you might like, as well as sheaves of parchment and pen and ink, if you feel the need to scribble down the odd note."

"Take him my thanks, would you?"

"Of course, my lord."

Rùnach waited until he'd pulled the door shut behind him before he peered into the basket to see what Nicholas had sent along. Along with tools for taking notes, there was a book on the detailed political geography of the Nine Kingdoms, a rather thick book entitled *The Etymology of Curses*, which left him smiling, and a slim, illustrated volume on sheep, the wool they produced, and spinning techniques used in turning those various types of wool into thread for weaving and yarn for knitting. Rùnach set the last aside for Aisling, should she be able to look at it without screaming, along with the book on curses, and opened the tome about the political geography of the Nine Kingdoms.

He couldn't say that in his youth he'd cared much for the political machinations of any given realm. His grandfather Sìle held a seat on the Council of Kings, of course, but he'd been a bit of a snob about the whole thing, something Rùnach had agreed with heartily. Most kings did have at least some spark of magic in their veins, but none to equal the might, majesty, and sheer beauty of Fadaire.

Well, those inhabiting the rather mysterious world of Cothromaiche might have disagreed, but King Seannair never came to any meetings and likely had no idea where his crown was, so Rùnach had never lumped him in with the others.

And besides, kingdoms changed, gained territory, lost territory, sometimes absorbed entire kingdoms into themselves or watched their lands disappear beyond their reach into someone else's realm. He supposed it might be an interesting exercise to see which kingdoms had begun as the only nine in the world, then become something entirely different. It might also be interesting, for the sheer sake of academics, to make note of who had written which history. He could guarantee that Sìle of Tòrr Dòrainn would have a far different view of things than Uachdaran of Léige. It wouldn't have surprised him at all to have found that his grandfather simply dismissed other realms if it suited his vanity and purposes.

He rose, fetched the table they'd used for supper, then set out ink, pen, and paper. Perhaps he would make a list of every kingdom of note, then jot down alongside each a brief list of the languages spoken within their borders. Just to give himself something to do, of course.

He glanced at the cot there in front of the fire that had banked itself a bit. The lure of sleep was almost too much to resist. A sleep that might actually leave him feeling as if he *hadn't* been sleeping on a rock would be a luxury he hadn't expected.

He looked at Aisling, lying there motionless, hardly breathing, then shook his head. Even an hour of searching might tell him things that would be useful. Even if all his knowledge did was help convince her that a provincial village that existed as nothing more than a speck on the map did not have the power to compel her to save it, his time would be well spent. A petty man styling himself as overlord did not require a mercenary with Weger's mark over his brow to find himself dispatched, though Rùnach was fairly sure he could simply go with her, approach the man, then threaten him with a harsh word or two to encourage him to trot off and look for less weak-kneed villagers to intimidate.

Because, after all, what sort of place with any culture at all could possibly leave a woman thinking that the touch of a spinning wheel would cause her death?

He leaned over, brushed the hair back from Aisling's face, then froze as she sighed something in her sleep. He thought it might have been *thank you*, but those were again words he'd never heard before.

A mystery indeed.

He frowned thoughtfully, then opened his book and began to read.

Twelve

❧

Aisling struggled to open her eyes, uncertain for a moment or two if she was trying to wake or trying to rouse herself from some sort of untoward illness. She had rarely suffered from any illness until she'd gone inside Gobhann. She supposed she could safely say she had woken before from all sorts of sleeps, from uneasy snoozes to hopeless, helpless descents into oblivion to escape the dullness and monotony of her life at the Guild, but she had never before woken from the sleep of death.

It occurred to her that she was not dead, she was very much alive. She ached from head to toe and her head felt as if someone had tried to pull her brain out of her eye sockets. Her eyes burned as if she'd been weeping for days, though she knew she hadn't. But other than those rather minor things, she felt remarkably good. She lay there for quite a while, thinking about life and death and the fact that she was partaking of the former instead of the latter. The more she thought about it, the warmer she felt.

But perhaps the fury of knowing that one had been lied to did that for a person.

Never touch a wheel, she had been told countless times at the Guild. *Death is the penalty for touching a wheel*, she'd had snapped at her time and time again. Those phrases had always been accompanied by the goriest of details about how death would come, not by the hand of some soul in power but from the wheel itself. But unless her senses had failed her completely, she hadn't lost her hands or her eyes or had her entrails explode out of her as retribution for her cheek.

She was whole.

She could scarce believe it, but there was no denying it. She opened her eyes and looked up at the ceiling above her. It was plain, though clean and nicely plastered. The bed she was lying on was terribly soft, so soft she had to admit that when she'd first found her senses, she had considered the possibility that she had been lying in some soft patch of the next world where pain would be no more. She felt the blankets under her fingertips and found those to be just as soft as the bed beneath her back, as if they'd been woven from something much finer and softer than silk, though she couldn't have said what. She was accustomed to rough cotton that wore at her fingers and left them bleeding by the end of the week.

She turned her head slightly and realized she wasn't alone. A white-haired man sat by the side of her bed, watching her. She blinked at the enormous golden crown on his head, partly because she couldn't imagine a king sitting by her bed and partly because the next time she blinked, the crown was gone but the man was still there. She frowned.

"Who are you, Your Majesty?"

He smiled. "Nicholas of Lismòr."

"Where is Lismòr?" she asked.

"It's a little university on the island of Melksham," he said without haste or irritation, sounding as if he had all the time in the world to answer questions that she realized she probably should have already known the answers to. "Just around the corner from Gobhann, if you look at the map the right way."

She considered that, then frowned again. "Am I dead?"

"Why would you be, my dear?"

Why, indeed? There were many deeds worthy of death in her country. Touching a spinning wheel was one of them. Crossing the border was another.

Yet there she was, still breathing.

"How did I come to be here?" she asked, deciding abruptly that that was an easier thing to contemplate than anything else.

"You were brought here," Nicholas of Lismòr said.

Aisling started to ask by whom, then realized there was some-one else in the room, someone standing in the shadows. It was Rùnach; she could tell that by his shape alone.

"Did he carry me here, Your Majesty?" she asked.

Rùnach made a strangled noise of some sort. Aisling looked at him, then at Nicholas.

"Did I ask amiss?" she asked.

Nicholas only shook his head, a faint smile on his face. "I'm sure he's just wondering about your form of address for my modest self."

"The crown over your head isn't very modest, if you don't mind my saying so," Aisling said. She rubbed her eyes briefly. "At least I think I saw a crown." She looked at Nicholas. "Am I dreaming?"

Nicholas reached out and patted her hand. "I don't think so, though any time you want to dream a crown atop my head, you certainly may. As for the other, you could simply call me Nicholas, if you'd prefer. Anything else might startle my students."

Aisling wasn't going to argue with him. Besides, she had prob-ably imagined the whole thing anyway. It had been that sort of fortnight.

"And to answer your question," Nicholas said easily, "Rùnach carried you here. You've been asleep for a trio of days. How do you feel?"

"Remarkably good, all things considered."

Nicholas laughed and it was as if the sun had come out from behind terrible clouds. He put his hands on his knees and rose. "I think something strengthening might be just the thing for you. I'll trot off to the buttery and see what Cook has in his stockpot. Rùn-ach, lad, keep her company, won't you?"

"How do you know Rùnach?" Aisling asked.

"I know his sister."

"Everyone knows his sister."

"She traveled a great deal recently," Nicholas said with a shrug. "You might like her, I daresay. Quite opinionated about things."

Rùnach snorted, but said nothing.

Nicholas put his hand briefly on Rùnach's shoulder in passing, then left the chamber, tossing a pleasant, "I'll return," over his shoulder as he did so.

Aisling watched him go, then looked at Rùnach leaning back against the wall near to the hearth, looking as if he couldn't decide whether to sit or bolt. He didn't move, though, as if he had at some point in his life perfected the art of simply leaning against a wall and becoming as still as death.

In time, it made her nervous. She cleared her throat finally.

"You needn't stay," she said. "I appreciate the rescue, but I know you have plans of your own."

He looked at her in surprise. "I'm happy to stay."

She realized then that she was supposed to be angry with him, but somehow she just couldn't quite muster up any enthusiasm for it. He could have clasped hands with her in a soldierly fashion at any point along their long slog through inclement weather and been off on his own, but he hadn't. He had walked with her, silent and grave, for his own perverse reasons, no doubt. And he had done her the favor of bringing her to a safe place after she'd had the temerity to touch a spinning wheel. That alone was enough to merit her gratitude, surely.

She thought about sitting up, then realized there was no strength in her limbs. It occurred to her immediately that perhaps she had rejoiced over her escape too soon. The truth was, she felt a great lassitude running through the entirety of her form, as if she'd been running the stairs at Gobhann without pause for days on end.

The other thing was, she wasn't seeing very well. First had

been that ridiculous crown on Nicholas's head and now it was a strange sort of something around Rùnach, something that glittered briefly as if it had been the echo of a dream. Of course, once she blinked again, it was gone.

It was very odd, that.

Then again, her life was full of things that made no sense to her. How was it that she should have longed so desperately for freedom, yet unless she succeeded in her quest, she was destined to lose that freedom precisely because of who she was? Surely she was nothing at all, not even worthy of notice by the very long reach of Bruadairian curses. After all, her family was not noble, though they had aspirations of appearing that way. She knew that because the Guildmistress had sneered it at her once, when she'd dared wonder aloud about them. And she wasn't even a part of that family any longer. Her parents had made that clear on her twenty-first birthday, when they'd come to sign her into slavery yet again.

She decided at that moment that if she ever managed to free herself completely from any and all curses, she would change a few things.

"Are you thirsty?"

She nodded. Rùnach pushed away from the wall and walked over to a table. He poured something into a silver goblet, then came to stand next to her bed. Aisling found herself helped into a sitting position, then watched over as she imbibed until her throat had stopped burning right along with her eyes. She was helped back onto her pillow, then left to herself whilst Rùnach returned the goblet to its place. Aisling watched him pick up a book and take his place in Lord Nicholas's chair.

"Shall I read to you?" he asked.

She looked at him in surprise. "Do I look like an invalid, then?"

He shook his head. "I simply thought you might be restless. A convalescence can be trying."

"Have you ever had one?"

"Once," he conceded, "and it was very tedious. A friend of mine read to me endlessly until I was able to hold a book myself. I think I would have gone mad otherwise." He frowned at the spine of the book he held, then opened the cover. "This appears to be the Tale of the Two Swords."

"Is that good?"

He looked at her in surprise. "Have you never heard it?"

Aisling thought there might come a day when she would reveal more than she cared to if she didn't learn to guard her tongue. "I'm sure I have," she said hastily, "but I've forgotten the details."

"Hmmm," was all he said. He glanced at her. "Would you rather sit up a little? I believe I can find another pillow or two."

"I can fetch—"

"Of course you shan't," he said with a slight sound of disbelief. "Here, hold this and I'll return posthaste."

She took the book from him, then watched him leave the chamber. For a soldier, he seemed to have rather lovely manners—then again, considering how few soldiers she knew, perhaps she wasn't a good judge of any of their ilk. The only men she knew, she realized, were Euan and Quinn, and she realized after being in Rùnach's company for several days that those two were rather foul-tempered and rude.

She had to admit, now that she could look back on their travels across Melksham from the comfort of being deliciously warm and alive, even temporarily, that Rùnach hadn't even been unpleasant on their journey—and that in spite of having found himself cast out of Gobhann.

She watched him walk back into the chamber and realized yet again that he was a rather intimidating specimen. She hadn't seen him all that often with Weger—she'd been too busy hanging her head over whatever bucket had been handy to notice, then fretting over how to get Weger to herself—but that last day they had seemed rather evenly matched. She wondered what had possessed Rùnach to go inside Gobhann when he was obviously fully capable of wielding a sword without instruction.

He helped her sit up, placed a pair of pillows behind her back, fluffed them, then took the book from her and sat down. He looked at her, then blinked in surprise.

"What is it?"

She would have shifted, but she was too tired to. "I'm sorry about Gobhann."

He smiled briefly. "You have nothing to be sorry for."

"But I drove you from it."

"Aisling, you had nothing to do with it, truly." He paused and seemed to consider his words carefully. "Weger has reasons for doing things, reasons that are too deep for us lesser men to comprehend. I daresay this is one of those times."

"Who was it who knew you there?" she asked.

"No one of import."

"The man who stabbed me?"

He studied her for several moments in silence, then smiled ruefully. "I think that we should make a bargain, you and I."

"A bargain?" she asked uneasily. The last time she'd agreed to a bargain—which, in truth, she really hadn't agreed to—she had wound up hundreds of leagues from home.

Though she had to admit her current locale was far more luxurious than anything she had ever imagined, even after surreptitious looks in Mistress Muinear's book of Fable and Lore, so perhaps bargains weren't all that terrible after all.

"Aye, a bargain," Rùnach said. "One question and one answer a day."

"Which will you offer?"

He blinked, then smiled. "You misunderstand me, lady. I'll have one of each, and so will you. And the answers must be completely truthful."

She opened her mouth to protest, but found there were no words to express how uneasy the thought of having to give him honest answers made her. If she gave details about Bruadair, she would die. Or so she'd been told.

Yet she hadn't died from other things . . .

"You know that you are perfectly safe here," he said quietly, "don't you?"

"For the day, at least," she managed.

"And you think you won't be tomorrow?"

"I hope I will be tomorrow," she conceded, "and I believe, my lord, that that is your question for the day."

His mouth fell open, then he laughed a little. "Very well, I will be more careful tomorrow, believe me. And I am no lord."

She smiled in spite of herself. "I'm channeling Losh, apparently. I apologize."

"Rather I should be flattered," he said, sighing lightly. "Now, I seem to have wasted my question, but you have not. What will you ask?"

"Is the man who stabbed me the reason Weger forced you from Gobhann?"

He took a deep breath, then let it out slowly. "Aye," he said, looking as if he would have preferred to be talking about anything else. "He is who Weger considered to be dangerous enough to send us both away."

She nodded, then froze. "Both?" she asked in surprise.

He looked at her steadily. "It wasn't me he stabbed, Aisling."

"But I'm no one," she protested. "I was simply in the wrong place."

"Possibly," he conceded. "Even though Weger didn't think so."

"And what do you think?" The words were out of her mouth before she could stop them. "Don't answer that," she said quickly. "I'm still half asleep."

He rubbed finger absently over the cover of the book he held. "I have to agree with Weger that you were in danger as well, though I've still to work out why. I wasn't thinking clearly when Weger roused us so gently from sleep, else I would have queried him more thoroughly." He looked at her then. "I have spent several years telling myself that I was working for the good of others, but the truth is, I was thinking of no one but myself, which would appall my mother were she alive to witness it. I apologize for the things I said that night. My conduct was reprehensible."

She could hardly believe her ears. "You don't owe me anything—"

"I owe you an apology," he said seriously, "and I'm offering it."

"But why would you bother with me?" she asked in surprise.

He said nothing; he simply looked at her in silence for far

longer than she was comfortable with. It came to the point that she had to say something, anything, to break the silence.

"You held my head whilst I was, ah, indisposed," she said quickly. "That erases anything you may or may not have said at any other time. Not that it—"

"It matters," he interrupted. "Because you are a woman, you were put into my care, and I failed to display the chivalry I should have. And before either of us thinks on that overmuch, let us turn to this rousing tale here in my hands. You can enjoy it along with the breakfast William has brought you. Here, lad, set it here and I'll see to serving her."

"As you will, my lord," the lad said, setting a tray down on a table that Rùnach pulled close to the bed. He made Rùnach a bow, then scampered off.

"Are you a lord?" Aisling asked, struggling to sit up a bit more.

"Why do you need a mercenary?"

She blinked, then smiled when she realized what he was doing. "I thought we were limiting ourselves to one question a day?"

"That might make for not much conversation, so perhaps we would do better to trade a question for a question, with the accompanying answers attached. And I'll answer yours in good faith. I am no lord, though I am curious as to why you need a mercenary."

"I told you why," she said, carefully.

"Did you?"

"That smells wonderful," she said, looking at what Lord Nicholas's page had brought. "I'm not sure I recognize half of what's there."

He filled a plate for her and handed it to her without comment. She looked at him eventually, because she supposed she couldn't sit with him in the same chamber and ignore him. He was watching her with a small smile.

"I know what you're doing," he said.

"Hedging?"

"Is that what you call it?"

She almost laughed. It had been so long since she'd had even the desire to smile, she hardly knew what to do with herself. There was just something about Rùnach that led her to contemplating all manner of things she had almost given up for lost. If she were to judge his condition by the scars on his hands and face, she would have assumed he would be bitter and angry, yet he wasn't. He was polite, solicitous, and possessing a dry sense of humor that left her wanting to smile in spite of herself.

She didn't answer, because she knew he didn't expect an answer. She simply ate everything she was given, wondering in truth if she had died and found herself in another world where the food was the best she'd ever eaten and the company quite decent.

An hour later, she was very full, the tale was finished, and she was ready for a nap. She didn't protest when Rùnach helped her lie down, nor when he sat back down in his chair.

"That was a lovely story," she said with a sigh. "I've always been fond of legends."

"Legends?"

She suppressed a yawn. "You don't believe those sorts of tales, do you?" She looked at him blearily. "In truth?"

His mouth worked for a moment or two, but apparently the fantastical nature of the tale had done its work on him as well.

"I should like to know how to wield a sword as Mehar did, though," she said with a sigh.

"As protection?" he said, apparently having found his tongue.

She nodded even though acquiring sword skill hadn't been in her plans. She'd had her hands full with trying to acquire an assassin. Only now she had not only the inability to wield a sword, but she had no one to send to Taigh Hall at the appropriate time—

Which, she realized, the peddler had said would be three months from the date he'd sent her off into the darkness. It wasn't possible that *that* was the end of her period of grace.

Was it?

In truth, she was becoming heartily sick of trying to determine just what the man had meant. She wished he'd written it down for her, so she could have read the paper over and over again until the ink was faded and the paper whisper-soft from being folded and unfolded scores of times. What did it matter if she had three se'nnights, three fortnights, or three months if the end result was she would be dead?

"Aisling?"

She focused on Rùnach. "What were we talking about?"

"You were giving me the details about the trouble in your village. What was it called?"

She blinked, then her mouth fell open. "I was not."

He smiled, a small, mischievous smile that was appallingly charming. She put her hand over her eyes in self-defense.

"Stop that," she said.

"It was worth a try."

She pursed her lips, then looked at him. "I was saying I wished I could defend myself, though I think a sword is beyond me. Perhaps a knife, though I'm not sure I could stab someone in the heart. Whilst looking them in the eye, that is."

"But you could do it from a distance?"

"Perhaps," she said. She considered, then looked at him. "Could you teach me to defend myself?"

He blinked. "Right now? With a sword?"

"Nay, later. With something else."

"Are you unsatisfied with what Weger taught you?"

"He taught me to poke a man in the eyes, elbow him in the gut, and hope I could run fast enough to escape whilst he was catching his breath," she said. "So, aye, I am unsatisfied with what he taught me."

Rùnach studied her for so long, she began to grow uncomfortable.

"Why?" he asked, finally.

"Because I am tired of being at the mercy of others," she said, because she was too tired to guard her tongue. "I never want to be so again." She looked at him. "Have you ever killed anyone, Rùnach?"

His mouth fell open. "You ask the damndest questions."

She watched him, but apparently he wasn't going to answer her. She turned on her side so she could look at him more easily.

He had the most remarkable pair of green eyes. She perhaps

wouldn't have known that sitting in a candlelit chamber if she hadn't spent the previous several days looking into his eyes and learning their color. The scar over his cheek, though . . . she looked away, because she realized she was looking too closely. There was something strange about it, though she couldn't say what it was—

She turned away from the whole thought because it was more scrutiny than he deserved. At least he hadn't been watching her watch him, though she supposed he was accustomed to it.

"Is anything as it seems?" she asked.

He stopped his idle flipping of pages and looked at her in surprise. "What do you mean?" he asked warily.

She would have shrugged, but she was too tired. "I'm not sure. It's just . . ." She yawned in spite of herself. "I thought things were a certain way. I was *told* things were a certain way," she amended. "And now I'm beginning to suspect they aren't that way at all." She looked at him seriously. "I think I've been lied to."

"About what?"

She shook her head. "You've already asked too many questions for the morning. And as for the other, in truth I'm not unhappy with what Weger tried to teach me, though I didn't learn it very well and it certainly didn't help me any when I truly needed it. So, aye, I would like to learn something else, if I have the time. But not the sword."

He studied her for a moment or two in silence. "I'll think about other things whilst you nap."

"Am I napping?"

"You look like you're considering it."

She yawned again before she could stop herself. She perhaps would have disagreed with him and tried harder to keep herself awake, but for the first time in over a month, she found herself contemplating sleep without fearing she was falling into death.

She struggled to focus on him. "What will you do?"

"Oh, I have a little project I'm working on."

"What sort of project?"

"A mystery."

She had a mystery for him, and that was why in the world she was still alive when she was supposed to be dead. She frowned.

"Is it possible to tell when someone is lying?"

He studied her, more closely than she cared for. "Why do you ask?"

"'Tis a mystery."

He grunted. "I daresay. And aye, I suppose there are ways to tell. You could take the miscreant in question and threaten him with a blade until he blurted out the truth. With others, simply making note of when they're speaking is enough to tell you what you need to know."

She considered that. "What if the soul in question seemed trustworthy, but you now doubt his truthfulness?"

"This *is* a mystery," Rùnach said. "I would, of course, need all the details in order to know how best to advise you."

She shook her head. "I can't give you the details."

"Does it have to do with your mercenary?"

"It might."

"Then I suppose you'll have to ferret out the truth yourself," he said with a shrug. "Lord Nicholas's library below is quite extensive."

She nodded, then felt her eyelids begin to close. She settled herself more comfortably, then sighed deeply. "Is he a king?" she murmured.

"Why do you ask?"

"I saw a crown on his head," she murmured. "Gold, heavy, adorned with all manner of gems and filigree . . . and . . . runes—"

She wasn't sure he answered. It was almost enough to bring her back to herself to find out why he asked, but the pull of sleep was too strong.

She felt herself falling into darkness and didn't try to stop herself.

Thirteen

❧

Rùnach sat in the buttery of the university enjoying a spectacular stew and gave thought to many things that intrigued
him. His own life was a mystery he was happy to put off for a bit,
but there were so many other things to investigate that he didn't
lack for things to mull over.

Such as why Aisling of a place yet to be determined had
thought she was going to die when she touched a spinning wheel,
or why she had been so desperate to speak to Weger each night
before midnight for those first pair of days in Gobhann, or why
she had given that up and settled for counting on her fingers when
she thought he wasn't looking.

If those things weren't interesting enough, there was the mystery of why she was so reluctant to tell him anything about her
past, her village, or the particulars of her errand. In honor of that,
he had spent a fair bit of the day making a painfully detailed list of
kingdoms, counties within kingdoms, and kingdoms that were
kingdoms no longer. He was frankly quite appalled to see how

many other lands Neroche had absorbed over the centuries, which
he would absolutely poke Miach about when he saw him next. He
hadn't begun to even consider the languages of each area, much
less speculate about the variations in those languages that had no
doubt occurred over hundreds of years.

Perhaps less puzzling, though, was the identity of that fat
chestnut-colored cat rolling on the floor in front of him and smirking.

"Do you care for more, sir?"

Rùnach looked up to find Nicholas's cook standing there, two
large bowls of stew in his hands. He couldn't in good conscience
send the man away disappointed, now could he?

He was fairly sure his mother would have been quite pleased
with his recent recapturing of his good manners.

"Only if you will join me," Rùnach said politely.

"If you insist," Cook said, setting one of the bowls in front of
Rùnach and placing the other in front of himself before he sat
down happily and set to his meal without hesitation.

"This is delicious," Rùnach noted, "but unsurprising given the
exceptional quality of everything that comes from your kitchen."

Cook accepted the compliment with the modesty that was
obviously his trademark and motioned for one of his lads to refill
Rùnach's mug of ale. And once he had sampled his own wares to
his satisfaction, he settled himself with his own hefty bit of liquid
sustenance, then reached down and scratched their table companion behind the ears.

"Don't know where this lad came from, but he's the best mouser
I've ever seen," Cook said, beaming down at that purring fiend,
who was obviously prepared to accept any and all compliments.
"Don't have much use for feral male pusses as a rule, but in his
case, I've made an exception."

"I'm sure he appreciates it," Rùnach said dryly. He thought it
wise to pretend not to notice that the mighty mouser's purrs
sounded remarkably similar to equine snorts. He also decided that
purposely neglecting to tell the cook that his mouser wouldn't linger forever was actually the kindest thing to do.

He eventually thanked the cook for his excellent stew, left his horse turned feline savouring a bowl of heavy cream, and walked back along paths and past doorways to see how his charge fared. He was actually slightly surprised to find her pacing around the edge of the courtyard, swathed in a very luxurious cloak. He stopped alongside the lord of Lismòr, who seemed to be equally interested in seeing how she fared.

"She doesn't look unwell," Rùnach offered. "Definitely not dying."

Nicholas smiled. "Nay, not dying. Fighting a headache, I daresay."

"How do you know?"

"She said as much."

Rùnach smiled ruefully. "She doesn't tell me anything."

"Perhaps you intimidate her."

"I'm certain that's it."

Nicholas looked at him, clear-eyed. "Rùnach, my dearest boy, you forget who you are—"

"Were—"

"Are," Nicholas stressed.

"There is nothing of what I was in my veins," Rùnach said, managing it without too much bitterness. "I am simply a man who will live an extraordinarily long time to enjoy my terribly ordinary life. There is nothing to be intimidated by."

"I think others might disagree, but we'll leave that for the time being. As for the other, there is something to be said for the simpler pleasures of this world."

Rùnach leaned his shoulder against a pillar and looked at the uncle he hadn't known lived still until he'd encountered him at Mhorghain's wedding. It was odd how he felt as if he'd known Nicholas his entire life. "Is there something to be said for them, in truth?"

"Fine wine, good food, well-loved books," Nicholas said easily. "Children, if you can manage them, either your own or someone else's."

Rùnach took a careful breath. "I will thank you in my mother's stead for watching over Mhorghain for all those years. She would have been, and I certainly am grateful beyond what words might convey."

"It was gladly done," Nicholas said with a smile. "I imagine you would do the same for any of your nieces or nephews, though I suspect you'll have children enough of your own to love."

"Should I find a woman willing to wed me."

"Charm, Rùnach. Rediscover your charm."

Rùnach sighed. "I believe I left it somewhere in Seanagarra along with all my notes."

"I thought you left those on the plains of Ailean."

Rùnach pursed his lips. "Been having tea with the notoriously loose-lipped king of Neroche?"

"We chat from time to time," Nicholas conceded, "though you can thank Soilléir for that last tidbit."

Rùnach dragged his hand through his hair and started to speak, then watched Aisling disappear down a passageway. "Where is she going?"

"Why don't you go ask her?"

"I'd rather have a very strong drink in your solar."

"I didn't think you partook of anything very strong."

"I thought I would try, to see if it improved my sour self any."

"I imagine she's gone back to bed, so perhaps you would enjoy a brief glass of port in my solar before you go check on her. I'm sure we'll find something to discuss."

Rùnach imagined they would. He also supposed Aisling wouldn't be unhappy for a bit of privacy, so he followed Nicholas to a very luxurious solar and happily accepted the proffered spot on a sofa. The port was indeed fine, the fire very lovely, and the feeling of safety palpable.

He was happy he'd enjoyed all three for the quarter hour he managed before Nicholas handed him a particular ring and ruined them all.

Rùnach looked at his father's ring, that flat onyx stone set in a silver that never tarnished, then looked at his uncle.

"Where did you get this?" he asked.

"Ruith gave it to me, of course."

"Dare I ask why?" Rùnach said grimly.

Nicholas seemed to be considering his words rather more carefully than Rùnach was comfortable with. "I believe he thought I might find another keeper for it when the time was right."

"Me?" Rùnach asked with a weary sigh.

"It would seem so. And how fortunate that you've arrived just in time to take it with you."

"Foresight, my lord uncle?"

"A hunch."

"Which for you is the same thing," Rùnach said sourly. He shot Nicholas a look. "Why is it I suspect nothing ever happened within the borders of Diarmailt that you didn't see beforehand and plan for?"

Nicholas smiled. "What leads you to believe my sight was limited to my own borders?"

Rùnach laughed in spite of himself "You and Miach. You no doubt leave the Council of Kings all aflutter."

"I certainly don't," Nicholas said, "not any longer. No one knows I'm alive, which is as it should be. It saves Simeon the trouble of wondering what I think of how he managed to lose the crown to that damned Stefan of Wychweald. Greedy little wretch."

"Who?" Rùnach asked with a smile. "Your nephew Simeon or Miach's cousin?"

"Both, which is why Diarmailt is nothing more than a very wealthy duchy absorbed into a larger realm, to my eternal disgust." Nicholas sighed. "I imagine none of them cares any longer."

"Don't they?" Rùnach asked.

Nicholas shook his head. "Simeon has magic of his own, of course, and a great amount of it, but he's less worried about it than he is with the keeping up of the library. It leaves all the practical working of spells to the lads at Buidseachd, but I suppose there's nothing I can do about that."

"Things change," Rùnach offered.

"They do, don't they?"

Rùnach shot his uncle a warning look. "The only thing that's going to change with me is my plan to use Weger's mark to secure a position with some obscure lord who won't have a clue who I am. I've no interest in the inner workings of the Nine Kingdoms." He looked at the ring, then at his uncle. "And as such, this might be better given to someone else."

"Oh, I don't think so," Nicholas said. "You'll find a use for it eventually, I imagine. I wouldn't lose it, though, like you did your notes."

Rùnach blew the hair out of his eyes. "I didn't *intend* to lose my notes."

"You might want to find them sooner rather than later, you know."

Rùnach shook his head. "They were just scribblings. Nothing anyone would find to be useful. Nothing will come of it."

"So say all who regret things later," Nicholas said with a smile, "though in this case you may be right." He started to speak, then shook his head. "I don't know, Rùnach. My dreams are troubled of late."

Rùnach suppressed the urge to groan. First the ship's captain, then Weger, and now Nicholas. He held up his hand to ward his uncle off.

"Things are as they should be," he said firmly. "Ruith sealed my father into that pitiful little garden, Lothar's safely tucked into Gobhann, and all is right with the world."

"And your bastard brothers?"

"The keep at Ceangail—"

"Aingidheachd," Nicholas interjected mildly.

Rùnach looked at him evenly. "We never refer to it as such. Ever. We called it Doibhail."

"That was not the original name, which your father well knew," Nicholas said quietly. "There was evil there at that keep before he ever took the place for his own. You might as well call it by its true name." He looked at Rùnach seriously. "I believe, my lad, that you might do well to make calling things by their proper names a habit."

Rùnach suppressed the urge to get up and pace. Just hearing

the name, he had to admit, was enough to send chills down his spine. "Very well," he said, trying to match Nicholas's tone, "*Aingidheachd* is destroyed, which leaves my bastard brothers seeking shelter in the witchwoman of Fàs's potting shed, a place I understand Franciscus of Cothromaiche found to his liking recently."

Nicholas only smiled. "I can't say I've had the pleasure, though I understand she was passing fond of you."

"As unlikely as that is," Rùnach admitted, "there is truth to it. Then again, I believe I endeared myself to her warty-nosed self by building her an extension to her greenhouse with my own two hands and crafting a spell that endlessly watered her more delicate plants without her having to do anything."

Nicholas laughed a little. "And what possessed you to do either?"

"It annoyed my father," Rùnach muttered. "That, and she is, as you know, a meticulous journalist of the obscure and difficult to ferret out. I wanted a look in her library."

"Did she offer it?"

"Repeatedly." Rùnach couldn't help but smile a little at memories he hadn't brought to mind in years. "She is not as unpleasant a woman as she's rumored to be, her personal habits aside. Her sons give her a bad reputation." He shook his head slowly, then looked down at what he was holding in his hand. He considered, then looked at Nicholas. "I can't imagine this will come in handy as I will never, ever come close enough to *Aingidheachd* for it to be of any use."

"Ah, *never*," Nicholas said, rubbing his hands together, "what an interesting word."

"You know, Your Majesty, the only reason I'm not swearing at you right now is because I was taught to be kind to old men."

Nicholas laughed merrily. "Cheeky whelp."

"Does that mean you won't slay me for telling you you're a thoroughly obnoxious, interfering, exasperating . . ." Rùnach took a deep breath. "Good breeding prevents me from saying more."

Nicholas smiled. "Rùnach, my dearest boy, you are truly your mother's son." His smile faded. "The only thing that comforts me is that she saw you as a man. I know she was pleased."

"I daresay she wouldn't have been pleased with my having hidden in Buidseachd for so long," Rùnach said with a sigh.

"You did what you thought appropriate," Nicholas said. "And even I will admit that no time spent in the company of that young rogue from Cothromaiche is ever wasted."

"Young?" Rùnach said with a snort. "He's at least a pair of millennia older than you are."

"Ah, but I'm so much more mature and seasoned," Nicholas said with absolutely no concession to irony. "The burden of kingship, don't you know."

"Nay, Your Grace, I wouldn't know," Rùnach said, "thankfully."

Nicholas put his hands on his knees. "We can discuss that later, perhaps. I understand we have a very talented puss in the kitchen, decimating the mouse population. I think I should like to have a look at him."

"It's my horse. He was a gift from Sgath."

Nicholas winked at him. "So he said as he was lying on my hearth rug late last night, filling me in on all your activities. He is angling for a mighty adventure, in case you were curious."

"I wasn't."

"Bragging rights, I daresay, should he ever encounter his Angesand cousins." Nicholas nodded wisely. "That pony has plans."

"He's a menace."

Nicholas laughed and rose. "Take your ease here, nephew, until you grow weary enough to be abed. I wouldn't worry about anything untoward. There is protection enough laid over the university."

Rùnach looked at him sharply. "I wasn't worried."

Nicholas only shrugged. "Just making conversation." He walked over to the door, then paused with his hand on the latch. "I saw someone interesting walking along the road from Gobhann to Bere the other day."

"Dare I ask who it was?" Rùnach said, shifting on the sofa to look at his uncle.

"Acair of Ceangail."

Rùnach shrugged, ignoring how the solar had become suddenly so completely still. He didn't like the way even the fire had paused, as if it held its breath. It occurred to him that he might have seen Acair as well, though he couldn't bring himself to even begin to think about why his father's youngest bastard would have been walking toward Gobhann.

"Interesting," Rùnach managed. "Perhaps he was simply out for a stroll."

Nicholas lifted his eyebrows briefly. "He's a bit far from home, wouldn't you say?"

"I have nothing to say about the activities of my father's natural sons," Rùnach said evenly. "They're free to carry on as they please, without my interference."

Nicholas smiled briefly. "And so they are. If you think about it, though, you might want to mention it to Miach."

Rùnach looked at him sharply. "Why would I want to do that? And why would I see Miach?"

"Aren't you taking Aisling to Tor Neroche? I understand she's looking for a lad to do a bit of dirty work."

"Eavesdropping, Your Grace?"

"She talks in her sleep."

"I didn't hear her."

"You were too busy snoring in front of the fire," Nicholas said cheerfully, then opened the door and left the solar.

Rùnach scowled. He suspected that just making conversation was one thing the former wizard king of Diarmailt never did. If something was said, it meant more than was apparent at first blush.

Rùnach stared down at the ring in his hand and contemplated things he didn't particularly care to, namely family he didn't particularly want to claim. Díolain, the eldest of his father's bastards, was powerful, the rest of them powerful and foul-tempered, but Acair . . . well, he was a lad of a different sort altogether. He had inherited all of his father's charm, all of his cleverness, the bulk of both Gair and the witchwoman of Fàs's power, all seasoned liberally with terrifying ambition.

Rùnach had loathed him from the moment he'd been old enough to see him for who he was.

That he should be wandering around Melksham Island—

He shook his head. It was none of his affair. His half brothers didn't know he was alive. More to the point, there was nothing he could do to stop them from wreaking whatever havoc they chose to even if they did know he was alive. All he could do was help Aisling to Tor Neroche if that was where she chose to go, secure her a lad to rid her village of its pestilence, then find himself an equally obscure village to call home for the rest of his long, ordinary life.

He was tempted to leave his father's ring on Nicholas's side table but couldn't bring himself to. The only thing he could say about it was that he wasn't tempted to put it on, though he had never seen his father without it on his hand. He couldn't imagine what use Nicholas could possibly believe it would have for him, but he supposed he would be wise not to question it. It was best to just stick it in a safe pocket and forget about it.

Which he did as he rose and started to pace in front of Nicholas's fire. Unfortunately, that only distracted him for a moment or two before he had to address what vexed him the most at present. Well, perhaps that wasn't the right word for it. He wasn't vexed by Aisling.

She would have troubled his dreams, if he'd had any.

He simply couldn't fathom what was so important that a wench would travel however far she'd traveled to a place where she would be completely out of her depth in order to beg aid from a man notorious for not offering any. And now Weger had done her the very great favor of sending her off after another wild hare. In truth, there was no point in going all the way to Tor Neroche to find a mercenary, if a mercenary was what she needed. If all she needed was a lad to clear out a simple village, there was no reason he couldn't . . . do . . .

No reason he couldn't do it for her.

He felt a sinking in the pit of his stomach. It was the usual feeling he had whilst contemplating the doing of good he didn't particularly want to do.

Damnation, but the last thing he wanted to do was rush off to some rustic locale in the middle of some endless stretch of farmland and dispatch the local bully. He could see receiving a payment of several cages of live chickens he would have to then slaughter and cook. Worse still, he would likely find himself watching Aisling be fawned over by the alderman's most charming son who would woo and wed her whilst Rùnach turned the spit over his fire so his supper didn't burn.

It was almost enough to have him reaching for another glass of port.

A pity he hadn't yet finished the first one so he could have indulged in more.

He dragged his hands through his hair. Despite what he'd said to Aisling the day before, he didn't particularly want any detours from his well-laid plans. Though chivalry demanded that he at least get her off in the right direction, as well as perhaps escorting her to where she was going.

And solve a few mysteries along the way.

He turned the words she'd murmured over in his mind, blessing his mother—and his father, it had to be conceded—for passing on the ability to hear something once and have it memorized. He had never heard words such as those, but they weren't mindless babbling or the result of fevered dreams, for she'd said a handful of those words more than once. He shook his head. They obviously meant something. Now all he had to do was find out what.

He left his uncle's solar rather more confused than when he'd entered it. His life had been so simple at Buidseachd. Selfish, he supposed, but simple. Now he was being pulled into something that smelled rather strongly of a quest, by a woman whose only fault was that she'd been sent off into the wilds of the Nine Kingdoms to find someone to do for her village what they could not do for themselves.

He walked without haste to Aisling's bedchamber. He knocked

softly, then was slightly surprised to have her open the door herself. She looked weary but otherwise quite sound.

And rather less plain than she should have in order to properly masquerade as a lad.

"Will you come in?" she asked.

He leaned against the doorframe and smiled faintly. "I only came to fetch my gear, if it pleases you. I daresay you are well enough to dispense with my nursemaiding services."

She only held on to the door. "I appreciate your efforts on my behalf."

"It was my very great pleasure."

She looked at him solemnly. "Aren't we polite today."

"I could ask you questions that make you uncomfortable, if you'd rather."

She pushed the door open fully. "Fetch your gear and begone, foul blight."

He smiled. "How cheeky you've become. Feeling comfortable, are you?"

She sobered immediately. "I shouldn't—"

He pushed away from the doorframe and eased past her. "Of course you should. I'll get out from underfoot, then you'll have a lovely night's rest." His pack he had left in the bedchamber next to hers, so his fetching was limited to books and his scribblings. He gathered those up, then retreated to the door. He turned and looked at her. "You should feel comfortable here. Lord Nicholas has insisted."

"Has he?" she asked quietly.

He took her words, considered them very briefly, then shook his head slowly. "You and I, Mistress Aisling, should have speech together some day when nothing but frankness rules the day. I think you would feel much happier were you to unburden yourself to a trusted confidant."

She looked up at him. "Are you that trusted confidant?"

He hesitated only slightly. "I could be, if you willed it."

She looked at the books in his arms. "Do you think Lord Nicholas might allow me to have a careful look in his library?"

"Without a doubt," he assured her. "Shall I escort you there in the morning?"

"You would come with me? Willingly?"

"Of course," he said, surprised. "Why wouldn't—" He paused, then sighed. "Very well, I can see why you might think differently, but aye, I will come with you willingly. Quite happily, even."

She looked at him seriously. "I don't mind being alone, but company might be a pleasant change. If you've nothing else to do."

The unknowing was killing him. He could feel his mother standing behind him, leaning up to whisper in his ear, *you know what curiosity killed, don't you, my son?* His courageous, beautiful, brilliant mother who had been beguiled by Gair of Ceangail, then paid the ultimate price for trying to free her children from his evil. He couldn't begin to express how much he had loved her. She had been curious, understood what had driven him, dropped unsolvable riddles into casual conversation because she knew the solving of those riddles gave him pleasure.

Unmanly as it might have sounded, there were times he missed her desperately.

He pulled himself back to the conversation at hand, then smiled at Aisling. "I should likely drag whatever swordsman I can find in this bastion of scholars out to the garden in the morning and keep myself from turning to fat, but I'll seek you out afterward and see what you've found—and make sure you've been fed."

"Thank you," she said quietly. She looked up at him. "You needn't be kind to me, you know. I have my quest and all, which I should be seeing to fairly soon."

Perhaps he had behaved more boorishly at Gobhann—and all points leading up to those miserable few days in Gobhann—than he'd feared. He would have reached out and tucked hair behind her ear or touched her elbow or taken her hand but his hands were full of tools he fully intended to use to figure out exactly who she was, something she obviously didn't want him to know.

He was tempted to simply turn and bang his head against the wall until good sense returned.

She looked at him seriously for another brief moment, then she shut the door in his face.

He stood there for several minutes, wondering when it was he'd last had a door shut in his face. At least she had shut it quietly instead of slamming it.

And hard on the heels of that bit of dangerous curiosity came the thought that he had no time for a woman in his life at present, particularly one who didn't behave in ways he could understand. She wasn't elegant, didn't engage in delicate flirtations, and remained unimpressed by whatever rusty manners he had attempted to trot out for her inspection. She refused to divulge important details about her quest, fully believed heroic tales were naught but myths, and could set spinning wheels to flying without touching them.

And if he didn't get her out in the sunlight at least once and determine the exact color of her eyes, he was going to lose his wits.

He turned and walked away whilst he still could. He set his burdens down in the bedchamber he'd been provided, considered, then turned and walked back the way he had come, continuing on until he reached the courtyard. He ran bodily into his uncle, then caught the man by the arm and steadied them both.

"My apologies," Rùnach said grimly.

"And where are you off to in such a rush?"

"I need a run." Rùnach pursed his lips. "I don't suppose you have anything as pedestrian as lists here, do you?"

"I suppose we do." Nicholas pointed across the courtyard. "Follow that passageway past my solar and continue on. You'll find them easily enough, I imagine."

"Thank you." He started to walk away, then looked at his host. "No prying questions?"

"Rùnach, you wound me," Nicholas said, putting his hand to his heart. "And you have obviously spent too much time with young Soilléir. He has no sense of grace or propriety. I, on the other hand, have it in abundance."

"Thank you. Again."

"That, and I don't need to pry," Nicholas said easily. "I can see everything written right there on your face."

Rùnach would have cursed him, but as he'd said before, his mother had taught him to be kind to old men. So, instead, he made his uncle a bow, then turned and strode off before he had to hear another affectionate chuckle or think too long on a woman who left him scratching his head.

It was far safer that way, he was sure.

Fourteen

❄

Aisling wandered through the racks of books in Lismòr's library, trying not to look as overwhelmed as she felt. She had never in her life seen so many books, nor imagined that so many could exist in the same place. The keeper of the books, Master Dominicus, had sternly warned her not to touch anything, a condition of entrance to which she had agreed without hesitation. He had then demanded to know what she was looking for, but in that, at least, she had held her ground and refused to speak.

Because she was looking for the truth.

She had eaten a very lovely breakfast by herself, brought by Lord Nicholas's page William, which had shored her up for the day's activities but also left her feeling rather more irritated than she would have suspected. Who knew that such food existed and in such abundance? She wondered how she had lived twenty-seven years of her life on beggar's rations.

She was beginning to wonder quite a few things.

William had told her that she was free to wander about the

university, and he had been good enough to show her to the library. She had walked inside, then come to an ungainly halt.

She had stood at the door for several minutes, trying without success to shut her mouth. The sight that had greeted her eyes had been so overwhelming, she hadn't known even where to begin to look for what she needed. Not that she'd even had a clear idea of what that thing might be. She had considered earlier that morning trying to find out about the nature of curses and how to get out from under them, but the more she'd thought about it, the sillier the idea had seemed. Who would write a book about such a thing?

She had then decided perhaps she should seek out books about Bruadair, but it had taken her even less time to dismiss that idea. Given the secretive nature of her country, who would dare pen such a tome? No native would for fear of dying and no stranger would know enough to say anything useful. Even she, who had lived inside Bruadair's borders for the whole of her life, couldn't speak of anything but the Guild.

What she wanted was to find everything in a neat, tidy little tome that would tell her without mincing words that everything she had believed up until that moment had been true, that she could count on curses, that she had never once over the course of her twenty-seven years been lied to, and that the preceding two fortnights had been nothing but an aberration.

She wasn't quite sure what she would do if she found out that it had all been an elaborately staged lie.

After William had introduced her to Master Dominicus, then departed for safer ground, she had done her best to look trustworthy, which had perhaps worked in her favor. Master Dominicus, after delivering his warning to her, had gone back to his work of scolding students who were whispering loudly behind their hands.

Now, even after an hour of wandering about, not touching anything, she stood in the middle of the rows and rows of books and still had no idea where to even begin.

"Need help?"

She jumped a foot, she was sure of it, pulling three books off a shelf as she whirled around. The only reason she wasn't thrown from the library, she supposed, was that Rùnach caught those books and put them back where they belonged before Master Dominicus was the wiser. He propped his elbow on a shelf and looked at her.

"Searching for something in particular?"

She almost blurted it all out, right there in the section devoted to the science of insects. After all, he was a simple soldier, wasn't he? He had no reason to be interested in the political complexities of Bruadair, did he? He would listen to her tale, nod wisely, then . . .

He would think her mad, that's what he would think her. She would tell him of the curses laid upon those who dared leave or speak or spin and he would think her absolutely daft. And perhaps she was, daft to believe that she could come and go across the border as she pleased and not pay a price.

It was one thing to touch a wheel and survive. Perhaps the Guildmistress had feared she would lose her control of her weavers if they looked further afield for more interesting things to do with their hands, so she had invented a curse to keep them fearfully obedient. But crossing the border, now, that was a different thing entirely. Those were tales she had heard from more sources than just the Guildmistress. Even Mistress Muinear had told her that the secrets of Bruadair had to be protected, even if those secrets were kept by slaying those who dared cross the border without permission.

Perhaps she had been protected because she'd had a trader's license, or because the peddler had bargained for her life by some means she couldn't divine, or because she still had her errand to see accomplished—

"Aisling?"

She focused on Rùnach, then blinked at the sight. He was simply appalling to look at. More shocking still was that she hardly noticed his scars any longer. She wondered, absently, how it was he'd managed to avoid any entanglements to this point. Surely women threw themselves at him wherever he went, scars or no scars.

"Are you unwell?" he asked.

"Daft, rather," she said, putting her hand to her forehead. "Or at least I think I'm daft."

He smiled. She wanted to close her eyes when he smiled. She looked down at the floor, though Weger wouldn't have approved of that. He'd shouted at her scores of times—in a single day, no less—to keep her eyes up and focused on what was in front of her. A very difficult lesson for one who had spent the whole of her life with her gaze fixed to the ground so as not to draw attention to herself.

"Are you looking for something in particular?"

She started to blurt out *I can't say*, but something stopped her. It was odd, wasn't it, how outside the borders of her land there were countless others who went about their lives and business without living under the shadow of a terrible curse. She took a deep breath, because something was beginning to stir in her, something that felt quite a bit like the beginnings of rebellion. She had learned to control those feelings at the Guild, because she had watched what rebellion had cost others who had allowed it to grow and flower, but now . . .

Well, there was no one there to punish her for it, was there?

She looked at Rùnach, because Weger had taught her to keep her eyes up. She lifted her chin for good measure.

"I *am* looking for something," she said firmly.

Rùnach lifted an eyebrow. "Are you going to do damage to this thing when you find it?"

She looked at him narrowly. "Are you mocking me?"

"I wouldn't dare."

"Good," she said shortly. "And I suggest you don't get in my way."

He held up his hands slowly but said nothing.

She would have pushed past him and been on her way, but the truth was, she had no idea where to push past *to*.

"Might I help you find this something you're looking for?" he asked.

She wished she could stop biting her tongue, but in truth it was more difficult than she would have thought it not to speak her mind. She who had kept her mouth shut for so long. The difficulty was trying to describe what she needed without *revealing* what she needed.

"I am looking for tales of, well, tales that aren't of your usual sort. I'm not sure what to call them."

"What do these tales contain?"

"I need tales about, ah, well, perhaps elves, dragons, dwarves, that sort of thing." She looked at him. "You know. Myths."

He blinked. "Myths?"

"Well, of course myths," she said in surprise. "You don't believe in faery tales any longer, do you?"

"Well—"

"Creatures from myth such as I've listed," she said, wishing he would stop looking at her as if she had suddenly sprouted faery wings herself. "If possible."

He started to speak, then shut his mouth. He seemed to be wrestling with something. Perhaps he was accustomed to dealing with more soldierly and less wondrous subjects. Perhaps he feared he would not be able to aid her.

"Do you know how to find things in a library?" she asked gingerly. "I don't mean to put you on the spot, as it were."

He smiled, though she couldn't account for why. Perhaps he merely found everything that didn't find itself inside Gobhann to be humorous.

"I think I might be able to at least find you the proper section. After that, you're on your own."

She supposed it was a place to start. She trailed after Rùnach as he wandered through the stacks of books, selecting a handful of tomes that he carried back to a well-worn table for her. He set them down, then looked at her.

"Anything else?" he whispered.

She considered. "Is there anything, do you think, about the histories of the Nine Kingdoms?" She had no idea if Bruadair was considered part of the Nine Kingdoms or not, being such a secretive place, but she supposed it didn't hurt to ask.

"I'll find something, then leave you to your reading, shall I?"

She nodded, then watched him walk away. When she could no longer see him, she reached for the topmost book and opened it to read the first page: *Famous Elves, Dwarves, and Dragons of Legend.*

That seemed a promising enough place to start. She only hoped she could make her way through the thing without making so many noises of disbelief that Master Dominicus threw her out of the library.

L ater, and she wasn't sure how long that later was, she decided she had read enough. In spite of her brush with the Heroes of legend in that much coveted book of Mistress Muinear's, she could at least say those lads had been real. She had spent the day reading about things she couldn't possibly believe, elven creatures that lived in enchanted forests where flowers whispered and trees sang, dwarves that mined in stone that spoke their names and murmured their tales of glory and riches, dragons that turned themselves into horses and horses that turned themselves into dragons.

Ridiculous.

She reached finally for a history of the Nine Kingdoms that Rùnach had found for her. She opened it and looked at its contents. There were chapters involving all manner of locales she'd read about in other places. There would be, she could only hope, time enough in her future to peruse histories that might have less to do with otherworldly creatures and more to do with wars and monarchs. She blinked when she realized that one place seemed to have been blacked out in the list. It lay in the vicinity of both An-uallach and Cothromaiche . . .

She flipped back through the pages and found that a certain number of them—three, to be exact—had been torn from the book.

"Find anything interesting?"

Aisling shut the book with a snap, then put her hand over the cover. "Nothing," she said promptly. She looked at Rùnach and realized he was sitting around the corner of the table from her, reading something that was propped up against his knee, which was propped up against the table. He looked perfectly at ease, something she couldn't say for herself. She also had no idea how long he'd been there. "Nothing interesting," she clarified, "though I appreciate your aid."

He only lifted his eyebrows briefly.

"Have you been there long?" she asked.

He shook his head. "Not very. I actually just came back to see if you might want something to eat."

"Luncheon?"

"Dinner, actually. Lord Nicholas has invited us to join him in his solar. It will require, from what I understand, having the chamber infiltrated by orphaned lads at some point, but perhaps we will have finished our meal before then. Apparently the lads here have an uncommon fondness for tales of elves and their ilk."

"Is that wise?" Aisling asked seriously. "Filling their heads with rubbish of that sort?"

"Rubbish?" Rùnach echoed faintly.

She shrugged helplessly. "I think perhaps it might give them an unrealistic view of the world as it is." She paused. "Then again, I read more than I should have in my youth about Heroes and such."

He shut his book and looked at her with interest. "Did you? Care to enlighten me?"

"Don't you know any of those tales?"

"I fear that in my youth I was fed a steady diet of mythical characters engaging in mythical adventures, so my knowledge is sorely lacking about things of a more heroic nature."

She frowned at him. If she hadn't known better, she might have suspected he was poking fun at her. She frowned a bit more.

"Are you making sport of me again?"

He smiled. "Not at all. I'm curious." He set his book on the table. "Shall we walk whilst you're telling me about these lads and lassies?"

She supposed there was no sense in earning any more dark looks from Master Dominicus than necessary. He was obviously very particular about the conduct going on in his domain. She nodded to him, then walked with Rùnach out of the library and up the stairs.

"Where to?" she asked.

"The shore?" he suggested. "It isn't far and I have a cloak here for you. We could be there and back in less than an hour, well in time for a tasty supper."

"The shore," she repeated. "The seashore?"

"The very same."

She had never seen the shore before, nor the sea really, save what she'd seen of it aboard Captain Burke's ship and in the courtyard of Gobhann. She agreed readily, accepted a cloak that was certainly not the one she'd worn at Gobhann, then walked with him along passageways and to a heavy gate set in the wall. She wondered why a university would need such a substantial entrance.

"Lord Nicholas is careful with his students, then," she mused.

"He takes in orphan lads, as well," Rùnach said, "and he's careful with all who come inside his gates." He had a quiet word with the gate guard there, then the gate was unlocked and held open for them to go through.

Aisling found the path rocky enough that she had to watch her feet, not that she likely would have seen anything anyway. It was very foggy and rather rainy, actually, though she wasn't inclined to turn back and Rùnach didn't seem bothered by the weather.

"Are there any other libraries of note in the world?" she asked, because those three missing pages in that book bothered her. She didn't suppose it was possible that she might find the same book elsewhere, but it didn't hurt to ask.

"Chagailt," he said with a shrug, then turned back to watching the path. "I suppose there are books enough at Tor Neroche. There is a very useful library in Beinn òrain."

"Beinn òrain?"

He stopped then, and turned to look at her. "Have you never heard of it?"

She shook her head helplessly. "Never. What's there?"

"It is a city in the east that hosts the schools of wizardry."

She would have smiled, or chided him about his imagination running off with him, but it was clear to her that he was perfectly serious. She hesitated, then reached out to put her hand on his arm. "Rùnach," she said as gently as she could manage, "I'm sorry to tell you the truth, but there is no such thing as wizards, or magic, or other creatures from myth. I have no idea what they purport to teach there at that school, but it can't be magic."

He blinked a time or two, then he smiled gravely. "As you say." He tilted his head to one side. "Let's carry on, shall we?"

He had taken that well, which reassured her about his ability to listen to hard things and accept them. She could only hope she had that same skill.

It occurred to her, with a startling flash of something that didn't set well, that Weger had spent an inordinate amount of time during the apparent composition of his strictures talking about mages and how to either avoid them or rid the world of their pestilence, but perhaps that was a euphemism for something else.

"There is also, of course, the great library at Eòlas," Rùnach continued.

"Where?"

"Eòlas," he repeated. "The city itself is in Diarmailt, which used to be its own country but now is part of Wychweald, or so I understand. Eòlas was once a very great seat of learning. The library there is immense."

"Have you been there?" she asked in surprise. "I mean, you being a soldier of fortune and all that."

"Even a soldier needs to read now and again."

"Where are you from?" she asked without thinking.

"I was born in the mountains," he said with a shrug. "The place doesn't matter."

"Do you have siblings?"

"Yes, several. Not all are still living." He smiled faintly. "You are full of questions this afternoon."

"The library was a bad influence on me."

He smiled briefly. "And I believe that was three questions you asked me, which leaves me with three of my own."

"That was two."

"I don't count very well."

"I think you count very well," she said grimly.

He only smiled again. "I'll contemplate which answers I'll have and let you know."

She thought she just might be dreading them, but she couldn't bring herself to say as much. She continued to walk with Rùnach along flat ground that was rather softer and less manageable than what she was accustomed to.

"Have you ever seen the sea before?" he asked.

"On the ship," she said, watching her feet. "But that was only a brief glimpse before I spent the rest of the time hiding in the captain's cabin. And then I didn't have much of an opportunity when we docked in Sgioba." She paused. "I don't remember much about Sgioba, actually."

He paused, then turned and looked at her. "I'm sorry I didn't do more for you. I didn't realize then that you weren't a lad."

"My disguise was so good, then?" she asked lightly.

"Nay, I am so stupid," he said with a smile. He held out his hand for hers. "Come with me, but keep your eyes closed. I think the sun has cleared away the fog closer to the water. You'll have a better view of things there."

She put her hand into his, then closed her eyes. She followed him until he stopped, then felt him squeeze her hand. She looked.

And she lost her breath.

Nay, she lost her soul, or who she had been up until that point. She moved past Rùnach and continued on until she could go no further without walking out into the sea itself.

Rùnach had been right. Whatever fog there had been was apparently limited only to the university and the path leading up to it. From where she stood, the sun was shining, sparkling on the water in front of her, sparkling on the endlessly rolling waves. The roar was almost deafening. She put her hands to her ears for a moment or two, then pulled them away slowly. The roar was no less, but she expected it that time so it wasn't as startling.

She stood there, the waves lapping every now and again at the toes of her boots, and felt tears streaming down her face. She remembered after a bit that she wasn't alone, though she wasn't sure how she could have forgotten. She looked to her left to find

Rùnach standing there. He was watching her, his green eyes full of something she couldn't quite name. Pity, perhaps. Kindness, definitely.

"You *haven't* seen the shore before, have you?" he asked gently.

She shook her head. "I've never seen anything before."

He clasped his hands behind his back. "Are you going to tell me any more than that?"

I cannot was almost out of her mouth before she stopped herself, because perhaps it wasn't exactly the case. She was still breathing, which considering all the things she had done that she had been forbidden to said quite a bit. She looked at him.

"Have you ever seen the sea before?" she asked.

He smiled. "A time or two. Not as often as I would have liked, but a time or two."

"What was your home like?" she asked.

"That's two questions."

"You look distracted."

He smiled and a dimple peeked out at her from his unscarred cheek. "You are more devious than I give you credit for being. I am keeping a tally, you know, of all the questions I answer. I'll expect a like number of answers from you."

She stared at him for a moment or two. It was difficult not to sneak looks at the sea, but he didn't seem to mind.

"Why?" she asked, finally.

"Because you are a mystery."

"And do you care for a mystery?"

"I am obsessed by a good mystery," he said frankly. "Reason enough to pry a few answers out of you however I'm able."

"And what if I'm not inclined to give them?" she asked, her mouth suddenly dry. She had to take a deep breath, then another, and remind herself that she lived still. She had not been struck down by touching a wheel, had not died after less than a month because she hadn't found a swordsman, and likely wouldn't die in another few days' time when her third fortnight ended.

"Then I'll wonder about you silently."

"In truth?" she asked, surprised.

He smiled, looking a little surprised himself. "What else would I do? Beat the answers from you?"

"I don't know," she said slowly. "I don't know what soldiers do."

He shook his head. "I have never in my life raised a hand to a woman except to rescue a falling hair ornament. You might hedge all you like, if you like."

"Hmmm," she said, frowning. "Your mother must have been a well-bred lady."

"Why do you say that?"

"She seems to have taught you decent manners, for your being a mere soldier."

"She tried," he agreed. He looked out over the sea. "And she loved the sea as well, I daresay. Water, streams, lakes, she was pleased by it all. But then rivers of—" He closed his mouth abruptly. "She fancied the sea, I daresay."

She turned and looked at him. "How long ago did you lose her?"

He took a deep breath and dragged his hand through his hair before he bowed his head and slid her a look. "That answer will cost you dearly."

Her first instinct was, as always, to say nothing. But the truth was, she lived and breathed still. She could tell him perhaps a bit about herself without revealing too much about anything that would bring a curse down on her head. She took her own deep breath. "Very well."

"I'll go first," he said. "My mother died twenty years ago, though I vow it feels like yesterday."

"How did she die?"

He was very still. "My father slew her and half my siblings. Time has done the rest of that terrible work, I suppose."

She shut her mouth and put her hand on his arm. "I'm so sorry."

"I am too," he agreed. He shook his head, then reached for her hand and drew it through his arm. "Let's walk whilst you spew out the answers you owe me. You'll be more comfortable that way, I'm sure."

She was becoming, she had to admit, rather accustomed to his courtly manners. At least she thought they were courtly manners.

It was what a Hero from legend would have done, offering his companion his arm. All she knew for certain was that she never thought she would be accorded such a courtesy. She looked at him.

"I'm not sure you should worry about my comfort," she managed, "not after that question."

"But I do. And now that I've bared my soul, I think you should worry about my comfort and do the same."

She watched the sand as they walked. It was almost impossible not to. Odd, though, how it almost looked as if there had been footprints there before theirs. She shrugged that aside and glanced at Rùnach.

"My parents sold me to a weaver's guild when I was eight."

His mouth fell open. *"What?"*

"They came back to fetch me on my ten-and-fourth birthday, or so I thought," she said. It was surprising how comforting the feel of someone walking next to her could be whilst relating details that she'd never voiced out loud before. "Instead, they had come to borrow against another seven years of my labor."

"Were they that destitute, then?" he asked quietly.

She smiled, because it was in the past and she had taken to heart Mistress Muinear's advice to never give her parents even the briefest moment of thought. It was enough that they had stolen her freedom for so long.

"I had thought so, though the fineness of my siblings' clothing spoke otherwise." She shrugged. "I have the feeling they simply wanted me out of the way, for their own reasons. And so another seven years passed, as years do, until I was a score-and-one and they came again—"

"Aisling," he said, sounding stunned, "you needn't go on."

She shot him a look. "Weak-kneed?"

He smiled sadly. "Nay."

She took a deep breath and let it out, ignoring that it felt as if it had shuddered out of her. "I will come of age at a score-and-eight, which is—" She paused and thought about it for a moment or two. "In another pair of months, unless I'm counting amiss. I had planned for the day, of course, because once I had attained my majority, they could not sell me. I had been out for my afternoon of liberty when, to my surprise, I saw a richly dressed couple in the, ah, village coming out of a, um, pub, and realized to my horror that 'twas them." She looked at him quickly. "My parents, that is. And there was only one reason they would have come to—" She had to take another deep breath. "There was only one reason they would be anywhere near where I was."

"What did you do?"

"I ran." She stopped and looked out over the sea. "I would do it again."

"There is no shame in it," he said quietly. "In running, that is."

"Shame isn't what I feel," she said, pulling her hand away from him and rubbing her arms. "Terror, perhaps." She frowned. "There are other things as well, but I'm not sure how to name them." She looked at him then. "I think I would like to see my parents slaving away in a mine. What would you call that?"

"Justice," he said dryly.

She smiled faintly. "Aye, perhaps." She looked out over the sea. "Even with everything else, I don't regret running, for it provided me with this."

"It is beautiful," he agreed.

She watched the water sweep up into a spot on the shore, some arbitrary place carved out of the sand by previous oceanic forays. She watched the water swirl, then reached out and traced above it in the air with her finger.

The water leapt up and began to spin under her hand like a wheel.

She continued to spin it, because the feel of the water under her hand pleased her. Then she turned it, because it pleased her more to have it look less like a plate and more like a flywheel. It occurred to her that she was spinning, but since it wasn't a wooden wheel, she supposed it wouldn't count. And since she certainly wasn't dead, she let that thought continue on its way. Her head was full of the sharp tang of sea air, and she was at peace. She continued to spin the water idly when it would begin to slow . . .

And then she realized what she'd done.

"What," said a garbled voice from next to her, "in the hell is *that*?"

Aisling closed her hand and pulled it close to her. The water fell to her feet, splashing her boots. She looked at Rùnach and felt his stillness become hers.

"I don't know," she whispered.

He started to say something, then cursed. He yanked her behind him and drew his sword.

She found herself in fog before she knew it was hard upon her. She heard Rùnach fighting with an unknown quantity of men, but that lasted perhaps less time than it might have if they all hadn't been deafened by the sea rising up and roaring in a voice that had her sticking her fingers in her ears.

Only that wasn't the sea.

She was knocked off her feet before she could identify what was sweeping down from the sky over them, roaring to deafen the sea itself. She lay on her back, winded, with Rùnach half sprawled over her, and gaped at the beast that flew low over them, the gems on his breast blinding her, his roaring deafening her, the fire spewing suddenly from his gaping jaws coming close to singeing her. Screams suddenly filled the air, but they were not her screams, nor were they Rùnach's.

And then there was silence save the sound of the sea.

She felt for Rùnach frantically, because he hadn't moved, then realized he was still breathing. He was sopping wet from the waves, but then again, so was she. He was gasping, but then again, she was as well.

"What in the bloody hell was that?" she wheezed.

He laughed. "A dragon. And *bloody* isn't a ladylike term."

She had help to her feet, then she was again pulled behind Rùnach as he walked forward to see what was left of those who had apparently had nefarious intentions.

There was no one there.

"Bloody hell," he breathed.

She looked around his shoulder, then up at him. "I don't think that's a ladylike term."

"I'm not a lady."

"Well, even *I* could tell that." She watched him resheath his sword, then didn't argue when he took her hand and pulled her away from the sea.

"We'll come back," he said. "With a guard," he added, not entirely under his breath.

She couldn't imagine why anyone would find either of them important enough to assault more than one random time, but she wasn't going to argue. She sloshed along with Rùnach at something of a run. By the time they'd reached the gates of the university, she was breathless and terrified. She stopped him.

"We didn't just see that."

He shook his head. "Of course not. Dragons are mythical beasts."

She looked at him seriously. "Have you ever seen a dragon?"

"Aye, just now."

She thought she just might have to sit down soon. She laughed a little, because she couldn't help herself. She looked at him. "I'm beginning to think I have been misled about several things."

He took her by the hand and pulled her along through the gate. "Let's go dry off and have supper. I'm sure Lord Nicholas has a tome or two he would let you have. You can decide then for yourself what the truth is."

"I think I might have learned enough about dragons for the day."

He smiled. "I imagine you have."

"I also think I need some way to protect myself besides hiding behind you."

"I'll think on it and let you know. After supper."

"Thank you, Rùnach."

"You're welcome, Aisling."

She walked with him, feeling rather sandy, sodden, and overwhelmed. She felt a little bit as if she weren't exactly part of the world any longer. She had told a man she hardly knew details about her life she had never told anyone else. She had pulled water up out of the sea and turned it into a flywheel, then set it spinning.

And she had just seen a dragon.

She supposed that changed everything.

Fifteen

❧

Rùnach paced through the passageways of Lismòr well before dawn. It might have had to do with the fact that he hadn't slept much, if any, or it might have had to do with the fact that he'd been overtaken the afternoon before by a handful of ruffians he hadn't noticed coming and it had taken a bloody dragon—his uncle, he assumed—to swoop down out of the sky and rescue his sorry arse.

Or it might have been that an unmagical, indentured weaver from an obscure village she refused to name had drawn up a handful of seawater and turned it into a wheel that she'd set to spinning as easily as if it had been made of wood.

He ran bodily into the lord of Lismòr before he realized his uncle was standing there watching him pace around the perimeter of the inner courtyard. Rùnach blew out his breath.

"Forgive me, Your Grace."

Nicholas only put his hand on Rùnach's shoulder. "I have a hot fire and warm cider in my solar."

"I suppose that is an improvement over a hot fire on the strand yesterday," Rùnach said sourly, "a fire that fair singed the backside off my trousers."

Nicholas shrugged, smiling unrepentantly. "An interesting tale then, I'm sure. Why don't you join me in comfort and tell me of it?"

Rùnach went with him, but knew there was no point in relating a tale his uncle had had the starring role in. He'd heard all manner of reports in his youth about Nicholas, of course, beginning and ending with the fact that Nicholas had been, in his own youth, a notorious shapechanger, no shape too humble or too complicated for him to don. Perhaps he had little cause to exercise what Rùnach was sure was a prodigious talent, save for the opportunity to rescue the odd relative now and again. Rùnach couldn't say he blamed him for seizing the opportunity when it presented itself.

He followed Nicholas into his solar, made himself comfortable on that lovely sofa, and happily accepted a cup of cider. He sipped, then looked at his aunt's husband.

"You have an excellent cook, though that seems a pedestrian thing to call him."

"He prefers it thus," Nicholas said with a smile. "That sort of underestimation leads to cries of surprise and delight upon the tasting of his fare, which cries are truly the lifeblood of his art. Now, tell me what you think of the choice Ruith made about your father?"

Rùnach would have choked, but he had learned very quickly in Nicholas's presence to not be at ease whilst partaking of anything liquid. It was surely the only thing that saved the man's carpets at present. Rùnach coughed discreetly, sipped, swallowed, then set his cup aside.

"To lock him in a little hovel in the middle of Shettlestoune where his life will be nothing but scratching a meager existence from his pitiful garden?" he asked. He shrugged. "'Tis fitting. I can only assume Ruith dug him another well for water after he'd tossed all my sire's magic down the first one and sealed it shut."

"I don't think he merely sealed it shut," Nicholas remarked.

"Nay, Your Majesty, he used a Cothromaichian spell of essence changing and turned all my father's power into solid rock. Which, I suppose, is how it will remain for the rest of eternity unless someone with those spells and the power to use them changes everything back to what it was and gifts my father's magic back to him, but even then it wouldn't be quite the same, would it?"

"I wouldn't know," Nicholas said primly, "not possessing those spells myself."

Rùnach laughed a little in spite of himself. "My lord Nicholas, I daresay you have magic enough to terrify the masters at Buidseachd just with what you already know."

"But not enough to terrify Soilléir into giving me things I sincerely doubt even Seannair can remember any longer," Nicholas said with a snort. "I am assuming *someone* in Cothromaiche has their birthright spells hidden away, but perhaps not." He smiled at Rùnach. "It must have been amusing to at least see what Soilléir could do, even if you were prevented for the moment from working those spells yourself."

"For the moment?" Rùnach echoed, pained. "You are too kind. Magic is forever lost to me, Your Grace, but I have been resigned to that for many years now. The seeing, though, is more difficult."

Nicholas frowned. "What do you mean?"

"I can no longer see anything," Rùnach said. "Well, save ordinary things at night." He shrugged, though that cost him quite a bit. "Nothing of a magical nature, though. It was no great loss, I daresay."

"When, my dearest boy," Nicholas said, sounding dumbfounded, "did that disaster befall you?"

"At the well."

"Are you certain of that?"

Rùnach closed his eyes in spite of himself, because suddenly the vision was too strong. He stood at the edge of an ordinary glade, watching events he had intended to stop spiraling completely out of control. He watched his father gather all his sons around him, frown as he looked for his youngest son and daughter, then turn and beam with approval on one of Rùnach's younger brothers who had distracted their sire with questions about the mighty magic he was preparing to show them.

Because the focus was and always had been their sire.

Rùnach could remember dozens of conversations he'd had with his older brother Keir about how to help their sire finish himself off. He knew Keir had had scores of the same sorts of conversations with their mother, though Rùnach had never sat in on any of them. Even though her lads had not been children any longer, Sarait had been ferociously determined to shield them from their father's evil as best she could.

As daunting and impossible a task as it had been.

Rùnach had, he would admit, spent more time than perhaps he should have out in whatever training field he could find, pitting himself against the finest swordsmen he could lure out with him, and this after having worn through several peerless swordmasters. And when he hadn't been driving himself into the ground physically, he had been pouring over books of spells, taking for his own what served him, honing them endlessly into something better, more powerful, simpler, and more deadly.

He hadn't slept all that much.

So when he'd stood in a circle around that well with his mother and four of his brothers, he had thought himself quite prepared to counter whatever came his way.

How arrogant and deluded he had been.

His father had, with a single word spoken, either killed outright or stripped three of his younger sons of all their power. Rùnach couldn't remember and had never cared to find out. Gair had laid the same spell on him and Keir, but Sarait had spared his elder brother the brunt of it and Rùnach had thrown up his own defense, which had been woefully inadequate for the job. The well had opened, the evil therein geysering up toward the heavens and hanging there for what had seemed an endless moment, frozen in time.

It was then Rùnach had realized that his father had loosed something he couldn't control.

The truth was, he had never heard his father spew out so many spells in such a short time, not even in the heat of his cold angers. He had known with a finality that had left him ill that his father was not going to manage to do anything but kill them all. He had exchanged a glance with Keir, done exactly what they'd planned, which was for Keir to engage their father and for him to protect their mother, leaving Ruithneadh to see to Mhorghain.

Only things hadn't gone exactly as they'd planned.

Sarait had pushed him aside, then put herself between them and Gair to use on their father spells Rùnach hadn't realized she'd possessed, but she'd tripped and started to fall into the well. Rùnach could see with perfect clarity each moment that had passed from then on. He had reached out and caught his mother as he'd heard her begin closing the well. His father had continued to scream spells, spells that proved useless against what he'd loosed.

Sarait had shielded them from the brunt of the evil that had fallen down like an enormous wave, but that had left her so over-extended magically that when it had crashed down on them, it had wounded her fatally. Rùnach realized that someone had succeeded in closing the well only because they—either Keir or his mother, he couldn't remember which it had been—had closed it on his hands, the force of that closing pulling him down and grinding his cheek against the stone as he fell. He had seen one last tableau of his mother there, dying, Keir half broken and weeping, and his father crumpling to the ground, a victim of his own arrogance.

And then he had known no more.

He pulled back to himself and looked at Nicholas. "At the well, Your Majesty?" he asked hoarsely. "Aye, I daresay it was there that I ceased to see."

Because by the time he'd come back to himself and realized his hands had been pulled free of the stone, he had no longer been able to see the spells covering the glade. He had crawled with his broken hands and ruined face all the way to Buidseachd where he'd known there was one man who would hide him and heal him, if healing could be done.

Of course, it hadn't been possible, but he had learned to live with his challenges. He flexed his hands that were now useful in spite of their webs of scars and smiled at Nicholas.

"I don't miss it," he added easily. "Seeing, that is."

Nicholas only studied him in a way that made Rùnach nervous.

"You know, Rùnach," Nicholas said slowly, "though I wasn't there for your youth, I had the occasional conversation with your mother and Desdhemar of Neroche, who both knew you quite well."

"Did you," Rùnach managed, trying to sound as uninterested as he truly felt. "I shudder to think about what they said."

Nicholas shrugged. "Desdhemar told me that she and Sarait couldn't decide what unnerved Sìle more, watching you endlessly hone your sword skill or knowing that you were in his library, tinkering with his spells and pushing them in directions they hadn't been meant to go."

"Corrupting the perfection," Rùnach said lightly. "Aye, he was unhappy enough about that, I suppose."

"Actually, I think he was—and still is—enormously proud of you." Nicholas sipped at his cider. "That's probably why he shouted at you so loudly after the wedding."

"Heard that, did you?" Rùnach asked.

"Lad, I would imagine *Droch* heard that all the way in his comfortable lair at Buidseachd," Nicholas said with a dry smile. "And in spite of his fury over your choice of potential occupations, he loves you deeply. That's obviously why he put runes on your hands."

Rùnach blinked. "What?"

Nicholas looked at him in mock surprise. "Can you not see even *them*?"

Rùnach looked at his hands before he could stop himself, but of course he could see nothing. He couldn't see anything, hadn't seen anything for a score of years, had absolutely no desire to see anything for the rest of his life.

"Is that a poor jest, uncle?" Rùnach said shortly. "I fail to see the humor."

"I think you fail, my boy, to see much of anything," Nicholas said without rancor. "Let me change that for you."

Rùnach opened his mouth to do he had no idea what—protest, perhaps, curse his uncle, surely—but it was too late. He heard the spell come rushing out of Nicholas's mouth—and unfortunately saw it as well—and couldn't find the breath to damn his mother's brother-in-law before things changed for him. Dramatically. As if someone had turned on a light after he had been standing in darkness for years.

A score of years, to be exact.

He realized he had shoved himself backward so hard that he had tipped over Nicholas's fine sofa only because he almost sent himself through the window. He stood pressed against the wall of Nicholas's solar and looked at the things he hadn't seen before: spells tucked discreetly in the corners, the shimmer of Diarmailtian glamour stretched out above his head, things woven into the fire . . .

Runes on the backs of his hands.

He held his hands up in front of him and gaped at them, scarred and only recently made useful again. There were runes of Tòrr Dòrainn there, runes placed on him to protect and shield.

Runes to give him strength when he had none of his own left.

"Turn it off," Rùnach said hoarsely.

"Turn off what?" asked a voice next to him.

Rùnach looked to find Aisling standing there. He realized only then that she had her hand on his arm and she was looking at him as if she had seen a ghost. She transferred her look, which then turned into a frown, to Nicholas.

"You have vexed him, my lord," she said, sounding slightly displeased.

"Nay," Rùnach managed, "nay, he hasn't." He pushed himself away from the wall with hands that his grandfather had obviously marked at some point—no doubt when he had been unconscious thanks to either Ruith or Miach's fist under his jaw—and walked over to right the sofa. He tried to ignore the fact that Aisling had her hand under his elbow, guiding him as if he'd been approximately eight hundred years old. He sat where she put him, made polite conversation, had more cider, all the while feeling as if he were standing outside himself watching a very normal dawn turn into morning.

"Aisling, my dear, I don't suppose you would do me the very great favor of fetching something from the library for me, would you?" Nicholas smiled at her affectionately. "I think you are the only one I would trust with my more valuable tomes, knowing your love for books."

"But what of Rùnach, my lord? Will you look after him?"

"Of course, my dear."

"Then, as you will, my lord."

Rùnach couldn't watch her go. In fact, he hadn't watched her at all. He had spent most of the time with his eyes closed, that he might not see. He did, however, look over his shoulder to make certain she had left Nicholas's chamber.

Then he fixed his uncle with a steely look.

"Turn it off," he said, barely able to restrain his fury.

Nicholas only lifted an eyebrow. "Would you care to know what spell I used?"

"No," Rùnach said shortly. "I just want you to reverse it."

"It was, my dear Rùnach, a spell of clarity."

"Unclarify me then, damn you!"

Nicholas shrugged, then undid the spell. Rùnach knew he had, because in spite of himself, he'd listened to and memorized both spells Nicholas had used. The magic in Diarmailt was of an odd kind, not elegant like Fadaire, nor full of twists and turns and hidden things such as they used in Durial. It was simple, deceptively so, and full of meanings that were only seen after the spell had been spoken.

Rùnach was, he found, utterly unsurprised that Nicholas's spell had not muddied what it had clarified.

"Did it not work?" Nicholas asked innocently.

Rùnach couldn't even find the energy to curse him as he so richly deserved. He drew his hand over his eyes, but that only reminded him of what he'd seen on the backs of his hands. He turned his hands over and looked at the runes there.

"At least he didn't put you in line for the throne," Nicholas offered. "Unlike your sister."

Rùnach blinked. "Mhorghain wears the runes of ascension?"

"As does Miach," Nicholas said, "though I imagine Làidir will have something to say about that when your grandfather gives up his crown. But for the moment, aye, they both wear them. I believe they have served them very well up to this point. As for you, I can only speculate on what your grandfather laid upon you, not being an expert in Fadairian runes, of course. I suppose you would know what they represent."

"I suppose I might," Rùnach said unwillingly, "but I'm not sure I have the stomach to look at them, not even now that I have no choice."

"I suggest you don't look in any polished glasses either, then," Nicholas said mildly. "I believe he placed something there over your brow as well."

"Damn him," Rùnach grumbled. "'Tis no wonder Weger's mark wouldn't take."

"You can't be surprised," Nicholas said with a smile. He looked at Rùnach, then sobered. "I can only say to you what I think your mother would have said to you and that is that you have mighty gifts that you have, quite understandably, hidden away for twenty years. I believe the time has come for you to use them."

Rùnach dragged his hand through his hair, feeling rather more grateful than he likely should have that his hand was able to accomplish such a pedestrian task. "For what purpose, I can't imagine."

Nicholas shrugged. "I suppose you will discover that in time."

Rùnach looked at his uncle for several moments in silence. "Why is it I think you know what lies before me?"

Nicholas pushed his lips out a bit, as if he considered just how much—if anything—he should say. Then he shrugged. "I see many things and hear more."

"Such as Acair of Ceangail wandering about Melksham, looking for a place to take tea?" Rùnach asked sourly.

Nicholas lifted his eyebrows briefly, but said nothing.

"Your Majesty, I think you forget who I am. I have no magic, very little sword skill, and my father is safely tucked away where he can't do anything but shout at his neighbors. There is no great task for me to accomplish, no feat worthy of song, nothing but the simple life of a simple swordsman carving out an unremarkable existence wherever I choose to land."

"Wearing the runes of Tòrr Dòrainn on your hands."

"I didn't choose those."

"And ofttimes, Rùnach, we don't choose the events we're faced with, we are chosen to face them."

Rùnach let out a gusty sigh. "I don't think I can stomach any more of this conversation."

"Then let's turn to another one," Nicholas said mildly. "You were pacing this morning. Why?"

Rùnach was so unbalanced that he could scarce bring himself to form words. He rose and went to stand in front of the fire because he had to do something besides sit. He rubbed his hands over his face, then looked at his uncle.

"She spun water."

Nicholas looked at him as if he hadn't heard him.

"Water," Rùnach clarified. "Just as she touched air and set that wheel to spinning in that poor, terrified granny's house days ago. She stood over a pool of seawater, drew it up as if it had been a thread, then set it to spinning."

Nicholas frowned thoughtfully. "That is interesting."

"It is, isn't it?"

Nicholas merely waited. Rùnach waited as well until he couldn't simply stand there and not speak.

"Well?" he demanded.

"Well, what?" Nicholas asked politely.

"What do you think?"

"I think that your idea of teaching her to use a bow is a very good one."

"I don't believe I said anything about teaching her how to shoot."

"You mutter under your breath. Your sister curses under her breath, so perhaps you are an improvement."

"Did she ever curse you?" Rùnach asked crisply.

Nicholas leaned back and looked at him tranquilly. "Only when I pushed her too far, but what are uncles for if not to push you in directions you don't particularly want to go?"

Rùnach bent his head, rubbed the back of his neck, then looked at the former king of Diarmailt. "Forgive me," he said quietly. "You have been nothing but gracious—"

"And vexing," Nicholas said with a smile. "Rùnach, my lad, I don't take anything personally any longer. I've forced you to consider directions in which you didn't want to go, shown you things you didn't want to see, pried into your privacy with shameless abandon. I deserve everything I have in return—ah, Aisling, my dear, you've returned. Come and sit. There's a very fine cider here that Rùnach could pour for you."

Rùnach hadn't heard her knock, though Nicholas obviously had or he wouldn't be standing there by the door, welcoming her inside his solar. He led her over to his sofa. Rùnach poured her something to drink, realizing with a start that he should have been more grateful for the ability to do that. It had been difficult for him for longer than he wanted to think about.

He was beginning to think he should have been grateful for quite a few things he hadn't been able to do before.

"This is a rather thin volume," Nicholas said, taking the book from Aisling and smiling at her, "but contains interesting things. I understand that you're particularly fascinated by myths."

She looked terribly uncomfortable. "A foolish thing, isn't it, for a woman of my age."

"My dear, there is no limit to a body's desire for a good tale full of things that fire the imagination," Nicholas said easily. "I myself enjoy that sort of thing, even now that I'm in my dotage." He reached over and handed her the book. "You keep that, Aisling my dear. I think you might be the only other person in all the Nine Kingdoms who could possibly appreciate it as I have all these years."

She looked at him in shock. "But Master Dominicus told me it was the most rare and valuable book in the library below."

Nicholas smiled at her. "I have the feeling that you might be just the gel to be the keeper of such a rare and valuable tome. Wouldn't you agree?" He looked at Rùnach. "I had the armorer select a bow for her, and one for you if you care to brush up on your skills. It is waiting for you in the lists. I imagine it will still be there if you care to have breakfast before you begin your labors."

Aisling looked as if she might soon weep. "That is too generous, Lord Nicholas."

"My dear, if an old man cannot do now and again for those who pass through his gates, of what use is he? These are simple gifts that hopefully will serve you well." He looked at Rùnach. "Perhaps you would care to escort this lovely gel to breakfast."

"Happily," Rùnach said. Perhaps if he managed to get himself out of his uncle's solar, he would manage to get himself away from that damned spell and stop seeing things he didn't particularly care to.

He sighed. It wasn't that he didn't care to see. It was that he knew what it would feel like to lose that sight if the spell didn't hold—or if the undoing of it actually did what it should have.

Nicholas walked Aisling to the door, chatting pleasantly with her. Rùnach found his cloak and drew it around his shoulders. Unfortunately, the motion didn't dislodge anything he'd recently acquired, such as the ability to see with perfect clarity the runes engraved on the backs of his hands.

"How are you, Rùnach?" Nicholas asked politely, standing back so Rùnach could reach the door.

"Clarified."

Nicholas looked at him. "It won't fade, you know. That clarity."

Rùnach put his hand on the heavy wooden door and looked at his uncle. "Why?"

Nicholas smiled very faintly. "Of what use is an old man," he said very quietly, "if he cannot give simple gifts every now and again to those who pass through his home?"

Rùnach closed his eyes briefly. "I didn't expect this."

"I know, my boy." He put his hand on Rùnach's shoulder. "I know."

Rùnach took a deep breath, nodded to his uncle in what he hoped Nicholas would understand was thanks he couldn't voice, then left the solar and pulled the door shut behind him. He found Aisling standing there, looking down at the book in her hands. He almost asked her for a peek at it, then thought better of it. It was her gift, not his. He smiled at her when she looked at him.

"Food, then archery?"

She nodded. He offered her his arm, then walked with her to the buttery. He could only hope the only thing magical he was able to see there was the results of whatever Nicholas's cook had had on the fire.

He was, he reminded himself, looking merely for an ordinary life. A useful garrison. Good ale in the evenings. Work to do that he could actually do. It would be, he reminded himself further, a welcome change from all the years he'd spent living in a moldering old castle surrounded by all kinds of wild, student-created magic he hadn't been able to see.

"Dragons," Aisling murmured, shaking her head. "I think there is quite a bit in here about dragons."

Rùnach imagined there was.

She looked at him. "Do you think there will be tales of elves as well?"

He nodded. He imagined there would be. He could only hope that would be the only place she would find them for the foreseeable future.

He wasn't quite sure what she would do when she found out he was not exactly what he'd told her he was.

Sixteen

❋

Aisling stretched the great bow, sighted the bull's-eye on the target, then released the arrow as she'd been taught.

Her arrow split Rùnach's right down the center.

She looked at him and lifted one of her eyebrows. "Ha," she said.

"I taught you that," he pointed out.

"And I'm the one who learned it."

He laughed a little. "And you've learned a great deal in a very short amount of time. Shall I fetch our arrows and we have another go?"

She started to say *aye*, then found that she couldn't ignore the obvious, which was that she had been at Lismòr too long. She thought it might have been nine days, but she wasn't entirely sure. It was perhaps double that if she were to count the days she'd simply slept after Rùnach had carried her there.

She found Rùnach was watching her seriously, which she found slightly alarming.

"What?" she asked.

He didn't move. "I have been thinking that perhaps we should consider our plans. I'm not sure we would want to stay here forever."

She had to disagree with him there. She had relished every moment of every day she had spent at Lismòr because she had, for the first time in her life, felt that her life was almost her own. She had trained with the bow in the mornings, walked along the shore in the afternoons, then joined Nicholas's lads for rousing tales in the evening. Just last night, he had told one about an obscure girl who found a sword and a king to wed whilst looking for other things entirely. It had contained less magic than the tale the night before, so she had approved, though she had been somewhat unsurprised to listen to a dragon make an appearance.

She paused. She too had seen a dragon, so she supposed she couldn't condemn Lord Nicholas for telling tales about them.

She had also enjoyed decadently hot fires and the best meals she had ever eaten in the whole of her life. If that had been everything, that would have been enough to leave her looking back on her days at Lismòr with wonder, but there had been more in the person of Rùnach of somewhere in the mountains he would not name. She looked up at him and wondered how it was that only a handful of days could leave her feeling so at ease with him.

And leave her with so many questions about him.

He seemed perfectly comfortable with the lord of Lismòr, as if he were accustomed to chatting easily with men of power and significance, though he had seemed equally as comfortable with the rabble in Gobhann. And it didn't seem to trouble him to spend his mornings with her, teaching her how to use a weapon she had never touched before in her life.

"Who are you?" she asked suddenly.

He blinked, then smiled faintly. "No one of consequence."

She waved an arrow at him. "I like a good mystery as well, just so you know."

"I think I should be afraid."

She pursed her lips. "You don't seem to be afraid of anything."

"Oh, I wouldn't say that," he said quietly. "I'm afraid of quite a few things."

"Prying questions?"

He laughed a little. "Aye, those to be sure." He started to speak, then shook his head. "The other things aren't worth speaking of." He slung his bow over his shoulder. "Where shall we go now?"

"Right now?"

"Nay, when we leave Lismòr."

She looked at him in surprise. "Are you asking me?"

"I am asking you."

She looked at him quickly, just to see if he was preparing to burst into gales of laughter for having put her on, but he was only watching her steadily. And gravely.

"Ah, I was originally feeling a fair bit of haste," she began slowly. "For particular reasons I'm not at liberty to divulge."

"And now?"

She hardly knew where to begin. She had walked inside Gobhann's gates, sure that the only path to freedom lay through an agreement forged with Scrymgeour Weger. But now she had seen that people lived, ate, passed the time in their glorious libraries full of books, all without answering to anyone or fearing a curse that hung endlessly over their heads should they simply step across an arbitrary line in the dirt.

It made her wonder about those who had held sway over her over the years, if they knew any better or were simply parroting lines they had learned themselves. The Guildmistress had warned her to never touch spinning wheels, but had that been a lie or simply something the woman had believed for so long that she had never thought to question it? And the things she'd been told at the pub by Euan and Quinn and the rest of their mates, rumors of the fierceness of the curse attached to the borders, could those have been simply things repeated until they had passed into legend?

She could hardly bear to think that her entire life had been covered and hedged about and smothered by lies told to . . . what? Keep her where she was? Keep her from asking questions? Keep her from thinking for herself?

And then there was the peddler who had sent her on a quest, thrown her into a world she had no idea how to manage, forced her halfway across the world—

Well out of the way of the reach of anyone from Bruadair, as it happened.

She looked up at the sky, feeling a faint mist full of the smell of the sea fall upon her skin. It was, she had to admit, glorious, so glorious that she wasn't sure what she would do without feeling it again.

"There is the sea touching other places, you know."

She looked at Rùnach. "Is there?"

"Aye," he said with a small smile. "There is coastline along all Neroche's eastern edge, actually. Shall I draw you a map?"

She shook her head. "I've seen one." Though she had to admit now that she wasn't at all sure that that map had been accurate. Nothing else had been. She looked at Rùnach. "Perhaps you should, but perhaps not now." She paused. "Should we take our leave—well, I should take my leave." She couldn't bring herself to look at him. "I'm not sure what your plans are."

She looked at him in time to see him draw his hand over his brow and rub the spot over his eye where Weger had attempted to brand him like a prized milch cow—and failed.

"I was thinking," he began slowly, "that perhaps I would make a journey to Chagailt." He looked at her and for a change his green eyes were rather pale. "There is, as you know, a rather lovely library there."

"Have you ever been there?" she asked.

"Chagailt?" he echoed. "It is the summer palace of the kings of Neroche, which makes it a rather exclusive locale. Scholars and seekers of truth are, however, allowed into the library without hesitation." He rested his bow against his shoulder, the other end of it resting on the ground. "You might find answers there."

She realized he hadn't answered her question, but she suspected he had done that on purpose. She wasn't sure she wanted to know why. "Am I looking for answers?"

"I don't know," he said. "Are you?"

"I'm not sure what I'm looking for any longer."

"I thought you were looking for a swordsman," he said slowly, "but perhaps that has changed."

The only thing that had changed was her intense desire to go back to that very comfortable bed Lord Nicholas had provided her and pull the covers over her head. She looked up at the sky again, wishing that she could, just for a few days, live for herself. Nothing hanging over her head, not the fate of Bruadair in her helpless hands nor the finding of a mercenary capable of instigating a palace coup left to her meager devices. She sighed deeply, then looked at Rùnach.

"Have you ever known there was something you needed to do, but found yourself dreading it with everything you were?"

"Once or twice," he said.

"What did you do?"

He looked at her steadily. "I did what needed to be done."

"Was the price steep?"

"Very."

She clutched her own bow, wishing her task was nothing more than learning to place an arrow where she wanted it to land. "Did you ever want to run?" she whispered.

He smiled, but it was a pained smile. "I'm not sure I want to answer that."

"Do you think Heroes ever want to run?"

"Only if they come from Neroche."

She blinked, then smiled. "They seem to send a preponderance of lads trotting off into the gloom, don't they?"

"I believe there must be something in the water there," he said dryly. He reached out and tucked a lock of hair behind her ear, then froze when he seemed to realize what he'd done. He carefully pulled his hand away and lowered it to his side, as if he thought she wouldn't notice if he were slow enough. He nodded to his right. "There is a bench over there, lady. Perhaps you would care to sit and take your ease after your morning of heavy labor."

She wasn't going to argue with that. She allowed him to take her bow and quiver of arrows from her, then walked with him and sat down on that very comfortable bench.

He set their gear aside, then looked at her. "Will you tell me what your quest is, Aisling?"

"I told you," she said. "I must find a swordsman to save my . . . village."

"Is that all?"

She clutched the edge of the seat of that lovely wooden bench, took several deep, steadying breaths, then looked at him. "I am to send this mercenary to a predetermined meeting place before a certain amount of time has passed."

He nodded, as if he weren't surprised by it.

"This presents a bit of a problem," she continued slowly, "given that whilst I had a bag full of gold at one time, I have that no longer. I could perhaps hire out as a weaver and earn more, but I fear it would take me a great deal of time to earn enough."

"Do you enjoy weaving?"

"I'd rather stick hot pins in my eyes," she said, before she thought better of it. She looked at him quickly. "I mean—"

"Just that, I imagine," he said with a faint smile. "And I can't say that I blame you, given your circumstances." He considered for a moment or two, then looked at her. "And if you don't find this lad within this certain amount of time?"

She wanted to tell him. Indeed, if she could have blurted it all out right there in Nicholas's lists, she would have. But all she could do was look at him, mute.

"Something dire happens?" he suggested.

She supposed a nod wouldn't fell her where she sat, so she nodded. Just once.

"Then I believe I have a thought."

"Is it a useful one?" she managed.

"It isn't one about how many questions I want to pepper you with and how many answers I intend to pry out of you whilst you're otherwise occupied," he said with a smile, "which makes it a useful one, I suppose."

"My answers aren't very interesting ones."

"I'll be the judge of that," he said, half under his breath, then he smiled. "Let us do this. Let's make our way to Chagailt, then take our ease briefly in the library there. We might find a few of the answers we're both seeking."

"Are you seeking answers?"

He smiled. "I have a question or two that I could happily find an answer to."

"Another mystery?"

"The same one."

"What one is that?"

He smiled, then rose and started toward the target. "Can't say," he threw over his shoulder.

"Can't, or won't?" she called after him.

"Take your pick."

Impossible man. She watched him collect their arrows, then examine the one of his that she'd destroyed. He shook his head, then walked back and collected her as well.

"Lunch," he said, sounding thrilled by the prospect.

"Thank you," she said, as she walked with him off the field.

"For what?"

"For coming with me."

"It is my pleasure."

She looked up at him as they reached the buttery. "Why are you?"

"Do you mind if I do?"

She shook her head.

"Then it's settled."

It was only as she had finished her lunch that she realized he hadn't answered her question, nor did it appear he intended to. Worse still, she wasn't sure she wanted him to. Perhaps he was coming with her out of pity, or boredom, or a secret nefarious desire to rush into Bruadair himself and overthrow the government to install himself as king.

Though of any of the thoughts she'd had over the past month, that was easily the most ridiculous.

She stood on the edge of Lismòr's beautiful inner courtyard, waiting for Rùnach to come back from the library where he'd gone to fetch her a book or two he thought she might like, when she realized she wasn't standing where she was, she was standing at a crossroads. She almost looked over her shoulder to see if someone might be standing behind her, breathing lightly, waiting for her to realize the gift she'd been given.

Freedom.

And a man willing to help her discover how to keep it.

She looked up into the flat, grey sky and wondered if there were such things as curses, and quests, and . . .

And dragons.

She felt something sink into her soul, something that felt quite a bit like courage. She put her hand on the pillar she was standing next to, found it solid beneath her touch, and began to wonder things that she supposed might be the death of her, but she couldn't help but wonder them just the same.

What if the peddler had lied to her?

What if her entire life had just been one lie after another?

What if she were free?

She blinked when she realized Rùnach had come to stand in front of her. She looked at him seriously.

"Are things as they seem to be?"

He blinked in surprise, then smiled. "You keep asking that question."

She only waited, because she wasn't sure she dared begin to think about her reply.

He chewed on his words for a moment or two, seemingly looking for just the right ones. "I don't know," he said, finally. "I suppose that depends on what you think things seem to be."

She supposed the only way to find that out was to find out everything she could about Bruadair. She had begun a halfhearted search the day before, but she could see now that it would take more than just halfhearted searching to discover what she needed to.

Because until she knew the truth, she would spend her days living in fear of the cold hand of doom falling upon her.

She looked up at him. "I'm not sure of anything right now."

"Then you should find answers."

"Are there answers to be found, do you think?"

He smiled, handed his book off to a page who happened to be trotting by, then offered her his arm. "I think a walk along the shore might provide us with a few. If not, there is always the library at Chagailt. It is, you know, a convenient stop between here and Tor Neroche."

She wondered what was worse, being under a curse, or not having words to thank a terribly handsome, chivalrous, mysterious man for his kindness.

All she could do was take his arm.

They left at sunset. Aisling had thoroughly enjoyed her final walk along the shore, though the air had chilled her more than she'd thought it would. She had spent most of her time feeling the ocean against her hands, though she hadn't touched it.

Not since she'd sent it spinning, of course.

Nicholas walked with them out the front gates she hadn't remembered coming in. He was having a conversation with Rùnach that she hadn't been paying attention to but supposed she had better lest something come as an unexpected and unpleasant surprise.

"Perhaps," Nicholas was saying, "but there is something to be said for traveling under the cover of darkness."

Aisling looked at Rùnach to find him looking at the lord of Lismòr with a very grave expression.

"I think we've been fairly anonymous so far," he began slowly.

"Save for your time in Gobhann."

Rùnach sighed. "Other than that, who would know? Who would care?"

Aisling felt a chill go down her spine. "Who would care about what?" she asked. She could hardly voice the thought that occurred to her suddenly, but she had to. "Is someone looking for . . . someone in particular?" *Like me,* she wanted to add, but she couldn't bring herself to say the words, because they were so ridiculous. No one knew her; no one could possibly care about her.

Which meant that Nicholas was concerned about Rùnach.

Nicholas smiled easily. "I'm overly cautious, my dear, about my guests and their travels. I'm sure you and Rùnach will be just fine. He is a very skilled swordsman, which will serve you well. And you have your bow, don't you? I daresay you'll manage between the two of you."

She nodded, though the thought of someone pursuing Rùnach was one that suddenly filled her with dread. She looked at him searchingly, but found he looked anything but worried.

"Now, as to how you'll travel," Nicholas began, then he fell silent.

Aisling heard the very sudden sound of the rushing of wings. She reached for an arrow, but Rùnach stopped her with his hand suddenly on her arm. She would have protested, but she followed his gaze—just to know from whence their doom might be coming— and felt her knees give way. Rùnach caught her, then steadied her with his arm around her shoulders.

"What," she wheezed, "is that?"

"I believe," Nicholas said pleasantly, "that it is a horse."

"But it has wings!"

"A pegasus, then," Nicholas amended.

"Where did he come from?"

"I'm not exactly sure," Nicholas said thoughtfully. "He's not mine, that much I know."

Aisling leaned against Rùnach and watched as the horse—ah, pegasus, rather—made several enthusiastic circles before he came to earth, tucked his wings modestly, and bowed his head to Rùnach. She leaned harder.

"I think he likes you."

"And I think he likes *you*," he said. "How do you feel about flying?"

The only reason she didn't land on her backside was because Rùnach was holding her up. She began to shake, because that was what a sensible woman did when faced with something that terrified her.

"I believe I'm going to stop reading," she whispered. "I'm afraid to ask what might leap from the pages next."

Nicholas laughed merrily. "My dear, I suspect that won't stop these things from appearing in your life. You seem to attract them."

"I like them better in books," she said, though she found to her surprise that at the moment that wasn't exactly true.

She could hardly believe her eyes, but she couldn't deny what she was seeing. There standing before her was the most magnificent horse she'd ever seen. Admittedly, the only horses she had seen before were the ones befouling the streets of Beul, who were nags, and Rùnach's mount, whom she hadn't had a very good look at. She walked over to the horse standing five paces in front of them, feeling as if she were walking in a dream, then reached out her hand to stroke the blaze on his long, elegant nose. He didn't seem to mind it. And when she stepped to the side to look at his profile, he turned his head just so, presumably so she might catch him on his best side. She looked at him, then looked at Rùnach.

"He looks a great deal like your horse." She paused. "And I could be wrong, but he sounds as if he's purring."

"It's a mythical noise," Nicholas said firmly, sounding as if he knew of what he spoke. "If it sounds feline, that's a coincidence. It's actually something only the pegasus does, or so I've read. I'm sure you'll find that confirmed in your research. And look, how polite of him to provide you with reins. Aisling, I'll hold your gear whilst Rùnach gives you a leg up."

She looked at Nicholas and laughed, because she couldn't do anything else.

"This is a pegasus," she said in wonder.

Nicholas took her hand and tucked it under his arm. "And so he is, my dear."

"Is he Rùnach's horse, do you think?"

"I daresay he might be," Nicholas said, "though perhaps we can assume Rùnach didn't know about these unusual talents he has. He seems to be prepared to carry you where you want to go, however, so I think you should take advantage of what he's able to do, wouldn't you say?"

Aisling wasn't at all sure she wanted to get up on that beast's back, but there didn't seem to be any avoiding it. She settled herself in the saddle, took the reins, then shivered when Rùnach climbed up into the saddle behind her. There was something rather too final about knowing that once he was up in the saddle with her, there was no turning back. She suspected she might spend the entire journey feeling as if she were nigh onto falling off.

She didn't want to think about all the places to which—or heights from which—she might fall.

She managed to nod at Nicholas, but that was the extent of her thanks. She was fairly sure Rùnach had made polite conversation with their host, but she didn't hear any of it. All she could do was clutch the entirely useless reins and the pommel of the saddle at the same time and hope she wouldn't scream when the pegasus's wings unfurled and he leapt up into the sky.

But she didn't scream.

She fainted.

She knew this only because she realized after she'd woken that she had woken from something, but by then it was too late to even scream. She simply sat in the saddle with Rùnach's arms tightly around her and gasped.

"You know," he said loudly into her ear, "you'd best stop with that, else you won't ever catch your breath."

"We're off the ground!"

"Well, aye, we are," he agreed, "but you are when you're riding as well. What's the difference?"

"Several hundred feet!"

"Oh, perhaps more than that—"

"Be silent, you fool!"

He laughed. She would have elbowed him sharply to accompany her suggestion, but she didn't want to knock him off because then she would go with him. So she clutched his forearms that were wrapped around her and tried not to shriek. She closed her eyes, because that seemed the wisest thing to do.

Eventually, though, she found herself growing accustomed to the rushing of wind in her ears and the security of Rùnach's arms around her. She ventured a look down and realized how far up off the ground they were. That was every bit as startling as she'd suspected it would be. She looked over her shoulder at the horse's wings and blinked. Then she blinked again, but it was still there, something trailing from them.

Magic, no doubt.

She felt as though she were lost in a dream. She considered, reconsidered, then cast caution to the wind. She reached out and trailed her fingers in whatever the horse was flying them through.

Her fingers left streams behind them, just as the horse's wings had done.

Rùnach made a garbled noise of some kind.

"Do you see that?" she managed.

He only tightened his arm around her briefly in answer.

She was dreaming. It was the only explanation that made sense. She had been cast up into the night and somehow thereafter into a dream. She would wake on the morrow and everything would be the same as it had been. Perhaps she would even find herself back in Beul, at the Guild. She would walk quietly from her dormitory to the enormous weaving room with its endless rows of looms, take her place in her assigned spot, and begin her daily task of weaving a never-ending amount of dull grey cloth that would have none of the painfully beautiful sparkle that the threads her fingers seemed to be drawing out of nowhere did.

The thought of that almost brought tears to her eyes, she who had never wept in her life.

"Am I dreaming?" she asked aloud.

"I don't think so."

"Is there a way to be sure?"

He laughed a little. "At the moment, I'm not sure. We're hundreds of feet—"

"Don't say that!"

He laughed again, a rumble in his chest that was surprisingly soothing. "We're sitting safely and comfortably on the back of a horse with additional, unexpected appendages, traveling just barely off the ground, and you seem to be trailing your fingers through strands of something I'm not quite sure should be there."

"Can you see it?" she asked.

"To my everlasting surprise, I find I can. And if we aren't dreaming, we certainly should be." He tightened his arms around her briefly. "There are always answers. We just have to find out where to look."

"You'll help me?"

"Yes, Aisling, I will help you."

She couldn't imagine why, except that he loved a good mystery. She supposed she had a goodly amount of them to solve.

Perhaps there was reason to travel together a bit longer after all.

Seventeen

꧁

Rùnach walked along the smooth stone path that led to the front
doors of Chagailt and sighed in pleasure. Not only was the
palace itself exceptionally lovely, but the gardens were renowned
throughout the Nine Kingdoms for their beauty and variety. He
supposed that shouldn't have been surprising given that they had
been designed by Iolaire the Fair, queen of Neroche and daughter
of Proìseil the Proud, a former king of Ainneamh. Rùnach had been
to the palace several times, but that had been in his youth. He had
forgotten how impressive the castle was and how lovingly tended
were the grounds.

He looked at Aisling walking alongside him, staring mute at
the castle rising up before them. He wasn't sure if she was overwhelmed or just exhausted. He couldn't fault her for either. He
was weary from being awake the whole of the night, but that had
been his choice. He had been torn between the desire to make sure
his companion didn't fall out of the saddle and the diversion of

watching her touch magic that he could, to his continued surprise, see running beneath her fingers.

He thought he might have to send a thank-you along to his uncle, when he could properly express his gratitude.

Iteach had been left in the forest surrounding the keep to see to his own affairs and Rùnach had carried on with Aisling on foot. He wasn't quite sure how he would present himself to the inhabitants of the keep, given that there might be one old soul who might mistake him for his father, or his uncles on either side, or perhaps even for himself. To further complicate matters, he had no idea how to explain his hesitation to Aisling.

Because he had the feeling she wouldn't like finding out he'd been, ah, hedging.

He had gone out of his way to simply avoid answering things he couldn't respond to with the truth. He had heard in great detail just how angry his sister Mhorghain had been when she'd found out that her now-husband Miach had lied to her about his identity. Then again, Mhorghain had thought mages were evil. Aisling just thought mages were myths. There was a difference there, though he wasn't quite sure how to qualify it.

The only thing that saved him at present was that it was raining and he had to keep his hood up over his head to keep the weather off his face. He was accustomed to hiding, so it was no trouble. It did remind him uncomfortably, however, of how often he'd done it in the past.

He wondered, absently, if his scars bothered Aisling.

And he wondered why he was wondering.

"This is very . . . large."

He looked at his companion to find her still wearing that look of absolute astonishment she had put on the day before and not taken off since. He pulled her hood up over her hair and nodded.

"It is," he agreed.

"And you think they'll allow us inside?"

"Scholars are never turned away."

She made a little noise that sounded a bit like a laugh. "I'm hardly a scholar."

"Pretend."

She looked up at him. "I don't know how."

I know you don't was almost out of his mouth before he could stop himself. And that was, he had to admit, one of many things about her that intrigued him almost beyond his power to resist.

"Do you?" she asked.

He met her eyes. "Do I what?"

"Know how to pretend to be something you're not?"

He managed not to catch his breath because he had, as he was loath to admit, become very good at pretending. He had done it in one form or another for the whole of his life. First he had feigned interest in his father's mighty magic when all he'd wanted were his damned spells so he could learn how to counter them. Then he'd pretended to be a servant at Buidseachd, so he could keep himself alive. His reasons had been understandable, he supposed, but he had to admit he was growing tired of it.

At the moment, though, he thought spewing out all the details about himself and his family would be rather ridiculous. Aisling wouldn't believe him in the first place and in the second, she wouldn't care.

There are those in the world who might care very much to learn you're alive . . .

Nicholas's murmured words to him before he swung up onto Iteach's back had haunted him for most of the night. No one would care, least of all a simple weaver from a place apparently too humble for her to want to name. He couldn't imagine that anyone with any more importance in the world would be interested, not even his bastard brothers. After all, what did he have that they could take? Magic?

Knowledge?

He pushed aside that thought, because it was troubling, and wished however briefly for power enough to at least defend himself from lads possessing more than sword skill. But because he had nothing more than sword skill and little enough of that, he shoved aside all his troubling thoughts and concentrated on the woman at his side.

"I think I can pretend to be a scholar with enough effort," he said. "What of you?"

"I thought I would just be quiet and follow along."

He smiled. "I imagine we'll get on well enough, then. At least we're not bristling with weapons. They'll most likely let us in."

Or so he hoped. He continued to walk with her, knowing he had been marked long before then. He had no spell of Un-noticing to use, and they had left their weapons carefully hidden in the forest where Iteach would or wouldn't honor his promise to keep an eye on them. It made him nervous not to have anything save his hands with which to defend them both should the need arise, but there was nothing to be done about it. He would simply have to throw himself on the mercy of the steward and pretend to be nothing more than a simple scholar. That, at least, he thought he could manage well enough.

He walked up the front steps as if he had a right to and knocked on the front door. It opened slowly and a liveried servant stood there.

"Yes," the man intoned.

"Scholars," Rùnach said easily, "seeking the library, if you please."

"Very well. Your names?"

"Our errand is private," Rùnach demurred.

The guard looked them both over, scowled, then bid them wait where they were. Rùnach kept his hands in front of him where they could be clearly seen and waited. There was nothing else to be done.

It wasn't long before someone arrived at the doorway, preceded by complaints about preparations being interrupted. Rùnach soon found himself facing none other than Sgoilear of Chagailt, keeper of the king's private books. He continued to complain to the servant who had fetched him, then he stopped long enough to glare at them both.

"I am very busy," he said briskly. "Who are you and what do you want?"

Rùnach lifted the hood back from his face and spoke quickly, because he knew there was no possible hope for secrecy unless he enlisted aid where he hadn't anticipated needing to. "We are humble, nameless scholars," he said firmly, "seeking but a handful of hours in the general library."

Sgoilear of Chagailt looked at him for a moment or two, then his mouth fell open.

"Our errand is private," Rùnach repeated. "Not even my companion here knows anything about it."

Sgoilear shut his mouth with an audible snap. "Simple scholars," he managed.

"Aye," Rùnach said, nodding until Sgoilear began to nod with him. "If we might beg this time for research that cannot be done elsewhere, we would be most grateful."

"Of course," Sgoilear said faintly. "No one is denied entrance to Chagailt's library. Especially—"

"Simple scholars," Rùnach finished for him.

"Simple scholars," Sgoilear repeated, even more faintly. He beckoned weakly, then gave a guard a hearty shove out of their way. "They need the library. I'll see them there."

"Very generous, Master, ah—"

"Sgoilear," Sgoilear said, looking at Rùnach as if he'd just run into a pillar and was still stunned from the encounter. "Keeper of the king's books. But surely you—"

"Aye, I have heard tell of you," Rùnach agreed quickly. "Your reputation amongst those of a scholarly bent is flung far and wide. How fortunate Neroche's king is to have you minding his tomes."

Sgoilear apparently realized his mouth had fallen open again, because he shut it and nodded. He said nothing more, but continued to steal looks first at Rùnach, then at Aisling, who had removed her hood as well. To his credit, he didn't blurt out anything untoward or gape any longer. Rùnach suspected he would not escape the palace, however, without having had speech with the man.

Rùnach looked about him and wondered slightly at all the activity. He looked at Sgoilear.

"Is there a reason for all the cleaning?"

"King Mochriadhemiach is bringing his bride here for a visit," Sgoilear said. "Queen Mhorghain, but you—"

"Had heard tell that His Majesty was recently crowned and wed," Rùnach interrupted. "Aye, I had heard. Of course, there is great sadness for the passing of King Adhémar, but I am sure Neroche is safe in the hands of his youngest brother."

Sgoilear managed to nod. "He has been tireless as archmage. We feel we are in the best of hands now that he has taken the crown."

Rùnach nodded, then exchanged a polite smile with him before Sgoilear's attention was drawn away by someone in a panic about something only Sgoilear could attend to. Rùnach glanced at Aisling to find her wearing a look that was slightly skeptical.

"Archmage?" she whispered. "What does that mean?"

He considered how best to explain it to a woman who didn't believe in either mages or magic.

"It's complicated," he said, because that seemed simpler.

She looked satisfied enough with that answer. Actually, she looked utterly overwhelmed. Rùnach reached for her hand and wrapped his around it.

"The palace is large, isn't it?"

"I've never seen its like."

"The library is smaller."

"What a mercy."

He shot her a smile, then continued along with her behind Sgoilear, who was now engaged in a very spirited discussion with a woman Rùnach didn't recognize about how many of his librarians she was poaching to iron linen napkins when he needed them for the freshening up of several things His Majesty and his bride might care to read during their stay. The head housekeeper, which Rùnach decided she had to be, was not having any of it.

"Our new queen," she said crisply, "is the granddaughter of Sìle of Tòrr Dòrainn and will have certain expectations. She will not sit down to table and find her linens crumpled!"

Aisling leaned close. "Who is Sìle of Tòrr Dòrainn?"

Sgoilear's ears were apparently more refined than his negotiating skills. He came to a full stop and turned to look at her.

"Why, he is the king of the elves," he said, dumbfounded. "The elves of Tòrr Dòrainn, of course. Queen Mhorghain is his granddaughter. Didn't you know?"

Aisling, to her credit, didn't snort, but Rùnach glanced her way and had a knowing nod in return. He supposed he would hear something about the deluded nature of the librarians at Chagailt at some point, but hopefully that point would be when there weren't such eager ears listening. He only winked at Sgoilear, had a look of disbelief in return, and happily took up the march behind the keeper of the royal books again once the man had found it in himself to carry on.

It didn't take long for them to reach the library. Rùnach supposed he should have been surprised that they were to be simply turned loose inside it, but he realized he could see the faintest shimmer of spell hanging over the door. He imagined someone would know if they tried to poach anything.

He knew, however, that he would not escape scrutiny so easily. He sent Aisling off into the chamber, noted that a fire was being hastily stoked for her pleasure, then turned to look at Sgoilear by means of the werelight the librarian had kindled for them both.

"Prince Rùnach," he whispered in a garbled tone. "We are honored by your presence."

"Honored enough, I hope," Rùnach murmured, "to keep my visit a secret."

Sgoilear's eyes were very wide. "I hesitate to ask."

"I would as well, actually," Rùnach agreed. "I'm helping my companion with a quest. Very important to maintain absolute secrecy."

"As you will, Your Highness."

Rùnach smiled, shook the man's hand, and pretended not to notice when Sgoilear winced slightly—in sympathy, no doubt—at his scars. He didn't volunteer any information. He simply thanked Sgoilear for his discretion, then went inside the library to see what had become of Aisling.

She was standing with her back to the fire, looking around her as if she'd never seen books before. He came to stand beside her, sighed in pleasure, and steamed a bit thanks to the dampness of his cloak.

"We can begin our search whenever you're ready," he said easily. "I told the librarian we were on an important quest. I imagine we'll have as much peace as we care to have."

"I'm not sure how long I'll manage to stay awake," she admitted.

Rùnach smiled. "I believe there is a couch over there—a recent addition, I daresay—just right for the weary scholar who doesn't want to leave his research too far out of reach."

She looked horribly tempted. "Think you?"

"I do." He set his pack on a table near the hearth. "I'm not weary," he said easily, "so why don't you take a turn first. I have things I'm curious about."

She hid a yawn behind her hand. "I should say no, but I find I can't. I didn't sleep well last night."

"You were busy dreaming," he said with a smile.

"I think I was screaming," she said wearily.

He laughed a little. "Well, that too, perhaps. A small nap might be just the thing for you."

She stretched out on the sofa, then didn't protest when he took off his cloak and spread it over her. "You're very kind."

"You're very easy to be kind to."

She only looked up at him with eyes that he still couldn't decide the color of, though he had taken his share of looks at them on the shore in the sunlight and in the mist. They weren't blue, nor were they green, nor a combination of both. He supposed it might take a bit more study to decide.

He smiled down at her, wished her a good rest, then wandered about the shelves, pretending to look for things until he was certain she was asleep. Then he went directly for what lexicons he could find.

It took him less than an hour to realize that whatever tongue she had been speaking was a tongue not described in any of the books he'd found. He found a handy wall to lean against and considered things he simply hadn't had the heart to before.

He had brought his map with him, the one he'd made of the
Nine Kingdoms and how they had changed over the years. The
unfortunate truth was, the Nine Kingdoms was an enormous collection of lands and peoples. There were lands that remained as
they always had—Neroche, for instance, Durial, Meith, Tòrr
Dòrainn—and others that he'd mapped out easily at Lismòr.

The Council of Kings was made up of nine kings—or, rather,
eight kings and a queen—but there were places that considered
themselves outside the bounds of that council and wouldn't have
frequented it if forced. His grandmother's homeland of An Céin
was a good example. Her father had diplomatic relations enough
with his elvish neighbors, the elves of Tòrr Dòrainn, and to a lesser
extent the nobility of Ainneamh, but King Beusach never would
have treated on any level with a dwarf or a mere man. But a king
he was, and a powerful one.

There were also kingdoms that had been absorbed by other
places. Diarmailt was proof enough of that. Rùnach wasn't entirely
sure that his cousin hadn't gambled away the crown to Stefan of
Wychweald in a game of chance. Wychweald was less of a kingdom than it was a tributary of Neroche, and Stefan currently wore
a title that Miach no doubt considered just above a courtesy. Pen-
rhyn had been in the early days of the world a rather small but
very powerful place. Now all that came from it was a very tasty
sour wine and a great deal of noise about how its seat on the council had always belonged to the kings of that land and so it should
always be. Rùnach suspected there were quite a few who disagreed.

He glanced at Aisling, saw that she slept still, and decided perhaps it was time to be a bit more serious about narrowing things
down. He fetched his map out of his pack, spread it out on the table,
and decided he would start from the west and work his way east.

He immediately dismissed Melksham Island. They spoke sheep
and irrigation there, which was understood readily enough when
emphasized by the point of a sword. Meith had its own tongue, true,
but his aunt was wed to the king of that land and he had learned

well not only the common tongue, several variations of it, but their particular language of magic. Aisling had not come from Meith.

By the time he had cut the world in half and satisfied himself that there was nothing that fit what he'd heard come out of Aisling's mouth, he had a pounding headache and knew he needed either sleep or food.

He walked over and found Aisling with her head on her pack, her hands tucked under her cheek, swathed in both her cloak and his. He fetched a chair to sit in so he might watch over her for a moment or two. Nothing more.

He supposed that if he was to judge her by worldly standards, he wouldn't have said she would garner a second look on any busy street in any busy metropolis. She was not beautiful in the way his aunts and cousins were beautiful, painful to look at, with the magic shimmering in their veins seemingly rendering them unattainable. She was also not lovely in the same way his grandmother Eulasaid was, or any of her daughters, his aunts, or his cousins, half-elven, half-wizardess get, every last one of them worthy of the rapt attentions of the finest portraitist.

Aisling was not.

She was something else entirely, something that words seemed unequal to describing.

Her hair was a very pale blond, hanging around her face unevenly, as if whoever had cut it had done it not at all well. Perhaps she had done it herself in order to escape that terrible life of servitude she hadn't asked for. He supposed there were souls enough in the world who suffered that fate. It gave him pause that he couldn't bring another of them to mind.

He wondered how it was she could touch air or water or night sky and stir them all as if they were solid substances he could have touched himself. And if the situation in her village had been so dire, why had she, an untrained, unskilled lass, been sent to find someone to rescue them? Why not send a seasoned swordsman to do the deed? And why all that haste to find a mercenary only to have that haste be abandoned?

And why was it when he looked in her eyes as he was doing now, he felt as if he had stepped out of time and space and was looking into dreams?

"Were you afraid I would run away?" she asked.

He realized he was likely sitting too close to her to be considered polite, but who could blame him? He felt a certain sense of protectiveness where she was concerned. Sitting nearby on the off chance she required aid was simply the chivalrous thing to do.

"Something like that," he managed.

She sat up and dragged her hand through her hair. "I'm not sure if I feel better or worse."

"I think food might help either way," he said. "Let's seek out the kitchens and see what's available."

"Did you find what you were looking for?"

"Not yet, but I will."

"I imagine so," she said through a yawn. She handed him his cloak, then hesitated suddenly. "I have no gold to buy food."

"I have enough for the both of us."

She looked at him, her expression very grave. "I'm not sure how to repay you."

"Secrets?" he asked lightly.

"I wonder if they need a floor scrubbed instead?"

"I imagine they will feed us out of pity," he said wryly. "We'll discuss floors and secrets later when the need truly arises." He rose wearily to his feet and held out his hand to help her up. "Let's be off before we haven't the energy to get there."

She nodded and followed him out of the library. He had left their packs behind, but he imagined no one would walk off with them. The lesser librarian's magic would see to that.

He walked with Aisling along passageways and outside through the gardens to reach the kitchens. He realized only as he'd left her behind for the third time that she seemed to find something rather interesting about the greenery. He stopped and walked back to where she was plucking something off a budding rosebush.

"What is it?" he asked.

She held up a single strand of silver, no thicker than a strand of hair, though obviously fashioned of an otherworldly substance. "I keep seeing these."

He was almost speechless at finding that once she had the magic in her hand he could see it as well. "Interesting."

She studied it, then looked at him. "Camanaë."

He felt for somewhere to sit down and only succeeded in putting his hand into the middle of a very thorny rosebush. He cursed, sucked on his thumb, and tried to look casual.

"What?"

"That is what this . . . is," she said, looking at him helplessly.

"Is it?"

She swallowed, hard. "Is it magic?"

"Ah—"

She waited for him to finish. He couldn't. All he could do was stare at her and remind himself that he was far too old to be squirming under the piercing gaze of a woman who could draw strands of magic out of thin air.

Her eyes narrowed. "That is my question for the day and you must tell the truth."

He might have believed she wanted the truth if she hadn't sounded as if she would rather have heard anything but.

He took a careful breath, then nodded. "It is."

"How do you know?"

He knew he either had to lie or say nothing. So he said nothing.

"But there is no such thing as magic," she protested, looking as if she were very near to weeping.

He could only look at her, because there was nothing he could possibly say to make the truth any easier to bear. He just didn't understand why the knowing of it grieved her so.

She looked away, down at what she held aloft on her finger. "It isn't fashioned from anything," she said, her voice barely audible. "It just is. As if it were a thread from a cloak snagged on this as someone walked by." She looked at him, then. "What is Camanaë?"

Rùnach felt a little winded. "It is a type of magic," he said, when he thought he could speak easily. "It is also a place, very small, tucked in amongst other places."

She dangled the strand of magic from her pinched thumb and pointer finger. Even Rùnach could see how it sparkled in spite of the lack of sunshine. It was, he had to admit, a very beautiful magic. He was partial to Fadaire because it was his birthright and it was extremely powerful, but he was also heir to Camanaë through his father's mother, who was the granddaughter of the wizardess Nimheil, who had woven her tears into a famous blade, the name of which he honestly couldn't bring to mind at the moment. That might have been because Aisling was looking at him as if he had answers she might want to have. That look made him unaccountably nervous.

"It is very elegant," she said with a frown.

"It is an elegant magic," he agreed, trying to look about surreptitiously for a place to place his arse before he landed full into that damned rosebush. "Matriarchal, as it happens. I think it might have been Friona of Camanaë to first lay her hand on the spring of power in that land and claim it for her own. Her husband, if I remember aright, had just eaten most of a half bushel of overripe peaches and found himself indisposed for the afternoon, else he might have found the spring first and the destiny of that realm would have been forever changed."

She shut her mouth, then smiled. "You can't be serious."

"I am," he said, finding he had to smile in return. The woman was, he had to admit, so earnestly grave most of the time that when she smiled, she became . . .

Beautiful. She became beautiful.

"I think you need to eat," she said suddenly. "You look unwell."

He wasn't sure he wanted to think about how he looked. *Besotted* was definitely not the word he was searching for. He nodded firmly. "I think I might be feverish. Perhaps we would both benefit from food and a place to sit."

"All this talk of legends leaves one hungry for something substantial, does it not?"

He would have argued the point with her, but she looked at him so quickly and with such a haunted look in her eye, that he couldn't.

"Absolutely," he said. He offered her his arm. "Shall we?"

She looked at his arm as if she had no idea what to do with it, though he was certain he'd escorted her thus before. Then again, with that woman, he was honestly not quite sure what was dream and what wasn't. He reached for her hand, tucked it into the crook of his elbow, then nodded up the path.

"Things will seem easier with a full belly."

She nodded, though she didn't look convinced. She looked at the thread of Camanaë she had laid back onto the rosebush, shook her head slowly, then didn't protest when he led her away.

Two hours after having managed a meal for them without garnering undue notice and managing further to get himself back to the library before he couldn't stay awake any longer, he woke and wished he'd had an entire night's sleep and not just a nap. He sat up, rubbed his bleary eyes, and found Aisling sitting at the table with a rather large stack of books.

She was reading, though looking rather less than pleased with her efforts. He pushed himself to his feet with a groan, stumbled over to the table, and collapsed into a chair around the corner from her. He forced himself to sit up with his elbows on the table.

"What are you looking for?" he asked with a yawn.

She started as if he'd poked her with a hot fire tong. She shifted. "Nothing in particular."

"Which is why you're so irritated at not being able to find it."

She looked terribly uncomfortable. Rùnach couldn't say he was a particularly adept reader of faces—though Soilléir had certainly been a master at it—but he could spot a lie coming at him from fifty paces.

"I am looking for myths."

He leaned back in his chair and propped his ankle up on the other knee, trying to look as unassuming as possible. These were details he found himself rather more interested in than perhaps he should have been.

"Myths?" he asked casually. "What sort?"

She shrugged, though she looked very nervous and didn't manage it as smoothly as she would have liked. "Things that don't exist. You know what I'm talking about."

"I've forgotten."

She glared at him. "Wizards, bejeweled caverns under the mountains belonging to dwarves where they pluck already faceted diamonds from the ceiling to spend in creating even more lovely halls, perhaps dragons. Elves too, though I'm willing to allow that there might be the odd thing I've read about that might exist." She looked at him seriously. "A pegasus, for example."

"There is that," he agreed.

"I still don't believe in magic."

"I know."

She sat back and looked around her. "Have you ever seen so many books in one place at one time? Well, save Lismòr, of course."

He almost didn't know how to respond. The library at Lismòr was very well stocked, he had to admit, but it paled in comparison to the library at Buidseachd, a place he had haunted for a score of years. He had heard tales that the library in Diarmailt contained so many books it took a small army of librarians to simply reshelve them all.

The thought made him a little light-headed, truth be told.

"You're overwhelmed as well," she noted.

"Aye," he agreed, for he was, and not just by the thought of all the things he could discover with the right amount of searching.

She looked around. "I have looked in the most obvious places here. I may have missed something, given that this library is so large."

Rùnach had to bite his tongue to keep from telling her that these were only the books put out for public use, that the king of Neroche had a vast library on the second floor for his own personal use, for then she would wonder how he knew that and that would lead to questions he simply didn't want to answer at present.

She would think him a myth, no doubt.

"And you can't let me help you?" he asked, though he didn't have to see her shake her head to know what she would answer.

"Nay, but I thank you just the same." She paused. "I think I might need to search elsewhere."

"Tor Neroche, perhaps?"

She put her hand over the uppermost book. "I might find what I'm looking for there." She looked at him carefully. "A mercenary for my quest as well, perhaps."

He nodded, though he wasn't as sure as he should have been about the potential for either finding the facts she needed or the mercenary. What he was sure of, though, was that Miach would have ministers from all over the world haunting his halls, trying to curry his favor. If there were a place in the whole of the Nine Kingdoms where he could casually mention a word or two and have an answer about its origins, it was Tor Neroche.

"When should we leave?" she asked.

"Now," he said. "I'll help you stack books."

"But you won't look at them?"

He looked at her seriously. "Is your errand so secret then, Aisling?"

She let out her breath slowly. "I don't know anymore," she said, sounding more weary than he'd ever heard her. She shook her head. "I just don't know any longer what to believe."

He watched her tidy up her small piles of books, carefully put Nicholas's book in the leather pack he'd given her and filled, no doubt, with useful things, then simply stop and look at him. He settled her cloak around her shoulders, took her pack and his in his hand, then escorted her from the library.

There were none but the night guards to see them out the front door, but he thought that might have been a boon. He stood on the front steps of Chagailt, looked out over the landscape that was revealed thanks only to the heavy clouds that seemed to shimmer with a light of their own, then looked at Aisling.

"One question."

She took an unsteady breath, then nodded.

"If you tell me the details of your errand, what will happen to you?"

Her expression was very grave. "I will die."

He almost fell off the steps. Perhaps even more surprising than her answer was that he had absolutely no doubt that she believed it fully.

He wasn't sure that he didn't as well.

He stared at her, trying to mask his surprise, then took a deep breath, reached out, and gathered her into his arms. He was quite sure that she had never in her life been held, perhaps not even by her parents. She was stiff as a plank, but she wasn't pulling away and she wasn't screaming, so he thought perhaps he hadn't terrified her beyond measure. He released her, then fussed with her cloak, pulling her hood up over her hair and adjusting the cloth over her shoulders. He would have to add thanks for new, quite serviceable clothing in that note he had yet to pen to the former king of Diarmailt.

"Let's be off, shall we?" he said quietly.

She was looking at him with absolutely enormous eyes. "Very well," she whispered.

It was all he could do not to hug her until she begged him to cease. Instead, all he could do was smile, reach for her hand—which didn't seem to trouble her—and walk down the stairs with her.

He turned them toward the forest and hoped that his horse was waiting. He didn't particularly care to think about the walk they would have if he wasn't.

I will die.

He suppressed the urge to shake his head. The woman was a mystery. And as he'd admitted before to more than one person, he loved a good mystery.

With any luck, he thought he might manage to limit his interest in her to solving hers.

Eighteen

❧

Aisling woke to the feeling of falling. She jerked and managed to keep her seat only because Rùnach was holding on to her so tightly. She dragged her sleeve across her eyes, then looked into the wind, trying to get her bearings. The sky was rapidly lightening, so she knew she had slept yet another night away whilst Rùnach had obviously not. The only sleep he'd had in the past three days had been when his horse had deigned to descend from his heavenly lea to feed and water himself. She had spent that time demanding that Rùnach sleep at least an hour or so whilst she stood guard over him with his sword drawn.

Of course, she'd had no idea what she would do if a ruffian attacked, but the sword had made her feel fierce.

She leaned back and shouted over the wind. "What are we doing?"

"I saw something," Rùnach said loudly. "Someone waving at us from down below."

She couldn't imagine how he could have seen that with the

rising sun blinding him, but she wasn't going to argue. She had to admit she was grateful to be flying and not walking, but still the thought of getting out of the saddle and using her own legs for a bit was a welcome one.

Their mount didn't seem to be particularly eager to land, but he was nothing if not obedient when Rùnach insisted. He took his time at it, however, as if he saw something that made him unhappy. Aisling didn't see anything untoward, though she was surprised to find they had left the plains behind and had now come up upon a more mountainous and forested sort of terrain. She had never seen its like before, so she wasn't unhappy to have a closer look.

Once the pegasus had landed, she swung her leg over the saddle and slid down to the ground before Rùnach could stop her. She was so grateful to feel solid earth under her feet, all she could do was hold on to the horse's saddle and wait until her legs were steady beneath her. She heard Rùnach jump down behind her, then felt his hand briefly on her back.

"Stay here," he said quietly.

She lifted her head and looked at him in surprise. "Why?"

He simply shot her a warning look and walked away. She considered, then removed her bow and quiver of arrows from off the saddle. There was no sense in not protecting Rùnach if she were able to, though she imagined by the way he had his hand on his sword, he wasn't going to need all that much protection. Why he felt the need for that when he'd been the one to decide to land, she didn't know.

She eased around the pegasus's nose, then stood there, an arrow fitted to the string. The horse put his nose in her back, as if he were telling her he would keep her safe.

She looked past Rùnach and was surprised to see a lad standing there thirty paces away, a lad she recognized. She walked over to stand next to Rùnach before she thought better of it.

"'Tis Losh," she said in surprise.

"What is he doing here, I wonder," Rùnach murmured. He glanced at her. "Stay behind me."

She nodded, though she had a hard time not looking at Losh. It was such a surprise to see him there, she could hardly fathom it.

Rùnach walked forward. "Losh, is it?"

"It is," Losh said, looking both exhausted and unnerved. He pointed behind Rùnach. "And what would that beast be, sir? A demon horse, perhaps—"

"Nay, nothing so exotic, I assure you," Rùnach said. "Why are you here, lad?"

Losh came closer and held out a sheaf of paper. "I was sent from Lord Weger to give you this. He said he thought you would be coming this way and to wait for you." He paused. "'Twas a terrible journey, this one."

"Did you *walk*?" Rùnach asked in surprise.

"Nay, took the ship as far as Magh, then bought a horse and rode like the wind."

Rùnach took the sheaf of paper but didn't unfold it. "Good of Weger to think of us."

"He is a generous sort," Losh agreed. He looked over Rùnach's shoulder. "And about your horse, my lord—"

"Common enough in some parts, I'd imagine," Rùnach said.

Aisling listened to them make idle conversation, but somehow the words grated against her ears. Not Rùnach's actually, but Losh's. She realized she hadn't spent perhaps enough time with him to know, but there was something about him that was . . . dark. She listened to him speak of his journey and found herself rather surprised that Losh had managed it, though she supposed if Weger had demanded it of him, Losh would have walked on hot coals.

"But how much does a horse like that cost, my lord?" Losh asked, wide-eyed.

"Oh, I wouldn't know," Rùnach said easily. "He was a gift. And I am no lord."

"Oh," said Losh, shooting Rùnach a sly look, "you aren't, are you? A pity for you that I know exactly what you are."

Aisling watched as Losh disappeared and in his place stood a man with a terrible scar down one cheek. It was red, angry, matching perfectly his expression.

Rùnach grabbed her arm, crushing the sheaf of paper in the process, and hauled her behind him.

"We have nothing you want," he said calmly.

"Oh, you think not?" the other man said in a deceptively calm voice. "I think I'll be the judge of that."

Aisling looked around Rùnach's shoulder and saw something come tumbling out of the other man's mouth, words that were black, barbed, dripping with something that she instinctively shrank away from. She recognized the words; it was the common tongue, only corrupted, twisting and turning. It reached out toward Rùnach like a mighty rushing wind, poised to swirl around him and take him prisoner.

And then she realized with a start that the man facing them was the same one who had stabbed her through the heart with a blade.

She stepped around Rùnach and fitted an arrow to the string. The man saw her do it, paused in his evil spewing, and laughed. That was worse, for the things that appeared in the air to join in his mirth were—

"Don't look," Rùnach warned.

"Oh, can she see?" the man asked, looking frankly quite delighted. "Perhaps there is something here I want after all."

"When I'm dead," Rùnach said calmly.

"Given that you have nothing to give me, as you've said, then perhaps that would be the kindest thing for you," the man said. "Can you see what I'm doing, little lad, or is it just your wee wench there with the sight? Shall I make it visible for you and whomever else might be looking?"

"I don't think either of us cares," Rùnach said dismissively, "given that anything you do would be—what is the word I'm looking for? Ah, yes, I have it now." He looked at the scarred man coolly. "Less."

Aisling felt the arrow fall from her fingers and the bow from her hands. The words that were coming out of the man's mouth were worse than the ones before. Those had been barbed, dark, dripping with poison. These were full of despair, hopelessness, and an almost overwhelming suggestion that she and Rùnach both simply give up. She felt rather than saw Rùnach take half a step backward, as if he'd been assaulted by a wind so strong he couldn't stand against it.

Aisling realized at that moment that there was something she didn't want to accept as truth but could no longer deny.

Magic existed.

And the man in front of them was a master at it.

Before she thought better of it, she put the flat of her hand toward him and set air to spinning. Perhaps it was Fate—or, more likely, simply luck—but part of the man's spell became caught up in her flywheel. She knew that wasn't the proper way to spin anything, but it didn't seem to matter. The wheel of air didn't seem to mind that it was pulling into itself threads of despair. Aisling reached for the hopelessness, trying to pluck a single strand out of the wave of it that was about to fall upon her and Rùnach both.

Her hands caught fire.

She looked down at them and couldn't see anything, but they burned with a heat that simply wouldn't abate.

The man facing them laughed.

"Well, what do we have here?" he said, snapping his fingers and destroying her wheel of air. "How in—"

Aisling watched in surprise as he stopped speaking. The words he had been building into such a towering wave of evil fell to the ground in front of him, writhing like snakes for a moment or two before they simply stopped moving and lay still. She looked at the man in time to watch his eyes roll back in his head. He listed to the left, then continued to list until he fell over onto the ground.

Another man, a younger man, stood behind him, holding on to a stout club. Rùnach blew out his breath, then put his arm around her and pulled her close.

"Are you unharmed?"

"I don't know," she said, finding it difficult to be clutched by

Rùnach and keep her hands free of his cloak. "Is that one friend or foe?"

"Friend, assuredly," Rùnach said. He pulled back, then caught sight of her hands. "What in the bloody hell happened to you?" he exclaimed.

She gestured helplessly toward the fallen man, but could find nothing to say. The pain was so intense, she could hardly breathe. She felt the world begin to fade. That, she supposed, was a boon, for it dulled not only the fire on her hands but the sight of what had been left behind by that . . . man's . . . well, whatever it was he had spoken that had come out so foully.

"Miach, help her," Rùnach said, his voice sounding very far away. "Her hands are burned."

Aisling watched the man she assumed was Miach step over his fallen foe, then walk across the polluted ground. She looked down, wondering how he would keep the words from attacking him, then blinked in surprise. Where he had passed, he had left footsteps behind, footsteps of gold and silver. He dropped the club, rubbed his hands together, then smiled.

The footsteps suddenly disappeared along with the remains of the other man's spell.

As well as the pain in her hands.

Aisling looked at him in surprise. "Who are you?"

He opened his mouth, then looked at Rùnach. "Who am I?"

Rùnach gestured toward him with less elegance than he usually used. "This is Miach. Miach, this is Aisling." He reached for her hand, then sighed in relief. "Healed, aye?"

"When the words on the ground disappeared, so did the pain," she said, though she thought she perhaps might like to wash her hands rather soon. She looked at Miach. "Was he a mage?"

"Who?" Miach asked, looking quickly at Rùnach. "A mage?"

"That man there," she said, pointing behind him. "The one who used—" She started to say *magic* but she simply couldn't bring herself to. "I'm not sure what he used. He was, however, masquerading as someone we know, else we wouldn't have landed." She looked up at Rùnach. "Would we?"

Rùnach shook his head firmly. "We wouldn't have." He reached out and clapped a hand on the other man's shoulder. "I think we might be well served to find a refuge nearby. Any ideas?"

Miach said nothing. He simply pointed back over his shoulder, his eyes very wide.

Aisling followed his finger, then felt her mouth fall open.

A castle sat on a bluff, overlooking the valley below it. Well, actually it didn't overlook, it guarded. She moved closer to Rùnach, because she thought she might like to have something to lean against if she felt any fainter than she did at present.

"What is that?" she managed. "*Where* is that?"

"Tor Neroche," Rùnach said, putting his arm around her. "Seems a handy enough place to go, don't you think?"

She inched closer to him. "Will they let us in, do you think?"

"One could hope. Perhaps Miach will find a way to sneak us in through the stables."

"Absolutely," Miach said without hesitation. "Easily done."

Aisling found it difficult to look away from the fortress in front of her. She could hardly believe she hadn't noticed it, though it was true they had landed at sunrise and she had been slightly preoccupied with impending doom. All she could do was look at the keep and try to keep her mouth from hanging open in astonishment. It wasn't so much a palace as it was a bastion of security.

"Do you like it?" Miach asked mildly.

She looked at him and found he was as difficult to look away from as was the keep, though for different reasons. He was terribly handsome, to be sure, but she had almost grown accustomed to Rùnach's face, so this Miach's handsomeness didn't affect her. There was something else about him, though, something she couldn't find a name for . . .

She let her curiosity slip past her without holding on to it and concentrated on what he'd asked her. She nodded toward the castle. "I've never seen anything like it." She considered it a bit longer. "I'm not sure it cares what I think."

"You might be surprised."

She looked at Rùnach. "We would be safe there, wouldn't we?"

"We would."

The thought crossed her mind that she shouldn't accustom herself to any sort of security, not from Tor Neroche, not from Rùnach, but at the moment and after the morning she'd had already, she was thoroughly glad for both.

She realized suddenly that the men she was standing with knew each other perhaps better than she would have thought to suspect, if the looks they were exchanging were any indication. She decided to question Rùnach, though she knew she would pay a price for it in answers herself.

"How do you know him?"

Rùnach sighed lightly. "He's wed to my sister."

"That's handy," she noted.

He smiled. "Aye, it is, actually." He released her and handed her her bow and arrow. "And since we know him and he has at least access to the stables, I think perhaps we should be off sooner rather than later."

She took her weapon but couldn't move. "What will they think when we arrive on that?" She nodded toward their pegasus, on the off chance Rùnach hadn't understood what she'd been getting at.

Rùnach looked at Miach. "Well?"

Miach only smiled faintly. "I imagine they've seen all kinds of things that would unnerve and unsettle more rational lads and lassies. I wouldn't worry."

Aisling looked around her, then frowned. "Where is your horse, Miach?"

He gestured to the trees a fair distance away. "Left him there, of course, in the interest of stealth."

She was vaguely dissatisfied with that answer, though she wasn't sure why. She frowned thoughtfully, then looked at the note the man pretending to be Losh had handed Rùnach. "What does that say?"

He unfolded the sheaf of paper, then shook his head. "'Tis blank, of course." He looked at the man lying there unconscious, then at Miach. "I'm not sure what you intend to do, but I cannot aid you with that one."

Miach clasped his hands behind his back and smiled briefly.

"Not to worry. Perhaps Mistress Aisling would care to stow her gear, as it were, then you two could be off on the rest of your journey? I'll catch up as quickly as I can."

Aisling nodded, then walked over to attach her bow to the pegasus's saddle.

Iteachhhhh . . .

She jumped a little, then looked around her. It occurred to her with a bit of a start that the voice in her head belonged to Rùnach's horse. She stepped up to stand at the side of his head and look him in the eye. "Iteach?"

He tossed his head and whinnied.

She put her hand to her head to stop it from spinning. Truly she was going to need time at some point where she could sit and try to unravel truth from fiction, fact from legend. She stroked his nose and looked around her, trying to distract herself.

That was when she saw the body.

She walked past Iteach, if that's what his name truly was, and over to a young man who was lying still as death on the ground some thirty paces away from where she'd been standing. She realized as she drew closer that it was none other than Losh himself. She sank to her knees next to him, then put her hand out and touched his cheek only to find it was still warm.

But she suspected he was dead.

She jumped to her feet and stumbled backward. She had never seen death before. It wasn't something that happened in Bruadair, at least not where anyone could see it. She stared down at the lad in horror, then realized there was something tucked into the collar of his tunic. She thought it might have been a sheaf of paper, but she didn't dare reach for it.

"Rùnach," she called, only to realize he was standing next to her. He put his hand on her arm and pulled her back, away from the body.

He squatted down next to Losh, then put his fingers to the boy's neck. He paused, then bowed his head and sighed. He looked up at her.

"Dead," he said quietly. "And recently gone, unfortunately."

She swallowed with difficulty. "That man killed him, didn't he? That man with the scar."

Rùnach nodded. He reached out and closed Losh's eyes, then paused. He very carefully pulled the sheaf of paper out from the lad's tunic, then read it. Aisling looked over his shoulder and read it as well. If Losh had perhaps come looking for the both of them, there was no reason she shouldn't know why.

> *Rùnach, Lothar escaped and is looking for you. Heard rumor he isn't the only one, now. And you won't be the only one they're after, trust me.*
>
> *SW*

Aisling glanced at Rùnach. He was looking off into the distance as if he saw things she could not. He suddenly folded the missive and tucked it into a pocket.

"Let's go."

"Wait," she protested, "what did any of that mean?"

He looked at her seriously. "What it means is that we should seek the shelter we've been offered until I decide what we'll do."

"What did he mean, *you won't be the only one they're after*?" she asked.

"Weger is cryptic," he said. "We'll take it apart later, when we're safe."

She stopped him before he tried to take her elbow, presumably to steer her in the direction he wanted her to go. She gestured to Losh. "What will we do with the body?"

"We'll ask Miach to ask a handful of lads to come bury him."

She didn't move. "Who did Weger mean by Lothar?" She hadn't had much time to read, she would admit, but she had pulled out the small, very rare book Nicholas had gifted her and read for a bit whilst Rùnach slept for those very brief periods of time. "The only Lothar I've ever heard mentioned was the son of Yngerame of Wychweald."

Rùnach stopped trying to steer her and simply looked at her. "What else do you know about him?"

"He has been the enemy of the kings of Neroche for . . ." She had to take a deep breath. "For centuries. The book Lord Nicholas gave me claimed he was a mage." She looked up at him searchingly. "That can't be the same man Weger was talking about." She paused. "Can it?"

Rùnach dragged his hand through his hair. "It can."

She gestured to the fallen man behind them, the man who had spewed out such vile words that had seemed so much more than mere words. "Who is that man?"

"The black mage of Wychweald," he said quietly. "Lothar."

She wanted to smile, to dismiss his words as a jest, but she knew he was absolutely serious. All she could do was stand there and try not to shake. "But mages . . . they don't exist."

He only looked at her, silent and grave.

"I think I recognized him," she said unwillingly.

"That's because, love, he is indeed the one who stabbed you at Gobhann."

She had known it, of course, but hearing it put into words was substantially more unsettling than she would have thought it might be. Rùnach's hands were immediately on her arms, which she supposed saved her an undignified sprawl. She held on to his forearms until she thought she could stand on her own. She also drew in an unsteady breath that if she hadn't known better she would have sworn felt a bit like a sob. She looked up at Rùnach.

"Nothing is as I thought it was," she whispered.

He reached out and tucked hair behind her ear and this time he looked less uncomfortable. "Aisling," he said very quietly, "there are many things in the world that *are* as you think they are. But then there are some that aren't. This might be properly classified as the latter."

"I'm not sure if I want to weep or find those responsible and . . . and . . ." She looked at him. "I'm not sure what I want to do. I just know it wouldn't be *that*." She gestured at the fallen lad. "Not that. Why would Lothar of Wychweald do that?"

"Because he is a black mage and that is what they do."

"Is that why there was evil coming out of his mouth—nay, you've no need to answer that. I think I can divine that on my own, thank you just the same."

He was gaping at her. "What did you say?"

"Those words," she said. She frowned. "Couldn't you see them?"

He took a deep breath, then nodded. "A few of them. I could feel their effect more than see them, though." He put his hands very lightly on her shoulders. "I also saw your wheel."

"I didn't know what else to do."

"You purchased us the time we needed," he said grimly, "for which I am very, very grateful, though I'm sorry you had to be a part of any of it." He sighed and reached out to put his arm around her shoulders. "Let's be off, unless there's anything else you want to tell me."

"Your brother-in-law left footprints in Lothar's evil."

He flinched. "Did he?"

"Gold and silver ones," she said. "Very lovely."

He looked a little winded. "Anything else?"

"The pegasus's name is Iteach."

He bowed his head and huffed out a bit of a laugh, then looked at her. "And how in the world do you know that?"

"He told me so."

He shook his head, still smiling. "Woman, I am going to go very far into your debt one of these days and leave you with no choice but to answer an endless list of my questions. And the first will be, who *are* you?"

"I don't know," she said honestly. "No one of consequence."

"That's mine and you can't have it," he said with another smile. "You'll have to find something else to say." He nodded toward Iteach. "You go discuss it with Iteach whilst I finish up with Miach. The sooner we're behind Tor Neroche's puny walls, the happier I'll be."

"Puny?"

He only shook his head, squeezed her shoulders, and deposited her with his horse before he walked off to talk to Miach about things she suspected she would very much like to hear but wasn't sure she could stomach at present.

She made certain her bow was securely fastened to the saddle, then reached into the saddlebag and came up with a curry comb. She put her hand on Iteach's nose and looked him in the eye.

"Shall I pretty you a bit before we make our grand entrance?" she said lightly. "It is Tor Neroche, after all."

He purred at her.

She smiled in spite of herself and set to work. She had a dozen questions she wanted answers to, but since all of them seemed to lead back to black mages and magic, she wasn't sure she could ask any of them.

Iteach bumped her elbow, distracting her. She smiled at him, grateful for the interruption, and set to her work.

And she couldn't help but wish Rùnach would hurry.

Nineteen

❖

Rùnach looked over his shoulder and saw Aisling grooming his horse. He decided that there was no time like the present to convince his brother-in-law to keep his bloody mouth shut. He walked over to find Miach wrapping Lothar in spells even Rùn- ach could see the echo of. Miach looked up at him.

"Perhaps Gobhann is less secure than I dared hope."

"Perhaps Weger was more distracted," Rùnach said grimly. "I have no idea how Lothar escaped, but I wouldn't doubt there was both subterfuge and death involved."

Miach straightened and looked at him. "I'm sure I'll have the details eventually."

"What will you do with him?"

"I'm still thinking about it. He's secure enough for the moment."

Rùnach wasn't too proud to show a little gratitude, though he drew the line at falling upon his brother-in-law's neck and bawling like a bairn. "I appreciate the rescue," he said, though that seemed an inadequate expression of just how grateful he'd been.

Miach only shrugged. "I think your lady had things well in hand, actually, but I was happy to do my part." He slid Rùnach a look. "Are you going to explain what I just saw, or must I guess?"

"Neither," Rùnach said with a weary smile. "Ask me later."

"Might I ask now what you're doing here?"

"Can you stop yourself?"

Miach smiled at him. "I'm pleased your time in Gobhann didn't sour you."

"I won't say what it *did* do to me, though I suppose I wasn't there long enough to be truly corrupted by the place."

"Well, you seemed to have acquired a lovely gel over there." Miach blinked innocently. "Does she have any idea who you are?"

"None," Rùnach said. "She's lived a rather sheltered life."

"How sheltered?"

"She believes elves, dwarves, and dragons are figments of fevered bardly imaginations."

Miach looked at him for a moment in silence, blinked as if he were trying to decide if he'd heard things aright or not, then smiled. "I'm not exactly sure how to respond to that."

"Trust me," Rùnach said dryly, "I'm still working on something appropriate myself." He glanced at Aisling, found she was still busy with Iteach, then turned back to his brother-in-law. "Might we seek refuge at Tor Neroche in truth? We are, as you have seen, somewhat vulnerable at the moment."

"Do you need anonymity?"

"It seems to have worked well for those who have gone before me," Rùnach said pointedly.

Miach raised his eyebrows briefly. "That is definitely something you should rethink, but I'm happy to humor you. My only suggestion would be that you keep your hood pulled up around your face if you decide to wander the halls. I think you look more like your mother's side of the family than your father's, but that's just me. There are several, I imagine, who would recognize you just the same."

"And will you keep your hood up around your face as well, or just avoid the entire problem by keeping us in the stables?"

"I could try to lie," Miach offered.

"You're terrible at it. Always have been."

Miach shrugged. "Fortunately my need for subterfuge and hedging has passed, though I can see your need for both has not." He paused, then looked thoughtfully at Iteach. "I would venture to say that lad is Angesand get, perhaps out of Nimheil's stables?"

Rùnach blew his hair out of his eyes. "Who don't you know?"

"Oh, I've never met Nimheil," Miach said quickly. "I haven't hit upon the proper hostess gift yet, though I was thinking your sister might be enough. We're planning a visit." He looked at Rùnach with another frown. "What have you told your lady there about your steed?"

"Nothing. Nicholas made up a tale of some sort that I honestly can't remember at the moment. And she's not my lady."

Miach studied him. "How much do you like her?"

Rùnach attempted a dismissive smile. "Do you think I would fall in love with the first woman I met after a score of years as a monk at Buidseachd?"

"I don't know," Miach asked. "Would you?"

Rùnach decided it was perhaps wisest to just ignore the question lest he be forced to state the obvious, which was that his brother-in-law was a bloody romantic. "All I ask is that you make whatever you do believable," he said, "if for no other reason than I don't want her hurt. That is answer enough for your loose tongue."

"Hmmm," Miach said, sounding far too interested in things he should have left alone.

"Don't make me thrash you in your great hall in front of your entire family," Rùnach warned. "And don't think I wouldn't."

Miach only smirked in a way that annoyed Rùnach so much, he thought he might seriously consider making good on his threat, then pushed past him to go talk to Aisling. Rùnach turned to make certain his sister's husband wouldn't make things dodgier than they already were.

He watched Miach greet Aisling with chivalry that did him credit, though Rùnach had to remind himself that there would be questions as to why he had bloodied his brother-in-law's nose if he didn't restrain himself. He also had to remind himself that he had indeed passed a score of monkish years behind very tall walls and he certainly could not become entangled with the first female he encountered upon his release. He also had to remind himself that he could, if he wanted to, take his place as one of Sìle's grandsons and live a very exclusive, very pampered, very *mythical* life full of the most beautiful of kings' daughters come to tempt an elven prince.

They might even have been able to overlook his scarred face and ruined hands, if the inducement had been generous enough.

"You have magic."

Rùnach dragged himself back to the present to realize that Aisling was speaking. Not only was she speaking, she was studying Miach with a type of scrutiny that should have made both him and his brother-in-law very nervous.

"A little," Miach conceded.

Aisling reached out and plucked something off Miach's shoulder. Rùnach found that, as usual, he could see it once it was in Aisling's hand. Miach obviously could as well, for his eyes fair fell from his head. Aisling was only staring at what she was holding draped over a finger. She looked at Miach.

"I'm not sure," she said, looking very pale and slightly ill, "but I think this is a strand of magic."

"Is it?" Miach said faintly.

"'Tis purple."

"Is it?"

"Is it yours?"

"Ah," Miach said helpfully.

Aisling put it back on his shoulder, then patted him. "You might want to be more careful where you walk so you don't pick any more of those up. I think only royalty is supposed to use purple, aren't they?"

Miach started to babble something. Rùnach didn't bother trying to make sense of it. He simply gave his sister's husband a bit of a shove and put himself in front of Aisling.

"He's always getting into things he shouldn't."

Miach cleared his throat. "It comes from being wed to *his* sis—"

Rùnach elbowed Miach firmly in the ribs. "I think we should

be going. I think Iteach agrees. Fortunate for us, isn't it, that he has wings?"

Aisling looked at them both as if they'd lost their wits. She turned and walked off, casting Lothar an uneasy look.

"Brilliantly done," Rùnach muttered.

"What was I supposed to say?" Miach asked defensively. "Who the hell *is* that?"

"I have no idea," Rùnach said. "I have no idea where even to begin in determining that."

"Is there a reason that you don't want her to know who *you* are?"

Rùnach shrugged and attempted a lightness in his tone he most certainly didn't feel. "There is no point, for what is there to know? I have marginal skill with a sword and a long and gloriously ordinary life stretching out in front of me."

"For hundreds of years."

"I'll worry about that later," Rùnach said dismissively. "And since that is the case, I've told her nothing, because there is nothing to tell."

"No sense in trying to convince her of the reality of myths, eh?"

Rùnach pursed his lips. "Something like that."

"Why are you here with her, then?"

"Because she's looking for a swordsman to save her village from a cruel, usurping overlord, and after Weger threw me out of Gobhann, I decided it might be a good use of my time to look after her until the deed was done."

Miach shut his mouth. "I see."

"I don't dare hope for that." He nodded toward Lothar. "What about him, in truth?"

"You two go on ahead. I'll bind him and stuff him in that crofter's hut over there, then set spells over him for the moment."

Rùnach looked at him in surprise. "Can you?"

Miach lifted an eyebrow. "Do you mean will I or am I able to?"

Rùnach dragged his hand through his hair. "Sorry, Miach. I don't doubt your abilities."

Miach put his hand on Rùnach's shoulder. "I wouldn't blame you if you did, actually, and you would be justified in it. As it happens, however, I am fairly good with unconscious mages and I'm continually surprised by what the land aids me in doing."

"Adhémar was an ass."

Miach smiled. "Aye, well, there is that. He could have been a better steward of things, but perhaps he was looking elsewhere."

"Aye, toward the nearest tap." Rùnach looked at Lothar, then at Miach. "It isn't as if I could help you any, short of driving my sword through his heart."

Miach shook his head slowly. "He owns some of Sosar's power, if nothing else. I'm not sure your cousin would want it back now that it's been mixed with Lothar's, but I can't decide that for him." He smiled grimly. "It would be easier to do him in, perhaps, but something stops me."

"Your annoying desire to do good at all costs," Rùnach said with a sigh, "which I have to admit I admire."

"You should," Miach said cheerfully, "since I learned it at your knee. Ah, here is our lady fair and your horse who looks primed and ready to flap off into the distance."

Aisling was indeed leading Iteach by the reins. She looked at Miach with a frown. "You don't think they'll mind if we come?"

"I think I can guarantee that you will be quite welcome," Miach said, "and I'm sure accommodations are to be found elsewhere besides the stables. Let me tidy up here, then I'll hurry on ahead. You two take the long way, won't you? There is a plethora of lovely vistas in the area."

"That is very kind," Aisling said quietly.

Miach opened his mouth—no doubt to weave more of his very dangerous lies—but shut it. Rùnach supposed that had been thanks to the glare he himself had offered.

He gave Aisling a leg up, swung up behind her, and exchanged a final look with his brother-in-law. He didn't doubt that Miach had arrived in some form not his own and would return to Tor Neroche in precisely the same way, well before he and Aisling managed to reach the road leading up to the keep. He could only hope that the front gate guards would allow him in without an excessive and unnecessary number of questions.

He left Miach to his work, turned Iteach back to the south where they wouldn't have to watch either Lothar or Losh as they leapt into the sky, and gave his pony his head.

He was extremely grateful for the rescue.

He just wished he hadn't needed it.

An hour and a bit of vista viewing later, he was walking up to the front gates with both Aisling and his pegasus-turned-horse in tow. Aisling hadn't said anything when Iteach had shed his wings, though Rùnach supposed he shouldn't have been surprised. She had been riding a pegasus for three days and she had just seen Lothar of Wychweald in all his glory. Perhaps she'd simply become numb to things of an otherworldly nature.

The massive front gates were standing open, but that didn't surprise him. There were magical safeguards there enough, he supposed, and the barbican was simply bristling with well-weaponed men-at-arms. If there had been an assault in truth, an enormous steel portcullis would have dropped immediately and heavy metal gates would have slammed shut behind it. Miach's defenses were not only intimidating but thorough.

He was very relieved to find there was an escort waiting for them, an escort who asked no questions but simply bid them follow him along a more discreet route to the stables.

The servant waited whilst every last one of the stable lads gathered around Iteach to loudly admire him, which he accepted as merely his due. Rùnach turned him over to the stablemaster, who looked as if he'd just been offered the chance to tend to the Fleet of Angesand himself. Rùnach picked up his gear and Aisling's and followed the servant to what he hoped would be a tack room that would be at least free of mice.

What he found, however, was a surprisingly luxurious chamber with a window that looked out over a garden. The bales of hay that were seemingly serving as furniture were covered by plain but clean blankets, two baskets of food were sitting on a low table, and there wasn't a mouse in sight. There was, however, his sister standing there, waiting for them. He set his burdens down just inside the door, then reached out and pulled her into his arms. He hugged her tightly, then kissed her on both cheeks before he released her.

"I didn't expect to see you here," he said, feeling pleased.

"Nor I you," she said, smiling, "yet here we both are." She looked around him and held out her hand toward Aisling. "I'm Morgan, Rùnach's sister."

Rùnach knew that was what she had been called for the whole of her life he hadn't been a part of, so he knew he shouldn't have been startled by it. It was what Miach called her and what she called herself when she wasn't wearing a crown. He supposed there was no point in wishing things could have been different for the both of them. All he could do was be grateful she had been looked after during her youth, in some fashion, and that she now had Mochriadhemiach of Neroche to keep her safe at present.

He could only wish that events in his own life would work out so well.

Aisling shook Mhorghain's hand, studying her as if she couldn't quite decide how to take her. "I am Aisling."

"You both look as if you need a decent sleep," Mhorghain said, waving them on to a bale of hay, "but perhaps food first. This isn't grand, but Miach says you both have come recently from Gobhann, so I imagine you won't be displeased with what's available." She shook her head. "Even I will admit that the food Weger provides for his students is barely edible."

"Especially when 'tis laced with lobelia," Aisling said grimly.

Mhorghain frowned in displeasure, then looked at Rùnach. "Did you beat Baldric properly for his cheek?"

"Didn't have to," Rùnach said cheerfully. "I just told him I was your brother and that seemed to be enough. Anything you have there, though, I'm sure will be a vast improvement over the unidentifiable substances we were favored with there. I will warn you, however, that we have also been a handful of days at Lismòr and Lord Nicholas's cook was outdoing himself at every meal."

Mhorghain shook her head. "I'm not sure this will compare,

but at least it's hot. Sit, the two of you, and let's dive in. I think that's Miach coming along the passageway."

Rùnach sat with Aisling, then attempted to put on his best manners for breakfast. Though Nicholas had thoughtfully provided them with rations for a long journey, Rùnach hadn't been above wishing for something fresh and hot.

Along with his meal, he soon found himself also enjoying things he hadn't had the time nor the heart to think about properly over the past fortnight. First was hands that worked as they should have. He had made do in Buidseachd, grateful beyond measure for the delicate restoration Soilléir had affected, but still doing little more than making do. He supposed Soilléir could have wrought a change of essence and healed him completely, but Soilléir had demurred—for his own unfathomable reasons Rùnach hadn't had the energy or the cheek to question. But now, to be able to do the simple tasks of holding a cup without worrying he would drop it, or pouring wine easily, or grasping the hilt of a sword with strength . . . aye, those were unexpected and very welcome gifts.

As was the pleasure of simply sitting back and enjoying the company of souls he was passing fond of. He watched his sister chatting earnestly with Aisling, though he couldn't have said at the moment what they were discussing. He was too busy watching Mhorghain and wondering how it was possible she could look exactly like their mother but be so much herself instead. Almost as entertaining was watching little Mochriadhemiach of Neroche unable to tear his eyes away from her.

Rùnach shook his head wryly. That one had been trouble from the very beginning, trailing along after his own mother, Desdhemar the Fair and Devious, from the moment he'd been able to toddle, learning all her most appalling habits of poaching spells she shouldn't have been adding to her collection. Rùnach wasn't sure who had begun the association, but there had come a time when Miach and Rùnach's younger brother Ruithneadh had combined forces. He could bring to mind without effort a score of occasions when he'd happened upon Miach and Ruith hiding in a corner, plotting their next adventure.

He supposed, looking back on it now, that Desdhemar and his own mother Sarait had kept Miach and Mhorghain apart simply for Mhorghain's safety, though perhaps they'd known that the youngest prince of Neroche would have fallen for her even at a tender age and then the course of events would have been forever altered. It was perhaps enough to know now that Miach loved Mhorghain and would keep her safe. Their mothers would have been content.

Miach realized he was being observed, looked at Rùnach in surprise, then smiled gravely, as if he knew exactly what Rùnach had been thinking. Which Rùnach supposed he did.

And he supposed if he thought any longer on it, he would grow maudlin past the point of anyone enduring him, so he concentrated on listening to the animated conversation going on between his sister and his, er, well, whatever she was.

"I keep seeing these strands everywhere," Aisling said, waving her hand about, a hand that wasn't very steady. She looked at Mhorghain. "I think I'm going mad."

Rùnach found himself the recipient of a look from his sister that, to his surprise, he had absolutely no trouble understanding. He lifted one shoulder in a helpless shrug. He hadn't had any idea what to say to Aisling without saying far more than he cared to. Mhorghain scowled at him, then shifted so she was facing Aisling squarely.

"You must know the truth."

Aisling looked as if she might be ill. Rùnach agreed wholly with the feeling, though he supposed the warning looks he was sending his sister were never going to be heeded. He jumped a little when he realized Aisling was looking at him.

As if she had become accustomed to looking for him.

He was in trouble.

"She is your sister," Aisling managed. "What truth is she going to give me?"

"I have no idea," Rùnach said. "She does have all Weger's

strictures memorized, though, so I suppose that should ease us both a bit."

Aisling looked no less unsettled, which Rùnach could understand. He put his hand on her back and smiled gravely at her. She relaxed slightly—he felt her do it—then nodded and turned back to look at Mhorghain.

"I am ready."

Mhorghain, to her credit, didn't so much as put on even a hint of a smile. Then again, Rùnach had the feeling she herself had been in Aisling's shoes at one point and knew exactly how the poor gel was feeling.

"I didn't believe in mages either," Mhorghain said bluntly. "I had been raised for as long as I could remember by mercenaries. They had no dealings with magic, unless you call their ability to intimidate and terrify those they came upon with their frowns alone magic."

Aisling nodded.

"Even at Lismòr, there was no talk of anything unusual," Mhorghain continued, "and you can only imagine Weger's opinion on the matter."

"Magic is a prissy, unmanly way of going about one's business," Aisling repeated dutifully.

"Exactly," Mhorghain agreed. "So, whilst I was willing to allow there might possibly be such rot in the world, I wasn't convinced."

Rùnach continued to trail his fingers over Aisling's back, though he wasn't sure if it were more to soothe her or himself. He exchanged a glance with Miach. Thinking about Mhorghain's past was difficult, primarily because it was unsettling to think about how little any of those who had known where she was had been willing to interfere in the course of her life. Not even twenty years of watching Soilléir of Cothromaiche watch events unfold in the world and remain still had erased his first instinct, which was to march out onto the field and change things to save others pain.

"What convinced you?" Aisling asked very quietly.

Mhorghain sighed deeply. "I was asked by Nicholas of Lismòr

to carry a knife to the king of Tor Neroche. It turned out to be Queen Mehar's knife—do you know of her?"

"Rùnach read me the Tale of the Two Swords at Lismòr," Aisling said, "but I thought it was merely a legend."

Mhorghain shook her head, her expression serious. "I thought as you did whilst I was there, but I came to learn that it wasn't so much fiction as it was a faithful retelling of actual events." She smiled briefly. "Holding the knife in my hand was useful in convincing myself of that fact, as you might imagine. Also difficult to deny was the fact that it was slathered with magic."

"How did you know that?" Aisling asked, sounding as if she had absolutely no desire to have the answer.

Mhorghain looked at her steadily. "I could see it."

Aisling leaned back against Rùnach's hand so hard, he flinched. She looked at him in surprise. "Oh, I'm so sorry."

He shook his head and started to pull his arm away, but she shook her head quickly.

"Please, don't."

He wondered if it were possible to throw something very hard at the king of Neroche and not find himself hanged in the courtyard at dawn for his cheek. He settled for glaring at his brother-in-law who was blinking owlishly and doing what he obviously considered his damndest not to smirk. Rùnach ignored him and put his arm around Aisling's shoulders. He didn't protest when she turned a bit and used him as a sturdy place to lean against.

He imagined when she found out the truth about him, she wouldn't be using him as a place to lean, she would be using him as a place to stow any number of her very sharp arrows. That would hurt, because she was an astonishingly fine archer.

He also suspected he wouldn't care for what it did to his tender heart.

Aisling took a deep breath. "If I ask you questions, Morgan," she said quietly, "will you tell me the absolute truth?"

Mhorghain frowned. "Has my brother not been answering your questions?"

"He ignores many of them."

Mhorghain pursed her lips. "Unsurprising. At least he doesn't hedge, for which he deserves some credit." She shot her husband a pointed look, then turned back to Aisling. "And aye, I will answer whatever you ask as truthfully as I'm able. If I cannot answer your question, I will tell you that plainly."

Aisling was trembling. Rùnach would have wrapped his arms around her but didn't dare. He did, however, catch the throw that Miach tossed to him and pulled it over Aisling. What he wanted to be doing was bolting through the door so he didn't have to look at her when she realized all the things he hadn't told her—

Then again, what would he have told her? He had no magic, no claim to any elven throne, no power except the ability to smell a clue in a row of books all the way across an enormous library.

"Are there curses?"

He came back to himself in time to hear his sister snort.

"Of course not."

"In truth?" Aisling asked in surprise.

Mhorghain shrugged. "Spells, I suppose, but not curses." She looked at her husband. "Have you a different opinion?"

Miach shook his head. "I don't believe in curses."

"Weger said the same thing," Aisling said, sounding as if she couldn't quite bring herself to believe it.

Mhorghain tapped the mark over her brow. "Trust Weger. He knows these kinds of things."

"Then what of other things?" Aisling asked. "These creatures of myth?"

"What would those be?" Mhorghain asked.

Rùnach realized that his sister had seen him trying to shake his head slightly in warning but she was thoroughly ignoring him. He looked at Miach, who only leaned back against the wall and put his hands behind his head. He closed his eyes and looked perfectly at ease.

"Elves," Aisling said, "dwarves, those sorts of creatures."

Rùnach was somewhat satisfied to see Neroche's monarch lose his smile thanks to his bride's elbow in his side. Mhorghain looked at Aisling seriously.

"You have led a very sheltered life, haven't you?"

Aisling took a deep breath. "I've been in a weaver's guild all my life. Well, all my life I can remember."

"I understand completely," Mhorghain said promptly. "Nicholas gave me a marvelous education, for which I am most grateful, but I was in Gobhann for six years. That was enough to lead me to disbelieve anything I couldn't poke at with my sword." She paused. "I understand, though, that you can see quite a few things others can't."

"Aye," Aisling said uneasily. "I touched a spinning wheel in an old woman's house, fainted, then woke with this . . . ability."

"Well, it might serve you in a good skirmish, so I wouldn't shun it," Mhorghain said. "And about the rest, well, do you want the truth? Can you bear the truth?"

Aisling laughed a little, a very little. "I'm not sure I want it, but I think I must have it."

"Then I'll give it to you," Mhorghain said matter-of-factly, "but no more than that, lest it prove too difficult at present." She leaned forward with her elbows on her knees and looked at Aisling very seriously. "Elves do exist, as do dwarves, and mages. Some are good, some are evil, but all have magic." She shrugged. "It doesn't change the world, though, does it?"

Aisling took a deep breath. Rùnach watched her as she pulled away from him and shifted slightly so she could look at him.

"Do you have magic?"

He took a deep breath, then shook his head. "I don't."

"Does your horse?"

"Yes."

She frowned slightly, then looked at Mhorghain. "Do you have magic?"

Mhorghain didn't flinch. "Yes."

"Does Miach?"

"Yes."

"Is it evil?"

Mhorghain reached for Aisling's hand. She held it, hard, for a brief moment, then released her. "Aisling, not all magic is evil, not all mages are evil. There is magic that is . . ." She took a deep, steadying breath. "It is so beautiful, it would leave you weeping." She started to say more, then shook her head. "To tell you anything else would be to tell you too much, I think." She looked at her husband. "They are weary and need more than just a picnic here in the hay. Can you not use your influence and find them a place to wash and rest?"

"Already done," Miach said, uncrossing his ankles and sitting up. He put his arm around his wife's shoulders. "I understand hospitality has been extended and a servant awaiting their pleasure. I'm sure discretion is still advised as they traverse the halls, but since their errand is a private one, perhaps that will suit."

Rùnach stood, helped Aisling to her feet, then embraced Miach briefly, slapping him perhaps with more vigor than necessary on the back of the head in return for the smirks barely suppressed. He shot his brother-in-law a warning look as he released him, then reached out and pulled his sister into his arms.

"Thank you," he whispered against her ear.

She only hugged him tightly, then leaned up and kissed his scarred cheek.

"I like her."

He had nothing to say in response to that, because he did too. Unfortunately, nothing would come of it. She had a quest and he had an ordinary life in front of him. He could only imagine her fury when she discovered exactly what he was . . . or, rather, had been.

Mhorghain looked at Aisling, then very carefully put her arms around her and embraced her briefly. She pulled back and smiled at her.

"It is difficult," she said honestly, "to realize that the world is not what you thought it was. I'll promise you this, though: it will grow easier with time."

"Have you always had magic?" Aisling asked, her voice not quite steady.

"Heavens, no," Mhorghain said promptly. "Didn't know I had it, and I would have cut it from my veins if I'd been able to when I found out I did. It can be useful now and again, though I prefer seeing to things with my sword." She looked at Aisling closely. "Do you have any, do you think?"

Aisling shrugged helplessly. "I don't know. I don't think so." She glanced at Rùnach, then back at Mhorghain. "I can spin."

"That's handy," Mhorghain noted.

"Water," Aisling added. "And air, I think." She looked at Rùnach. "Would you say that's all?"

"I would say that Miach needs to go find a drink before he chokes to death," Rùnach said, giving the king of Neroche a bit of a shove in the right direction. He looked at Mhorghain. "She has some unusual gifts. What they mean, I couldn't possibly begin to guess."

"You might have more success at that after a nap," Miach said with a smile. "Morgan and I have our duties to scamper off and see to. We'll catch up for supper, if you like."

Rùnach nodded, thanked his hosts for their hospitality, then waited until his sister and her husband had closed the door behind them before he looked at Aisling.

"Shall we?" he asked politely.

She smiled faintly. "Your sister is very kind."

He smiled in return. "I thought you might like her. Let's see if we can't take advantage of what hospitality we've been offered, then perhaps have a nap. I'm exhausted; what of you?"

"Terrified," she said frankly.

He gathered up their gear, pulled his hood over his face, then opened the door for her. "We're safe here, Aisling. The world can turn a bit longer without us, I imagine."

She looked up at him seriously. "And yet it still turns and time grows short."

He made the appropriate noises of agreement and ushered her out the door, but adjusted his plans as he did so. He would indulge in a bath and wee nap, but then he was going to take up the hunt again.

For her sake and his.

Because she had taken Lothar of Wychweald's spells and spun them on a wheel of air, and it just didn't seem possible to him that an unremarkable girl from nowhere in particular should have that skill.

Twenty

Aisling was beginning to wonder if she would ever manage to keep her mouth closed. She was fairly certain she'd been gaping since they had landed without fanfare a goodly distance from the castle and ridden under its walls that leaned out just the slightest bit, as if the keep itself wanted to make certain anyone brave enough to ride under them understood just how perilous their situation was. That had been just the beginning of the things at Tor Neroche that had left her astonished.

First, there had been that very frank conversation with Rùnach's sister, Morgan. She had spoken about the most appalling things—magic, mostly—as if they were as normal as the endless training that went on inside the unforgiving walls of Gobhann. She'd still been shaking her head as she'd been separated from Rùnach—a rather alarming turn of events, actually—and led off to a chamber where she'd luxuriated in a bath better suited to the needs of a princess. She'd wondered briefly if commenting on the fact that the water was hot instead of icy cold and clean instead of less-than-pristine had been inappropriate, but the servants had been too discreet to react.

She had been swathed in a luxurious dressing gown and offered a seat in front of a roaring fire after which her hair had been combed for her and allowed to dry as she had been left briefly alone with her thoughts. She had wondered just what it was that Miach did in the castle that had won her such delights, but decided perhaps it was better not to know.

She had then been offered the choice between a gown or a tunic and leggings. She had hesitated, but the lure of the gown's fabric had just been too strong to resist. She'd put skirts on over leggings, just in case she needed to make a quick getaway. She had been draped in a cloak that was very light yet so deliciously warm she thought she might never want to take it off. A liveried servant had been waiting just outside the door to take her to she knew not where, but she had followed him just the same.

All of which led her to where she was at present, standing outside a heavy wooden door and watching it be opened by someone who at first glance looked like a prince.

She realized with a start that it was just Rùnach. He thanked her escort, then took her hand and drew her inside a chamber that was so large, her mouth resumed its previous posture of hanging open. She turned around in a circle, looking upward toward a ceiling that she couldn't make out clearly because it was so far above her. The chamber itself was no less magnificent. It wasn't particularly large, she supposed, but it was extremely fine, full of comfortable places to sit, an enormous hearth at one end, and murals of heroic scenes painted upon the walls.

She started to ask Rùnach why they'd been given such a place of luxury, but she made the mistake of looking at him.

He'd had a bath as well, she could tell, and been dressed in clothing that was very discreet, but very well made. She was, after all, a weaver, and could spot poorly made cloth from fifty paces. She realized he had shut the door behind her and was simply leaning against the wall, watching her.

"What?" she asked uneasily.

He shook his head with a smile. "Nothing. Just watching you and wondering what you're thinking."

She gestured weakly to the chamber. "This is . . . well, it is . . ." She had to take a deep breath. "I thought Lismòr was spectacular, but this is something else entirely. That is to say, I've *read* about glorious things of this nature, but I never thought to experience them for myself." She looked up at him. "I feel like I'm *in* one of those tales, if you know what I mean."

He winced, closed his eyes briefly, then looked at her. It was terrible, she decided abruptly, that a man should be so perfectly beautiful. She had stopped seeing his scars long ago. All she saw at present was someone who had been kind to her for reasons she couldn't fathom. He would go off, she was sure, to be fawned over by beautiful women, but for the moment, she was surprisingly glad he was standing there in front of her.

He had, she had to admit, the most amazing pair of green eyes she had ever seen.

Which had absolutely nothing to do with her current quest, of course. She ruthlessly recaptured her good sense and reminded herself of the task before her. She had to find a swordsman willing to go to Bruadair with only the hope of riches and glory as motivation, though now that she was standing there perfectly comfortable and no longer hungry, she had to face the truth she had known full well before but hadn't been willing to acknowledge. To get a soldier to Bruadair she would either have to tell him where to go or lead him there herself. And if she told him where to go, she would fall under the curse and die. But if she led him there herself, she would be captured, labeled a renegade, and put back in the power of her parents and the Guild, because her birthday wasn't until summer, and until the sun set on that birthday, she was not legally emancipated.

Death of her body or death of her soul. It was no wonder she had avoided thinking on it before.

"Aisling."

She pulled her gaze away from nothing and looked up at Rùnach. "Aye?"

He was still leaning against the wall, but she suspected that was a casual pose designed to put her at ease.

"I think I could help you," he said carefully, "if you would give me a few more details about your village."

She shook her head. "You know why I can't."

He looked at her gravely. "Death if you don't find a swordsman, death if you speak of your village, death if you flee the Guild. Is it a land of death, then?"

"I don't know," she said helplessly. "I only saw the inside of the Guild and the pub where I went on the sixnight's end. I don't think the people were happy, but who is?"

He looked at her in astonishment. "Why, many people are, I daresay."

"How can they be?" she asked. "Working from dawn to late in the evening, one day a week where there is freedom from endless, unrelenting greyness, but having not enough money to do anything but pay for a meager meal and go back to a terrible bed in an overfilled dormitory to sleep uneasily until rising and doing it all over again the next week?"

He looked at her as if he'd never seen her before. "Was that how it was?"

She reached for the door. "I think I need to walk."

He caught her before she opened the door, then turned her to face him. He put his hands gently on her shoulders. "Please let me help you."

"I cannot," she said. She looked up at him and realized that her eyes were burning, she who had never wept, not even as a child. "I don't want to die."

He drew her gently into his arms. She began to have trouble breathing, but perhaps that came from gasping for air. And she supposed that came from realizing that for the first time in her very long, weary existence, she was being presented with the opportunity to feel safe courtesy of a man who was offering that safety simply because he was kind.

She let out her breath slowly and allowed herself to indulge in something besides an intense urge to flee. She considered for a moment or two, then slowly put her arms around his waist. It shouldn't have been difficult. She had, after all, ridden on a pegasus for the better part of four days with Rùnach's arms around her, though she supposed that was just his making sure she didn't fall off.

Yet another courtesy offered where he hadn't needed to.

"Thank you," she said finally. She pulled away from him and attempted a smile. "Very kind."

He smiled gravely, as if he were thinking things he simply couldn't put into words, then reached out to tuck her shorn hair behind her ear. He met her gaze. "Does it bother you if I do that?"

She shook her head.

"Was it long?"

"Once," she said with a shrug. "Not any longer."

"It is still beautiful," he said quietly. He took a deep breath, then clasped his hands behind his back. "You don't have to go back there, you know. To wherever there is."

She clutched that dreadful hope for the space of approximately four glorious heartbeats before she realized she had to let it go. "I think I must."

He shook his head, then took her hand and pulled her over to sit down in one of the chairs placed by the doorway. He sat down next to her and looked at her seriously.

"I think you could safely ink *the reality of curses* in the back of that very rare book of myths Lord Nicholas gave you," he said seriously. "And I would put that in the back simply because it's far less possible than anything else you would read there."

"But why would anyone lie about such a thing?" she asked in surprise.

"I don't know," he said frankly. "Why *would* someone lie about such a thing?"

She looked off at the fire across the room, glanced at the scenes of heroic battle painted with great care and no doubt at great expense on the walls, then looked back at Rùnach.

"Because they want to keep their people powerless," she said slowly, "or because they have something they want to keep hidden."

"Exactly."

She wrapped her arms around herself. It was suddenly rather chilly. "I don't understand why anyone would do either."

"Neither do I," he agreed, "but that doesn't change the truth of it. There are many who have no greater wish than to cause harm to those around them, by whatever means."

"Like Lothar?" she asked reluctantly.

"He is a good example of it," Rùnach said. "And as for your situation, unless there is a spell laid upon your land that would have the power to follow you all over the Nine Kingdoms—" He looked at her, then shook his head again. "I don't believe in curses."

"And if it were a spell instead?"

"Then I think you would see it. Don't you?"

She started to speak, then shook her head. She had spent too many years believing fully that she would pay a very dear and exact penalty if she spoke out of turn. She wanted to believe Rùnach was right, but she couldn't bring herself to. After all, what did Bruadair have that anyone would want? There was no magic, no beauty, nothing but endless drudgery. She half wondered, when she allowed herself to wonder, if Sglaimir enjoyed any of his luxuries in that ugly, unrelentingly grey keep she had only ever seen the faintest glimpse of one day when she had been feeling particularly feisty and wandered a few streets from where she should have been.

She looked at him. "I cannot risk it."

He smiled, as if he understood, then looked at her silently for a bit, as if he were trying to come to a decision. "What if you were to prove it to yourself? Which is, I believe, what you've been trying to do in various libraries."

"There is that."

"Then let's make a bargain, you and I. We'll start from opposite ends of the library below. Whoever reaches the middle first with all the answers wins a prize."

She smiled in spite of herself. "And what would that be?"

"Your life," he said succinctly, "and my sanity." He stood and held down his hand. "Shall we?"

She put her hand in his and looked up at him. "You are a very kind man."

"And as I've said before," he said, pulling her to her feet, "you are easy to be kind to. Let's be off, gel, and see what the bowels of Tor Neroche have to offer."

"Will they allow us in?"

"We'll put on our best scholarly miens," he said cheerfully. "That worked out well the last time, didn't it?"

She had to agree that it had. She took his arm, because he offered it, and walked with him out into the passageway.

And she hoped she would find what she needed.

Three hours later, she was tired, cross, and overwhelmed. She had stumbled to a halt initially just inside the library doors—they were a pair of doors that opened grandly, instead of a single one that opened normally—and spent a good five minutes simply trying to catch her breath. *Bowels* had been, she suspected, a deliberate misuse of the word, because whilst she and Rùnach had definitely descended steps to reach the library, they had not ended up in a dark, unpleasant little room. She had no idea how the king of Neroche—who she understood was in residence and sincerely hoped she wouldn't encounter and have to make polite conversation with—had managed to make his library so gloriously full of light, but it was so. If the story of Queen Mehar was fact and not fiction, then the rulers of Neroche possessed magic. Given the marvels of the monarchy's library, she had to concede that their magic might have certainly been on display in the bowels of the keep.

Unfortunately, her search had yielded absolutely nothing. The only mention she had found of Bruadair had been one made a score of years earlier when King Frèam had sat on the Council of Kings and contributed not a single word to the proceedings. Every single history she had read had contained nothing about Bruadair, not even the slightest mention. For all anyone knew, the country didn't exist. If she hadn't spent the first twenty-seven years of her life there, she might have begun to doubt as well.

Rùnach was sound asleep in a chair on the opposite end of the table from her. She rose, walked down to his end, then sat and looked at him.

She had no idea how old he was. He didn't look much over a score-and-five, though she suspected he was older than that. His dark hair was the perfect foil for his fair skin. She was admittedly rather new at admiring exceptionally handsome men, but she supposed it didn't take much practice to note the pleasing breadth of his shoulders or, well, anything else, for that matter. She put her elbows on the table, propped her chin on her fists, and looked until she thought she could consider herself quite properly dazzled.

And then she noticed a dimple appear suddenly in his cheek.

She kicked him under the table, because he deserved it, the lout. He opened his eyes and smiled.

"Flattering."

"I was bored."

He laughed softly and sat up, dragging his hands through his hair. "You are a cruel gel, Aisling. Let's take ourselves out to the lists and you can vent your ire on a target instead of me. My heart is too tender to endure it."

She would have said she doubted that, but she didn't, actually.

He stacked his books in a tidy pile, then looked at her. "Find anything useful?"

"Not a thing."

"Neither did I," he admitted, "which is why a bit of time sticking arrows into targets that resemble my brother-in-law might bring us both pleasure."

"What has he ever done to you?" she asked with a smile. "He's a lovely man, and he quite obviously loves your sister."

"Hence the problem," Rùnach said with a snort, "though you realize I'm not serious. We'll find something equally as interesting to use, I'm sure."

She walked with him from the library and down passageways and hallways. And then she heard a sound. She put her hand out on Rùnach's arm, stopped him, then turned and looked for the source of the noise. She left him standing there and made her way back down the passageway, turning down a little hallway that terminated in a modest doorway in what she was sure was in a more obscure part of the castle.

She knocked, was invited to enter, then came to a teetering halt.

How so many windows had been fit into one wall, she couldn't have said, though she was grateful for it. It made the riotous colors of wool piled in baskets beneath them all the more glorious. But that wasn't what caught her attention.

It was the spinning wheel in the middle of the little room.

A woman sat there, spinning, singing to herself as she did so. Her hair was snowy white, her hands worn and wrinkled, but her eyes were a bright blue, as full of life as they had likely been when she'd been a girl.

"Ah, a fellow spinner," she said, stopping her wheel and rising to come take Aisling's hands. She turned them over, then frowned. "No stains, though, from freshly dyed wool. Perhaps you've been spinning other things of late, eh?"

Aisling heard a choking noise, but it wasn't coming from her. It was coming from Rùnach, who was standing behind her. She turned to look at him, but he was simply standing there, looking rather winded. Aisling frowned briefly at him, then turned back to the old woman.

"I've never spun wool."

"Then perhaps 'tis time you began." The woman inclined her head. "I am Ceana. And you are Aisling."

Aisling felt her mouth fall open. "How did you know?"

"I know many things," Ceana said wisely, "though I rarely speak of them." She made a sweeping gesture with her arm. "Please come in and make yourselves comfortable. I don't often have company, so you are most welcome. What would you care to see?"

Aisling had no idea where to begin. She looked around the chamber, so full of light and color . . . then looked at the old woman helplessly. "I don't know."

"Why don't we start with my showing you how to spin wool,

my dear." She glanced at Rùnach. "You may come along as well, my lad, if you care to."

Aisling wondered if Rùnach would refuse, but he simply nodded, clasped his hands behind his back, and followed along behind them as if he had nothing better to do with his afternoon.

For herself, she felt as if she had walked into some sort of earthly paradise where everything was like nothing she'd ever imagined before. She found herself taken in hand and shown where the wool was separated, picked, then carded into batts ready to spin into thread.

She frowned, knowing where that was going. "And then you must weave it?"

The old woman chortled happily. "Well, of course, gel. What else would you do with it?"

"I'm not fond of weaving," Aisling said. If she was going to be in paradise, there was no reason to not be honest.

"Neither am I," Mistress Ceana said promptly, "which is why I never tell anyone I can. I am a spinner, you see. What would those weavers have to work with if not for my art?" She paused. "I will knit, I'll allow, if the wool is particularly fine and I have need. But I would far rather spin."

Aisling almost smiled. "Do you choose the colors?"

"That art lies in a different room," she said, taking Aisling by the arm. "Come with me and I'll show you."

Aisling looked over her shoulder. Rùnach was standing there, leaning against the wall with his arms folded over his chest, watching her with a small smile.

"Bring your lad, if you like," Mistress Ceana added.

Aisling felt her cheeks grow hot. "He isn't my lad."

"Nay," the woman said thoughtfully, "he's a man, isn't he? And a powerful handsome one. Come along then, young man, and try not to leave my workers swooning over your pretty face."

Aisling looked at Rùnach quickly, but he was only smiling ruefully. He pulled the hood of his cloak over his head, but she suspected it wasn't because of the fairness of his face. It grieved her, she had to admit, that he felt the need to do that because of his scars.

She could have told him it was unnecessary.

She spent a very pleasant hour learning how to dye, how to choose what wool to blend together, what sort of sheep and goat produced what kind of substance, and what types of each Ceana thought most fine. Eventually she found herself back where she'd started. She stood next to Ceana's wheel and looked at it.

"What are you spinning now?"

The woman put her hand on the flywheel. "The stuff of dreams, my gel. Wool so soft it will make the queen herself sigh in pleasure to wear it."

Aisling nodded. She hadn't touched a wheel since the one that rendered her senseless—

"I have another wheel," Ceana said, "over there under the window. Be a good lad and fetch it for us, would you, young Rùnach? Aisling, my dear, pull up a stool here next to me. We'll have a lesson, shall we?"

Aisling looked at Mistress Ceana in surprise. "How did you know his name?"

The old woman only smiled enigmatically.

Aisling looked at Rùnach, mute. He smiled briefly, fetched what was required, then set the wheel down in front of Aisling. She looked at it and felt a little as if she were staring death in the face.

She looked down at her feet, because that was what she was accustomed to doing.

"There's a leader already tied, my dear. I'll show you what to do with it."

Aisling looked up and met Rùnach's eyes. He was watching her steadily, as if he would have given her some of his own courage if he'd been able.

She kept her gaze locked with his, then reached out and touched the wheel.

And she breathed still.

She smiled.

Rùnach smiled in return, though his eyes were full of tears.

"Tenderhearted, is he?" Ceana said gently.

"Very," Aisling agreed.

Rùnach smiled at her once more, a smile she understood completely, then turned to Ceana and made her a low bow. "I'll leave my lady in your care, then, for an hour or so. Manly business, you know."

"A trip to the larder, I imagine."

Rùnach laughed. "Aye, I daresay. What might I bring back with me?"

"Enough for three, me lad," Ceana said, sounding pleased. "Spinning is hungry work that requires the occasional infusion of delicate edibles. You'll want to watch and admire, though, which is why we'll need food for us all."

"I'll return posthaste."

Aisling watched him turn and walk away. She realized Mistress Ceana had joined her in the activity. The old woman looked thoughtfully after Rùnach as he closed the door, then at Aisling.

"You know who he is, don't you?"

"A soldier," Aisling said, feeling a little startled, though she couldn't deny that the more time she spent with Rùnach, the less she thought him simply a soldier. "I once thought he was a lord, but he claims he isn't." She shrugged helplessly. "I don't know and he won't tell me."

"Hmmm," Ceana said thoughtfully. "Well, he has his reasons for keeping things secret, I suppose, but don't we all?" She looked at Aisling. "You have secrets, my gel. Deadly ones."

Aisling found absolutely nothing to say to that.

"Not to worry," Ceana said with a smile. "I am an old woman who knows how to keep her own counsel. There are no great tasks left for me in this world but to take my pleasure at my wheel and pour my love for all things beautiful into my yarn. I have often wished, though, that I could spin other things. The blush of love, the scent of roses on a warm summer's afternoon, the first chill of fall as it settles in the trees." She looked at Aisling. "Dreams, perhaps."

"Dreams," Aisling whispered. "Why would anyone want to spin dreams?"

Ceana smiled. "'Tis just a thought that came to me just now. I don't know why." She fingered the wool she was holding, a royal purple shot through with golden threads. "If I *truly* had my wish, I would spin all those things out of thin air, then string an invisible loom with them." She smiled at Aisling. "I might even be tempted to weave, then."

"They would have to be fairly lovely things to convince me," Aisling said doubtfully.

Ceana laughed. "I'm sure they would, my gel. I'm sure they would." She rubbed her hands together briskly, suddenly. "Let's be about our work, Aisling. I have much to teach you and time is short."

Aisling reached out and gingerly touched the wheel again, on the off chance the curse hadn't noticed her cheek the first time. But the result was the same, namely nothing at all. The wheel was simply wood under her hand, nothing more. She took a deep breath, then looked at Mistress Ceana.

"I am ready."

"I think, my gel, that you are."

Twenty-one

❧

Rùnach paced through the hallways of Tor Neroche, finding that doing so was far more unsettling than it should have been. The last time he'd been there, he'd been a youth of ten-and-three, come with his mother who had made the journey to visit the queen just after Mhorghain's birth. He thought he remembered them having put Mhorghain and Miach to nap together in adjoining cribs, but he could have been wrong. He'd been too busy making clandestine forays into the library whilst enduring priggish lecturing from the crown prince Adhémar about sneaking into places he shouldn't have to know for certain.

He thought he might have pointed out to Miach's eldest brother that filching his father's sour wine was a more grievous sin than looking for something to read, but he couldn't be sure. He *was* fairly sure, however, that he'd bloodied Adhémar's nose at one point, but that had been nothing more than he'd deserved. He had been, he had to admit, a bit hot-tempered in his youth. Fortunately a score of years locked away in Buidseachd had tempered that a bit.

Now, he simply felt cold as he walked through the passageways and felt as if he were walking over his own grave.

At least Aisling had found something pleasant to do. Actually, perhaps *pleasant* was grossly understating it. The wench was obsessed. Fortunately, she had found in Mistress Ceana a kindred soul who was equally enamored of all things woolly. Rùnach had seen them both fed lunch, napped on a cot Mistress Ceana had insisted be brought in and set under the window for his pleasure, then dragged himself to the kitchens for supper for the three of them.

He'd started to ask Aisling if she didn't want to at least take a walk after supper, but he had watched her blossom right there before his eyes, as if she'd been a seed that had been planted in some magic-saturated soil. He had taken her hand, bowed low over it, extended the same courtesy to Mistress Ceana, then left them to their work.

He'd considered the library, but his afternoon's labors there had been too useless and depressing to return to. Though he'd tried to make it seem a bit of a contest earlier in the day, sitting with Aisling at opposite ends of a very long table, and exchanging the occasional knowing look, it had seemed less and less like a game and more like death waiting for him around the corner.

He had to have answers and he had to have them soon.

He paused at the bottom of a long, circular stairway and looked up into the darkness. No one barred his way, so he began to climb. He climbed until he could climb no more and stood on a landing outside a door. He knocked, because he at least had that much good breeding left in him.

"Come!"

He opened the door and found none other than the illustrious king of Neroche sitting in front of his fire. Miach was looking at him in a way that suddenly made him very nervous.

"Waiting for me, were you?" Rùnach managed.

"I thought you might be wandering abroad this evening," Miach said with a smile. "Is your lady still spinning, or has she worn her spinning mistress out?"

"She's still there, but I told her I would fetch her in an hour and insist that she sleep." He shrugged. "And speaking of the opinions of women, what does your bride think of your spending your evenings in your hovel here?"

"I made a special trip just for you, so she approves. And just so you know, I don't spend *all* my evenings here."

"Of which I imagine she also approves," Rùnach said, shutting the door behind him and casting himself down into the empty chair in front of the fire. "Our mothers are pleased with the match, I'm sure."

"Are you?"

"I am." He accepted a cup of ale from his brother-in-law, sat back, then sighed. "Get on with the bludgeoning."

"Me?" Miach asked innocently. "Why would I bludgeon?"

Rùnach pursed his lips. "Because you are who you are and you know Soilléir of Cothromaiche very well. I am continually appalled by the similarities between the two of you."

Miach only watched him steadily, a small smile playing around his mouth. "You know what she is, don't you?"

"Who?"

"Aisling."

Rùnach shot him a look. "A girl, thank you. I haven't been so long at Buidseachd that I can't recognize one when I see one."

Miach looked at him for a moment or two, then rose and set his cup on the mantel. "Very well, think what you like. I'm going to bed."

Rùnach gaped at him. "That's it?"

Miach only raised his eyebrow briefly. "Lock up when you've stewed enough, would you?"

Rùnach pondered that.

He was still pondering the next day in the lists. He didn't like to reduce his life to simple reports worthy of an assistant bard's practice diary, but there had been little progress to speak of on any front. He had slept a discreet distance away from Aisling in front of their fire, then escorted her to Mistress Ceana's chamber at first light. He had encountered one of Miach's older brothers in the passageway, which had left him grinding his teeth as he realized Mansourah of Neroche had taken one look at Aisling and apparently fallen immediately under her spell. It hadn't helped matters at all when Mansourah had introduced himself and Aisling had realized he was the soldier Weger had recommended she seek out. Rùnach had sent Mansourah one way and Aisling the other. Knowing she was closeted with Neroche's master spinner—and hoping that wasn't a mistake of epic proportions—had left him free to trot out to the lists to try to find answers.

His sister was terrifying the garrison, so he took the opportunity to terrify the hapless king of Neroche. He was happy to find that he remembered several things Weger had taught him, though less than surprised to find Miach knew those same things. He finally leaned on his sword and looked at his sister's husband.

"I'm biting. What is she?"

"A girl."

Rùnach growled. At least he thought he growled. It was difficult to tell what he was doing when all he wanted to do was wipe the smirk off Miach's face.

"You know," he said shortly, "you annoyed me when you were a lad. You haven't improved since then."

"I repaired your hands."

"And left me with a broken tooth thanks to the rivet in the leather strap you gave me to chew on whilst you were about it!"

"I fixed that as well."

Rùnach looked over his shoulder to make sure no observant gel with shorn hair was standing behind him, eavesdropping with abandon, then leaned closer to his brother-in-law. "Let me lay out for you, King Mochriadhemiach, all the problems that sit arranged pleasingly on a trencher before me. Perhaps then you can stop smirking long enough to examine them with me."

"You're testy."

Rùnach ignored him. "Why no one saw fit to tell me that Lothar was lounging negligently at Gobhann, I don't know—"

"Didn't we tell you?"

"Nay, you bloody well didn't tell me!" Rùnach shouted. He took a deep breath. "Nay, you didn't tell me, but no matter. I found that out all on my own. Somehow he managed to free himself and find me, all whilst I was singularly unable to protect a helpless woman."

"She's not helpless." Miach smiled. "She is lovely—and all the more lovely for not thinking herself so."

Rùnach frowned. "You shouldn't be looking."

"I'm scouting out a future sister-in-law," Miach said mildly. "I'm just wondering if you understand the path that lies before her."

"And you do?" Rùnach said shortly. "And just so you know, I'm not sure I'm equal to expressing how desperately I would like to loathe you for your damned sight."

Miach only smiled briefly, then his smile faded. "There is something stirring," he said slowly. He hesitated, then looked around himself. "I don't think it wise to speak of it here." He paused. "Something slippery that I can't quite see."

"Heaven help us, then."

"Or you, rather," Miach said seriously. He chewed on his words a bit longer, then shook his head. "I'll say no more at present. I think you should be careful, both with yourself and with that gel of yours."

"She is not mine," Rùnach said, though it was odd, wasn't it, how he found that he was wondering where she was and what she was doing. He would have put his hand to his head to check for undue warmth there, but then Miach would have thought he was feeling for Weger's mark.

"I suppose you could ask for aid," Miach mused. "In keeping both you and Aisling safe."

"From whom?" Rùnach asked grimly. "You, newly wed? Ruith, newly wed and fresh from a battle with my sire? One of my elvish cousins who would shudder delicately at the sight of anything to do with anything created from anything but Fadaire?"

"I only said you *could*," Miach pointed out, "I didn't say you *should*."

"Can I assume you have suggestions for me?"

"Perish the thought," Miach said, holding up his hand in sur-render. "I was just making idle conversation."

Rùnach chewed on his words for quite some time before he spoke again. "Who is she?"

"How would I know?"

Rùnach suppressed the urge to take his fist and plow it into Miach's nose. "You're obnoxious."

"My wife doesn't think I'm obnoxious."

"She's dazzled by your crown," Rùnach said, though he knew nothing could be further from the truth. He sighed deeply. "Very well, I concede the battle. Where do I go to find out who she is?"

"You're asking me?" Miach said, blinking owlishly. "What would I know of anything?"

"I didn't allow Rigaud and Gille to beat you often enough. A mistake I shall obviously pay for long into my old age." He inclined his head. "If His Majesty will excuse me?"

"Where're you off to?"

Rùnach only snorted at him and walked away, because it was safer that way—for Miach. He walked back to the keep, pulling his hood over his face yet again, and continued on to his chamber. He had a wash, donned fresh clothes—for which he would unfor-tunately have to thank Miach—and made for the library.

He started down into the bowels of the castle and had to admit he was rather glad that he could trot down the stairs instead of having to limp down them, and that his hand as it skimmed along the metal railing could not only feel the terrible chill of the iron but grasp it occasionally as the need arose. He walked in, nodded to the head librarian, then went immediately to where he thought he might find what he was looking for.

He had only been at it for a quarter hour before a small, sharp-eyed man appeared as if by magic by his side. Rùnach realized too late that his head was bare and his face uncovered. He stopped himself midway in pulling his hood forward and looked at his companion.

"I am a simple traveler," he said, shooting the man a look that said he would be wise to agree, "and am here thanks to the king's graciousness. Who are you?"

The man's eyes were alight with excitement. "I am Feòcallan," he whispered, "special researcher to His Majesty, King Mochri-adhemiach, who is a kind and generous ruler, especially benevolent to those who love books."

Rùnach almost smiled. "So he is," he agreed.

"What might I help His—er, I mean, the *goodman*—what can I help him find?"

Rùnach found himself, for a change, without a single idea. "I'm not sure," he admitted. "I'm looking for something, but I'm not sure what."

"I fear, Your—ah, I mean, *sir*, that we don't have a section entitled *Not Sure What*."

Rùnach was terribly tempted to laugh. "I imagine you don't." He considered, then looked at the librarian. "I don't suppose you have a list of all the wagon trains that routinely converge on Istaur and from where they originate, do you, Master Feòcallan?"

"We do, Prince—um—" Feòcallan frowned fiercely. "Forgive me, sir. Habit."

"Which does you credit."

"Take your ease by the well-tended fire over there, Your Highness," Feòcallan said, "and I shall bring you what you need."

Rùnach looked at him. "Do all your patrons receive such courtesy?"

Feòcallan looked at him seriously, then leaned closer. "With all due respect, Prince Rùnach, they do not." He pulled away. "I can keep a secret, but disrespect is impossible."

Rùnach looked at him. "Who told?"

"No one, Your Highness. I have a ready ear for tales."

"My face?"

"Only hastened the elimination of suspects, Your Highness."

Rùnach laughed a little in spite of himself. "Very well, Master Feòcallan, show me where I might take advantage of your hospitality. It will be most welcome, I assure you."

• • •

He spent the afternoon looking at trade routes and eliminating them one by one. He leaned his chin on his fist and stared off into the distance, unseeing. That first night in Gobhann when she had been so desperate to see Weger, to talk to him, Aisling had said something about midnight—

And three se'nnights.

Rùnach looked at the map. It had taken Aisling six days to sail from Istaur to Sgioba and then walk to Gobhann, which would have left her, as it had happened, needing to talk to Weger that night to manage her three se'nnight schedule. If that was the case, that left a full fortnight for her to come from her home to Istaur.

He thought back to when he'd first seen her in Istaur. She had been relatively clean save her clothes and her feet, and she hadn't been limping, which meant she couldn't have been walking for the previous fortnight. He looked at Istaur on the map, then slid his finger east to a distance that might represent a fortnight's walk. The arc that distance then encompassed included the beginning of the plains of Neroche, a portion of Shettlestoune, and much of Meith. But he could say with certainty that that language she had spoken hadn't come from any of those places.

He considered a bit longer, then looked up and caught Feòcallan's eye. The man leapt forward as if he'd been called upon to lead the charge against Lothar and all his minions whilst the former were all bound and all that needed to be done was make a show of victory. Feòcallan drew up a chair without being asked and looked at Rùnach eagerly.

"Aye, Your—"

"Ahem," Rùnach said pointedly.

Feòcallan bowed and scraped. "Forgive me, sir. What do you need?"

Rùnach considered. "I need this information in the strictest confidence."

"Of *course*, Your H—er, I mean, sir."

He tapped Istaur on the map. "If one were to travel to Istaur, or, rather, let's say one were leaving from Istaur and traveling a fortnight, how far could one go by horse? Or wagon?"

Feòcallan studied the map. "On horseback? It would depend upon the horse, but this"—he drew an arc with Istaur as its focus—"might be possible with a horse who could do ten leagues a day. Perhaps half that again for a very fleet horse." He looked at Rùnach. "You would know better than I what a very fine horse is capable of."

Rùnach smiled briefly. "I have led a charmed life where they are concerned, I will admit." He looked back at the map. "But many things can befall a steed, can't they? Unless, I suppose, you had fresh animals waiting at certain points along the road, as do very fleet . . ."

He found that words were flowing away from him, as if they'd been cast upon a rapidly flowing stream.

"Carriages," Feòcallan finished for him. He looked at Rùnach with a puzzled frown on his face. "There are those to consider, I suppose, if one has enough gold to spare."

"I don't suppose you might have a list," Rùnach began slowly.

"I'll see."

It took the man less than a quarter hour to return with a very thin logbook. He handed it to Rùnach. "This I think might suit your purposes, Y—er, my good sir. The truth is—" He shifted uncomfortably. "The truth is, there is a certain reputation associated with many of those sorts of transports, but rapid flight is the tie that binds, as it were. I won't say that all who choose that method of transportation are ruffians—"

"Or smugglers," Rùnach said wryly.

Feòcallan lifted his eyebrows briefly. "Exactly. There seems to be, however, always a great amount of secrecy about the passengers." He looked at Rùnach meaningfully. "Gold buys many things."

"It does indeed, Master Feòcallan." He smiled at the man, then opened the book, trying not to notice how his hands were shaking. He flexed his fingers, then began to read.

A carriage from Istaur would take him in a fortnight or thereabouts to, in no particular order, Tor Neroche, Diarmailt,

Tiùrr—no doubt thanks to the vast stretches of farmland lying along the southern route—and Beul.

He frowned thoughtfully. Beul was . . . He frowned again. He had no idea where the hell Beul was, but he would find out. He looked back on the map he had, but it wasn't as detailed as he would have liked. He trailed his finger along the arc, looking at cities and villages within that distance, but saw nothing that piqued his interest overmuch.

He closed the books, stacked the maps, then thanked Master Feòcallan for his aid and left the library, wondering how he might narrow things down. Aisling belonged—or had belonged, rather—to a weaver's guild, but it had occurred to him earlier that morning that a small village wouldn't have a guild. In his experience, that sort of thing was reserved for a larger city.

A large city within fourteen days' hard travel from Istaur.

He paced along passageways, thinking, until he stopped. He stopped because he had run bodily into something immovable. He thought to apologize, then realized whom he had encountered.

Mansourah of Neroche, that damned flitting butterfly.

"Rùnach," Mansourah said, looking rather more interested than he should have. "What a pleasure—"

"Where have you traveled?" Rùnach interrupted.

Mansourah blinked. "What?"

"I want a list of countries visited," Rùnach said, trying to smile politely but fearing it had come out as more a baring of teeth, "not conquests made."

Mansourah put his hand over his heart. "You wound me, truly you do."

"I would love to in truth, but then you'd be too dead to tell me what I want to know." He put his arm around Mansourah's shoulders and turned him so they were facing the same way, then pulled him along. "Let's walk and you'll talk."

"Chummy, aren't you?"

"I need information. I'm willing to pretend to like you in order to have it."

Mansourah smiled. "She's very pretty."

"She isn't pretty," Rùnach said grimly. "She's past that, some-how, and that isn't what I want to talk to you about." He looked around him to make sure no one would pay him any heed, then put his question to Mansourah. He put it to him in Fadaire, on the off chance he was overheard by an idle servant. "Say, *I'm a stupid git* in all the languages you know east of the mountains and tell me afterward what languages they were."

Mansourah laughed a little, but obliged him.

Rùnach stopped, listened, then held up his hand. "Wait. That last thing, what was that?"

"Deuraich," Mansourah said, looking at him as if he'd lost his mind.

Rùnach walked on, pulling him along. "How much of it do you know?"

"I'm fluent, but I'm fluent in everything." Mansourah smiled pleasantly. "It's a gift."

"You're annoying," Rùnach said, feeling that the point needed to be made, "but useful, I'll admit it. Where is it spoken?"

"Bruadair."

Rùnach stopped walking. He stopped walking because he'd almost tripped over his own feet and gone sprawling. He turned and gaped at Miach's older brother. "*What?*"

"Bruadair," Mansourah repeated. "Why, is that a problem?"

"Less of a problem than a surprise. Are you certain?"

"Of course."

"Say something else," Rùnach commanded. "Say *thank you.*"

Mansourah obliged him.

Rùnach saw stars. "Impossible—nay, don't give me the word for that, you fool." He dragged his hand through his hair. "Impossible."

"Why?" Mansourah asked. "What?"

Rùnach shot him a look. "Nothing. Thank you. You've been very helpful." He turned and strode away.

"I can continue to be helpful—"

"Not," Rùnach said distinctly, "in the way you think you would like to be helpful."

"When I determine what that means, I'll argue with it," Mansourah said, trotting alongside him. "I think you need a drink."

"I already had a drink."

"Not that watered down swill Miach pours." Mansourah nodded. "Down the passageway, my friend, and into my luxurious chambers."

Rùnach supposed a quarter hour and something to drink wouldn't change the events of the world. It might allow him a bit of peace for thinking if Mansourah could shut his mouth for that long, which he seriously doubted.

Aisling was speaking Deuraich?

"What does it mean?" he asked Mansourah. "*Deuraich*? The word itself, not the language."

"It means *water*," Mansourah said, opening his door.

"I wonder why?"

"Because the whole country is practically nothing but coastline," Mansourah answered, "and what isn't on the coast is so dotted with lakes, I'm surprised anyone can walk a league without getting soggy. Well, save in Beul, which is, I have to admit, an absolute hellhole." He shot Rùnach a look. "Have you *ever* looked at a map, Rùnach?"

Rùnach slapped him briskly on the back of his head on his way to accepting what he was quite certain would be a very fine glass of something that looked rather strong. He wouldn't be able to finish it, but that was likely something he should think about later.

"I have," he said, sipping and finding his eyes watering madly. "Bloody hell, Sourah, what is this rot?"

"Something I made myself."

"I hate to ask what's in it."

"I wouldn't," Mansourah advised. "And I'm having you on. It's strong ale from Uachdaran's cellars. Have you never had it before?"

"Never, and I hope to never have it again." He set the glass down and collapsed in a chair in front of Mansourah's fire. "What do you know about Bruadair?"

Mansourah sat and stretched his legs out. "I know where the ousted king and queen are at present, but other than that, not much at all. They're a tight-lipped, clannish bunch, those Bruadairians." He shot Rùnach a look. "Soilléir would know quite a bit more about their country, I imagine, not that he'd tell you. 'Tis bad luck to speak of it."

"Nay, that's your brother's full name," Rùnach said absently. He considered for a moment or two, then looked at Mansourah. "Do they let visitors in?"

Miach's brother shook his head. "No one in, no one out. Unless you're a trader, of course, or an envoy they particularly want to impress, but even then you're under tight control for as long as you're inside the country."

"Why is that, do you suppose?"

"Are you serious?" Mansourah asked with a laugh, then his mouth fell open. "You *are* serious. How can you not know this?"

Rùnach felt something slither down his spine. "Know what?"

"Your sister-in-law is Bruadairian royalty in exile and you don't know this?"

Rùnach cast about for something to say. The best he could come up with in a tight spot was, "ah . . ." He cleared his throat and made another attempt. "You mean Sarah?"

"You only have one sister-in-law," Mansourah said with a snort. "And as for the other, those Bruadairians are dreamweavers, you idiot."

Rùnach blinked. "What?"

"Just what I said."

"What utter rot," Rùnach said without hesitation. "How do you weave dreams?"

"Well, I don't know that part," Mansourah admitted. He looked at Rùnach and shrugged. "They just do."

"To what end?"

"I have no idea."

Rùnach looked at him coolly. "You've been extraordinarily helpful."

Mansourah raised his glass. "Cheers."

Rùnach glared at him, then heaved himself up out of his chair and strode across the chamber.

"I told you what language that was," Mansourah called after him. "Why did you want to know?"

"I always want to know," Rùnach threw over his shoulder.

"Where did you hear—oh, damnation, this is vile stuff—"

Rùnach left him to his choking.

He supposed the most sensible thing to do would be to go back to the library and look up everything he could find on Bruadair. Somehow, though, he had the feeling he would simply be peeling books from off Aisling's stack about the same country and then the jig, as they said, would be up.

"Ah, sir?"

He turned and found one of the king's pages standing there, holding a folded note very carefully between a surprisingly clean thumb and forefinger.

"This is for you, ah, sir."

Rùnach smiled pleasantly and took the note. He sent the lad on his way with thanks and a coin, then opened the note and read it. He considered, then decided perhaps it was time to pry a certain gel away from her wool.

Before the jig was up.

Twenty-two

❧

Aisling sat on the same stool she'd been sitting on for the past . . . well, she wasn't sure how long she'd been sitting there. Since the previous afternoon, she supposed, save for when Rùnach had forced her to eat or insisted that she come sleep. He had been so polite about it that she hadn't wanted to argue.

But she hadn't wanted to walk away from her wheel.

Her first attempts at making yarn had been, she had to admit, absolutely dreadful. Mistress Ceana had insisted that even the thickest most uneven yarn had its own beauty, but she couldn't see it. What she wanted was perfect, thin thread that she could then ply into something she could use for things that would be worth saving.

She looked at the last of the roving she was spinning and watched it as the bobbin turned, putting in the amount of twist she allowed, then pulling the yarn onto itself. She reached out and stopped the wheel, marveling at the feel of the smooth wood under her hand. She looked at what she'd spun, then looked at Mistress Ceana.

"Well?"

Mistress Ceana peered at it, then smiled and looked at her. "Beautiful."

"The wool I started with was perfect."

Mistress Ceana shook her head with a smile. "You underestimate your gift, my gel." She covered Aisling's hand with one of her worn, wrinkled ones. "I'll ply it for you, shall I? I think you might have somewhere to go for the evening."

Aisling looked up to see the door open. Rùnach peeked inside. "It is safe?" he asked.

Mistress Ceana laughed merrily. "Of course it is, my lad. Have you come to fetch your lady for supper?"

"If she can be pried away from her art," he said politely. "Just for an hour or two, if possible. We've had an invitation I think we should accept."

Aisling found that her cheeks were unusually hot. She put her hands to them, which seemed particularly foolish, but what else could she do? Rùnach was fetching her as if she'd been some sort of grand lady. It was utterly ridiculous, but he seemed to think nothing of it, so she supposed she shouldn't either. She rose, then looked down at Mistress Ceana.

"Thank you," she said, "though thanks seem particularly inadequate for what you've taught me."

Mistress Ceana waved away her words gently. "It was my everlasting pleasure, my child. Come again tomorrow, if you have the chance, and we'll begin your lessons in dyeing. Anything else you need to do with a wheel, you can learn on your own."

Aisling thanked her profusely, though, again, it seemed not enough. She allowed Rùnach to wrap her up in her cloak and fasten the catch under her chin. When he offered her his hand, she put hers into his without thinking. She smiled once more at Mistress Ceana, then walked with Rùnach out into the passageway. The door closed softly behind them.

She looked up at him. "She has been very kind."

"You're easy to be kind to."

She found that she couldn't move, because he was wrong. She

took a deep breath. "I have terrible thoughts about my parents," she admitted, "and the Guildmistress."

"Well," he said slowly, "I didn't say you were perfect."

She looked up at him in surprise, then realized he was laughing a little at her. She pursed her lips but continued on with him.

"Where are we going?"

"Miach managed to forage for supper, or so I understand. I thought we might pass a pleasant hour or two with him and my sister. Or, rather, with my sister."

She smiled. "You're terrible to him."

"He expects it," Rùnach said dryly. "We might even convince him to tell us a few tales. He's not completely without merit as an entertainer."

"Does he know many tales?"

"Scores, but then again, he's done nothing useful with his life but memorize tales, so that's understandable."

She followed him along passageways, up and down stairs, and finally up a dizzying set of circular steps to a tower chamber. She hesitated on the landing and put her hand on his arm to stop him before he knocked.

"What does he do here?" she asked quietly. "It must be something important, to have these privileges. Wouldn't you say?"

He put his hand on the doorframe and looked at her seriously. "I'm not sure you want to know right now."

"Is he dangerous?" she managed.

"Very," he said honestly, "but noble."

"He bears Weger's mark as well, doesn't he?"

Rùnach nodded.

She took a deep breath. "I don't think I want to know anything else about anyone," she managed. "I definitely don't want to see anything else."

"Then come sit next to me, keep your eyes on your supper, then you may use my shoulder as a fine resting place for your head whilst you close your eyes and enjoy all manner of tales to delight and astonish." He smiled gravely. "Will that suit?"

She almost looked down, but she decided that she was finished with that sort of business. She lifted her chin, though it cost her a great deal.

"I have the feeling," she said unwillingly, "that this is the calm before the storm."

He lifted one eyebrow briefly. "I would argue with you, but I cannot. I've been thinking the same thing." He looked at her in silence for a moment or two, then opened his arm, the one that wasn't resting against the doorframe.

She walked into that embrace as if she'd been doing it the whole of her life.

"I am becoming far too accustomed to this," she said lightly.

He wrapped both arms around her and rested his cheek against her hair. She didn't know which one it was, so she reached up without looking and felt the other cheek. It was unscarred.

"The scars are terrible," he said very quietly.

"I don't see them."

He laughed a little, though it sounded quite a bit like a groan. He pulled back and looked down at her. "I think we should knock before I do something."

"What?"

"If you don't know, I'm not going to enlighten you," he said dryly. He kept his arm around her shoulders and knocked lightly. "Let's see if Miach is in good form tonight. If not, we'll throw things at him."

She didn't particularly think they should, but she wasn't going to argue. The door was opened and they were welcomed inside.

The chamber was small, but she supposed that said nothing about it for it seemed very luxurious to her. She stood just inside the door and tried not to gape.

There was a hearth set into the wall to her right, but the rest of the chamber was nothing but windows. The sun had set, but twilight left enough light to see by. She walked over to a window and looked down over the castle, then up and out to the sea. She supposed if she had tried hard enough, she might have been able to smell it as well.

She watched the faint lights below her for a moment or two,

then turned and looked at the chamber and its occupants. Miach and Morgan were sitting together on a sofa on one side of a low table placed there in front of the fire. There was enough food there to feed a dozen people. There was a spot left for her on the opposite couch, or so she dared assume since Rùnach was still standing, waiting for her to come and sit. She started to, then froze. She looked up, then frowned.

There, pressed against the ceiling far above her head was . . . a spell. She stood in the middle of the chamber and turned around slowly. The spell was a diaphanous thing, scarce visible, that fell from the ceiling to the floor. It wasn't under her feet, for there was another sort of spell there, something she couldn't quite name, though it seemed to be woven into the very floorboards. It was very old, indeed.

She looked at Rùnach. "There are spells here."

"For protection, no doubt," Rùnach said promptly.

Aisling walked over to the wall, smoothed her hand over the magic woven there, then smiled in spite of herself. It was beautiful and it was indeed for protection. She had no idea who had put it there, but she wasn't going to complain. She walked back over to Rùnach, smiled at him, then sat down where she was invited to. Rùnach poured her a glass of wine and started to hand it to her.

"What did you see?" he asked.

"A spell of Fadaire."

She caught the glass before he dropped it.

"It isn't evil," she added, "if that's what's worrying you."

"Nay," he managed, "nay, nothing worries me."

She looked at Miach and Morgan, but they were busily filling their plates, so she thought perhaps she should do the same. She served Rùnach, who seemed rather rattled, then helped herself.

The meal was just as lovely as everything she'd eaten in the palace. She was terribly tempted to ask Miach how he'd managed it, but she just couldn't bring herself to. She hadn't lied when she'd told Rùnach she felt as if she were standing on the edge of a storm. She didn't want to think that her days wouldn't carry on as beautifully as they had been for the previous two days, but she knew better.

She didn't want to count, but had to. She had five days left, five days left to find a man to agree to her bargain. She knew she should have been looking since she'd arrived, but learning to spin had been . . . well, there had been only one other time over the course of her life in which she had felt such absolute peace.

And that had been half an hour earlier, in Rùnach's arms.

"What are you thinking?"

She jumped a little when she realized he had leaned over to whisper in her ear. "Nothing useful."

He sat up and patted her shoulder. "One more night, Aisling, one more night of peace before we turn to more difficult things. Take your ease and let us see if Miach can demonstrate his raconteuring skills to our satisfaction."

Miach rubbed his hands together, then flexed his fingers. "What will you have tonight. The Two Swords?"

Morgan groaned. "Not that one, not again. I don't care how much I love you, there is simply too much romance in that tale for my tastes. Choose something else."

"And preferably without a lad from Neroche in the lead role," Rùnach said with a snort. "There is only so much of that a man of taste and accomplishment such as myself can be prevailed upon to endure."

Aisling laughed a little before she could help herself. She jumped a little when the other three looked at her in surprise. "Sorry," she said quickly. "I didn't mean to give offense."

Miach only smiled. "I don't think we've heard you laugh before. If this is what it takes to draw it from you, I'm happy to paint Nerochian lads in their most unflattering lights all evening."

"That won't be hard," Rùnach said with a snort. "Miach, choose something interesting."

"Something with bloodshed," Morgan said firmly.

Aisling found that Miach was looking at her expectantly.

"Well?" he asked. "Have you an opinion?"

She might have felt foolish at another time saying what was on the tip of her tongue, but she knew that Morgan at least wouldn't think her so. She looked at Miach seriously.

"Something about elves."

"Excellent choice," Miach said, sounding pleased. "We'll skip the lesser elves of Ainneamh and strike out for the most exclusive lot of them all, the inhabitants of Tòrr Dòrainn."

Aisling glanced at Morgan, but she didn't seem to be rolling her eyes or making noises of disbelief, so Aisling thought she might manage the same.

"Whilst there are many elves who have had many adventures," Miach continued, "I believe we will begin with a young, strapping lad named Sìle. Of course he is not as young now, but in his youth he was a tremendous adventurer and more ready with a sword than you might suspect. Not to Weger's standards, of course, but Gobhann did not exist when young Sìle was honing his skill in the lists, so we'll just have to allow that he made do with what he had."

"Adventures?" Rùnach asked, sounding as if he might be choking.

"You might be surprised, though how you could have missed them being such a lover of tales yourself, I don't know," Miach said. "Settle in, my friends, and prepare to be astonished."

Aisling realized at one point during Sìle's adventures that her eyes were growing slightly heavy. She shifted, felt Rùnach take her hand and pull her closer, then made use of his proffered shoulder. She was convinced she would fall immediately asleep.

But to her surprise, and though she closed her eyes, she made it through all of Miach's stories. She supposed part of it was because Miach was, as promised, an excellent teller of tales. She felt as if she were standing next to Sìle as he plighted his troth with his beloved Brèagha after satisfying her father with deeds worthy of song. She delved beneath the earth and rock with the dwarves of Durial, wandered the halls of the schools of wizardry, sat at the table and watched a king of Meith risk everything in a single game of chance for the thing he wanted most.

The other thing that kept her awake, she supposed, was Rùnach idly stroking the back of her hand. And where nothing else had induced her to open her eyes, that did.

She looked down at her hand in his, then turned her hand over so his was visible. She supposed she should have thought better of it, or considered the consequences of her actions, but perhaps she had been too long out from under the Guildmistress's iron rule. She looked at his hand, then reached out and traced the scars there.

She supposed there was no point in trying to quantify them, for they were too innumerable for that. It was as if his hands had been caught under a hopelessly unforgiving weight and he'd had to pull them free by sheer determination alone. She lifted her head and looked at him, realizing only then that he was watching her. She smiled gravely.

"I'm sorry."

He shook his head but said nothing.

"It must have been painful."

"It was."

"Hmmm," was all she could find to say. She smiled as best she could, then put her head back on his shoulder. She forced herself to pick up the thread of Miach's current tale, but she couldn't concentrate on it.

She wondered what had happened to Rùnach's hands.

It was almost midnight when she found herself swathed in her usual, ridiculously luxurious dressing gown, and sitting in front of the fire in the chamber she'd been given. Rùnach had asked her that first day if she preferred to have a chamber of her own, but she'd found the thought rather unsettling. It was a little surprising how quickly she'd become accustomed to having him within sight, as he was at present, sitting across from her and working on fletching an arrow. She knew he was making more for her, which she found somehow quite overwhelming.

"Rùnach?"

He looked up and smiled. "Aye?"

"Thank you," she said, gesturing inelegantly at what he was doing. "That is very kind."

He smiled ruefully. "My brother would be appalled by my efforts, being as he is the far superior fletcher, but I'll do what I can. I suppose you can blame me if your arrows go astray."

She smiled, because he made it easy to smile, then considered the truth that had been nagging at her for most of the evening.

"Rùnach?"

He looked up again from his work. "Aye?"

"Miach didn't tell us any tales about black mages."

"He didn't," Rùnach agreed.

"Do you know any?"

"The better question would be, do I want to tell you any?"

She smiled. "Aye, that would be a better question."

He continued to work for some time in silence. He finally looked up, considered her, then sighed. "You're not going to let me out of this, are you?"

"I'm curious."

He smiled, as if the word had a particular meaning for him beyond the norm. He looked at the arrow in his hands, then set it and his knife aside. He leaned forward, rested his elbows on his knees, then looked at her.

"Which black mage did you want to know about?"

"Are there many?" she asked in surprise, then she scowled at his pained smile. "You realize, of course, that 'tis only the past pair of days that I've begun to believe they might exist. I haven't had time to make a list of their names."

He shook his head. "I'm not sure that's a list I would care to make for you."

"The worst offenders, then."

"In truth, Aisling?" he asked, wincing. "There are so many other things we could discuss that would be a far better use of this lovely fire and our full stomachs."

She looked at him steadily. "I think I need to know."

He rubbed his hands over his face briefly, then sighed and looked at her. "Very well. There is Lothar of Wychweald, whom you already know," he said wearily. "Droch of Saothair—"

"His father was Dorchadas, wasn't he?" she asked.

Rùnach looked slightly startled. "Aye, he was. How did you know?"

She shrugged helplessly. "I don't know. I've heard his name mentioned somewhere. But that isn't important." She waved him on. "I'm sure there are more."

"Wehr of Wrekin," Rùnach said, sounding as if he would rather have been talking about anything else. "Gair of Ceangail, of course."

She shivered. "I *have* heard of him."

"Have you?" he asked in surprise. "Where?"

She caught herself just in time before she revealed that Mistress Muinear had on an occasion or two been prevailed upon to terrify and unnerve a few select inmates with darker tales of myth and legend. Gair had been a particular favorite, though she had to admit she hadn't thought about him in years.

"I wasn't able to read many books about legends and myths and that sort of thing, but there was one that, ah, spoke of . . ." She looked at Rùnach and simply shut her mouth. She couldn't lie with any enthusiasm, so perhaps there was no point in lying at all.

He smiled. "Keep your secrets, if you like. I'm sure I'll pry them from you eventually."

And she was just as certain he wouldn't, but perhaps they would leave that for later.

"About whom shall you hear about from my very meager supply of lore?"

"Gair."

He sighed, as if he hadn't expected anything else. She knew Gair's tale, of course, and had always thought it the unabashed work of fiction it had to be, but after seeing what she'd seen come out of Lothar of Wychweald's mouth in the valley just outside the keep, she had begun to seriously doubt her thoughts.

Rùnach recounted the bare minimum of details, as if he were reading from a text he didn't particularly care to commit to memory. She heard many of the same things she'd heard before, that Gair had lived a thousand years before he'd wed himself the daughter of the king of the elves, had several children with her, then—

She stopped Rùnach. "Wait, that isn't how I heard it told. I was told that he wanted to take over the world and found a source to do so in a glade."

Rùnach looked at her seriously. "And what else did you hear?"

"That it was a well of power," she said, "which is, of course, ridiculous, but there you have it. Power does not exist in wells made for water, nor does it run through streams, or underground, or, well, anywhere." She paused. "Does it?"

He lifted one shoulder in a hesitant shrug. "Who is to say?"

She certainly wasn't the one to ask. She waved him on. "What happened then?"

"As the tale goes," he said slowly, "he opened a well of evil, found it too much for him to control, then lost his own life along with all his family members in an instant."

"Well," she said, "at least that's the end of him."

He nodded but said nothing.

She was vaguely dissatisfied with that, but she was weary, so she decided that her unease and discomfort was merely due to needing sleep. She looked at Rùnach and tried to smile.

"I think I must retire."

"Here by the fire, perhaps?"

"Aye. I can see to a pallet—"

"Of course you won't," he said promptly. He smiled at her. "You, Mistress Aisling, are far too independent for my chivalry. Go fuss with your hair or whatever it is you gels do to prepare for long hours of beauty slumber and I will see to your luxurious couch."

"Thank you," she said quietly.

"It is, as always, my pleasure."

She moved out of his way and went across the chamber on the pretense of making ready for bed. In truth, all she could do was think about that poor family of Gair's who had been slain. She wondered about Gair's wife, Sarait, and why she had left the splendor—admittedly simply rumored, not verified—of elven halls to link her life with a man who loved evil and not good.

She supposed Sglaimir was of that ilk, though she had never met him and couldn't verify if his reputedly unpleasant qualities were due to magecraft or not.

She watched Rùnach thoughtfully for a moment or two, then remembered something he'd said once about his family having been slain by his father. Perhaps he understood, then, the horrors that might be perpetrated by a father with too much power and lack of pity. At least his father hadn't had magic—

But Rùnach's sister Morgan did.

Aisling realized she hadn't slept enough. Picking through the threads of conversation and memories and words that swirled around her was difficult. Perhaps she had heard Morgan awrong. She couldn't say she knew anything about magic, indeed she hardly believed in its existence, but it was odd that it should skip Rùnach to find home in Morgan.

Then again, what did she know? She was a simple weaver from a country no one could possibly care about, charged with a quest that was far beyond her ability to accomplish, enjoying for a very brief time the chivalry of a man who would no doubt very soon take up his own business. He hadn't, after all, promised to do anything past getting her to Tor Neroche. What he would do now was anyone's guess.

She didn't have the luxury of wondering about her future. It had been a very lovely pair of days and she was very grateful for the refuge, but the sword of doom still hung over her head. She was even more convinced of that now that she'd had an evening full of fantastical things that her companions apparently believed were completely true.

Five days. She had five more days before the three fortnights had slipped into memory.

She would be about her quest first thing in the morning.

Twenty-three

Rùnach made his way along passageways, up and down stairs, until he reached the great hall. The hour was appallingly early, but he hadn't been able to sleep. It wasn't that his dreams had been troubled, for he never dreamed. It was just that there were threads that had been woven into his life that had suddenly begun to form a pattern.

A pattern he didn't care for.

He supposed he wouldn't have given any of those threads any particular thought except to dismiss them as quickly as possible if it hadn't been for all the tales Miach had told them the night before.

He would give his brother-in-law credit for knowing some of the most obscure and pointless stories full of romance and ridiculous heroics. And those hadn't even been the stories about Heroes from Neroche, which Rùnach was fully convinced had been so shamelessly embellished over the years that they bore absolutely no resemblance to the actual events.

But there had been one tale, one simple, random tale of a lad from Diarmailt who had once upon a very long time ago had an adventure he hadn't cared at all for simply because he'd been a scholar who had mistakenly handed a greedy mage something he hadn't meant to and hadn't had the means to get it back. The mage had been Dorchadas of Saothair, father of the resident evil at Buidseachd. The scholar had been some lad Rùnach had never heard of, which had likely been for the lad's own good, for he would have gone down in history as one of the biggest fools ever born.

Rùnach was quite sure Miach hadn't told the tale to poke at him, but rather to prove to Aisling that there was indeed evil in the world and mages willing to use that evil to their own ends. But it had left him thinking on things he would rather not have thought on.

He stopped in front of the doors to the great hall. He was faintly surprised to find the guards not only opening the door for him but bowing as they did so. He realized then that he had once again forgotten to shield his face. He suppressed a sigh, nodded politely to them both, then walked into the hall.

He found the king of Neroche sitting on the edge of the high table, swinging his legs back and forth as if he'd been a lad of approximately eight summers. He was talking to his now-eldest brother, Prince Cathar, who was the only one of the pair to have any respect for the trappings of his office for he at least had his feet on the floor.

Cathar turned immediately to see to whom the footfalls belonged. Rùnach wasn't surprised to see that his right hand was twitching. Miach was fortunate to have such a brother standing at his side, ready to defend him. Cathar clasped his hands behind his back and inclined his head politely.

"Prince Rùnach."

"Prince Cathar."

Miach laughed a little. "And now we have the formalities over with, let's move on to other things. Why are you up so early?"

"I couldn't sleep," Rùnach said. "You?"

Miach shook his head. "Too much on my mind."

"Anything besides romantic fluff?" Rùnach asked politely.

Miach considered. "A pair of things, actually," he said slowly. "The first isn't anything you don't already know." He picked up a sheaf of paper from off the table. "Here, read this."

Rùnach accepted the missive from his brother-in-law, read it as he'd been bid, then sighed. "Well, it was lovely of Weger to let you know Lothar had declined further hospitality at Gobhann. A pity he couldn't have let us know a bit sooner, or how the deed was accomplished. There is such nuance to *escaped*."

"Sending Lothar to Gobhann probably wasn't a very good idea in the first place," Miach said, "though at the time it seemed the easiest solution. That, and I couldn't help but think it would bring Weger a bit of pleasure to be able to give his grandsire back a bit of his own. But now the burden lies again with me to see to him, which is as it should have been from the start."

Rùnach couldn't disagree, but he didn't suppose Miach needed to hear that. He waited, but Miach wasn't moving. "Well?" he prompted finally, when it looked as if Miach wasn't going to do anything but continue to sit there, swinging his legs back and forth. "You said there were two things. What's the other?"

Miach looked at him, his pale eyes full of something another might have called concern. "A puzzle," he said. "I'm not sure I know what to make of it."

Rùnach watched Miach reach behind him, then hand over a sheaf of paper, all without comment. Rùnach took it, then frowned. It looked as if part of it had been torn—and not very well. He looked at Miach, but the king of Neroche only shrugged. Rùnach frowned again, then read:

This poor wizardling here refused to give me what we bargained for, but now I know where to go to have it.

Fair warning

Rùnach dropped the sheaf of paper with the same alacrity he would have a live asp. Cathar leaned over and retrieved it, then set it on the high table, without comment.

"Interesting, isn't it?" Miach asked. "It would appear that someone found our guest in the crofter's shed. Lothar was—how would you describe it, Cathar?"

"Worse for wear," Cathar said succinctly.

"Lothar was worse for wear," Miach repeated. "And I believe he was so angry at having a note pinned to his tunic, he tried to tear it apart with his teeth."

"Did you find the missing piece," Rùnach asked faintly. "The bit after the *fair warning*?"

Cathar shook his head. "I was too busy trying to stay out of Lothar's way. He is bound, but he can roll and kick."

Rùnach walked away. He realized he was cursing, but it seemed to help keep him where he was instead of being scattered in a thousand different directions, so he kept at it. He turned and walked back to the table.

"This is very bad."

Miach looked at him in surprise. "Well, I'll admit it isn't good that Lothar was found, but surely the note means nothing—"

"Acair wrote that," Rùnach said flatly.

Miach looked at him for a moment or two, then blinked. "What in the hell are you talking about?"

"Acair of Ceangail," Rùnach said.

"I know who you meant," Miach said, slightly impatiently, "but I'm not sure why you would think of him. He's dead."

Rùnach folded his arms over his chest, because he thought it might give him something to do besides wring his hands. "How do you know?"

Miach exchanged a brief frown with Cathar, then looked back at him. "After that last battle, we went inside the keep to fetch out Adhémar and Adaira. Cathar found a note in Lothar's study written by Acair saying he had traded Gair's spell of Diminishing for Lothar's help in ridding Ceangail of the rest of his brothers."

"He lied," Rùnach said promptly. "He never had that spell to give."

"I didn't imagine he had," Miach said slowly. "I simply assumed that Acair had tried to double-cross Lothar and paid the price."

"Did you see a body?" Rùnach demanded.

"I wasn't looking for a body—"

"Then he's not dead."

Miach looked at him as if he were mad. "Rùnach, this is Lothar we're talking about. You know what he's capable of."

"You would know better than I," Rùnach said, not intending the words to wound, "for which I assure you I grieved with Soilléir every day you were locked in his dungeon. And because you were witness to what I only heard reports of, tell me exactly how many bodies of mages Lothar had destroyed did he not put on display somewhere, either in his hall or on his land."

Miach was motionless. "How could I possibly know that?"

"Very well," Rùnach said carefully, "how many mages that he destroyed *in front of you* did he put on display where you could admire them every day?"

Miach closed his eyes briefly. "Every last one."

"Precisely," Rùnach said. "If Acair had died, his corpse would have been dressed in velvets and displayed outside Lothar's front door until the sea had rotted it to mere bones and tatters. Such a trophy would never have simply been buried."

Miach pulled back, as if he'd just encountered something fragrantly vile in his supper. He considered, then shook his head. "I want to believe you, Rùnach, truly I do, but there was no possible way to escape that chamber."

"The seventh and final son of Gair of Ceangail and the witchwoman of Fàs?" Rùnach said flatly. "He has the full force of the power both parents possessed, and he's devious as hell. I'm not sure any of us knows exactly what he's capable of."

Miach considered, then looked at Cathar. "I suppose that chamber in Riamh where we found Acair's note earlier this spring wasn't exactly freshly dusted, was it?"

Cathar shook his head. "I would imagine no one had been there for several fortnights, at least."

Rùnach started to speak, then shook his head. He dragged his hand through his hair, then finally surrendered to the urge to pace. Miach's floor was made for it. Lovely blue slate with just the right amount of smoothness to make it beautiful but the occasional patch of rough stone so that a man with things troubling him didn't slip whilst about his pacing and fall upon his arse.

He stopped and looked at Cathar.

"How much worse for wear?"

"Do you want me to describe it for you?" Cathar asked, sounding as if he would have liked nothing better. "Lothar was extremely bruised and battered, but more interestingly, he was almost out of his head with rage. I would imagine whoever had found him had kicked him around quite a bit, then stayed to chat. And that note was pinned to the front of him as if he'd been a wee lad whose mother had sent him off to school with a message to the master?" He smirked. "A truly lovely piece of work, that." He shook his head, then let out a long breath. "And whilst this has been lovely, all this Fadaire is giving me a headache. If you two lads will excuse me, I need a drink. I'll let you know, brother, if I hear anything else."

Rùnach realized only then what he was speaking. He watched Cathar make Miach a low bow, had a firm hand on his shoulder in turn, then watched Cathar stride purposefully from the great hall. He looked back at Miach who was only shaking his head wryly.

"He bows to annoy me."

Rùnach smiled in spite of himself. "He has always loved you unreasonably. I daresay you couldn't ask for a better advisor."

"He is one," Miach agreed. "And here is my other."

Rùnach glanced over his shoulder to see his sister walking across the hall toward them. He leaned against the table, because every time he saw her, he was startled yet again. A little support for his poor form wasn't unwelcome.

"You think she looks so much like her, then?" Miach murmured.

"My mother? Aye, she does. But they are very different." He

looked at Miach quickly. "Not that Mhorghain isn't elegant or lovely."

Miach laughed a little. "You don't need to explain yourself to me, brother. I knew your mother too. I daresay she would be proud of how you've both turned out." He hopped down off the table and drew his wife into his arms. "You're up early."

"You were gone and I had the feeling you were about business I wanted to be a part of." Mhorghain looked up and met his eyes. "My love."

Miach laughed a little, kissed her thoroughly, then linked his fingers behind her back, keeping her trapped. "Very well, you've properly wooed me right from the start. Though the only reason you'll stay is because this doesn't involve you."

Mhorghain rolled her eyes, pushed out of her husband's arms, and gestured for him to sit back up on the table. She put her hand on the table, then looked at Rùnach purposely. "Well?"

Rùnach waved Miach on. "You tell her. I think I haven't the stomach for it."

He did, however, listen to Miach's very brief recounting of the events so far, because he couldn't help himself. He helped himself to a bit more pacing, but that didn't ease him.

"You're convinced it was this Acair," Mhorghain said slowly.

"*Fair warning* was his preferred signature," Rùnach said, trying to keep his lip from curling. "The arrogant little bastard."

"I believe, Rùnach, that he's at least fifty years older than you are," Miach ventured.

"Yet he looks not a day over a score," Rùnach muttered. "He gets that from his father."

"What does he mean by *now I know where to go*," Mhorghain asked slowly. She looked at Miach. "Is he talking about a place, do you think, or a person?"

Rùnach rubbed his hand over his face. "I don't know."

"Then what do you think he wants?" she pressed. "Specifically."

Rùnach looked his sister full in the face. "The spell of Diminishing, as always."

She wore the same what-*is*-that-in-my-stew look that Miach had just recently worn. They had obviously already spent too much time together. She managed to shake off her disgust more quickly than her husband, but he supposed that came from all that bracing discipline learned at Gobhann.

"Mages," she said in disgust. "What an unruly lot."

Rùnach exchanged a very brief smile with Miach. Some things never changed, apparently.

"So, what you're saying," Mhorghain continued, "is that Acair had gone to Riamh to trade the spell of Diminishing—which he didn't have—for Lothar's aid in casting everyone out from Ceangail—which he wasn't interested in." She looked at her husband. "That makes no sense, unless he intended to attempt to wrest Lothar's spell of Taking from him and start his collection with that."

"That's possible," Miach agreed.

"But how did he know where to find Lothar this morning?"

Rùnach swore. He realized he should have paid better heed to his first suspicion, which was that he had indeed seen his bastard brother walking toward Gobhann that morning on Melksham Island. Perhaps Acair had indeed overheard Miach talking earlier in the year about where Lothar was to be sent. If so, it was also possible that he had been loitering outside Weger's gates, perhaps even waiting for Lothar to come out. And if that was true, he had likely followed Lothar with the intention of having a little tête-à-tête out in the open where he might not be so easily bested.

Which boded ill for them all, actually.

Rùnach took a deep breath. "I think I saw Acair on Melksham."

"*What?*" Miach said incredulously.

"I thought I was mistaken," Rùnach said slowly, "but now I'm beginning to think perhaps not. Nicholas suggested as much, though I scoffed at it."

"And you think Acair knew Lothar was at Gobhann?" Mhorghain asked in surprise. "How is that possible?"

Miach looked at her grimly. "I wasn't careful when discussing where to put Lothar," he said. "I have no idea who might have been listening." He looked at Rùnach. "I hesitate to say this, but if Acair knew Lothar was in Gobhann and was possibly waiting for him, could he have seen you leave the keep?"

"Impossible," Rùnach said, though he realized there was hardly any sound to the word. He started to speak, then shook his head. "Aisling and I left in the middle of the night. Besides, Acair thought I was dead. They all thought I died at the well. If he had known I lived, he would have attacked me in Buidseachd long before now."

"Unless he thought you had the spell of Diminishing and could best him," Mhorghain pointed out.

"I'm sure that has given more than one mage uneasy dreams," Miach said.

Rùnach knew he had been pacing. He was fairly sure that his feet knew they were still supposed to be taking him across that lovely blue grey slate, but somehow he suddenly found himself standing, rooted to one spot. He turned and looked at his brother-in-law. "What did you say?"

Miach looked at him with a frown. "I said the thought of someone with Gair's spell of Diminishing taking his power has likely given more than one mage nightmares—"

Rùnach shook his head sharply. "That wasn't how you said it. What did you say, exactly?"

"I don't know," Miach said, holding up his hands in surrender. "Something about dreams, mages, magic—how the hell do I know what I said?"

Rùnach rubbed his hands over his face and sighed wearily. "Forgive me. I've heard too much about dreams of late, I suppose, and rivers of things running where they shouldn't be."

Mhorghain frowned. "Things running?"

"Rivers," Rùnach said crisply. "Rivers of dreams running through a captain's belowdecks, rivers of unease running through Weger's empty head—"

"I imagine that's just supper," Miach put in helpfully.

Rùnach glared at him, then turned to his sister. "Rivers of something he cannot name troubling the sleep of the former wizard king of Diarmailt. Lothar killing an innocent lad to get to me. Why?"

"You were in the wrong place at the wrong time," Miach said firmly. "That's all. And this business of dreams . . . well, what does it have to do with anything?"

Rùnach felt his entire world grind slowly, almost imperceptibly to a halt. He stood there, simply breathing, until he thought he could form words that for some reason seemed to be lingering just outside his reach.

"What did you say?" he managed, finally.

"I said, *What does this business of dreams have to do with anything,*" Miach said, looking faintly alarmed. "Why do you ask?"

Rùnach felt the floor become slippery beneath his feet, as if it had suddenly become a river itself. He looked down and saw the spells lying there, glittering as if they'd been water sparkling in the sunlight as it slid over flat rocks. He took a deep breath, then looked at his brother-in-law. "Because I've been in your library," he said hoarsely.

"What did you discover?" Miach asked.

"Bruadair."

Miach no doubt thought he was doing a smashing job of keeping his thoughts to himself, but that little twitch at the corner of his mouth was almost enough to inspire Rùnach to do damage to him.

"Stop smirking," he growled.

Miach only blinked. "I don't know what you're talking about."

"And I don't know what either of you is talking about," Mhorghain said, looking at them as if they'd both lost their minds. "What is—"

"Don't say the word," Rùnach said sharply.

She looked at him as if she'd never seen him before. "What *are* you going on about?"

Miach reached out and pulled her over to sit on the high table next to him. "In this, I think it might be wise to humor your brother. The place he mentioned, which discretion suggests we not name aloud, is not unfamiliar to any of us, actually. Sarah hails from there, though she wouldn't remember anything about it."

"Oh," Mhorghain said, drawing the word out. "I see."

Rùnach found that he was being observed by the pair of them as if he'd turned out to be a much more interesting scientific experiment than they'd thought before. He scowled at them, but they only continued to study him.

"That is an interesting place," Miach remarked. "Many lakes, very difficult to get in and out of. I'm curious as to why you've mentioned it."

"You bloody well aren't curious," Rùnach said shortly.

Miach started to speak, then shut his mouth. He even went so far as to hop off the table and look a bit more like a man with responsibilities. Rùnach looked over his shoulder to find none other than that irrepressible flirt, Mansourah of Neroche, striding into the great hall as if he had something important to say.

Fortunately for them all, he said nothing. He merely handed Miach a scrap of something. It had been well mauled, as if it had been ripped off a larger piece of paper. Miach took it, looked at it, then his face shuttered.

"Thank you," he said quietly.

"I thought you might want to see it," Mansourah said, his expression equally guarded. "I know Cathar had been as thorough as possible, but my curiosity got the better of me."

Rùnach was beginning to hate that word. He swore, then looked at Miach. "What did you find?"

Miach handed him the rather ragged scrap without comment. Rùnach looked down.

And then he wished quite desperately for somewhere to sit, for on that scrap of paper was scrawled a single word. A name, really. He didn't have to match it up to put the whole message together.

Fair warning . . . Rùnach.

"He knows you're alive, obviously," Miach said.

"I don't know how," Rùnach said hoarsely.

Miach looked at Rùnach slowly. "Perhaps he saw you on Melksham after all." He paused. "Or perhaps he found the notes you lost on the plains of Ailean."

Rùnach thought he might be ill very soon. "No one would spend the time to gather them up, much less make sense of them. No one could know I wrote them."

"Unless they knew your hand," Miach ventured, "as Acair might have. He could have been following you before. I suppose in the end, it doesn't matter. 'Tis obvious he plans to follow you now."

Rùnach felt the world around him begin to spin. Dreams, Bruadair, Acair of Ceangail sending a message to him, losing his notes, finding himself in the company of a woman who spun things out of thin air—

"I think," Miach said suddenly, taking the tattered scrap out of Rùnach's fingers, "that you might want to keep this all to yourself for a bit."

"Why?" Rùnach demanded.

Miach looked at his wife. "I don't think this is going to go well, do you?"

She sighed lightly. "I don't think so either."

Rùnach found himself rather unwilling, all of a sudden, to turn around.

Because he had the feeling he knew what he would find there.

Twenty-four

❧

A isling stood in the middle of what she could only assume, having merely read about that sort of thing in books, was the great hall of Tor Neroche. It felt a little as if she'd stumbled into a dream, but perhaps that was the nature of the place. Or perhaps she was still trapped in the dreams she'd been having the night before, dreams of black mages and evil and things that troubled her. She had dreamed of rivers running under rock, carrying along with them everything that was beautiful and sparkling, terminating in an enormous lake that was full of black, poisonous water.

She had risen from her bed to find herself alone. She had dressed in gear meant for traveling, because she had felt the overwhelming need to flee. It had occurred to her as she had forced herself to sit and warm herself briefly in front of a fire obviously built up for her comfort that she was perhaps slightly overwhelmed. She had spent the whole of her life closeted in a building with just enough light to see by, soaking up every hard fact she could when she was allowed freedom from the terrible drudgery of her work. Anything of a more mythical nature had been limited to those rare peeks into Mistress Muinear's book of lore.

Yet now, over the past two days, she had heard more about things she had believed to be the stuff of dreams than she had during the entirety of her life.

She had the feeling there were other things about to become reality for her, things she wasn't going to like.

The great hall she had been allowed inside was spectacular. The floor was a polished, bluish stone that looked as if water were running over it, though it wasn't slick beneath her feet. Perhaps those were spells. At the moment, she was honestly past telling.

Fireplaces flanked the hall along with one massive hearth placed boldly behind the raised dais. Above the equally impressive hearth hung two swords, crossed. They were glowing, one blood red, one icy blue, and both were covered with runes that sparkled gold and silver.

She decided that she had definitely wandered into a dream. Swords did not glow. Water did not run dry over pavement. And people she knew as simple members of a very large castle didn't loiter negligently around the lord's table as if they were sitting in their own kitchen.

She felt herself floating over to them as if her feet weren't quite touching that stone that was covered with water that wasn't there. It was strange how the water made a sound—

That wasn't the stone, that was the language the four souls in front of her were speaking.

She stopped several feet behind Rùnach and listened to it, drinking it in, feeling it fill a place in her soul she hadn't realized was so parched. They stopped too soon for her taste and Rùnach spun around to look at her in surprise. She stepped to her right so she could see him and the rest of them at the same time.

They looked so different.

She realized there was something shimmering in the air there in front of her, something that surrounded the four in front of her, a spell of Un-noticing, fashioned from Fadaire. She drew a circle with her finger, sending the air spinning, then pulled a thread out of that . . . spell . . . shining there before her and put it onto a bobbin she created out of more air.

Perhaps that time with Neroche's spinner hadn't been wasted.

The spell unraveled so quickly she could hardly control the uptake—indeed, she found she couldn't control it at all. The bobbin overflowed within moments and spilled out onto the floor, leaving her wondering what to do with it now. It sparkled with gold and silver runes that spoke of power and might. She watched that magic pooling there, then reached out to still her flywheel. She felt it come to a halt beneath her fingers. The magic lay there for a moment or two, then she breathed out and it vanished away. She looked up at the quartet standing before her.

They were watching her, openmouthed.

The fourth soul there, Miach's older brother Mansourah, she thought, wished them well and walked away. Aisling didn't bother with him. She turned first to Morgan, because while she hadn't had many conversations with Rùnach's sister, she had found her very much to her liking. Plainspoken and sensible, definitely a product of Weger's best efforts. Plus, she tended to recite the same strictures Aisling had memorized, which was comforting.

Only now, Morgan didn't look at all like a soldier. She was sitting on the table, clutching its edge, and looking as if she would have preferred to be anywhere but where she was. Aisling looked at her face. There was a mark above her brow, Weger's mark that seemed to be a dark, steely sort of silver color.

But above that, upon her brow, sat a crown. It was a beautiful thing, filigreed silver, and adorned with diamonds and pearls. However, it wasn't the crown of a princess.

It was the crown of a queen.

Aisling looked at her in stunned surprise. "You're wearing a crown."

"Well," Morgan said faintly, "not now."

"You're not just a simple farmer's wife," Aisling managed.

Morgan looked at her, then shook her head slowly. "I'm afraid not."

Rùnach started toward her, but Aisling held out her hand and he stopped. She found that she was starting to feel a slight bit of something she hadn't felt in quite a long while. It wasn't hurt or even surprise.

It was anger.

She didn't want to believe it, but she was beginning to suspect that the three in front of her had lied to her. There was obviously far more to them than they had let on. If they had known who they were and they had declined to say anything—

She looked at Miach, who also had a crown hovering over his head. "Who are you?" she demanded.

He looked at her, his very pale blue eyes troubled. "Mochriad-hemiach," he said quietly. "King of Neroche."

"Are you sure? You look very young."

"I feel very old at the moment," he said with a sigh, "but yes, I'm sure."

"And your lady wife?"

"Mhorghain," he said, glancing very briefly at Morgan, "grand-daughter of Sìle, king of Tòrr Dòrainn."

"Why didn't you say something?" she asked him, pained.

"Because your friend here asked me not—*oof*."

She was surprised how Rùnach had managed to get his elbow into Miach's—nay, Mochriadhemiach's—ribs from where he stood, but perhaps he was quicker than he had let on before. He was also a bigger liar.

"Again, this isn't going to go well," Miach murmured.

Aisling walked over to stand in front of Rùnach. "Who are you?"

"No one of consequence—"

He didn't manage an *oof*, likely because he was too stunned to do so. She heard his neck snap back, watched his eyes roll back in his head, then watched Miach catch him before he cracked that head on the side of the lord's table. Miach lowered him with relative gentleness to the floor. She shook out her hand because it felt as if she'd just cuffed a stone wall. Weger would have been impressed that his training had served her so well, but she found she was nothing but heartsick. She looked at the king of Neroche.

"He lied to me," she whispered.

"You could consider it that," Miach ventured, "or you might call it hedging."

Morgan pushed off the table and drew Aisling's arm through hers. "It doesn't matter, does it, Aisling? Let's leave these lads to their parsing of words and go off to find something to drink."

Aisling would have protested—she was slightly curious as to whether Rùnach would wake again or not—but Morgan gave her no choice but to walk out of the great hall. The queen of Neroche was very persuasive.

That lasted until they were just outside the hall doors, because her anger gave her strength she hadn't realized she had. She looked at Rùnach's sister, fully intending to be quite direct about what bothered her, but then she saw the expression on Morgan's face and felt all her anger dissipate. She was left with nothing but a chill that settled deep into her soul.

"I shouldn't have hit him," she said, wrapping her arms around herself. "He didn't deserve it. Not truly."

Morgan smiled briefly. "I can't say that I blame you. I doubt he will either."

Aisling took a deep breath. "I was angry."

"I've done worse," Morgan said with a shrug. "Shall I tell you of it? I guarantee you'll feel better after you know."

"I can't stay," Aisling said quickly. "And not because of . . . well, not because of what just happened."

Morgan hesitated. "I think you would be safer here."

"I'm not safe anywhere," Aisling said frankly. "There is a curse of death laid upon me."

"As I've said before, I don't believe in curses. Yours was likely just something made up by some black mage—or *any* mage, actually—with delusions of grandeur who thought he could oppress your people with a few clever words."

"I wish I could believe that—"

"Then believe this," Morgan said seriously. "You are not prepared to face alone what lies outside the keep. Rùnach would be appalled by the thought. Or, he would, if he were conscious to express an opinion."

"But my errand is not his," Aisling said slowly. "He promised Weger he would bring me as far as Tor Neroche, but I know he has other things to be doing."

Morgan looked at her in surprise. "Why did you want to come here?"

"I was sent to procure a mercenary."

Morgan lifted her eyebrows briefly. "Gobhann was a good place to start, then, I suppose. Was there no one there to suit?"

Aisling shook her head. "Weger didn't think so. He told me to come here."

"Then he had his reasons," Morgan said promptly. "We could go look over the garrison here, if you like. Then you could send that lad off on your errand and remain here in safety."

What Aisling wanted to do was find somewhere to lie down—preferably in Mistress Ceana's weaving room—and sleep until she could wake and have everything make sense. Either everything she had been told was a lie, or it was the truth. If it was the truth, then she had four days left in which to find and convince a man to meet the peddler at Taigh Hall. And if it were all a lie, then it didn't matter where she went or what she did.

Though she was beginning to wonder how anyone with the power to slay her would know when and if the bargain had been struck.

She looked at Morgan. "I am beginning to have doubts about several things."

"Are you?"

Aisling nodded. "I think I must go. I need to find the truth."

Morgan sighed. "I understand that, perhaps better than I'm able to tell you at the moment. Where will you go to find this truth?"

"Diarmailt, I think." Aisling frowned thoughtfully. "Rùnach said there was a very important library there. I think I might at least begin to acquire the truth I need in such a place."

Morgan looked at her in silence for another moment or two, then looked around her. A page sprang immediately to her side.

She leaned down, whispered in his ear, then ruffled his hair before he ran off. She linked arms with Aisling.

"I think you might be right. Let's go to the stables. I'm always happier out of doors. Thomas will bring your gear—or do his best to, that is. We'll chat whilst we wait, if you don't mind."

Aisling didn't suppose she minded much of anything at the moment, so she walked arm in arm with the queen of Neroche and jumped every time someone bowed to her companion.

It didn't take long for them to reach the stables. Morgan asked for Iteach to be groomed and prepared for a journey, then sat down with Aisling on a bale of hay. The stable lads seemed to not quite know how to take their queen, which Aisling found rather charming, all things considered. She supposed she should have been annoyed that Morgan had been just as deceitful as the rest of them, but the truth was, she hadn't been. She had promised to give the absolute truth for the questions she thought she could answer and she hadn't answered the ones she presumably would have been forced to lie about.

Perhaps Rùnach had done his best to do the same thing.

"I told you before that Nicholas had sent me on a quest to take Mehar's knife to the king of Neroche," Morgan said, "but I didn't tell you everything. Do you care to hear it now?"

Aisling nodded. Truth was truth, wherever she found it.

"Then what I didn't tell you was that in my company north was not only Adhémar, the king of Neroche himself, but Miach as well. I didn't know either of them, of course, because Adhémar was traveling in as much disguise as he could muster, and Miach was pretending to be a farmer."

Aisling considered, then smiled briefly. "I can imagine that."

"He doesn't exactly put on airs, does he?" Morgan said, sounding as if she thoroughly approved. "Unfortunately, being one of Weger's devotees, I had made no secret of my loathing for mages. This problem was made worse by Miach's becoming convinced he knew the past I had forgotten, the one that cast me in the role of youngest daughter to one of the worst black mages in history."

Aisling blinked, realizing the connection she hadn't made before. "Gair of Ceangail? He is your *father*?"

Morgan lifted her eyebrows briefly. "If you want to be exact, then yes."

"Rùnach's too," she said, feeling slightly horrified.

"Actually, that's true as well," Morgan agreed, "though Rùnach is nothing like him. As for the other, the particulars of our journey here are unimportant, but let's just say that Mehar of Angesand's sword—"

"The one in the great hall that glows with a blue light?"

Morgan looked faintly startled. "Aye, that one. And when I first saw it in the great hall, it not only glowed for me, it sang, then it leapt off the wall into my hand. I turned around and found Adhémar and his six brothers standing on the other side of the high table. It was then that I was told he was the king and realized that Miach was his youngest brother, the archmage of the realm and a liar of the first water."

"Ah," Aisling said, beginning to suspect that things had not turned out well for Miach. "What did you do?"

Morgan shifted uncomfortably. "I'm not proud of this, but I was so angry—" She had to take a deep breath. "Well, I took Mehar's sword and slammed it against the table, shattering it into hundreds of shards."

Aisling felt her mouth fall open. "What did you do then?"

"I ran."

"Ah," Aisling said, finding the word surprisingly satisfying. She looked at Rùnach's sister and felt as if she were truly seeing her for the first time. "Then you do understand."

"I do understand," Morgan agreed. "Miach followed me, eventually, when he could. We came to an understanding."

Aisling sighed. "I don't know if I can ever come to an understanding with your brother."

"Why not?"

Aisling rubbed her hands, because they pained her a bit. Too much spinning, perhaps. At least her skin was soft from the lanolin in the wool, not scratched to bits from the coarseness of thread spun from who knew what. She looked down at her hands until she thought she could look at Morgan and not say too much.

"He is a prince," she said finally, "and I am nothing at all."

Morgan shrugged. "That is not how my brother thinks, though perhaps that may not be as clear as it should have been. But I understand your hesitation. His scars are quite off-putting—"

Aisling looked at her sharply only to realize that Morgan was watching her with a half smile that wasn't quite teasing but was definitely knowing. She pursed her lips.

"I don't see them anymore."

"I didn't imagine you did."

"He lied to me."

"Before or after you told him the absolute truth about yourself?"

Aisling blinked, then smiled. "You spent too many years at Gobhann."

Morgan laughed a little. "I fear Weger ruined me for polite company, 'tis true. But perhaps you can see where Rùnach might have a bit of room for hedging. As for this curse you seem to believe in, all I can say is that Weger would tell you to find out the truth of the matter for yourself. Though I imagine Rùnach has suggested the same thing already."

"He has," Aisling said slowly.

"And if something in your country needs to be changed, Weger would tell you to see it changed. If you've the courage for it."

Aisling looked down at her hands, hands that had done things she'd been forbidden to do for the whole of her life, and wondered what else her hands might do. She looked at Rùnach's sister. "I don't yet," she said, "but I think I might do well to find it."

Morgan slapped her hands on her knees. "That was exactly what I wanted to hear. I will tell you, though, that I don't think you should go alone."

"I don't think there's a swordsman alive who would come along with me when I could not guarantee either payment or success."

"You might ask Rùnach, you know. He's handy enough with a blade."

"I don't think he's going to want to talk to me anymore."

"Now that you clipped him under the chin?" Morgan only laughed. "He deserved exactly what you gave him and more."

"He'll be furious when he wakes."

"He won't," Morgan said cheerfully. "He'll consider it penance." She shot Aisling a look. "He is a bit bossy, though, and will likely dictate your actions to you, which you may not want. Best disabuse him of that notion right off. As for anything else, I'll do for you what I can."

Aisling managed a smile. "You're very kind."

"Blessed," Morgan corrected, then she smiled. "And here is my page with your gear. I think you should steal my brother's horse. I've had him saddled for you, as you can see."

"Rùnach won't be happy."

"They never are," Morgan said with a wink. "Always overattached to their horseflesh, but Rùnach will survive."

Aisling took the satchel and her bow and arrows from the lad who bowed respectfully, then moved to stand a discreet distance away. The satchel contained nothing but Ochadius's book and the book Nicholas of Lismòr had given her, but it was enough. She looked at Morgan.

"I think this is all I need."

"Perhaps you'll find other things in your saddlebags," Morgan said. She looked at Aisling. "If you want one suggestion, it would be that you find out who you are, and very quickly before someone you won't like does."

"Does that happen?"

"I'm afraid it does."

Aisling didn't want to know how Morgan knew, so she didn't ask. She simply stood and waited until she heard the sound of horse hooves.

Iteach whinnied when he saw her. Aisling was so surprised, she felt her eyes burn with tears she couldn't manage to shed.

"He knows me," she murmured.

"Of course he does," Morgan said. "Likes you too, apparently. Look at that lovely saddle he's conjured up for you."

Aisling looked at Rùnach's sister. "He has magic."

"I would hazard a guess he does," Morgan agreed, "but Rùnach admitted that already, if memory serves." She turned and faced Aisling squarely. "I want you to know, Aisling, that you may come back here any time you like. You will always be welcome in our hall."

It took a moment before Aisling could find her voice. She looked at the queen of Neroche and attempted a smile.

"Thank you," she managed. "It is a very great gift."

"I understand needing a place to land," Morgan said. "I was very fortunate to have such a place in my youth. I'm pleased to be able to provide the same for you here. As for anything else, what can I do?"

"Don't tell Rùnach where I've gone," Aisling said. "He'll just follow me and jam up the works."

"Men tend to do that," Morgan agreed.

"He doesn't like me very much."

Morgan smiled. "Oh, I wouldn't say that."

"He'll like me even less when he finds out I've poached his horse, but I'll send Iteach back when I'm finished. You could apologize for the theft to him, if you like."

"I'll think about it," Morgan said with a smile. "We'll see how he behaves when he wakes."

Aisling returned her smile, accepted reins, then led Iteach out of the stables into the courtyard. She climbed on, waved to Morgan, then held on as the horse leapt up into the air. She supposed it said something that she merely gasped instead of shrieking.

Life was, she had to admit, full of things she hadn't expected.

She landed two hours later, because she'd seen something in a clearing below her that she thought she might have to have a closer look at.

Rùnach, as it happened.

Iteach wasn't particularly enthusiastic about landing, but she insisted. She had forgiven Rùnach before Morgan had even told her details about her own little scuffle with Miach's family sword. It had taken but another hour to make her think that she had leapt where she should have looked first. When she'd seen the man in the clearing below, looking up into the sky, she'd known that she'd been given a gift.

She would have landed in the clearing, but Iteach balked. She supposed if she managed to get him on the ground, that was perhaps all she could ask for. She slid off the saddle when she was able, took a moment to gather not only her legs beneath her but her thoughts in her head, then walked into the clearing to find Rùnach standing there with his back to her.

He was a little more travel-stained than she remembered him being, but perhaps he had come in haste. That was almost enough to bring a smile to her face.

"Rùnach?"

The man was very still, then he turned around.

It was at that moment that she realized she had made a very serious mistake.

Twenty-five

✳

Rùnach woke. It took him a moment or two to realize that no one had bothered to pick him up off the floor where he'd fallen when he'd been felled—

By a slip of a girl who had apparently learned more at Weger's bony knee than he'd suspected.

He looked up to find Miach in the same place he'd seen him before, sitting on the lord's table, swinging his legs idly back and forth, as if he simply didn't have anything better to do. Rùnach sat up, clutched his head until it stopped spinning, then glared at the king of Neroche.

"What in the hell was that?"

"You," Miach said, "being bested by a wraith of a wench who I will tell you is absolutely furious."

"She was hedging as well," Rùnach muttered.

Miach laughed a little. "Rùnach, my friend, if you haven't learned for yourself that it is a far different thing when they do something than when we do the same thing, then there is no hope for you. I suggest a quick trot after her and an apology."

"Where did she go?"

"I have no idea. Ask Morgan."

Rùnach staggered to his feet, then had to lean back against the table. He watched his sister saunter into the great hall as if she hadn't a care in the world.

"Where is she?" he rasped.

"Gone," Mhorghain said cheerfully. "Is there wine?"

Miach reached behind him and poured her a cup, which he then handed to her. He looked thoughtfully off into the distance. "You know," he said to apparently no one in particular, "there is something very different about that gel, but I can't quite lay my finger on what."

"She spins air," Mhorghain said. "That's something different."

"And she pulled my spell of Un-noticing right off its frame and spun it into something that is no longer there. Interesting, wouldn't you say?"

"I would," she agreed. "Very interesting, that."

"I've been thinking other thoughts," Miach offered helpfully.

"Which ones, my love?"

Miach patted the spot next to him on the table, then put his arm around his wife when she hopped up to sit next to him. "You know what they do in Bruadair, don't you?"

"I'm not sure I do. Do you?"

Rùnach growled before he could stop himself. His sister and brother-in-law looked at him briefly before they continued their conversation with each other.

"They're dreamweavers."

"Dreamweavers?" Mhorghain echoed. "How interesting. How is it they weave dreams?"

"I'm not sure," Miach said thoughtfully. "There must be an art to it, wouldn't you suppose?"

"I would," she agreed. "It begs the question, does it not, where it is they get the dreams to weave? Someone has to spin them, I should think."

"I couldn't agree more—"

"They can't," Rùnach said flatly.

Mhorghain and Miach looked at him as one.

"They can't?" Miach asked politely.

"They aren't *allowed* to spin," Rùnach said, realizing he was coming very close to growling again. "The penalty for spinning is death."

"But," Miach said slowly, fixing him with a look Rùnach couldn't quite decipher, "your lady can spin and not die, can't she?"

"Well, of course she can—" Rùnach stopped, then felt as if he'd just run into Aisling's fist again. His mouth fell open. "What are you suggesting?"

Miach shrugged. "She spins air."

"And spells," Mhorghain added helpfully. "That's unusual. I wonder what the penalty for *that* is." She looked at her husband. "Because didn't you say they weren't allowed to spin there in Bruadair?"

"No, Rùnach said that. Didn't you, Rùnach?"

Rùnach found that he was beginning to regret having regained consciousness. "What are you saying?"

"I think you should go get her now," Miach suggested, "and do your damndest to keep her safe."

"I was already planning on that."

"And don't lie to her anymore," Mhorghain added.

Rùnach was tempted to clack their heads together, but it was his sister after all and he was a gentleman. He was willing to sharpen his tongue on her husband, though, without the slightest regret. He opened his mouth to do just that, but Miach held up his hands before he could even start.

"Don't shout at me," he said evenly. "I didn't let her go; I've been here watching over you. Blame Morgan."

"Coward," she said, elbowing him companionably.

"He's cranky," Miach said with a shudder. "I don't want to tangle with him in this mood."

Rùnach turned a dark look on his sister. "What is this *go get her now* of which your husband speaks?" he asked with an attempt at politeness. "I suppose I don't dare hope you managed to talk her into stomping about safely in a chamber here until her pique has subsided, can I?"

"She wanted to leave the keep," Mhorghain said. "Who was I to stop her? She's a woman full grown and obviously about some noble quest."

"To Diarmailt," Rùnach said through gritted teeth. "The library at Diarmailt. You sent her off to that hellhole by herself!"

"Nay," Mhorghain said reasonably, "I sent her off with your horse."

"*What!*"

"You're awfully interested for a man who said he didn't care for her," Miach said.

"I never said I didn't care for her."

"Then perhaps you weren't vocal enough in your declarations of affection," Mhorghain offered. "That's important, you know."

Rùnach threw up his hands and left the great hall. It was either that or tell both his sister and her husband exactly what he thought of them.

Which was that they were a very lovely couple and he envied them their happiness to the very depths of his soul.

By the time he reached the chamber he'd been sharing with Aisling, his own fit of pique had subsided to be replaced with something that left him feeling cold enough that he had to stand in front of the fire for several minutes before he thought his hands would work as they should.

He couldn't follow her, because if he did, he would lead Acair to her.

And if Acair had any idea what she could do . . .

He forced himself to pack his gear without emotion. He started to leave the chamber, then saw what had been left on the table there.

It was the yarn Aisling had spun. Mistress Ceana had turned it into a skein and tucked a pair of knitting needles into it. He considered, then placed it carefully in the top of his pack. He left the chamber and started back through the castle. He didn't bother to cover his face, for what need was there? He wasn't going to put

Aisling in danger by being anywhere near her, so it didn't matter who knew where he was.

He continued to repeat that to himself as he made his way out to the stables, drawing the perfect sensibility of that around him like a warm cloak. After all, who could fault him for his reasoning? Aisling would be fine. In fact, she would be far better off without him than she would be with him. He had nothing to offer her, no means to see to her, no way to keep her safe, not even a plan to elude those he could hardly fathom would be looking for him.

Besides, he didn't care for Aisling. She had none of the social graces he had come to expect in his women, no regal pedigree, no long list of suitors she had rejected in order to be free to receive his attentions.

But she could spin air.

By the time he reached the stables, he had a blinding headache. He squinted against the faint sunlight and wasn't terribly surprised to find his sister and her husband waiting for him. A horse stood there as well, wearing wings on all four hooves. He looked at Miach.

"Dare I ask?"

"I wouldn't," Miach advised, "and definitely don't tell Hearn when next you see him. Luath will carry you where you need to go, then you might send him back. I don't want to answer to Hearn for your activities."

Rùnach blew out his breath. "Thank you."

"You should also, if I might be so bold," Miach said carefully, "wear a spell of Un-noticing. You never know who might be watching."

"And then how will Aisling see me?"

Miach looked at him knowingly. "Going after her, are you?"

Rùnach drew his hand over his eyes. "Aye, fool that I am." He looked at Miach instead of Mhorghain because he knew that his brother-in-law would understand perfectly the thoughts that tortured him. "With a black mageling on my heels and absolutely no way to protect her."

"I could possibly, with enough effort and thought, make it so the spell took a wee rest when you were within a certain distance of your love. If you like. Or, even better, have it respond to your voice. You could call it or dismiss it at will. It won't protect you, but it will hide you."

Rùnach closed his eyes briefly. "You are too generous."

"My worst fault."

"And annoying."

Miach laughed and gave him a pair of useful words to use with the spell he cast over him. "This will cover your lady as well when you meet."

"If we meet."

"Fly hard," Miach suggested.

"And be careful," Mhorghain said quietly.

He pulled her into a quick, tight hug, slapped her husband on the back of the head, then mounted and held on as Luath leapt into the air without any of the grace of Iteach. He wasn't entirely sure Miach hadn't instructed the beast to make the journey as rough as possible.

He wouldn't have been surprised.

An hour later, he was walking into a glade. His weapons were behind him, his pack hidden in the woods, his mount long gone. He saw Aisling first, sitting on a log, facing a man who was sitting across a small fire from her. It was the same tableau he'd seen from the air, but it was substantially more distressing to see it right there in front of him. Aisling didn't look as if she'd been harmed, though she was very pale. He stopped with Aisling on his right, the fire in front of him, and one of his bastard brothers sitting on a log to his left.

At least it wasn't Acair. He supposed he should have been grateful for small favors.

"Well, who have we here?"

Rùnach looked at his half brother, sixth out of seven, and

forced himself to maintain a bland expression. "I imagine you'll divine that, with enough time."

Gàrlach shook his head, wearing a faint smile of disbelief. "I could hardly credit it when your little wench there blurted out your name, but miracles never cease."

"So they don't," Rùnach agreed. He nodded toward Aisling. "Do you mind if I sit?"

Gàrlach waved expansively. "Be my guest. I'll make tea, shall I?"

Rùnach supposed anything Gàrlach did to keep himself busy could only be considered a good thing, so he nodded, then walked over to sit down next to Aisling on the log. She was trembling.

"How are you?" he murmured.

"I've had better days."

"I can sympathize."

She looked at him. "Sorry I hit you."

"I fully intend to exact an excruciating penalty."

She blanched. He realized immediately that perhaps she hadn't told him nearly as much as she should have about her past. He shook his head just the slightest bit.

"Do you care to know what it will be?"

"Not particularly, but if you must tell me, say on."

He smiled briefly. "You must allow me from this moment on to shamelessly coddle you at all times."

She looked at him from rather bloodshot eyes. "You are a terrible man."

"Is that why you ran?"

"Nay, I ran because . . ." She sighed. "Well, you did nothing more than I did, but you're more important than I am, so it was worse."

He laughed a little. "When I come up with the reply that deserves, believe me, you'll hear it. Quite possibly quite loudly." He nudged her companionably with his shoulder. "Will you survive it?"

She blinked rapidly a time or two. "I truly don't understand why you are kind to me."

"Let's scamper off somewhere else, and I'll see if I can't explain it to you."

"Will we manage that, do you think?"

He tried to maintain an air of carelessness, but he feared he had failed to do it properly. "I don't know," he admitted. "I'm less armed for this than I would like to be."

"I have an idea."

He started to tell her *absolutely not*, but he realized he might not have a choice. "Let us have a bit of pleasant conversation here, then we'll conclude the interview. We'll see if your idea suits then, shall we?"

"Very well." She leaned against him. "Is that truly your brother?"

"Half brother," he admitted. "Appalling, isn't it?"

"I don't think he's very nice," she said very quietly, "though he did nothing untoward to me."

Yet was Rùnach's first thought, but he thought it might be wise to keep that to himself. If he didn't get them both away soon, the misery would be spread about equally.

Again, at least it wasn't Acair.

He accepted a china cup and saucer from Gàrlach, watched Aisling do the same thing, but knew he didn't have to tell her not to drink.

"It has been a year or two, Rùnach," Gàrlach said. "We thought you were dead. I'm surprised, since you seem to be quite alive, that you haven't made a visit."

"Oh, with this and that," Rùnach said waving a hand dismissively, "one neglects these sorts of social calls. You look as if you've been traveling. Somewhere interesting?"

"Shettlestoune," Gàrlach said, fixing Rùnach with a look utterly empty of all emotion. "I wonder if you know who I found there?"

"I've heard," Rùnach allowed. "How is the old rapscallion?"

"Let's just say Ruithneadh isn't going to want to be planning any pleasant strolls through Dòire any time soon," Gàrlach said with a smirk. "Father was not pleased with his current accommodations."

"And did you offer aid?"

"Are you daft?" Gàrlach snapped. "I don't want him free, I want his damned book!"

"Didn't you have his book?" Rùnach asked, frowning as if he were truly puzzled. "I thought it would be in the library at Cean-gail."

"It was initially, for all the good it did me," Gàrlach said curtly. "I could never find it. There was some damned spell on the spines of everything there."

Rùnach didn't suppose there was any use in telling him that the original idea for that spell of his father's that did indeed hide all the books there had been his and that he'd created a counter-spell that worked beautifully.

"What a shame," Rùnach said with a heavy sigh.

"Oh, I'm much less broken up over that than I was before," Gàrlach said smoothly. "Now that I have you."

"And what could you possibly want with me?" Rùnach asked, affecting an innocent look. "Recipes for teatime delights?"

"I believe I'll have your power first."

"I have no power," Rùnach said, then he heard his teacup shat-ter. That was likely because he had dropped it against something; a rock, most likely.

He had forgotten over the years just how powerful all his bas-tard brothers were. They might have been fools, but they were full of a terrible legacy. Gàrlach's ransacking of his soul was almost enough to kill him, truth be told. He felt Aisling's hand clutching the back of his cloak, keeping him from falling backward off the log. It took him a moment or two before he stopped seeing stars, but he managed it eventually.

"You're telling the truth," Gàrlach said, sounding stunned.

"I told you so," Rùnach gasped.

"No matter," Gàrlach said coldly. "I know what you have mem-orized."

"Sorry, don't have that either," Rùnach managed. He stood up and pulled Aisling up with him. "We have to go *now*," he whis-pered frantically, "or we won't manage it at all."

She was shaking so badly, he wasn't sure which of the two of them would fall over first. He stepped in front of her, then turned to give her time to get over the log without being in his half brother's sights.

The spell slammed into his back, sending him sprawling over Aisling and the log both. He staggered to his feet, braced for the next volley, certain it would mean his death. But at least it would allow Aisling time to flee—

But instead, she began to spin.

He vowed right there that he would find a way, any way, even if he had to beg spells that worked on their own without anything from him besides pulling them from his pocket, to keep her safe.

His brother froze, watching as she created an enormous wheel from air.

She spun fire, pulling the spells Gàrlach was soon spitting out as quickly as possible into that fire, then sending what she was spinning around him as if he'd been a simple bobbin made just for her purposes. Rùnach realized he was gaping at her just as his half brother was, but the truth was, he couldn't help himself.

The fire continually swirled around Gàrlach, leaving him standing there helpless in the midst of a vortex of his own spells. Rùnach felt Aisling fumble for his hand and pull him along with her. He stumbled after her, ignoring the shouting going on behind him, not daring to ask how long she could make it last.

Iteach appeared in front of them suddenly, looking very fierce. Rùnach stumbled with Aisling to fetch their gear, speaking the word that called to Miach's spell as they went, hoping fervently that it would work as promised. He hooked gear onto Iteach's saddle, then boosted Aisling up onto his back. He crawled up after her with much less grace, but the new howls of outrage he heard from Gàrlach left him feeling slightly less panicked than before. He and Aisling were obviously quite safely invisible.

Iteach leapt up into the sky and climbed fiercely on wings Rùnach couldn't remember having seem him acquire. It was not a pleasant ascent, but Rùnach didn't think to ask for a better. He was too busy trying not to lose what was left of supper from the night before, though he couldn't decide if that was from the unpleasantly turbulent ride or the aftereffects of his bastard brother's ministrations.

He simply closed his eyes and held on to Aisling as tightly as possible until his head stopped swimming and Iteach settled down into something a bit more measured. He would have loosened his embrace but when he started to, Aisling clutched his arms and shook her head.

After an hour, he realized he simply wasn't going to make it if something didn't change very soon.

"We have to land," he shouted over the wind.

She almost fell off the saddle. "Why?"

"Because I'm going to be violently ill and don't particularly want to puke down the back of your cloak."

She looked over her shoulder at him, then she smiled. "You're serious."

"Painfully. Miach gave me a spell, though, that will keep us covered. No one will see us."

"I know," she said. "I've seen it. But that man—"

"Details, later," he said, closing his eyes and praying he would make it back to the ground before he fell senseless. "Iteach, find a secluded . . . spot . . ."

The descent was worse than the ascent, as was the subsequent landing he made directly on his face as he fell out of the saddle.

He was, he decided after he'd finished retching past where any man should have had to in front of a woman he thought he might like to impress, going to have to rethink his strategy when it came to being out in the world. It was obvious that his plan to be a simple soldier was simply not going to work.

And that was the last thought he managed before he slid helplessly into darkness.

Twenty-six

❧

Aisling paced in the shadows of what could have charitably been called a glade but was perhaps better termed a very slim parting of trees that seemed determined to close back in above her. If she hadn't known better, she might have begun to suspect those trees were sentient.

Then again, given all the things that had turned out to be anything but what she'd thought they were, she wouldn't have been surprised.

She glanced to her left. There in the trees stood an enormous hound of such ferocious mien, she almost quailed. Well, she might have if he didn't occasionally look at her and wicker, as if to remind her that, aye, he was still, under all that fierceness, merely Rùnach's horse.

She finally sat down on a half-rotted stump and looked down at the felled son of a black mage who lay at her feet on a bed of pine needles that she hoped were as soft as they looked. She had been convinced that his brush with disgorging whatever it had been that had ailed him would be what finished him off. He lay where he had fallen simply because he was too heavy for her to move. So she'd drawn his sword and propped it up against her shoulder where she might have a better chance of simply bringing it down on a miscreant's head and rendering him unconscious enough that he could do further damage.

Now, though, Rùnach's sword was resting next to her on her right, Rùnach was resting next to her on her left, and she was trying to keep breathing normally instead of gasping in terror.

She did not care for black mages or their unscrupulous get.

She looked off into the trees, unhappily able to recall her encounter with Rùnach's half brother. She had realized when she'd seen his face that she had made a terrible mistake. And once she'd seen his face, she'd noticed that he wasn't quite as tall as Rùnach, nor as well built, nor as handsome, though he had been handsome enough. He had invited her to sit on a fallen log, fashioned himself a comfortable seat out of nothing, then created a small fire in front of her. She had supposed at the time she had been fortunate to have heard so many tales of magic or she might have been rather startled at what she'd seen. As it was, she had simply stared at a man she had no doubts belonged in some way to Gair of Ceangail.

Rùnach groaned suddenly, then swore. She knelt down next to him and turned him over, with help fortunately from the patient himself.

"I feel terrible," he managed.

"You look terrible," she agreed. "What did you eat?"

"Nothing, unfortunately," he said. "Here, help me sit up—"

"I don't think you're going anywhere for a while," she said firmly. "Stay where you are."

He looked up at her, then reached up and tucked her hair behind her ear. "You have," he said hoarsely, "the most amazing eyes I've ever seen."

"You're feverish."

He laughed a little. "Probably so, but not for the reasons you think." He dropped his hand, but only so he had hold of her forearm. "Thank you for the rescue."

"What—oh, that."

"Aye, that," he said. "The things you can do, woman, with thin air—" He coughed a little. "How long will what you spun last, do you think?"

"I have no idea," she said honestly. "I'm not even sure what that was."

"A miracle, wrought by you, to save my sorry arse," he said, patting her arm, then carefully pushing himself up until he was sitting. He put his hand over his face for a moment or two, then looked at her and smiled. "Thank you."

"Shall we consider it a trade for my having felled you in your brother-in-law the king's great hall?" she asked.

"Absolutely."

"I have questions for you."

He sighed. "I imagine you do." He slid her a look. "And yes, Aisling, I realize I won't be having any answers from you. I'm going to save my breath and not bother to ask."

"Thank you," she said quietly.

"You find me in a weakened and pitiful state," he said. "It won't last, so you'd best take advantage of it."

"Who are you?"

"You're not wasting any time, are you?"

She made herself comfortable on the bed of pine needles that she found was not at all sharp. "Talk."

He leaned back on his hands. "I am Rùnach," he said with a sigh, "second son of Gair of Ceangail and Sarait of Tòrr Dòrainn."

"You're an elf," she accused.

"Mostly," he agreed slowly. "Part wizard, if you want to be completely accurate."

She stopped herself just before she touched him. He caught her wrist before she could pull her arm away, then looked at her with a faint smile.

"Go ahead."

She shot him a warning look. "You're laughing at me."

"I am most definitely *not* laughing at you."

"I'm looking for pointed ears."

"I know."

She reached out and tucked his hair behind his ears, one side at a time, just as he'd done to her so many times in the past. She met his gaze.

"No telltale signs there."

"I guess you'll just have to take my word for it, then," he said solemnly.

She touched his scarred cheek before she thought better of it. He merely closed his eyes, which she supposed was just as well. That way, he wouldn't have to watch her try not to weep.

"You were at that well, weren't you?"

He opened his very green eyes and looked at her. "Unfortunately," he agreed. "It was a bit dodgy, truth be told."

She could only imagine. Mistress Ceana had given her the entire tale whilst they had been sorting through black woolen locks, though she hadn't divulged names. Aisling had thought that just as well. She knew the number and kind of the children, knew what had happened to Sarait and three of the brothers, heard that the youngest brother and wee gel had both disappeared into places that had hidden them for years.

"What happened to you there?" she whispered.

"Ah, well, nothing very interesting," Rùnach said with a shrug. "You know what my father did there, I believe. Someone—either my mother or my older brother—brought the cap of that damned well down on my hands without realizing it. I don't remember anything after that, though I suppose someone pulled my hands free. I knew there was nothing I could do for anyone. My younger brothers and my mother were dead, Keir was gone, my father washed away with the evil from the well—or so we thought—and Ruith and Mhorghain nowhere to be found." He smiled. "I found a place to land and there I've been for several years, making a nuisance of myself."

"Then why does your sister have magic and you don't?"

"My father took mine," he said, as easily as if he spoke of losing a pair of socks. "It was no great loss, I assure you."

She imagined it was, though given that just speaking of magic felt strange, she thought she might be better off not to comment. "Is that what that man was talking about?" she said, gesturing back the way they had come. "Taking magic?"

"'Tis what black mages do."

She looked at him searchingly. "Did he try to do it to you? There in that glade?"

"Hmmm," he said. "Passing unpleasant, that ransacking."

"Oh, Rùnach," she said quietly. She put her arms around him. She felt his arms go around her and his breath catch.

"Damn you, woman," he said with a miserable laugh, "you're going to be the first person in a score of years to reduce me to tears." She held him tightly. "I never weep either."

"Your eyes were red the other night."

She pulled back and looked at him with a frown. "They were not."

He smiled, took her face in his hands, then kissed the end of her nose. He released her, then staggered to his feet, as if he thought she might clip him again under the chin if he didn't. He swayed once, steadied himself, then held down his hands for her.

"Let's be off, wench, before we both wind up weeping. You're maudlin enough, I daresay, for the both of us."

She scowled at him. "You cad."

He laughed as he pulled her up to her feet and into his arms. "Thank you," he whispered against her ear. "For holding me together."

All she could do was return the embrace. It was impossible to tell him how often she had been comforted by his doing the same for her.

He released her, then very deliberately reached up and tucked her hair behind both ears. He studied her ears closely, then smiled into her eyes.

"I think I might see a smidgeon of pointy-ness there."

She pursed her lips. "Fetch your sword, lad, before you think too hard about it and hurt yourself."

He smiled in that particular way that showed off his dimple in its best light, fetched his sword, then looked at her. His smile faded. "We must decide on a destination, Aisling. And what to do."

"I don't know what to do now," she said slowly.

"*Stop poaching my horse* would be my first suggestion," he said, "for it makes it very difficult for me to follow you. As for where we go now, I think you might have a suggestion."

"The library at Diarmailt?"

He nodded. "I assumed that was where you were headed."

She stopped and turned to face him. "I have to know the truth. About—" She looked at him helplessly. "Well, about . . . you know."

"I know," he said quietly. "I'll help you look."

"I'm afraid the answers might get us both killed."

"Well, what's the use of a miserable fortnight spent in Gobhann if we can't trot out our fierce fighting skills to fend off feisty librarians now and again?" He cocked an ear toward the hound in the trees, then looked at her. "What shape shall Iteach take? He wants to know your preference."

She blinked. "Is he asking me?"

"He is asking you."

She hadn't but begun to imagine how he might look as . . . as a glittering black dragon, fierce and terrifying.

He was spectacular.

He scarce fit into the glade, which necessitated their backing up into the trees to give him room to properly spread out his wings. Aisling felt her mouth go dry. She looked up at Rùnach.

"Ah—"

He laughed. "Your choice, not mine."

"He'll terrify everyone we meet."

"Which will suit him perfectly," Rùnach said, "though Miach's spell of Un-noticing will unfortunately rob our good steed of as many howls of terror as he might otherwise enjoy." He reached for her hand. "Let's be off. I think you may be holding me for a bit of this trip. I'm still feeling a little faint."

She looked at him quickly, then felt her mouth fall open. "You liar."

He smiled, a small, mischievous smile that she was quite certain had sent more than one woman to her swooning couch.

"Stop that," she added.

"No," he said cheerfully.

She turned away. She started toward Iteach, then stopped in mid-step. She stood next to that terrifying creature from myth and looked up at another creature she had thought could be found only in myth. She took an unsteady breath.

"You don't believe in curses?"

He shook his head slowly.

"I was told I would die if I didn't find a swordsman to save my country within three se'nnights."

"And yet you breathe."

"I thought perhaps I might have misheard it," she said, watching his face closely, "but I don't think so. It could have been three fortnights, though."

"Which is finished when?"

"In four days."

"What else were you told?"

"That if I crossed the border, I would die."

"And yet you live." He reached out and smoothed the hair back from her face. "And you spin. A capital offense that one, wasn't it?"

She nodded.

He turned her to him and put his hands on her shoulders. "You, love, have braved Weger's gates, mythical steeds from legend, and two black mages with less than pleasant intentions, and you have survived them all. If you want my opinion, I think there is more to you than you suspect. And I don't think your destiny calls for you to be felled by a curse. But if you want proof, let's find answers."

"In Diarmailt?"

"In Diarmailt."

She paused. "And it would serve you as well?"

He shrugged. "As much as it wounds my pride, I won't be unhappy to lose myself in a large city for a bit and enjoy the safety of anonymity. If that losing allows us to search for an answer or two, so much the better."

"Because of that mage back there?"

He hesitated, then shook his head. "He isn't my worry. I have been given fair warning by someone else, and it behooves me to find out why."

"Rùnach," she said, finding she was rather more appalled than perhaps she should have been. "What are you talking about?"

"Where were you born, Aisling?"

She pursed her lips. "I can't say."

"Neither can I," he said cheerfully. "I suppose we'll both have to rely on the merits of King Simeon's library."

She gaped at him. He only winked and held out his hand.

"Let's go."

She supposed there was no point in putting off the inevitable any longer, either the ride or what awaited her at the end of the journey.

Rùnach had apparently been serious about her holding on to him, for she soon found herself sitting behind him. She supposed that was something of a boon, partly because she didn't have to watch as Iteach leapt up into the air through that impossibly small space between the trees and climbed mercilessly toward the stars, and partly because Rùnach blocked the wind quite handily.

And she had to admit there was something almost peaceful about putting her arms around his waist and resting her cheek against his shoulder. She was able, even in the strong light of late afternoon, to reach out her hand and trail her fingers through not only the spell they were covered with but the magic Iteach created as he flew.

It was nothing she'd ever expected.

She closed her eyes, finally, because she couldn't see any longer for her tears. She had started her journey with loss, loss of what was known, loss of Mistress Muinear, loss of any hope for a life free of the Guild. And then, beyond all reason, she had found her life filled by other things, things more beautiful and magical than she would ever have dreamed. Letting go of that life—

Well, she wasn't about to have a curse take from her what she'd so recently found. For the first time in all her twenty-seven years, she looked forward to the future. No matter the peril, or the uncertainty, or the possibility for meeting other things from myth she hadn't believed could exist, she was not going to surrender to a curse.

She had the feeling that she was going to find what she needed, and that had everything to do with the man in front of her who had done everything in his power to keep her safe.

Rùnach squeezed her hands. "There are always answers, Aisling," he said over his shoulder. "Always."

She had the feeling he might be right.

She only hoped she could bear the answers once she learned them.

Turn the page for a preview of Lynn Kurland's
first Novel of the Nine Kingdoms

Star of the Morning

Now available from Berkley Sensation!

One

Morgan of Melksham walked along the road, cursing both autumn's chill and her journey that caused her to be traipsing out in that chill instead of hunkering down next to a warm fire. This was not what she had planned. Her life had been proceeding quite nicely until she'd received the missive in the middle of a particularly muddy campaign in which she'd been trying to pry one of Melksham's nobles from a keep that did not belong to him. The message from Lord Nicholas had been brief and pointed.

Come soon; time is short.

Morgan didn't want to speculate on what that might mean, but she couldn't help herself. Was the man suffering from life-threatening wounds? Was his home under siege from nobles he had exacted donations from once too often? Had he had a bountiful harvest and needed an extra pair of hands to bring that harvest to the cellar?

Was he dying?

She quickened her pace, forcing her thoughts away. She would know soon enough and then that uncomfortable, unwholesome pounding in her chest would cease and she actually might be able to eat again.

She reached the outer walls of the orphanage just as the sun was setting. Melksham Orphan's Home at Lismòr had begun many years ago as a home for lads, but at some point it had also become a place of study that had brought together a collection of the finest scholars from all over the Nine Kingdoms. Nicholas, the lord of Lismòr, was the orphanage's undisputed champion and the university's chief procurer of funds.

Over the years, it had become different things to those who had experience with it. Many called it "the orphanage." Others referred to it as "the university." Nicholas simply called it "home."

Morgan agreed with the latter, though she never would have admitted it.

The outer walls of Lismòr soon rose up before her, forbidding and unfriendly. It made her wonder, not for the first time, why a university merited anything more than a sturdy gate. It was rumored that Lismòr hid many things, including chests of marvelous treasure. Morgan supposed those rumors could have been referring to the offerings that appeared each night on Lord Nicholas's supper table, but she couldn't have said for certain.

There were rumors, though, of another sort that swirled around Lord Nicholas. It was said that he never aged, that he conversed with mysterious souls who slipped inside the gates after dark and left well before dawn, and that he even possessed magic.

Morgan snorted. She had never seen any display of otherworldliness at the orphanage, and she'd lived there for many years. No doubt Nicholas's garden bloomed in the depth of winter because he was a damned fine gardener, not for any more magical reason. He was a man of great intelligence, quick wit, and an ability to convince others to fund his ventures. He possessed no magic beyond that.

Surely.

And surely his missive had nothing to do with his health.

She knocked on the heavy gate, then waited impatiently as a

single square of metal was slowly pulled back and a weathered face appeared, looking out suspiciously.

"Hmmm," he said doubtfully.

Morgan pursed her lips. "Aye, hmmm."

The porthole was slammed shut and the gate opened without haste. Morgan tapped her foot impatiently until the moment she could slip inside. She shut the gate herself, then looked at the gate-keeper.

"Is he dying?"

"Morgan," the gatekeeper said pleasantly. "You've been away long."

"But I have returned, in haste, and my hope is that it is not to attend a wake. Master James, is he *dying*?"

"Who?"

"Lord Nicholas!"

Master James scratched his head. "Not that I know of. I think he's holding court with the lads in his solar. Best to seek him out there, aye?"

Morgan could hardly believe her ears. Nicholas was well?

She wasn't sure if she was relieved that he was apparently hale and hearty or furious that he'd tricked her into coming by means of such a cryptic, panic-inducing message. One thing was certain: they would have words about the wording of future missives.

What she wanted to do was sit down and catch the breath she realized she'd been holding for almost a se'nnight. Instead, she nodded to the gatekeeper and walked weakly away. She would sit when she reached Nicholas's solar. And then once she recovered, she just might put him to the sword for her trouble.

She made her way across a rather large expanse of flat ground that the students and lads used to play games on, then continued on toward the inner walls that enclosed the heart of the university. Now, these were walls that offered protection against a foe. Morgan walked through the gate, casting a surreptitious look up at the heavy spikes of the portcullis gleaming dimly above her as she did so. Perhaps Nicholas was more concerned about the safety of his scholarly texts than he appeared.

Or perhaps he was concerned about the safety of his lads. She suspected she understood why. He had only mentioned once, in passing, that he'd had sons of his own at one time who had been slain. She supposed that since he hadn't been able to protect them, he felt compelled to protect others who could not see to themselves. Whatever the true reason, there were many, many souls that had benefited from his altruism. She certainly counted herself as one of them.

She threaded her way through many buildings and along paths until she reached the heart of Lismòr. It was an enormous building, with chambers and apartments surrounding an inner courtyard. Nicholas's chambers took up one half side of the building, and his solar happily resided in one of the corners. Morgan had spent many a pleasant hour there, conversing with an exceptional man who had made an exception in her case, allowing her to remain at the orphanage in spite of her being a girl.

Which was no doubt why she found herself standing not fifty paces away from his chambers, instead of at a siege that had been destined, thanks to much effort on her part, to yield quite a tidy sum. Her comrades had thought her mad for walking away; she had agreed, yet still she had packed her gear and left.

All because of a message from a man who had been like a father to her.

Morgan pursed her lips and continued on toward Nicholas's private solar. She would contemplate her descent into madness later, perhaps when she was sitting before a hot fire with a mug of drinkable ale in her hand and Nicholas before her to answer a handful of very pointed questions.

She stopped in front of a heavy wooden door, turned the handle, and slipped inside. The chamber was an inviting one, luxuriously appointed yet not intimidating. A cheery fire burned in the hearth, fine tapestries lined the walls, and thick rugs were scattered over the floor to spare the lord's feet the chill of cold stone. Candles in abundance drove the shadows back into their corners and sweet music filled the air.

Until she closed the door behind her, that is. The music faltered. The young man who plied his lute averted his eyes when she looked at him.

"Continue, Peter," said a deep voice, roughened by the passage of many years. "Now, lads, I seem to remember one of you asking for a tale."

The dozen or so lads strewn about the floor like so many shapeless garments were successful in varying degrees at tearing their gazes from her. Morgan was acutely aware of the filth of her clothing and the poor condition of her cloak. She looked about her for a place to sit. She settled for a corner and sank down onto the stool that had been handily placed there for just such a need as hers. She pulled the edges of her cloak closer around her and did her best to become part of the shadows.

Then she glared at the man holding court, for Lord Nicholas looked fit and strong and certainly in no need of anything from her.

He only winked at her and turned his attention back to his lads. "What will it be tonight?" he asked. "Romance? Adventure? Perilous escapades that should result in disaster but do not?"

"Peril," Morgan said before she could stop herself. "Imminent death. Something that requires an immediate and drastic rescue. Something that might include missives sent and travels made when apparently there was no need."

The lads again turned to look at her briefly, many of them slack-jawed, the rest looking quite confused.

"Oh, nothing so frightening," Nicholas said smoothly. "Lads? Any suggestions?"

"The Tale of the Two Swords," a young lad piped up.

Half the lads groaned. Morgan groaned right along with them. Too much romance in that one. Unfortunately, it was one of Nicholas's favorites; he would never do the decent thing and refuse to retell it.

"The Two Swords," Nicholas agreed readily. "So it will be."

Morgan rolled her eyes and leaned back against the wall, preparing to completely ignore all she would hear. Obviously, she would have no answers out of the man before he was ready, and if he held true to form, his nightly tale-telling would last for at least an hour. It was his ritual, repeated as consistently as the sun rising and setting each day. It gave the lads a sense of security, or so he said.

Morgan closed her eyes, wondering if she might be able to snatch a bit of sleep and block out the romance that would ooze out of the tale Nicholas was beginning to spin. But, despite herself, she found herself listening. Gilraehen the Fey was bold, Mehar of Angesand was beautiful, and Lothar of Wychweald was evil enough to make the most hardened of listeners shiver.

In time, the romance in the tale increased. Morgan was quite certain there would be tender sentiments exchanged soon between Gilraehen and Mehar—things entirely too sugary to be inflicted upon the hapless lads in the chamber. Morgan shot Nicholas a warning look, but he blithely ignored it.

She gave up and turned her attentions to the condition of her own hands. As she listened to Mehar placing her hand in Gilraehen's and giving herself to him as his queen, she pursed her lips. She herself hardly had time for such pleasantries; it was just as well, for no man would look at her hands, scarred and rough, and ask her to do anything with them besides curry his horse. A mercenary's life was not an easy one.

It was especially hard on one's hands.

"What of the two swords?" a lad asked. "The king's sword, especially." He paused. "I hear it is very sharp."

Nicholas laughed. "Well, of course the king keeps the Sword of Neroche. But the other—" He paused and shrugged. "The Sword of Angesand hangs in the great hall at Tor Neroche."

"But," another asked, sounding quite worried, "isn't the king afraid someone might make off with it?"

"Nay, lad, I daresay not. Before she died, Queen Mehar, she who fashioned the blade, laid an enchantment of protection upon it, that it would never be stolen. She also prophesied about several special souls who would wield that blade at a time of particular peril, but that is a tale for another night."

The lads protested, but not heartily. They were secure in the knowledge that the following night would bring more of the same

sort of pleasure. Morgan watched them file past her and understood precisely how they felt. She'd been orphaned at six, taken in
by a company of mercenaries for several years until she'd begun
her courses, then heartlessly deposited without a backward glance
upon Nicholas's doorstep at the tender age of ten-and-two. She
had had her own share of those long evenings passed in the comfort of Nicholas's solar, listening to him tell his stories. But she had
never, for reasons she never examined if she could help it, allowed
herself to luxuriate in that sensation of security.

There were times she suspected she should have.

An older lad, one who looked as if he spent far more time thinking about heroic tales than determining how he might become a
part of them by some time spent in the lists, stopped by the door
and turned back to Nicholas.

"I know the prophecy, my lord," he said quietly.

Nicholas remained seated in his chair, resting his chin on his
steepled fingers. "The prophecy?"

"Queen Mehar's prophecy about the Sword of Angesand."

"I imagine you do, lad."

"I can recite it for you—"

Morgan was about to tell him not to bother, but Nicholas beat
her to it.

"Not tonight, my son. I've a guest, don't you see, and you need
to be abed."

"I could speculate," the lad offered.

Nicholas rose slowly and walked over to stand by the door. "In
the end, my son, unless you are intimately involved in either the
doing of the deeds or the making of the tales, it is naught but
speculation. And since we are neither, we should leave the specu-
lating to others and retire to our beds before our nerves are over-
worked." He held the door open pointedly. "Good night, Harding's
son. Have a peaceful sleep."

"And to you, my lord," the lad said, then unwillingly made his
way from the chamber.

Nicholas closed the door and turned to look at Morgan. "You
came."

Morgan rose and looked at him narrowly. "Your missive said to hurry. I feared you were dying."

Nicholas laughed merrily and enveloped Morgan in a fatherly embrace. "Ah, Morgan," he said, pulling back, kissing her soundly on both cheeks, then drawing her across to sit upon his exceptionally comfortable settee, "I'm not dead yet. What a pleasure to see you."

Morgan scowled at him as she sat. "You asked me to come."

"Did I?" he said, sinking down into an equally comfortable chair.

"It sounded as if your trouble required my immediate attention."

"And so it does," he said with a smile. "But not tonight. Tonight you will eat, then go to your rest. We'll speak of other things tomorrow."

"My lord—"

"Tomorrow, my girl."

She frowned fiercely at him. "I made great haste away from a *very* lucrative bit of business, simply because you called. I've hardly slept in a se'nnight for worry that I might arrive too late and find you *dead*. I daresay I deserve to at least know why you wanted me here!"

He smiled. "Is it not enough for an old man to simply wish to see the daughter of his heart?"

Morgan felt a sudden and very uncomfortable burning begin behind her eyes. She rubbed them to ease the stinging and to give herself time to recapture her frown. She was better off in a pitched battle. She did not do well with these kinds of sentimental utterings.

"A pleasant visit does not seem a good reason to me," she managed finally.

"Doesn't it?" he asked kindly. "A pleasant visit, a se'nnight of comfort, a chance for me to make sure you're still alive?"

"I suppose," she conceded, but she wasn't sure she agreed. She did not need the luxurious surroundings she found herself in. She did not need the affection of a man who had taken her in as a scraggly, snarling, uncivilized lass who had been accustomed to sleeping with a dagger under her pillow and holding her own against men three times her age. She did not ever dwell with pleasure on those many years in Nicholas's care when he taught her of letters and numbers and the quiet beauty of the seasons changing from year to year.

She also did not think on him each time she drew the sword at her side, the glorious sword he'd had made for her and adorned with gems from his own personal treasury.

"Morgan?"

"Aye, my lord?"

"What were you thinking on?"

She sighed deeply. "I was contemplating my condition as an appallingly ungrateful wretch."

Nicholas laughed. "I daresay not. There is a chapel nearby, my dear, which you may use on the morrow for your penance. For now, fill this old man's ears with your adventures. We'll speak about other business tomorrow."

Morgan lifted her eyebrows. "Other business? Is that why you sent for me, in truth?"

"Tomorrow."

Morgan shot him a final, disgruntled look that he completely ignored, then she relented, and sat back against his dreadfully comfortable couch to give him the tales he wanted.

She told him of her travels, leaving out the more unsavory encounters. She told him of the places on the island she'd seen, the wonders she'd seen come in on ships at port, the tidy sums she'd earned.

"Obviously not of late," Nicholas said dryly, casting a look at her clothes. "A rough year so far, I'd say."

"Not the most profitable," Morgan agreed.

"I told you the last time you were here, my child, to marry one of Harding's sons, not fight the man's battles for him. He is notoriously stingy."

"Only because you've coerced so many donations out of him, my lord."

"Goodness," Nicholas said with a laugh, "you've been too many years out of polite company. Although it is all too true about the funds, we usually don't like to bring it up. Now you realize I have Harding's youngest here. He's a handsome lad."

"He's likely half my age."

"But he is rich."

"*Was* rich," she corrected. "I hazard a guess he will be less rich still once you're through with him—"

A discreet knock prevented her from discussing with Nicholas his extortionary techniques. Soon she found herself with a hearty repast sitting atop a table before her. Nicholas invited her to help herself, which she did without hesitation. It had been, after all, a rather lean autumn. Nicholas watched her thoughtfully as she ate.

"You know," he said casually, "there are richer prizes farther afield."

Morgan stopped chewing and looked at him. "What?"

"There are nine kingdoms, Morgan, my dear. The last time I checked, those nine kingdoms contained at least nine kings. I would imagine that any of them would be more than happy to pay you quite handsomely to raise your sword in his defense."

Morgan continued to chew. When she thought she could swallow successfully, she applied herself to her goblet of wine. "I don't fancy traveling," she said with conviction—the conviction of one who truly did not enjoy traveling.

"A pity," Nicholas said, admiring his own wine in the hand-blown glass goblet. "Gold, silver, renown. Glorious deeds." He looked at her placidly. "Hard to resist."

"And yet I manage," she said. "What are you about in truth, old man? I've resigned myself to a decent meal and pleasant conversation, but I only find one of the two here."

Nicholas smiled. "Finish your meal, my dear, then get yourself to bed. We'll speak on other things tomorrow. You'll stay for a bit, won't you?"

"Perhaps," she said, but she knew she didn't dare. Too many nights with her head on a soft goose-feather pillow and the rest of her under an equally soft goose-feather duvet would completely ruin her for hard labor.

"However long you can manage will be long enough," he said enigmatically. "Eat some more, Morgan. You're too thin."

She ate her fill, ate a bit more just in case, then sat back with a cup of the orphanage's finest and savored polite conversation for a bit. She and Nicholas spoke of the weather, of the harvest, of his garden that still produced a very fine grape even past the hard frost. Morgan learned of new lads who had come to be sheltered and of older lads who had come to study, then gone on to make their way in the world. All of it perfectly normal; all of it unremarkable and secure. It eased her heart.

All but the part of her heart that knew such peace was not to be hers for long.

She thanked Nicholas for the meal, bid him a good night, and walked with him to the door. He put his hands on her shoulders, then kissed both her cheeks. "A good sleep to you, daughter. You'll need it before you start your next journey."

"My next journey?" she asked blankly.

"Aren't you going on a journey?"

Ah, so this was where it lay, apparently. "I don't know. Am I, my lord?"

"An assumption, my dear," Nicholas said easily. "Sleep in peace tonight."

Morgan wondered if he had lost his wits, or it was that a decent meal and promise of a gloriously comfortable bed had robbed her of hers. She frowned at him, thanked him again kindly for his hospitality, then escaped his chambers before he could say anything else unsettling.

She had hardly made it ten steps from his solar when she was accosted by a voice from the shadows.

"My lady."

Morgan stopped and sighed. "I'm not your lady. I'm just Morgan."

"My lady Morgan." The lad from Nicholas's solar stepped out from the shadows.

He stood there, Harding's youngest son, squirming uncomfortably until he finally gained control enough of his gangly limbs to stop and look at her. Morgan was not given to shifting, having earned her own measure of self-control on the other side of Melksham Island where self-control was a particularly important subject to learn, but there was something about the moment that left her with an almost uncontrollable urge to rub her arms.

She managed not to. "Aye, lad?" she asked.

"Lord Nicholas won't speak to me about it," the young man whispered, "but I've heard rumors."

"Rumors are dangerous."

Apparently not dangerous enough to deter him. He leaned closer to her. "I heard," he whispered conspiratorially, "that the king of Neroche has lost his magic."

She felt her eyebrows go up of their own accord. "Indeed. And where did you hear that?"

"I eavesdropped on Lord Nicholas while he was discussing it."

Morgan waved aside his words. "He worries overmuch."

"I don't think so. 'Tis rumored the king also searches for a warrior of mighty stature to wield a sword for him." He paused, looked about him as if an enemy might be listening in, then leaned closer to her. "The Sword of Angesand," he whispered.

She blinked in surprise. "The what?"

"The Sword of Angesand. It was fashioned by Mehar of Angesand, who wove into it—"

"Aye, I know all about it," Morgan interrupted. That was all she needed, to have to listen to another of Nicholas's romantic and completely unsuitable tales while *outside* his solar. At least inside she had a warm fire to distract her. Here she only had a skinny, trembling lad who couldn't have been more than ten-and-two, who was making her cold just by looking at him.

"Go to bed," she ordered, "and forget what you've heard. The king is well. Indeed, all is well. I would say that listening to too many of Nicholas's stories has worked a foul work upon you."

The lad hesitated.

Morgan nodded firmly toward the dormitories. The lad nodded in unison with her, looking only slightly less miserable than before. He cast her one last desperate look before he turned and disappeared into the darkness.

Morgan snorted to herself. Rumor and hearsay. The lad was confusing fact with the stuff of Nicholas's evening's entertainment.

She put the matter out of her mind and sought her chamber, finding it just as she had left it two years earlier. Indeed, it looked just as it had for the six years she'd called it her own. She hadn't used it very often since going on to make her way to other places, but each time she'd returned, she had found it thusly prepared for her. She leaped into her bed with a guilty abandon she would regret in a se'nnight's time when she was reduced to rough blankets near a weak fire. She closed her eyes and promised herself a good, long march through bitter chill at some point in the future as penance.

But not tonight.

The king has lost his magic.

It couldn't be true. Morgan rolled over and pulled the covers up over her ears. The king of Neroche was as full of vile magic as ever, the Nine Kingdoms were safe, and she was indulging in a guilty pleasure she rarely allowed herself.

Surely all was well.